"The story of Dani and Brett captured me from the very first page and held me fast all the way through to the last. *When Love Arrives* is an engaging romance, but even more, it's a testament to the way God sometimes turns our best plans upside-down in order to give us something better. This book left me looking forward to Johnnie Alexander's next installment in the Misty Willow series!"

—**Ann Tatlock**, award-winning novelist
and children's book author

Praise for *Where She Belongs*

"This absorbing novel does more than just weave a story of romance; it creates an atmosphere of coming home. The town and its people feel like long-lost friends, and readers cannot help but invest emotionally in the plot's outcome. An added element of historical mystery swirls through the pages, alongside the more modern tensions also in play, and brings extra dimension to an already compelling story."

—*RT Book Reviews*

"Alexander deftly spins an emotionally charged contemporary romance with intriguing twists and turns. Masterful storytelling."

—CBA *Retailers + Resources*

"Alexander launches a promising trilogy that emphasizes the importance of home and the sense of belonging. An overarching theme of forgiveness for past sins runs throughout the novel. Friendship, romance, and a bit of family intrigue make this book impossible to put down."

—*Library Journal* Pick of the Month

WHEN LOVE
Arrives

Books by Johnnie Alexander

MISTY WILLOW

Where She Belongs
When Love Arrives

WHEN LOVE
Arrives

A NOVEL

JOHNNIE ALEXANDER

Revell

a division of Baker Publishing Group
Grand Rapids, Michigan

Published by Revell
a division of Baker Publishing Group
P.O. Box 6287, Grand Rapids, MI 49516-6287
www.revellbooks.com

Printed in the United States of America

Library of Congress Cataloging-in-Publication Data
Names: Alexander, Johnnie, author.
Title: When love arrives : a novel / Johnnie Alexander.
Description: Grand Rapids, MI : Revell, a division of Baker Publishing Group,
    [2016] | Series: Misty Willow ; book 2
Identifiers: LCCN 2016012622 | ISBN 9780800726416 (softcover)
Subjects: | GSAFD: Christian fiction. | Love stories.
Classification: LCC PS3601.L35383 W47 2016 | DDC 813/.6—dc23
LC record available at https://lccn.loc.gov/2016012622

16 17 18 19 20 21 22   7 6 5 4 3 2 1

To Mandy

I'd claim you as my own except your mom won't let me.

– 1 –

Praise be to the Lord, for he showed me the wonders
of his love when I was in a city under siege.

Psalm 31:21

LATE AUGUST

*B*rett Somers usually waited till after dark to take up his vigil outside the brick building. But not today.

Despite the warmth of the early evening sun, he shivered when a light, bluer than a clear summer sky, appeared through the rectangular panes of the ninth story window. Over the next few hours, random colors would appear in more windows and become more vivid, more numerous. In the darkness of night, the vibrant panes created a brilliant kaleidoscope of hope.

The hospitalized children controlled the color of their ambient night-lights unless, like the boy in room 927, they were in a coma.

Brett pressed his hand against his heart, but he couldn't ease the unbearable pain that threatened to break him in two.

If only the boy behind that lighted window would open his eyes. *I'd give everything I own if he would only open his eyes.*

9

Brett shifted his weight and leaned against his Lexus as footsteps ambled toward him. Finally.

He forced a smile. "How is he?"

"Still the same, man." A mass of curly red hair framed Aaron Wiley's round cheeks, and his blue eyes twinkled. No surprise that each Christmas he donned a white wig and beard for the young patients whose vital signs he monitored. "He just lies there, sound asleep."

Brett swallowed the sigh building up in his throat. "The accident was two months ago."

"Head traumas take time to heal."

"What about Meghan?"

"She seems to be doing better now that she's not spending twenty-four hours in this place. I overheard her talking about a church giving her an apartment, no charge." Humor twinkled in Aaron's gentle eyes. "Don't suppose you had anything to do with that?"

"She was going to end up in a bed next to him if she didn't . . ." Brett pressed his lips together.

"Take care of herself?" Aaron finished the sentence.

Brett grimaced. He wouldn't have to resort to these cloak-and-dagger tactics if Meghan weren't so stubborn. So unforgiving.

Not that he hadn't given her a good reason to despise him.

He pushed away from the car and retrieved a gift bag illustrated with zoo animals and balloons from the backseat. "Tomorrow's his eighth birthday. I want you to give him this."

Despite the blue and yellow tissue paper sprouting from the top, Aaron peered inside. "What did you get him?"

"It's not from me."

"'Course it isn't."

"Come up with something, okay? There has to be a group or some kind of foundation that donates toys to these children."

"A few." Like the big kid he was, Aaron slightly shook the bag as if trying to get a hint of what was inside. "They donate books. Hand-carved wooden toys. Stuffed animals."

"That works. It's a stuffed monkey. With an MP3 player inside."

"Good choice."

"Wearing an Ohio State football jersey."

Aaron grinned. "Even better." He held out his closed fist, and Brett obliged him with a friendly bump.

But the lightened mood quickly faded as a rain-tinged breeze swept along the quiet street. "She can't know it came from me. I'm depending on you."

"I'm always here for you, man. You know that." A rare frown pulled at Aaron's mouth. "But I can't do this anymore."

Brett closed his eyes as the words he'd been dreading settled like a boulder in his gut.

With anyone else, he'd pile on the charm. Or the pressure.

But Aaron wouldn't succumb to either. Besides, the certified nursing assistant risked his job every time he gave Brett an update. Even if the update never changed.

"I understand."

"You should just talk to her, man."

"I've tried." He slightly shook his head. "She hates me."

"Not used to that, are you?"

"No, Aaron. I'm not."

"Tell you what." The twinkle returned to Aaron's eyes, and his voice lowered to a conspiratorial whisper. "When he wakes up, I'll make sure you know."

"I'd appreciate it."

"I better go, man. My shift's about to start." Aaron's characteristic smile beamed as he cradled the gift bag. "Don't worry, she'll never know where this came from."

Brett nodded his thanks, and Aaron sauntered toward the hospital.

Suddenly light-headed, Brett bent over the trunk of the Lexus, his hands pushing against the black frame as the sigh finally escaped in an exhale of air.

If only he'd known she'd kept the baby . . .

He exhaled deeply again and shook his head.

If he'd known, he wouldn't have cared.

Not back then. Not when it mattered.

The camera shutter clicked multiple times in quick succession, then Dani slouched against the medical building across the street from the hospital. By the light of the sun's slanting rays, she checked the camera's digital display. The images of two men, a good-looking blond and an unruly carrot-top, appeared in the square screen. In the final image, the Adonis stood alone, his chin lowered.

Not an online photo scavenged from internet images, but the living, breathlessly handsome man himself.

When Dani looked up from the display, Brett's hands were interlaced behind his head. She caught a momentary glimpse of his pained expression as he lifted his eyes to the heavens.

Compassion stirred her heart, but it only lasted a single beat. Taking a few steps forward, she lifted the camera and took another quick succession of shots, though she wasn't sure why. She didn't need more photos of the guy.

Unless . . . She swatted away the thought, but it fought back. *Unless I could sell them.*

Given his recent celebrity, they might be worth something. And she desperately needed money.

Getting vengeance by humiliating him was one thing. But exposing his obvious pain to the world—she couldn't do anything that sleazy.

Could she?

It was bad enough she'd spent the past few hours waiting for him to emerge from his office building's parking garage so she could tail him. The thrill of playing detective had quickly evaporated into boredom.

When he finally appeared, she'd expected him to pick up a Barbie bimbo for a Friday night on the town. Her adrenaline raced as she prepared to follow him. But instead of going to a nightclub or restaurant, he'd driven to this children's hospital.

Why?

A blaring siren broke the brooding peace of the lonely street. Dani pivoted as an ambulance sped her way. The revolving red light throbbed as if toying with her. *Pain. Death. Pain. Death.*

The malevolent words kept time with each revolution, and her breathing accelerated as if racing the siren's crescendo.

Pressing her palm against her abdomen, she concentrated on deep inhales and exhales. This emergency had nothing to do with her. Nothing.

The ambulance slowed as it made a sharp turn and followed the curving drive around to the ER.

"Are you okay?"

Dani spun toward the voice and gazed into the most attractive blue eyes she'd ever seen. A faint smile creased the man's gorgeous face, revealing deep dimples.

Busted.

Her surveillance plan for learning more about Brett Somers's personal life hadn't included speaking to the guy. Heat crept up her neck and warmed her cheeks.

"I didn't mean to scare you." The smile disappeared. "You look a little pale."

Her voice stuck in her throat. Good-looking and self-assured, he was just the kind of man who made her stammer and trip over her own feet. The kind of man who either looked right through her or only noticed her because she'd done something clumsy or stupid.

Like secretly taking pictures of him.

His eyes narrowed. "Are you going to be sick?"

"Fine," she blurted, flushing again at the squeak in her voice. She cleared her throat. "I'm fine. I just don't like ambulances."

"Who does?"

She followed his glance toward the hospital. An assortment of colors shone through several of the windows.

"Taking photos of the lights?"

"Um, yes." She nodded to support the lie and forced a smile.

"Can I see?"

"No!"

He appeared taken aback by the force of her objection, but only for an instant. Holding out his hand, he smiled. "Please."

Her knees turned to jelly when his dimples reappeared. He obviously expected her to succumb to his charms. Most women probably did.

But no way could she show him the images she'd taken. He'd think she was a stalker.

Who was she kidding? She *was* a stalker.

Though for a very good reason.

"I'd really like to see them."

She couldn't let him know how much he intimidated her. Why couldn't she be poised and self-confident? Like Audrey Hepburn. No matter the circumstances, Audrey always said and did the right thing.

Of course she did. She had a scriptwriter.

Dani wished she had one too. With a quiet sigh, she straightened her shoulders and carefully placed the camera in its bag. "The pictures are personal."

He dropped his hand. "Which window?"

"Excuse me?"

"Which window is yours?"

She crinkled her eyes in confusion. "None of them."

"You don't have someone inside there? A sick child you're worried about?"

"No."

"So you take hospital photos for the fun of it?" His gaze bored into hers, and a hint of suspicion weighted his words. "Strange hobby."

Dani silently agreed. If that were the truth, it would be strange. She needed to distract him. Maybe engaging in conversation wasn't such a bad idea after all.

"Which window is yours?" She tried to sound nonchalant but doubted she had succeeded. Small talk with handsome men had never been her forte.

The brilliancy of his eyes faded, and he carelessly shrugged. "Just looking at the lights."

So he could lie too.

From her research, she knew he'd never been married. Since the death of his grandmother a few months ago, his only family members were a sister and a cousin, both single as far as Dani knew. So there should be no children in Brett's life.

Or maybe he was telling the truth, and the present he had given the other man wasn't for a patient but for someone on the hospital staff. Perhaps he was playing secret admirer.

The image of his earlier pained expression appeared before her as clearly as if she were staring at a printed photograph. His secret didn't have anything to do with romance. She gazed at the colored lights. Behind one of those windows was a child he cared about.

A mystery.

Feeling his eyes upon her, she met his gaze and awkwardly smiled. "I'm Brett Somers."

I know.

"And you are?"

Dani's eyes shifted, and she stared at the tan toes of her canvas shoes. Her mind flashed to the classic movie she'd watched last night.

"I'm, um, Regina Lampert." The lie surprised and emboldened her. Suddenly tickled by her audacity, she grinned.

His eyebrows lifted. "Regina Lampert?"

She nodded.

"As in *Charade*? Audrey Hepburn's character?"

Busted again.

"You know that movie?"

"Why wouldn't I?"

She mimicked his earlier casual shrug. "You just don't seem the type."

"What type?"

"The type to know about classic movies."

His eyes crinkled in amusement. "What type am I, Regina Lampert?"

"I don't know." *Careful, Dani. He can't suspect you already know anything about him.* "The never-alone-on-a-Friday-night type. The let's-jet-off-to-Paris-in-five-minutes type."

"Paris doesn't interest me." The amusement eased into a broad grin as he spread his hands. "And I'm all alone here. Besides, I never fly."

She nervously twisted the camera bag's strap, determined to ignore that last comment. "So how do you know so much about Audrey Hepburn?"

"I don't really. But my grandmother was a huge Cary Grant fan. I watched *Charade* with her several times. You?"

"Too many Friday nights alone, I guess."

"Pretty girl like you?"

Immediate heat burned her face.

"How many stars would you give *Notorious*?" he asked.

"Cary Grant and Ingrid Bergman's *Notorious*? I love it."

"It's playing at the Ohio Theater. Part of their summer classic movie series." He pulled out his phone and tapped at the screen. "We've got about fifteen minutes."

"Fifteen minutes?"

"Before the movie starts." He flashed that knee-weakening smile again. "I know we've just met, but I'm a respectable businessman. Successful too, I don't mind saying. I own a thriving property development company. And my cousin is engaged to the daughter of missionaries. We used to not-date, so she can tell you what a gentleman I am."

Dani's head spun at his quick patter.

His finger poised over his cell. "Shall I call her for you?"

As if it had a mind of its own, her hand shot out and covered the phone's screen to stop him. "You don't need to do that." Her fingers lingered against the warmth of his skin.

This could not be happening.

"Then you'll come? My treat."

"To the movie? It's probably sold out."

"I know the manager."

Of course he did.

"Come on, 'Reggie.'" He shoved his cell into his pocket and bumped her elbow with his. "Historical theater. *Notorious* on the big screen."

Twisting the camera bag's strap, she tried to think of another objection.

Just say no. N.O. One easy syllable.

But her voice didn't cooperate.

"A giant bucket of buttered popcorn."

He sounded so pitiful she couldn't help grinning.

"If it makes you more comfortable, we can drive separately. Where's your car?"

"Around the corner." She tilted her head to the side street next to the medical building. "Where's the theater?"

"Only a few blocks from here. So how about it?"

Maybe this wasn't such a bad idea. A movie meant little time for small talk, which meant she might find out something useful without giving anything away. Seeing one of her favorite movies on the big screen was a bonus.

"Okay," she said.

His dimples deepened. "Okay."

As they walked to her car, he gave her directions in case they got separated. She tried to pay attention, but her stomach tightened at what he must be thinking about her eleven-year-old Honda Civic. The rusted spots seemed to take on a noticeable and vibrant hue beneath the streetlamps.

Shoving her not-good-enough feelings aside, she unlocked the driver's door. So what if she didn't drive something new and shiny. At least she worked for what she had.

Until she'd gotten fired.

More accurately, forced to resign. But it amounted to the same thing.

Brett grabbed the door as she opened it and slid into the seat. "Follow me to the light and take a left."

"Got it."

"Good." He shut the door and waited.

The engine coughed, then smoothed into a solid hum. She lowered her window. "Something wrong?"

"Just wanted to be sure you got it started." \

"I usually do." Her voice held that defensive snap she hated.

"Usually?"

She swallowed a sigh and gazed up at him. "We're going to be late."

"You're right." He tapped the window frame, then jogged to his car.

A few moments later, she pulled onto the street behind his Lexus and gripped her steering wheel.

She was on this lonely street to spy on Brett Somers. How in the world had she ended up on a date with him?

– 2 –

Brett ushered "Regina Lampert" into the auditorium, then practically bumped into her as she suddenly stopped. He smiled, amused at her awestruck expression. The opulent reds and the golds of the historic theater never failed to impress.

"It's magnificent," she said softly.

"I'm glad you think so." While juggling their concession stand purchases, he placed his hand on the small of her back, then gently prodded her along. "My grandmother helped raise funds for its restoration a few decades ago. This theater was one of her favorite places."

"Is it one of yours?"

Brett shrugged noncommittally. "I haven't been here in a couple of years." Gran had been his date then. Now he was here with a girl whose name he didn't even know. All because the blare of an ambulance had yanked his attention to where she stood, her slender body appearing tense in the light of a lowering sunbeam.

Somehow her frailty had reminded him of Amy. A younger, less jaded Amy.

Apparently his big brother instincts had kicked in, because a moment later he was at the girl's side ready to offer a broad shoulder for her tears. That hadn't been necessary, but next thing he knew, he'd invited Miss I've-Got-a-Secret to a movie.

The mystery surrounding her was almost enough to tempt him to break his dating sabbatical.

Almost, but not quite. He didn't need the distractions of a romance when he had so many other things to figure out. Like how to persuade Meghan to give him a chance. To let her know he had changed.

The mystery girl paused beside a row of seats in the center section. "Is this okay?"

"Fine." He took his seat and glanced around. "I think we're the youngest people here."

"Do you care?"

"Nope. You?"

"I'm used to listening to a different drummer."

"Is that so?"

She nodded, a thoughtful expression in her eyes.

"I must say, you surprise me."

"Why's that?"

"You just don't seem the type." He purposefully kept his voice casual, though he knew exactly what he was doing. Teasing her. Baiting her.

"What type?"

"The spontaneous type. When's the last time you went on a date with someone you just met?"

"Never." Her mouth puckered in confusion, and she slightly shook her head. "But that doesn't mean I'm not spontaneous. I've just never been in a situation like this before."

"What's the last spontaneous thing you did? Besides giving me an alias."

Her eyes flickered as if she were considering and discarding answers. Finally, she swallowed and lifted her chin defiantly. "You don't know anything about me."

"I know your name isn't Regina Lampert. I know you don't live around here."

"Are you sure about that?"

"You have a Hamilton County license plate on your car. That's almost a hundred miles south. Do you live in Cincinnati?"

"Maybe I recently moved here and haven't had time to get new plates."

"Did you?"

Instead of answering him, she carefully unwrapped her hot dog and opened a mustard packet.

He leaned closer. "I know you don't have a serious boyfriend."

"How could you possibly know that?" The exasperation in her voice matched her puzzled expression. Her brown eyes appeared almost black in the auditorium's dim lighting.

"You're here with me. And you haven't checked your cell since we've entered the theater."

"Neither have you."

"No reason to."

"So you're not seeing anyone special?"

"Do you think I'd be here with you if I were?"

"I honestly don't know."

"So you've known me all of about fifteen minutes, and you've already labeled me as a modern-day Casanova?"

Her lips pressed into a tight line as her shoulders lifted.

"You don't trust men, is that it?" He tilted his head. "Tell you the truth, neither do I."

"You don't trust men?" Her voice sounded skeptical.

"Nope."

"Why not?"

"Maybe because I *am* one. I know how we are."

"So I shouldn't trust you?"

"You can trust me to be the perfect date. To see you safely to your car, safely home if you want, even if that means driving to Cincy." He flashed a smile. "You can trust me to be just like Peter Joshua."

Her lips curled upward. "Cary Grant's character in *Charade*."

"That's right. Did you know it bothered Cary when Audrey Hepburn was cast in the role of Regina? Because she was so much younger than he was?"

"I know he had them rewrite the script so she came on to him instead of the other way around."

"A movie trivia gold star for you."

"But you're not as old as Peter Joshua." Her eyes widened in fake innocence. "Are you?"

So the girl did know how to flirt.

"I'm almost thirty." He made a show of appraising her. "I'm guessing you're a few years behind."

"Five or six."

"Too young for me."

"So you prefer a woman closer to your own age?"

"Let's just say, I prefer a woman who's old enough to understand the rules."

"What rules?"

He hesitated, tempted to flirt and tease. But this was a one-time date, not a one-night stand. He had no intentions of playing The Game with this girl.

"The rules are complicated." And designed to break women's hearts. "Primarily, they are 'no commitments' and 'no recriminations when I walk away.'"

"I see." She turned away, but not before he saw the pink rise in her cheeks.

How had this conversation gotten so offtrack?

"Anyway, you can trust me to behave myself. *Regina*."

She didn't answer, and a moment later the lights faded. The low hum of conversation ceased as the screen flickered to life.

"It's Dani," she said in a low whisper.

Brett bent his head toward hers so they almost touched. A delicate fragrance, cool and flowery, surrounded him. "What?"

"My name is Dani."

"It's nice to meet you, Dani."

"You too, Brett."

As the trailer for an upcoming movie played on the big screen, Brett settled deeper into his plush seat and surreptitiously appraised the young woman beside him. Her brown hair, the color of darkest honey, partially covered her profile as she squirted a line of mustard along her hot dog.

If she was telling the truth about spending too many Friday nights alone it wasn't because of her looks. She might not be as beautiful as the women he dated, but her Bambi eyes and sun-kissed complexion gave her a classic girl-next-door freshness. Not to mention her tendency to blush.

Though not the gal for him, she was a nice distraction for one lonely night. In a couple of hours, Cary Grant would drive into the night with his leading lady safe in his arms. Then Brett would go his way and Dani would go hers.

Wherever that way might be. And as long as her clunker of a car didn't conk out on her.

— 3 —

*A*s the curtains descended over the screen and the lights came up, Dani hurriedly swiped away a tear.

"Are you crying?" Brett asked.

"Seeing this movie on the big screen . . ." She exhaled with delight. "It was absolutely magical."

"Not such a bad way to spend a spontaneous Friday night?"

"Not at all."

"I'm glad you agreed to come." He gathered their trash and stuffed it in an empty popcorn bucket. "Though if I'd planned ahead, I would have invited my cousin and his fiancée to join us."

He'd mentioned before that his cousin was engaged. An interesting nugget of information but not much help. An engagement certainly didn't explain why Brett was outside the hospital.

"They're nuts about these movies," he continued.

"Isn't everybody?"

"No one I've ever dated."

"I suppose most women prefer chick flicks."

"Do you?"

"Sometimes. But the classics are my favorites."

"They quote Cary Grant lines to each other."

"Who does?"

"My cousin and his fiancée." He pretended to gag. "Sickening, I tell you."

"Didn't you say earlier you dated your cousin's fiancée?"

"We 'not-dated.'"

"What does that mean?"

"Long story. And if I told you, you might want to slap me."

He didn't need to know she wanted to do that anyway. For a blissful couple of hours she had gotten lost in the black-and-white world of post–World War II intrigue. But the glamour of the evening had faded with the brightening of the lights. And so had the magic that allowed her to forget that the man munching popcorn beside her had pummeled her heart.

"I know you'll find this hard to believe, but I used to be a cad." He smiled, but a pained expression flickered in his eyes.

Again the image of him outside the hospital seared her thoughts. But she couldn't afford the luxury of feeling sorry for him. Right now, she couldn't afford much of anything.

The wordplay of her thoughts tickled her even though her dire financial circumstances too often made her sick to her stomach. But Brett must have taken her amused expression as a response to what he'd said.

"Told you," he said teasingly. "Hard to believe."

"Not really." She stood, pulling on her purse strap. Her bag knocked against the seat's cup holder, tilting her drink. Both she and Brett scrambled for the cup, but the lid popped off, and watered-down soda spilled onto his pants.

Could the floor open up and swallow her now?

"I'm so sorry." She grabbed a napkin, then didn't know what to do with it.

"I'm sorry," she said again, then wished she hadn't.

"You're always apologizing." The drunken voice echoed in her head. *"Take your sorries out of my sight."*

"Don't worry about it." Brett grinned as he took the napkin

from her. "It's not the first time a young lady has spilled soda on me at the movies. Though that particular young lady is only three."

The depth of those dimples made it impossible not to smile in return.

"You were at a movie with a three-year-old?"

"Why sound so surprised?"

"Because you don't—"

"Seem the type?" His eyes slightly narrowed. "Considering we just met this evening, you're making a lot of wrong assumptions about me."

"So, who is she?" She tried to sound nonchalant, as if the answer didn't really matter. But what if it did? Could the three-year-old be the child in the hospital?

If Brett did have a child in the hospital . . . She pushed aside the thought. Never would she use a defenseless child to get back at him. The very idea made her nauseous.

"She's a little monster disguised as sugar and spice and everything nice." He dabbed at his khakis, not that it seemed to do much good, then stuffed the useless napkin in the popcorn bucket with the rest of the trash. "My cousin is getting a wife and two daughters when he says 'I do.'"

"To the woman you not-dated."

"That's right. They're planning a Christmas wedding."

A sudden onslaught of jealousy ripped through Dani. She'd never seen this woman, knew nothing about her. But unexplained envy consumed her. Apparently Brett had a past relationship with her and now she was engaged to his cousin. Some women seemed to have all the luck when it came to men falling in love with them.

She turned away and walked toward the exit, sensing Brett following her. He probably thought she was behaving like that three-year-old. Or even worse. But she didn't care.

Except she did.

If she didn't already know what she knew about him, she'd be flattered he'd asked her out. He'd been polite, respectful, even fun. And she had enjoyed the movie. But she couldn't forget the other side of him she'd seen. The one that had stirred up painful memories and sent her sprawling into a dark abyss.

Suddenly unable to breathe, she clung to the strap of her purse as if to a lifeline. Air. She needed air. Squeezing between an older couple and the wall, she rushed through the door and into the lobby.

Brett caught up to her, placed his arm around her waist, and propelled her away from the departing crowd.

"Are you all right? What's wrong?"

She took a deep breath and focused on a vintage movie poster in its gold frame. Then breathed again and again. Slowly, the iron-clad grip on her chest eased.

"You look like you're about to be sick."

"I'm fine. Really, I am."

He searched her eyes as if trying to read her mind, then shook his head. "Then what happened?"

"I'm just . . . embarrassed."

"About spilling the drink? It was an accident. As much my fault as yours."

"I'll pay to have them cleaned." The words came out softer than she intended, and she cleared her throat.

"They'll wash." His voice was soft too, and he squeezed her hand. "Like I said, not the first time."

"But I'm not three."

"Wouldn't have asked you to the movies if you were."

Nor if he knew who she really was.

"You sure you're okay?"

"I'm sure." To avoid his gaze, she glanced around the lobby. "This theater is so beautiful."

"Picture-worthy beautiful?"

"Yeah." Her heart quickened as her photographer's eye set up imaginary shots.

"I think they have tours."

"That sounds like fun."

"Maybe we can catch one sometime."

His words sounded sincere, but something in his expression led her to believe he was only being polite.

She inwardly sighed at the sting of another rejection. On a lonely Friday night, this handsome man had asked her out. But he wouldn't again. Not that she'd accept if he did.

She slightly cleared her throat. "Watching *Notorious* on TV will never be the same."

"There is something special about seeing the classics on the big screen. Especially in a theater like this." He gestured around the lobby. "It has a history. Almost as if it's a character in its own story."

Startled, Dani caught his gaze and raised her eyebrows.

"What?" Brett asked.

"That was rather fanciful. You surprise me."

"Because I'm not the fanciful type?"

"I wasn't going to say that."

"You'd be right. I'm not. But after watching a movie like that, I can imagine living in the days when women wore stockings and men wore hats."

"Would you like to live in those days?"

"It was a simpler time, I suppose. Though the people living in them might not have thought so. Especially not during the war years."

"I suppose every generation has its challenges."

As they walked toward the theater's elaborate double doors, Brett's phone buzzed. He pulled it from his pocket and frowned. "You mind if I take this?"

"Of course not."

He nodded thanks, then answered the call. "Everything okay?" A pause. "You're where?"

Dani discreetly stepped away but surreptitiously glanced at Brett as he ran his hand over his eyes as if irritated.

"Do what you want. You always do." He jabbed at the screen, then joined her, an uneasy smile pasted on his face.

"Anything wrong?"

"That depends." He flashed his dimples.

"On what?"

"If you're free tomorrow night."

"Excuse me?"

"I have this thing to go to. A banquet. My sister just canceled on me, so . . ."—he shrugged helplessly—"I don't have a date."

"You were taking your sister?"

"Not to brag, but I'm one of the guests of honor. I wanted to make it a family thing. My cousin and his fiancée are coming too, so it's not really a date-date."

"I see." More than he realized. Her own ticket to the Up-and-Comers Banquet was tucked inside her purse. She'd bought it as part of her Brett Somers surveillance plan. But he didn't need to know that.

"So how about it? I know it's late notice, but you'd be doing me a big favor."

"Aren't you afraid I'll spill wine on your tux?"

He grinned. "It's not quite that fancy. I'm wearing jeans and a T-shirt."

"You are not."

"Suit and tie. So what do you say?"

Dani bit her lip and considered. Another chance to spend time with Brett. Another chance to humiliate herself by saying the wrong thing or doing something stupid.

But if she didn't go with him, she couldn't go at all. If he saw her, what excuse could she give for being there? Besides, it'd give her a chance to meet his cousin and the lucky fiancée. Maybe even find out why Brett was at the hospital.

"Why not?" Her cheery voice momentarily squashed the strident misgivings warring inside her. This might be a bad idea, but at least she had a lovely black dress to wear after yesterday's trek to practically every consignment shop in Columbus.

"Great." Brett sounded genuinely relieved. "You don't know

how much kidding I'd have to endure if I showed up without a date."

So that was his motive. The gleeful misgivings roared. "We wouldn't want that, would we?"

"You can't imagine."

Yeah. I can.

She shoved the painful voices into the deep place where she locked up all her hurts. More important matters needed her attention. Brett wouldn't be disgraced at tomorrow night's banquet, but before long she'd figure out the best way to teach him a lesson he'd never forget.

"I need your phone number and address." He tapped his phone. "D-A-N . . ." He looked at her expectantly.

"D-A-N-I."

He focused on the screen as he entered the letters. "Last name?"

"Prescott."

"Address?"

"Why do you want to know that?"

"So," he said, drawing out the syllable, "I can pick you up tomorrow."

"That's not necessary. I can meet you there."

"Where?"

Dani bit the inside of her lip. She'd almost slipped up with that one. "Wherever the banquet is."

"Would Peter Joshua let Regina Lampert drive herself to an important dinner? Besides, parking will be a nightmare. Trust me."

He had trapped her again. First into being his date to the banquet, and now she'd have to tell him where she was staying.

"You were right earlier. I'm not from around here."

"Aha! I knew it."

"I don't have an apartment yet, so I'm staying at this other place. But it's only temporary. Until I can find somewhere permanent."

Great. Now she was babbling.

"Makes sense. Where is it?"

"Baines Lodging. One of those pay-by-the-week places near the interstate. West of here, I think."

"That's not a great area." Furrowed lines appeared at the edges of his eyes. "Some of those places don't have a very good reputation."

"I wouldn't know about that." She feigned a careless shrug.

"I can recommend safer places."

Which would undoubtedly cost two or three times what she was paying. "I'm careful."

"Sometimes being careful isn't enough."

"Somehow I've managed my entire life without your help." She met his gaze, steeling herself not to waver under his intense expression. "I don't need it now."

Surprisingly, he looked away first, and her confidence level inched upward. Maybe she had what it took to handle a too-handsome guy after all.

He stared at his phone, then back at her. In that few seconds, something had changed about his demeanor.

"May I please have the honor of picking you up tomorrow night?" he asked. "I'd rather not take a chance that you'll stand me up too."

"I'm sorry your sister did."

"Amy does what Amy does."

"So this isn't the first time?"

"I don't want to talk about her." He held up his phone so she could see the Create Contact screen. "Address? Please?"

"I'd have to look it up."

"I'll do that. How about your number?"

She hesitated, and he pretended to glare at her. "After tomorrow night, I'll delete it. I promise."

"Okay, don't get testy." As she recited the number, he tapped his screen. A few seconds later, her phone buzzed.

"I sent you a text so you'd have my number. Just don't call and cancel on me."

"I won't."

"Promise?"

"Promise."

"Good." He pocketed the phone and lightly touched her arm. "Shall we go?"

Outside the theater, the sidewalk glistened beneath the black iron streetlamps. Dani shivered against the damp chill, a souvenir of the storm that had raged during the movie.

"Looks like we missed a downpour," Brett said. "How about a cup of coffee to warm you up? There's a diner down the next block. Famous around here for its homemade pies."

"Kind of late for coffee, isn't it?"

"It's the weekend. Stay up late, sleep late."

"Nice thought, but I better not."

"You got another date after this?"

Her cheeks warmed as she barely shook her head. "It's just . . . it's been a long day."

"Then I won't insist."

"Thank you." She headed toward her car, digging the key from her purse. Brett slipped it from her hand and unlocked the door.

"Do you know how to get to your place from here?"

"I have a navigation app."

"Good." He gingerly squeezed her shoulder, then pulled her into a casual hug. "Thanks again for coming with me. I wasn't looking forward to an evening alone in my apartment."

She awkwardly circled her arms around his waist. "Surely you have lots of friends you can go out with."

"Yeah, I guess I do. But none as appealing as you."

"You're teasing me."

"No, I'm not." His eyes captured hers. "Till tomorrow, Regina."

Unsure of what to say, she merely smiled and slid inside the driver's seat.

Brett leaned into the car. "Be safe."

"I will."

He nodded, then shut her door. After returning his wave, she drove away.

Somehow she'd survived the evening. But would she survive tomorrow's?

At least the movie had given them something to do. At the banquet, she'd have to engage in conversation not only with him but also his cousin and the fiancée. Brett hadn't even told her their names.

That alone was proof that, despite his flirting, he wasn't interested in her. Neither had he asked what she was doing in Columbus. Nor anything about her family or her career—not that she had much to say about either of those topics.

Maybe if she'd gone with him to the diner, they'd have had that awkward conversation. Now it might happen at the banquet.

And she'd have to be very careful how she walked the line between truth and falsehood.

– 4 –

*B*rett jammed his hands into his pockets as the taillights on Dani's car disappeared around the corner. Walking to his Lexus, he checked his phone. A few emails that could wait till he was back in the office on Monday. No missed calls. No texts.

No one missing him on a Friday night.

He might as well go home, though he was too wound up to sleep. Besides, just because Dani wanted to end their evening together didn't mean it was over. Beyond the Lexus, the diner's neon sign beckoned the departing theatergoers to drop in.

The hole-in-the-wall was a local favorite serving a limited menu of sandwiches and salads. But like he told Dani, it was best known for its sumptuous pies.

He perched on a stool and folded his arms on the counter. Though she had to be nearing forty, the waitress gave him a flirtatious smile. "What's your pleasure, handsome?"

"Apple pie a la mode."

"Coffee?"

"Why not?"

"Decaf?"

"No. Give me the good stuff."

"One cup of the good stuff coming up." She swished her hips, then pulled a mug from a shelf and poured his coffee. "What are you doing out alone on a Friday night?"

"My date and I were at the Ohio Theater. But she needed to go home."

"Honey, if that had been me, I wouldn't have let you out of my sight."

He politely chuckled. "Maybe I should have taken you to the movies instead."

"Anytime, honey, anytime. Now let me get you that apple pie."

"Thanks." He tested the coffee and almost burned his tongue. Strong and black. Just what he needed when he was already feeling out of sorts. What had happened to the days when he controlled his life? When he decided the beginning and ending of a relationship? When money seemed to solve any problem?

He didn't have to think hard to come up with that answer. Shelby had happened. Though he hadn't fallen in love with her, she had changed him. And then Meghan had come back into his life.

How could anything be the same after that?

He nodded appreciation as the waitress put the dessert plate in front of him. She watched as he took a bite. The warm pie oozed with tart apples and cinnamon. "Delicious."

"You need anything else, honey?"

He ignored the double meaning evident in her tone. "This is fine, thank you."

"You're welcome." She placed the check beside his plate. "Just let me know if you change your mind." The sashaying hips headed toward other customers.

Usually he was immune to harmless flirting, but tonight he almost needed the reassurance that he still had the famous Somers charm. Dani sure hadn't done anything to stroke his ego. All she did was blush. Kind of cute, really. But definitely a change from the self-assured women he usually dated.

Like Tracie. His former receptionist had been overly confident that an affair with the boss would open the door to a lifetime of wealth and privilege. As far as he knew, she'd done a fairly good job of spending his money in the few weeks she had his credit card. She could keep the stuff but not his heart. After all, she'd only been the last in a game that he and his buddies had perfected.

From their first kiss, Brett had known what Tracie had not. She would never be Mrs. Brett Somers. Self-absorbed women with their gorgeous bodies and beautiful faces were for showing off. Not for marrying.

Several weeks had passed since he'd arranged for the building concierge to remove Tracie's belongings from his apartment and change the lock. Tired of The Game, this time he'd hired an efficient, no-nonsense woman for the office.

His business associates, used to heady perfume surrounding them when Tracie handed them a cup of coffee and the occasional peek into her lace-adorned cleavage, had expressed their disappointment in his choice of a replacement.

But he didn't care.

Things had changed. He had changed. They'd have to get used to finding their not-so-innocent peeks somewhere else.

Which led his thoughts back to the enigmatic girl who had accompanied him to the movies.

Dani Prescott. Photographer of hospital lights. Classic movie aficionado. And somehow immune to the Somers charisma. He couldn't remember the last time he'd had so much trouble getting a woman's phone number.

Usually they offered their contact info without waiting to be asked. Then he entertained himself with imagining how many times his chosen victim looked at her phone, making sure it was on. Making sure she hadn't missed a message from him. Debated with herself whether to call him.

Always a game, and a game he always won.

Because he never called first.

Because the one who called first cared most.

And he never cared most.

Meghan Jensen McCurry plopped on the sofa and threw her arm over her head. She used to love Fridays. Without school the next day, Jonah could stay up later than his usual bedtime. On a rainy night like this one, they'd have made hot chocolate and snickerdoodles together before sprawling on their hand-me-down couch to watch a movie. Cozy nights that usually ended with the little boy falling asleep, his bare feet pressed against her legs.

She'd give anything to have those evenings back again.

Perhaps she should have stayed later at the hospital. But the sudden thunderstorm had sent her scurrying to the bakery before the weather got worse. The white box sitting on the counter held a dozen chocolate cupcakes. Jonah's favorite. A candle in the shape of the number 8 nestled inside. She wouldn't light the candle in the hospital, of course, but she'd put it in one of the cupcakes before singing "Happy Birthday."

Jonah would never remember, but she'd take photos so someday he could see what he missed.

Someday.

Let it be soon. Tomorrow even.

There could be no better birthday present.

A pastel green scrapbook lay on the sofa beside her. She picked it up and slowly opened the cover. Three photos of a red and wrinkly newborn adorned the first page. The pertinent information—date, time, weight—had been written in gold ink with a calligraphy pen.

The date a month earlier than expected. The weight an anxious, adorable five pounds, three ounces.

She turned the page and smiled at the first photo ever taken of her cradling the swaddled infant in her arms. His tiny face was barely visible between the blue cap and the striped blanket. Despite the overwhelming exhaustion, her own expression was one of awe and wonder. After several hours of intense labor, she'd given birth to the most beautiful boy who ever lived.

Love took on a whole new meaning.

Since no one else had been there to do the honors, the nursing staff took the photos. One of them went the extra mile by purchasing the scrapbook kit and placing the prints inside. They'd been kind to her at a time in her life when she desperately needed kindness. What would they think if they knew where Jonah was now?

If they knew why.

Unable to stop the tears, Meghan closed the baby book and clutched it to her chest. So many mistakes. So many stupid, stupid mistakes.

If only she hadn't gone to the Christmas party with AJ. Hadn't met Brett. Hadn't fallen for his deceitful charm.

She leaned her head back and let the tears run down her cheeks.

If she hadn't done any of that, she wouldn't have Jonah.

After leaving the diner, Brett meant to drive home. But several minutes later, he found himself turning into the complex where Meghan lived. He pulled into an empty space near her building and peered out the windshield at the third floor. A faint light shone behind the blinds.

Guess this was his night for staring at windows.

Not that Meghan gave him much choice.

At least his secretive plan to get her out of the hospital had worked. His pal Dr. Marc Nesmith had told Brett about a local megachurch that provided a few apartments for patients' families. They didn't have a vacancy but happily accepted Brett's offer to sponsor another one. Anonymously, of course.

His thoughts circled the same unending whirlpool. If only Meghan had told him the truth all those years ago. Had trusted him.

He shook his head, and the whirlpool swirled.

Back then it wouldn't have mattered. He knew it, and she knew it. That's why she had lied. Why she'd told AJ he, not Brett, was the baby's father.

But AJ hadn't been able to help her either.

Not when Anderson "Sully" Sullivan had other plans for his two grandsons. Plans that didn't include a social-climbing art student or her illegitimate child.

Brett shook his head again while biting the inside of his lip. Meghan wasn't a social climber. Just a naïve college coed who got caught up in a rivalry she didn't know existed. If she hadn't been AJ's date to their grandparents' annual Christmas gala, Brett would never have given her a second glance.

In a way, Dani reminded him of Meghan. The same nice-girl innocence. The same overeagerness to be viewed as sophisticated and worldly. It never worked.

He smiled remembering how awkward she had been when they first met. He'd have known Regina Lampert wasn't her name even if he hadn't been familiar with the movie.

Then, during the showing of *Notorious*, she scarcely took her eyes from the screen. Her contagious excitement and rapt attention enhanced his own enjoyment of the familiar film. Lucky break he'd remembered it was showing. And that she'd agreed to go with him.

Though if the situation with Meghan had taught him anything, it was that young women with stars in their eyes should be avoided. Somehow or another, they always trailed trouble behind them.

He probably shouldn't have asked Dani to tomorrow night's banquet. So much for his dating sabbatical. It had lasted all of two months.

A shadow moved past the apartment window, then the light went out. "Good night, Meghan," he whispered in the darkness. "Sleep well."

He backed his car out of the space and headed toward home. He lived in a ritzier part of the city than Meghan. Not that he didn't want her to have the best—he just knew anything that smacked of too much luxury would arouse her suspicions. He'd done the best he could to balance economy with safety. At least he didn't have to worry about her coming home late from the hospital.

Again, his thoughts slid to Dani. He wished he could say the same for her. But over the years, that area around the interstate had been featured in numerous news articles and reports. No one in their right mind would choose to stay there. Unless that was all they could afford. Was that the situation with Dani?

What was she doing in town, anyway? As he thought back over their conversations, both before and after the movie, he realized she'd never given him a reason. She never even told him what she did for a living.

Not that he had asked.

Perhaps he should have. But the truth was, he hadn't been that interested. He hadn't expected to see her again, to be involved with her in any way. No reason to care.

Except somehow he did.

Fat raindrops bounced across his windshield, then struck with a thunderous barrage. He flipped his wipers to the highest speed and braked as he approached an intersection. Lightning zapped nearby, and the traffic light disappeared. Simultaneously the streetlamps darkened.

Seeing no other headlights, he cautiously maneuvered through the intersection while pulling out his phone. He found Dani's name, then hesitated. His thumb hovered over the send button.

He couldn't break the rules of The Game.

Not for a slip of a girl who skulked around hospitals and spilled soda on his pants.

Not even if her dark eyes intrigued him with their secrets.

− 5 −

*D*ani froze as the lamp beside her bed flickered, then went out. By the dim light of her open laptop, she edged her way to the dark window and removed the blanket covering the ragged blind. With the streetlights out, the world beyond her bedroom was black and ominous.

Despite her assurances to Brett, she barely felt safe here in the daylight, let alone at night. Now the power outage made it an even scarier place. Even the name, Baines Lodging, was too close to Bates Hotel for her peace of mind.

The storm seemed to rise in power, the rain pounding against the window as if demanding entrance.

No taking a shower tonight.

She crawled back into bed, pulled the comforter over her knees, and stared into the darkness.

Why had she ever come here?

She glanced at the newspaper article filling the screen of her laptop. She'd read it so many times she practically had it memorized. And that was before Brett had asked her to be his date.

"Up-and-Comer Honorees Announced: Columbus's Top Thirty Young Professionals"

The splashy headline was followed by details about tomorrow night's awards banquet and information about the recipients.

Dani picked up the laptop and cradled it in her lap. With a click, Brett's enlarged photo appeared on the screen. Confidence radiated from his dimpled smile and direct gaze. This was a man who didn't shy from a camera. But why would he? He was gorgeous, and he knew it.

She set aside the laptop and picked up her camera. Despite the room's darkness, she managed to turn it on and slowly flipped through the photos she'd taken of Brett at the hospital.

What had he been doing there?

Since returning to her rooms, she'd been going through her notes, searching for something she might have missed or forgotten. But nothing new popped out.

She knew his home address—a posh apartment in an upscale high-rise—his office address, his alma mater, club connections, and even the basics about his sister and cousin. But children? Nothing.

Perhaps that was his Achilles' heel. A secret child who was sick.

Hopefully that wasn't his only secret. She needed to find something she could use to hurt him, but it wouldn't be that.

She flipped through the photos again, her eyes glued to the man's handsome features. The one of him staring into the sky especially tugged at her heart. But she couldn't let compassion for whatever heartache he had been feeling affect her resolve.

After clicking off the camera, she leaned back and closed her eyes. Maybe the evening had been a dream. But no. She had gone to a movie with Brett Somers and then he'd asked her to accompany him to the banquet, totally oblivious that she already had a ticket.

Fifty bucks she hadn't needed to spend. Maybe she could get a refund.

She shut off the camera and returned to her laptop. Thankfully, since the internet was out, all her research had been saved to a folder. After a couple of clicks, the video popped onto the screen. She had found the entire interview with Ohio's so-called most eligible bachelor shortly after a thirty-second clip became a "must see" sensation. Dani's co-workers, even the dragon-lady administrative assistant to the president, swooned as Brett Somers flirted shamelessly with the middle-aged interviewer.

Was Dani the only one with enough sense to wonder why this gorgeous wealthy man was still single? Behind the alluring dimples and engaging charm hid an ogre. And though she kept it to herself, she had the proof.

Each of the Up-and-Comer honorees had been interviewed by a television personality for a regional program's website. However, Brett's interview also aired on TV. The interviewer had obviously been smitten.

Perhaps the woman had realized she needed to make up for her unprofessional fawning by moving beyond narrative fluff. Or perhaps she hoped Brett could be wooed by her sympathetic handling of his parents' tragic deaths.

Whatever her motives, the interview had quickly descended into a dark pit as she urged Brett to share his feelings about the airplane crash that orphaned him and his sister. But instead of wallowing in sorrow, he lashed out at the airplane's pilot in barely controlled anger.

Dani set the cursor at the appropriate spot and hit play. Brett's familiar voice came through the speaker.

"That incompetent pilot killed—no, murdered—my parents. If she hadn't been killed too, she'd have spent the rest of her life in prison."

Stop. Rewind. Play. Stop. Rewind. Play.

Brett's words seared into Dani's brain like the refrain from a nightmarish song.

Thunder cracked, startling her, and she envisioned her mother's plane falling from the sky in ear-splitting terror.

She'd been orphaned that day too.

Though reluctant to lose even its small light, she slid the laptop to the floor, then huddled into a tight ball beneath the comforter. The only way to escape her pain was in the merciful bliss of sleep.

When she awoke, the sun would be shining, the electricity would be restored.

And maybe, just maybe, her heart wouldn't feel so dead inside.

Brett groaned and checked the time. Not even three o'clock. Flipping back the covers, he sat on the edge of the bed and pressed his forehead against the heels of his hands.

This would teach him to drink coffee so late. Though caffeine wasn't the only reason he couldn't sleep.

He'd come home after leaving Meghan's place, flipped on the lights, and poured a glass of cold water from the pitcher in his humming refrigerator.

But what had happened when Dani flipped the switch at her place? Did the room light up or remain in darkness? He should have called her when the streetlights went out at that intersection. Just to check.

His bare feet sank into plush carpet as he headed for the kitchen. Pulling a bottle of Scotch from a cabinet, he eyed the label. Liquor wouldn't shut up his nagging conscience.

Or tell him when he'd gotten one.

He placed the bottle back on the shelf, accidentally clanking it against a glass dessert bowl. He upended the dish, and a glittering amethyst and diamond ring fell into his palm.

Tracie's ring.

She'd left it in a teacup by the kitchen sink when the concierge had moved her out. Brett suspected she'd done it on purpose, an excuse to come back and see him.

But about two months had passed since their breakup, and she hadn't contacted him.

He probably should return it to her. Unless he was the one who had paid for it. Only his accountant knew how Tracie had spent his money during their short relationship. Life was easier when someone else handled the bills, and Brett didn't really care how much shopping she had done with his credit card.

But thinking about money led his thoughts to Jonah. Even if Meghan objected to the idea, Brett needed to establish a trust fund for his injured son. He'd already put it off too long.

Making a mental note to set up a meeting with his attorney, he plopped the ring back into the dish. Then he opted for orange juice instead of the Scotch and raised the glass.

"Happy birthday, Jonah."

He downed the juice, then returned to the bedroom. But he knew sleep wouldn't come. Not yet.

Pulling aside the floor-length drapes, he stared out the patio doors into the stormy night.

And prayed.

At least, he tried. This prayer thing was still new to him, and he wasn't sure he was doing it right. Especially at moments like this when the stakes were so high. What was he supposed to do to be sure God listened to him?

AJ had said the past didn't matter. But the past always mattered. And Brett's past certainly wasn't that of a saint. It broke all his business principles to expect God to grant him what he wanted when he had spent his days flouting anything to do with God. That just didn't make sense.

All of his adult life he had been the one in control. He was the one who planned and strategized and manipulated the outcomes.

But he couldn't out-manipulate God. And he couldn't control what happened to Jonah.

He has to get better, God. He has to come out of this coma. What do I have to do to make sure that happens?

The silence of the night surrounded him. A city asleep.

Maybe God was asleep too.

The ringing of Dani's phone woke her from a restless night's sleep. She opened one eye and glared at the clock's blank display.

Still no electricity.

She reached for the phone and answered without looking at the screen. "Hello?"

"Get up, sleepyhead." Brett's too-cheerful voice sounded through the speaker. "The day's a-wastin'."

"I thought the banquet was tonight," she said, her voice groggy.

"It is. But there are a lot of hours till then."

"How many hours?" She glanced at the clock on her phone: 7:49. "Do you know what time it is?"

"Too early, huh?"

"Only because I didn't sleep very well last night."

"Why not?"

"The electricity's out." Sitting up, she finger-teased her hair, then pushed it away from her face. "It's a little scary here in the dark."

When he didn't answer, Dani checked the screen to be sure they were still connected. "Hello? You there?"

"I'm here. In fact, I'm right here. Outside your building."

"What? Why?" Dani scurried to the window, then yanked too hard on the sash's cord. Hardware popped from the frame, and the yellowed window blind slanted as one side fell. Ignoring the crisis, she wiped condensation from the mottled glass with her sleeve. Brett's shiny Lexus was parked next to her beater, his headlights shining through the heavy downpour.

"I brought coffee. Okay if I come inside?"

Dani glanced around the bedroom. Its décor dated to before her birth, and she didn't think the place had been cleaned much since then either. The drafty building seemed to be permeated with the chill of the rain. But at this time in her life, financial considerations trumped comfort and cleanliness. She should never have told him where to find her.

Too late now.

"Dani?"

"Um, sure. It's the second floor, number 202."

"Heading your way."

The call ended, and she swiped at the window again. Brett emerged from the Lexus, yanked the hood of his jacket over his head, then sprinted toward the building.

Dani hurriedly changed into jeans and a light sweatshirt, then raised the blinds in the other room, part sitting area and part kitchen. There was nothing she could do to improve its lackluster appearance. Except burn it to the ground.

When Brett knocked, she slid the deadbolt and opened the door. Their eyes met, and he flashed his dimples.

No one should look so gorgeous this early in the morning.

"Hey, there," he said. "Sorry for waking you."

"That's okay. I needed to get up."

"It's dark in here. How long has your electricity been out?"

"All night."

"You should have called me."

"Why would I have done that?"

He shrugged, and she resisted the childish impulse to stamp her foot. "Why are you here?" she demanded.

"Told you." He held out a cardboard carrier containing four cups. "Coffee."

"Come on in." She stepped back so he could enter the grim apartment, her cheeks burning at what he must be thinking as he looked around the dump she called home.

"I suppose this is way below your standards." The words were out of her mouth before she could stop them.

He faced her, his expression neutral. "What do you know about my standards?"

She hesitated, then gestured to the cardboard tray. "One of those mine?"

"More than one if you want. I've got light roast, dark roast, café au lait, and hot chocolate."

"Whipped cream on that hot chocolate?"

"You bet." He handed her the cup, and she wrapped her hands around its warmth before taking a sip.

"Um, good. Thank you."

"You're welcome."

"You want to sit?" She gestured toward the sofa. Threadbare arms stuck out beneath the floral quilt draped over the back and seat cushions. Studying his face, she waited for his repulsed reaction.

But it didn't come.

"I know I'm taking a big chance here," he said. "But I thought we might spend the day together."

"Doing what?"

"First, breakfast. I know a little place in German Village with the best omelets you've ever had."

"The best, huh?"

"The very best." He tapped his coffee cup against hers. "Then, if this rain lets up, maybe I can show you around the city. How about it?"

Dani's eyes slightly narrowed. Perhaps she imagined it, but his voice, even the expression in his eyes, seemed close to pleading. That didn't seem likely, but there was only one way to find out.

"Why?"

"Why, what?"

"Why would you want to spend the day with me?"

"Why not?"

"Don't you have better things to do?"

He hesitated, tilting his head in thought for a moment, then seemed to make a decision. "Truth?"

This should be good. "Please."

"Nope."

"Nope? That's it?"

"I don't have anything better to do." He gave a self-conscious laugh. "I didn't mean it like that."

"How did you mean it?"

He took a long sip of his coffee, obviously buying time. Two could play that game. She swirled her cup, then took a drink. The whipped cream barely cooled the heat of the chocolaty beverage.

"I know it was presumptuous to show up like this. But it'll give us a chance to get to know each other before all the formality of the banquet. Unless, of course, you already have plans."

"I have plans." Plans to fine-tune her résumé and scour the not-working internet for job openings. If she didn't find something soon, her only other option was that sales position in Boise. Even the thought of making that kind of move churned her stomach.

"Anything that can't be changed?"

Plans, too, to find out more about the man who had publicly accused her mother of murder. And here he was, drinking his coffee without a care in the world and giving her another golden opportunity.

"I need a few minutes to get ready."

"Take your time. I'm going to step into the hall." He slipped his phone from his pocket. "I've got a call to make."

"Okay."

As soon as he left the apartment, she went to her bedroom, closed the door, and pressed her hands to her knees. She couldn't do this.

Inhaling a deep breath, she straightened, then slowly exhaled. She owed it to her mom to find a way to humiliate Brett. Maybe then the childhood nightmares that had haunted her since she watched the interview would go away.

If she had to spend the day with him to figure out a plan, so be it.

Which left her with one question: What did he really want with her?

Brett finished his call, then reentered the apartment. A weak rectangle of light from the single window filtered through the steady rain. Too bad the weather was so uncooperative. Otherwise they could have wandered through German Village or gone bicycling along the Scioto Mile.

Cautiously sitting on the edge of the quilt-draped sofa, he drank his lukewarm coffee. In the meager light, the place looked depressing. But it probably didn't look much better when the sun was shining. Why in the world did Dani move into a dump like this? Had what she left in Cincinnati been even worse?

His curiosity grew as he glanced around the room. No personal items or framed photos adorned the rickety end table. Only a couple of magazines. *Photographers Journal. The Smithsonian.*

He stood and examined the prints hanging on the walls. Trite, uninspiring stuff in cheap frames that probably came with the place. Strange that someone with such an interest in photography didn't showcase her own work.

The only nice piece of furniture was a slender, five-shelf bookcase. He scanned the titles.

Howard's End. Les Misérables. A collection of short stories by Edith Wharton. Novels by Jane Austen and Charles Dickens. A crate on the floor overflowed with more books.

He picked up a well-worn copy of *The Secret Garden* and opened it. The message inscribed on the flyleaf said:

Dearest Dani,
  Wherever life takes you, may you always have the delight of a secret place as full of beauty and wonder as you are.

                    With all my love,
                    Mom

At least she had family. So what was she doing in this dump?

One thing was certain. By the end of the day, he'd know.

The bedroom door squeaked open, and his welcoming smile broadened in appreciation. Her skinny jeans were tucked in ankle boots, and a loose-fitting top didn't hide the appeal of her body as much as she probably thought. Her brown hair, brushed to a fine sheen, hung loosely about her shoulders. Pink gloss shimmered on lips he'd enjoy kissing.

But that was *before*. He wasn't the same guy anymore.

"You look great."

"I've been told I clean up pretty well."

He slid his eyes over her, then grinned at her blush. "So you do."

The blush deepened, and she grabbed a lightweight jacket from a hook by the door. "Are you ready to go?"

"Let me ask you something first. What are you going to do if your electricity doesn't come back on before this evening?"

Confusion tensed her features. "It has to."

"But if it doesn't, it'll make it hard for you to get ready for the banquet, right?"

"I hadn't thought about it."

"Fortunately for you, I did. So why don't you bring everything you need and get ready at my place?"

Her eyes grew round from either shock or anxiety. He wasn't sure which.

"I don't think I can . . ."

"I thought you'd say that, so I made a backup plan. I called AJ—my cousin—and wrangled an invitation to Misty Willow for this afternoon."

"What's Misty Willow?"

"It's this really old house out in the country where Shelby lives with her two little monsters."

"Shelby?"

"AJ's fiancée." He feigned distaste. "The monsters are Elizabeth and Tabby."

"Isn't that being a little pushy?"

Dani rubbed her arms as if she were cold. Time to lay on the charm. He flashed his dimples.

"AJ and Shelby will be at the banquet tonight. The evening might be more fun if you met them at the farm first."

Dani tilted her head as if considering his logic. "Are you sure they don't mind?"

"Not at all. We'll have a great time. Plus we won't have to rush back here. We'll drive straight to the banquet."

"Okay. I'll get my dress."

"That's my girl."

He immediately regretted the too-casual phrase as Dani faced him, her lips tight. But instead of responding, she went to her bedroom.

Blowing out air, he rubbed the back of his neck. He needed to guard his silvery tongue with this one. His relationship with Tracie had begun when she'd approached him at the end of a workday with her blouse strategically parted in a blatant invitation. A move he'd been expecting since the day he'd hired her.

Dani would never do anything so obvious.

Not that it mattered. They'd spend the day together, then go their separate ways.

After all, he was on a dating sabbatical. And would be until his son was completely healed.

– 7 –

eghan stood beside the hospital bed and pushed the pale hair away from her son's forehead. His eyes seemed to move beneath the translucent lids, but she'd learned several weeks ago that the movement meant nothing.

"Happy birthday, Jonah," she whispered. "I have a cupcake for you. Chocolate. Your favorite."

The door to the room creaked open, drawing Meghan's attention. Shelby Kincaid stepped inside. "Okay if I come in?"

Meghan returned Shelby's smile. "Of course. Hi."

"I brought presents for the birthday boy." Shelby placed the colorful bags on a nearby table, then handed the smallest one to Meghan. "And one for you."

"Why for me?"

"A new tradition. Celebrating moms on their kids' birthdays. Do you think it'll catch on?"

"I doubt it, but it's a nice thought." Meghan cradled the bag, then narrowed her eyes. "It's not from Brett, is it?"

"Nope, and it's not from AJ either. It's only from me."

"Thank you. This means a lot."

Shelby turned her gaze to Jonah's still body. "How is he?"

"Nothing's changed."

"How are you?"

"Tired."

"You need a break."

"I know. But it's hard enough leaving the hospital at night. I'm not sure I can during the day."

"I understand that. You need to take care of yourself, though." Shelby tapped the gift bag. "Now open your present."

Meghan removed a small jewelry box from the bag, then opened the lid to reveal a silver chain with a cameo pendant. The ivory profile of a woman and child appeared against a navy blue background. Silver filigree edged the cameo. "Oh, Shelby, this is beautiful. You shouldn't have. But I'm glad you did."

"I'm glad you like it."

"I love it." Meghan fastened the necklace and touched the pendant where it lay against her throat. "How does it look?"

"Lovely." Shelby picked up a blue bag with yellow tissue paper. "This one is from the girls. They collaborated on a book. Elizabeth wrote the story, and Tabby drew the illustrations."

"I can't wait to see that." Meghan took the bag and gestured toward the bakery box. "Have a cupcake?"

"Kind of early in the morning, isn't it?"

"They're chocolate."

"Well, in that case . . ." Shelby opened the lid.

"I thought Jonah deserved a little party. Even if he's asleep."

"Of course he does." Shelby perched on the edge of the sofa while she peeled the liner from the cupcake. "Now don't get mad, but the green bag is from AJ."

"I guess I shouldn't be surprised."

"Jonah is his only . . ."—she hesitated then laughed—"his only first cousin once removed. I think. Anyway, he cares about him."

Meghan absentmindedly adjusted Jonah's blanket. If not for AJ, her son wouldn't be getting top-notch care at this premier children's hospital. But even though AJ had apologized for what had happened in the past, she hadn't quite forgiven him. And she definitely hadn't forgiven Brett. When she banned him from visiting, it seemed best to ban AJ too.

But that had been only a few days after Jonah's accident. She'd probably been too hard on both men, especially given her own treachery and deceit.

"Are you mad?" Shelby's voice sounded so pathetic that Meghan couldn't help but smile.

"No." She drawled out the syllable, revealing a hint of her Southern heritage, then giggled self-consciously. "You're the only friend I have here, so I can't alienate you."

"I'm glad of that. We all care about you, Meghan. You and Jonah both."

"I know you do. And I'm thankful. Really I am." She touched the cameo. "You're a good friend."

"I try."

"So tell me," Meghan said as she picked up a bag from the table behind her. "Do you know anything about this?"

"What is it?"

"It was here when I arrived this morning. The card says it's from the Bless This Child Foundation. Have you ever heard of them?"

"Can't say that I have."

"Me either. So I googled it."

"And?"

"It's a foundation for kids, but they specialize in carved wooden toys. Nothing like this."

"Then where did it come from?"

Meghan pulled out a stuffed monkey wearing an OSU shirt and wiggled it. "Kind of obvious, isn't it?"

"Brett." Shelby laughed as she reached for the toy. "Didn't he realize the OSU shirt would be a giveaway?"

"Apparently not."

"You know, Meghan . . ." Shelby hesitated as she straightened the tiny shirt. "Brett's not the same guy he was all those years ago."

"Why do I have so much trouble believing that?"

"Because he hurt you. But now he wants to do the right thing."

"And what is that, Shelby?" Despite her strongest efforts, Meghan's eyes misted. "What is the right thing?"

"I'm not sure any of us really knows. But he is worried about Jonah. And about you."

"He didn't care about me after I slept with him," Meghan said quietly. All these years later, his rejection still hurt. More accurately, her susceptibility to his feigned interest still hurt. If she could have foreseen the ripples caused by her desperate actions, she'd never have lied to AJ. At least she hoped she wouldn't.

"But that's not who he is anymore."

"How can you be so sure?"

"Finding out he had a son changed him." Shelby tilted her head in thought. "But I think it started before then. Maybe it was when his grandmother passed away. They were all deeply affected by her death."

"I remember her." Meghan returned the monkey to the bag. "She was kind to me at the Christmas party."

"Where you met Brett?"

"I was so stupid."

"You were young."

"And stupid."

"We all make mistakes. Do things we regret."

Meghan glanced at Jonah. Beneath his translucent lids were eyes the same enchanting blue as his father's. "Brett was so charming. So handsome. He took my breath away, and I just . . . I just let him."

"Believe me, I know how attractive he is."

"I bet you didn't fall into his arms." Meghan gulped. "Or his bed."

"Not his. But someone else's."

Meghan caught Shelby's gaze. "AJ's? That doesn't matter. You're getting married."

"It still matters, but I wasn't talking about him."

"Then who?"

"My husband." Shelby sighed heavily. "He was like no one I'd ever met before. Strong and handsome. It wasn't easy holding on to my beliefs, so we rushed into marriage. Less than a week later I knew it had been a mistake, but what could I do about it? And then Elizabeth came along and then Tabitha. I wouldn't give them up for anything, but . . . I do understand how easy it can be to get caught up in something that seems so romantic. So wonderful."

"Your husband. He didn't . . . hit you, did he?"

"No, nothing like that. Just little things that added up to me not really knowing him as well as I thought I did. And him not being the knight in shining armor I believed him to be."

Meghan's face relaxed into a small smile. "What about AJ?"

Shelby's expression immediately softened, and her eyes glowed. "He *is* my hero. And I love him with all my heart."

"I guess you're glad I ran away from him," Meghan teased.

Shelby's expression grew serious. "I'm so sorry for how he hurt you. You have to know how guilty he feels, how guilty he has always felt for not standing up to his grandfather until after you'd gone."

"But I should never have deceived him."

"We've all made a mess of things. In our own way. But now, God has brought us all together."

"You don't really think God made this happen, do you?"

"The accident? Of course not. But I believe God prompted AJ to look for you when you needed him most."

Meghan crossed her arms, shielding her heart from the truth she didn't want to face. It was easy for Shelby to talk about God. True, she had been through a lot. Apparently her marriage hadn't been that happy, and then her husband had been killed, leaving her with two little girls to raise on her own.

But things were working out great for her. She was engaged to a man who had turned out to be a better guy than Meghan ever thought possible. If only she could be as lucky as Shelby.

Instead she'd been gullible. Naïve. Stupid.

If she had not given in to Brett, she might be happily married to AJ now. She glanced at Shelby.

Except that she hadn't really loved AJ. Not like he deserved to be loved. She hadn't loved Brett either. And she didn't love her despicable ex-husband Travis.

Maybe she didn't know how to love. Except as a mother.

"I detest Brett, you know."

"I know."

"But sometimes it's hard. I have to work at it."

Shelby gave her a quizzical look.

"I look at Jonah, and he fills my heart with such joy. As much as I regret what I did, how can I be sorry for it when I have this amazing little boy in my life?"

"See? God gave you a precious little soul to light up your world."

"He has blue eyes. Did you know that?" She didn't wait for Shelby to answer. "I had forgotten how much his eyes looked like Brett's until he came here that night. It really shook me up. Anyone who saw them together would know Jonah is Brett's son."

"Brett knows it."

"So I should let Jonah have the monkey?"

"I think so."

Meghan smoothed the toy's furry head and straightened its sweater. "It has an MP3 player inside. Brett loaded songs on it. Lullabies, country and western, pop, jazz. 'Puff the Magic Dragon.' 'Jesus Loves Me.' Quite an assortment."

"That had to take time."

"Unless he hired someone to do it."

"Something tells me he didn't."

Meghan turned on the music and Kenny Loggins's "House at Pooh Corner" quietly played. "I love this song."

"Me too."

She nestled the monkey beside Jonah's pillow and glanced at the round wall clock. "I need to get to the arts and crafts room. They'll be waiting for me."

"Arts and crafts?"

"I volunteer there. Helping a few of the children pass the time. It passes the time for me too."

"Is it okay if I stay with Jonah for a few minutes?"

"Will you pray for him?"

"I'll pray for both of you."

"Thank you, Shelby. For the gifts. For being my friend."

"I'm always here for you. For both of you."

Meghan smiled her thanks, then bent over Jonah's bed and kissed his smooth forehead. With a wave to Shelby, she walked out of the room and leaned against the corridor wall. Maybe Shelby was right. Maybe God had a reason for bringing AJ and Brett back into her life. But why did he have to use Jonah to do it? Why was Jonah paying the price for all of her wrong decisions?

If only she'd stayed with AJ.

If only she hadn't slept with Brett.

And having made both those horrible mistakes, why in the world had she allowed Travis McCurry into her life? Allowed him to have anything to do with Jonah?

None of those questions could be answered. And neither could the most important one of all. Why had Jonah been in Travis's car? Her ex-husband had walked away from the accident. But not Jonah.

Because she hadn't been there to stop Travis from taking him, Jonah might never wake up again.

*D*ani stared out the windshield as Brett drove along the rain-soaked streets. The *thwack* of the wipers echoed the beat of her heart.

Her initial plan had been to discreetly observe the guy in his own social sphere at tonight's banquet. She'd be observing him, all right. Sitting right next to him. And not just tonight but the entire day.

She should be thrilled.

Instead, she felt like a fraud.

What would he think when he found out the truth? Who she really was. The reason she was skulking around the hospital taking photographs.

She'd expected, even wanted, to find an arrogant, conceited hedonist who thought only of himself. But Brett had gone out of his way on her behalf. Sure, he asked her to the movie because he didn't have a date on a Friday night. But, as promised, he'd been a gentleman. And loathe as she was to admit it, she'd had a good time.

Now he'd rescued her from a dreary day of the "poor me's."

Today could be, figuratively speaking, the answer to her prayer. If she found out something awful about him, something he didn't want anyone else to know, maybe she could coerce him into publicly retracting what he'd said about her mom.

She inwardly sighed. That hope was nothing more than a pipe dream. When had she ever forced anyone to do anything they didn't want to do?

"Gutless." Her stepdad's voice slithered in her ear. *"You won't amount to nothin' 'cause you can't stand on your own two feet."*

Besides, the women who'd drooled over Brett's interview video hadn't cared what he had to say about the crash.

But Dani cared.

She'd pored over the few documents she could get her hands on—news accounts, investigative reports, transcripts of witness testimony. But no matter how often she reviewed them, she was left with the unsettling feeling that there was more to the story.

The Federal Aviation Administration first ruled the crash an accident due to a mechanical failure. But Sully Sullivan would not accept that as an explanation for the deaths of his son and daughter. The case had been reopened, and it seemed the second investigation had been rushed to an unsatisfactory conclusion. At least from her perspective.

"Something wrong?" Brett's voice drew her from the past, a place she usually avoided. But his public accusation had thrown her back into its turmoil. The illusory respite she'd enjoyed during her college years had disappeared, and now her future appeared as dreary as the gray horizon.

"Dani?"

She started and glanced at him. "I'm fine."

"You're not nervous about meeting AJ and Shelby, are you?"

"Maybe a little."

"No need to be." He flashed a quick smile her way. "They'll love you."

Would they?

As he maneuvered alongside deep puddles, she studied his profile. Classically handsome cheekbones. Strong jawline. Self-confidence exuded from his every gesture, every movement. The perfect hero for a romantic love story. But only on the outside.

"You know, I don't think you ever told me what you do," he said. "Are you a photographer?"

"Not really." She slightly twisted toward him. "I'm kind of between jobs right now."

"Um," he murmured.

Dani read his thoughts as clearly as if he'd said them. *That explains the cheap place, the clunker. A charity case if ever I saw one.*

"What did you do?" he asked.

"You go first." She flicked a miniature OSU football hanging from his rearview mirror. It swung like a tiny pendulum. "I bet I know where you went to college."

"Business admin, communications minor, and MBA all from . . ." He tapped out a drumroll on his steering wheel. "*The* Ohio State University."

"Big fan, huh?"

"You know it. Ever been to a football game?"

"Not at OSU."

"We'll have to do something about that. Your turn."

"Bachelor's in liberal arts from the University of Cincinnati."

"Liberal arts? I should have guessed."

"Why do you say that?"

"Evening stroll in front of the hospital. Camera hung around your neck. The books in your bookcase." He gave her a sideways glance. "So before moving here, you were what, flipping burgers at McDonald's?"

She wanted to be offended, but his playful tone and the teasing glint in his eye refused to let her.

"I'll have you know I earned a legitimate and complicated degree."

"Of course you did."

"Really. I have three certifications."

"Wow me."

"Creative writing, historical preservation, and film and media studies."

"I'm impressed. And you do what with all that?"

She hesitated. The degree might be impressive, but her job history wasn't.

"Are you in the FBI?"

Her face softened as she gave a small laugh. "No."

"Then why so secretive?"

"It's just that I haven't found my place in the world yet. So there's nothing much to tell."

"Unless you're a trust fund baby, you must have been doing something for the past . . . when did you graduate?"

"In April."

Brett's eyes darted at her then back to the road. "This past April?"

"Surprised?"

"Just didn't realize . . ." His voice trailed off as he maneuvered into a tight parking lot. He found a space, parked, then half-turned toward her. "How many years did it take for you to get that complicated degree?"

"Five. Why?"

"Just wondering."

And estimating her age. She knew it as surely as if he had a calculator emblazoned on his forehead.

"So after graduation, you moved here?"

"Not exactly."

"Then what exactly?"

She'd known since last night that eventually he'd ask the question. And if he didn't, either his cousin or the fiancée would. All she could do was stick to the truth. At least until she couldn't.

"For my senior thesis, I produced a short film that aired on the Cincinnati PBS station. During my last year, they hired me part-time. After graduation, I was promoted to assistant producer."

"That's impressive."

"Not really. The actual day-to-day tasks weren't as exciting as my title suggested."

"So why aren't you still assistant producing?" He grinned mischievously. "Did you embezzle from petty cash? Run off with the station manager?"

Her lips parted in a small smile at his allusion to *Casablanca*. "Nothing like that."

"What then?"

Truth faltered, unable to withstand the weight of her secret.

"Victim of budget cuts," she said offhandedly. Her stepfather had been told the same lie in the vain hope he'd offer sympathy. Maybe even encouragement.

"After only a few months? That sounds odd."

"Yet true. If something doesn't turn up soon, I may be begging to flip hamburgers."

"Why move to Columbus?"

"I needed a change. Besides, I have an interview on Monday."

"Where?"

"At a bank. They need someone to help with social media marketing." She curled her lip. "Better than flipping hamburgers, right?"

"I'm not sure." He seemed to study her, his eyes appraising her own. "I have a hard time picturing you stuck behind a desk."

She shrugged and faced the windshield. The rain had lessened, but the sun's radiance was diffused by heavy gray clouds.

"You okay?"

Her throat caught, and she swallowed before answering. "Fine."

"Tell you what." He rested his palm on the back of her hand. Her first instinct was to pull away, but his comforting warmth seemed to soothe her seesawing emotions. "Let's declare this a forget-our-troubles day. No worries."

She gazed at him, allowing herself to get momentarily lost in the depth of his gorgeous eyes. "Do you have worries?"

In the space of a heartbeat, a cloud weakened his smile. "You'd be surprised."

"Tell me."

Pressing his lips together, he slightly shook his head. "If I did, you wouldn't want to spend the day with me."

"Sounds serious."

"It is."

"Something to do with last night's hospital vigil?"

"Long story."

"We've got all day."

Sadness lessened the light in his eyes. Suddenly she wanted to chase the gloom away, to soothe whatever pain gripped his heart. Without realizing it, she twisted her hand so their palms met.

He smiled, then gestured toward the restaurant. "I'm starving. Shall we go in?"

"Okay."

"The umbrella's beneath your seat."

"You aren't afraid of a little rain, are you?" she teased as she retrieved it. "Afraid you'll melt?"

"Afraid you will." He clicked open his door. "Stay there."

Always the gentleman. Opening her door, holding the umbrella as they hurried to the restaurant.

She could get used to being treated with such unfamiliar gallantry. But even if she could forgive him for what he'd said, he'd never consider someone like her for a serious relationship.

After they ordered a fruit sampler and omelets, Brett handed the menus to the waiter. Across the wooden table, Dani seemed to have retreated into a place he couldn't go. She was an enigma, this liberal-arts-grad/assistant-producer. Despite her quiet demeanor, he sensed a tornado spun within, whipping her mood from playful to sad to distant.

"I might be able to help with your job search. That is, if you'd rather forget the whole bank thing. I have a lot of connections."

"I'm sure you do."

"Is your résumé up-to-date?"

"Mostly. I planned to work on it today."

"It's my fault you're not getting it done. All the more reason for me to help."

"I appreciate it, but I doubt you can."

"Why not?"

"I've already been to the stations around here, both TV and radio. The only openings are for sales. If I wanted to do that, I'd be in Boise. I have a friend at a radio station there who told me about an opening."

Brett refrained from asking her why she hadn't checked out the local stations before she moved. The girl obviously had secrets, and he was intrigued by whatever she was hiding. But pressuring her wouldn't be as much fun as showing his so-called sensitive side. Women always told more than they intended when he used the subtle approach.

His practiced smile appeared, and he started to reach for her hand but picked up his water glass instead. The ice water cooled his throat as he berated himself. Whatever Dani's secrets, she wasn't his latest plaything. No more manipulation. No more insincerity.

He set down the glass and caught her gaze. "Sales can be tough, but you've got the necessary qualifications."

"No, I don't."

"You're young. Intelligent. Cute." He winked, unexpectedly enjoying the innocent rush of teasing her. "That'll get you in the door."

"That's nice of you to say, but I'm not sure how true it is."

"It's true," he assured her. "Then you just need to learn the secrets of closing."

"You know the secrets?"

"Of course."

"I thought you were in property development or investing. Something like that."

"But sales is part of what I do. I have to convince people to trust me with their money."

"I get the feeling you're really good at that."

"The company's growing, so I guess I am."

"It must be nice to have found your niche. To not have to worry about finances or how to pay for things or . . ." Her voice faded, and she stared at her hands.

"I enjoy what I do, but that doesn't mean I don't work hard. A land development deal is like a moving puzzle, and sometimes that puzzle has missing pieces. I have to gather them all together and put them in the right places."

"What if you don't?"

"Fortunately, that rarely happens. But when it does, I cut my losses, evaluate what went wrong, and then I don't make that same mistake again."

"You're very self-confident, aren't you?"

"I have to be. Who's going to believe in me if I don't believe in myself?"

"I guess that's one way to approach the world."

"It's worked so far." He picked up his phone and rotated it against the table. "Sully would be proud."

"Who's Sully?" she asked, as if she didn't already know.

"My grandfather. Anderson John Sullivan II."

"The Second? Not Junior?"

"Oh no. Definitely not a junior." Brett pretended to make a face. "Apparently, Anderson the First had high hopes his son and all the sons to come after would create a lasting legacy."

"A profitable business?"

"More than that." Brett frowned, not sure he wanted to delve much further into family history. Though what could it hurt? It wasn't like Dani was trying to surreptitiously ferret out any confidential information.

"Sully founded Sullivan Investments after he returned from the Korean War. Grew it almost single-handedly into his own little empire. I've worked there since I was a teen. And when he died, I inherited the company."

"He must have had a lot of faith in you."

"I suppose. Though he wouldn't have liked me changing the name."

"Then why did you?"

"I'm not a Sullivan. Plus, I wanted to put my own stamp on the company. Get a fresh start."

"But it's not really a fresh start if you're handed the whole kit and caboodle."

"I suppose not."

"So after a couple of generations, you ended your grandfather's legacy."

"I wouldn't say that. Besides, the name lives on. AJ is the fourth Anderson John."

If Sully hadn't sent Meghan away, she probably would have married AJ. He rotated his phone. And Jonah would have been the next bearer of the family name.

"What is it?"

He shook his head. This wasn't the time to be thinking of Jonah.

"I'm very aware that being born into my family has its benefits," he said. "I don't apologize for that."

"I didn't ask you to."

"Why do I feel you don't approve?"

"It seems odd that your grandfather left the entire company to you. What about your sister and your cousin?"

"Amy got money. AJ inherited Misty Willow."

"Must be nice." Tension edged her voice, and she bit at her lip. Obviously she regretted the snide comment as soon as she said it, but she lacked the poise to gloss over the awkwardness.

He placed the phone next to his plate with a slight thud. "You think you're better than me, don't you?"

"I never said that."

"You're looking down your nose at me because my grandparents left me a fortune."

"That's not true."

"Most people don't think so, but snobbery is a two-way street."

"You're calling me a snob?"

"I am." He tried to keep his tone light, teasing. But truth be told, he didn't like how she made him feel. As if his success had nothing to do with him.

But what could you expect from a liberal arts grad?

– 9 –

The waiter appeared with two piping hot plates. Dani eyed the cheesy golden eggs and inhaled the spicy warmth of mushrooms, ham, and peppers. "Looks delicious."

"Best ever," Brett said.

She took a bite and nodded. "You're right."

"When it comes to food, you can always trust me to tell you the truth."

"Does that mean I can't trust you about anything else?" She hoped he didn't detect the hardness lying beneath her teasing tone.

"That depends on what we're talking about," he said with exaggerated mystery.

"How about Misty Willow? You said your cousin inherited it, but I thought it belonged to his fiancée."

"He did and it does." Brett flashed his dimples. "Shelby's ancestors settled the land, but Sully acquired it several years ago. He left it to AJ, who sold it to Shelby. Before they were engaged."

"'Acquired'?"

"You picked up on that, did you?" He waved his fork in her direction before spearing a melon cube from the fruit sampler. "It's not a very flattering story."

"Now I'm even more curious."

"No one's really sure what happened. All those involved in the . . . transaction . . . have died." He hesitated, seemingly lost in thought. Or perhaps considering how much family history he wanted to tell her.

Dani sat quietly, a technique she'd learned when interviewing sources for her thesis project. Give people silence, and they'd find the words to fill it. And sometimes they filled it with words they didn't mean to say.

"Sully cheated Shelby's grandparents."

"How?"

"Like I said, no one's really sure."

"Your grandfather doesn't sound like a very nice man."

"It's true he had his faults. But he had a few good qualities too." One corner of his mouth turned up in a tight smile. "Besides, it all worked out. Shelby returned to claim the old homestead and got herself a husband."

"You make it sound so romantic."

"Romance is overrated. Though you're probably not old enough to believe that." He chuckled, seeming to visibly relax as he deftly steered the conversation away from his family. "Have you actually read all those books you've got?"

"Of course."

"How many times have you read *The Secret Garden*?"

"Several. Why?"

"I saw the inscription. Does your family still live in Cincinnati?"

The unexpected question sucked air from Dani's lungs. She sipped her water and forced her body to relax. *He read Mom's inscription.* Words written by the person he blamed for his parents' deaths.

"My father does." A half-truth. The man may have been her mom's husband, but he'd never been her father. At least not after Mom died.

"What does he think of your move?"

"I haven't told him."

"Why not?"

Dani paused, considering how to answer. If she told Brett the truth—that she'd spent more time in foster homes than with her stepdad or that she'd practically been on her own since she was seventeen—he'd only ask more questions.

"We seldom talk."

"What about your mom?" Puzzlement narrowed his eyes. "The inscription she wrote was really nice. Meaningful. Aren't you close?"

Dani scooched a bit of tomato around her plate with a fork. Everything within her wanted to lash out at Brett for saying something nice about the woman he'd publicly maligned. But to do so would ruin everything. Though she still wasn't sure what she hoped to gain by her deceit.

Information? Revenge? An explanation for all the unanswered questions that haunted her dreams? A reason why her childhood had been tragically ruined on one thunder-filled night?

"*The Secret Garden* was the last book she gave me. Before she died."

The sympathy in his eyes almost did her in. She pushed a sliver of mushroom beneath the leftover egg and pressed the fork against the table.

"I'm sorry."

Afraid to trust her voice, she merely nodded.

"I mean it, Dani." He grasped her hand, then twined her fingers with his. "I lost my parents when I was a teen. I know how much it hurts."

She stared at their hands, acutely aware that another land mine had almost blown up in front of her. As far as Brett knew, she was a stranger with no knowledge of his parents' deaths. Yet she had never asked about them, not even when they were talking about his family tree. Apparently he wasn't suspicious of her lack of curiosity.

Though hesitant to do so, she met his gaze. Grief, buried but never forgotten, tightened the muscles around his eyes. She recognized the pain—how often had she fought against it when sorrow threatened to surface?

"I'm sorry too," she said quietly. Surprisingly, she meant it.

For a moment, neither of them spoke, and Dani's pulse quickened. How easy it would be to give in to this man's charm. She should let go of his fingers, say something to break the spell. But she didn't.

The waiter neared to take their plates, and Brett let go of her hand. "We said a trouble-free day, remember?"

"So we did."

"Are you ready to go?"

"I guess so." Her voice was steadier than she would have thought possible. "Still a little nervous about meeting your family, though."

"Don't be nervous yet. We need to stop by my apartment first."

"Why?"

"You've got your formal duds, but I don't have mine." He placed a few bills on the table and stood. "Coming?"

"Do I have a choice?"

He grabbed her hand as she rose from her seat and tucked her arm into his. "What do you think?"

Grateful for how he'd lightened the mood and flattered by his teasing gallantry, she let him escort her from the restaurant. But as he closed the car door and sprinted around to the driver's side, his question echoed.

I think that if I'm not careful, I'm going to fall under his spell. But I can't, oh I can't. Not when he's caused so much pain.

Dani entered the foyer of Brett's apartment, then stopped. A plush sea of creamy carpet spread before her. She glanced at her rain-splattered shoes.

"Guess I should take these off."

"The housekeeper would probably appreciate it." He knelt and lifted her foot. "Allow me."

"You don't need to—"

"Wouldn't want you to dirty your hands."

"Are you kidding me?"

He bent his head but not soon enough to hide his grin. Dani had no choice but to allow him to untie and slip off her ankle boot.

"Now the other one," he said.

"This isn't necessary."

"I know." He removed the boot while stifling a yawn.

"Tired?"

"To tell you the truth, I didn't sleep very well last night."

"Thunder keep you awake?"

"Something like that." He placed the boots by the door, slipped off his own shoes, then headed for the kitchen. "Have a seat."

She followed him and perched on a stool by the counter. While he washed his hands, she swiveled to face the living area. Dark wooden tables and shelves were softened by a long upholstered couch and matching chairs. Silver-framed photographs and assorted sculptures adorned shelves on either side of a massive television. On one wall hung a giant canvas of a beautiful but mysterious landscape.

"Can I get you anything?" Brett asked. "Water? Juice?"

"I'm fine, thank you."

"So what has you so deep in thought?"

She swiveled toward him and grinned mischievously. "I was expecting stuffy. Maybe even pretentious. But this? It's comfortable. Upscale, but comfortable."

"Those two things aren't exclusive you know."

"I'm not so sure. Sometimes the rooms in decorating magazines look so . . . museum-ish."

"Museum-ish?"

"You know what I mean. Everything is beautiful, everything is in its place. But how does anyone really live in a room like that? I wouldn't even want to."

"But you could live here?"

She opened her mouth, then closed it again. From the mischievous glint in his eye, she realized he'd meant to fluster her. And he'd succeeded. Then his expression clouded, and she followed his thoughts to the two-room dump where he'd found her.

"I had a cute apartment in Cincinnati," she said. "It was on the third floor of what had once been a magnificent house. The ceilings slanted at odd angles and the closet was no bigger than your refrigerator. But it was cozy and charming and"—she paused, soaking in the memory of her refuge—"peaceful. It was peaceful."

"Why did you leave?"

"Told you. To find a job."

"And you couldn't do that in Cincinnati?"

"It was time for a change."

She boldly met his gaze and lifted her chin, a silent challenge to back off.

He seemed to study her, his thoughts hidden behind an impassive mask until his expression softened. "I'm glad you came to Columbus."

"Why?" she said warily.

"Just am. And I'm glad you approve of this place." He gestured toward the apartment's large interior. "Though Amy deserves most of the credit."

"She has good taste."

"In most things."

"What does that mean?"

"Nothing really."

"Are you still upset with her for backing out of the banquet?"

"Not at all." He stared at her. Appraising her. By his wolfish expression, approving of what he saw.

The fake.

She self-consciously pushed her rain-dampened hair behind her ears and rushed to change the subject. "Does she live here too?" she blurted, though she already knew the answer. "Your sister?"

"She has her own place on the other side of town. She's a lobbyist."

"She works?" This news came as a surprise. Though Dani had focused her attention on Brett, she'd found information on Amy too. But nothing about a career.

"Of course she works."

"You said she'd inherited money, so I thought . . ."

"Told you. You're a snob."

"I am not a snob." But his sister was probably a Brett clone in high heels. A diva. A diva princess with her nose in the air.

He beat a rhythm on the counter. "Snob," he said in a singsong voice.

"So why did you get the family business all to yourself?"

"That's how Sully wanted it." He glanced at the clock on the stove. "It's a bit of a drive to the farm, so we should be leaving soon. Will you be all right by yourself while I pack my suit?"

"Sure." Truth be told, she could use the break from the conversational land mines. Being with Brett was exhausting.

"Turn on the TV if you want. I'll be right back."

She glanced at the giant television, then wandered to the shelves and picked up the nearest photograph. A slightly younger Brett smiled directly at the camera, his arm around a slender woman. Her blonde hair hung straight beneath a blue mortarboard cap, and she held a single yellow rose. Amy. The family resemblance was too striking for her to be anyone else.

Dani scanned the other photographs but didn't find what she was seeking. Most were snapshots of Brett with either Amy or an elderly couple. Probably his grandparents. A man with brown hair appeared in a few. The cousin?

However, not a single photograph showed anyone who could be either Brett's mom or his dad. It was as if they no longer existed.

Except as a memory.

- 10 -

Inside the master bathroom, Brett brushed his teeth, then gargled. He'd finally identified the unease that had been niggling at him since they'd left the restaurant. The weak spot in his plan for him and Dani to spend several hours with AJ and Shelby. Jonah.

Though his name might not be mentioned by any of the adults, no one could foresee what Elizabeth or Tabby might say. The girls didn't know all the sordid circumstances, but they had been told about the sick little boy in the hospital.

Their dad-to-be's nephew. Their uncle-to-be's son.

Not exactly nephew and uncle, but that's how he always thought of the relationships. He and AJ might be cousins instead of brothers, but along with Amy, AJ was the only family he had.

Brett clutched the edge of the vanity and puzzled out his dilemma.

He could cross his fingers, hope for the best, and spend the day on edge. Or he could tell Dani the truth and relax.

Besides, keeping Jonah a secret seemed disloyal. As if he was trying to hide his son from the world. And that wasn't true.

He wasn't ashamed of Jonah.

Only ashamed of how he'd acted toward his mother.

Brett stared at his reflection and cleared his throat. "Dani, I need to tell you something. I have a son."

He shook his head and tried again. "By the way, I have a son."

Pressing his hands against the marble vanity, he slouched over the sink.

Help me, God. Why can't I do this? It should be so easy.

An unexpected warmth flowed through him, and when he looked into the mirror, his reflection somehow appeared straighter. Stronger.

Is that what it felt like for God to answer a prayer?

He wasn't sure. But one certainty steeled him. Whatever words he used, telling Dani about Jonah was the right thing to do.

After splashing his face with water and running a brush through his hair, he headed for the living room. Dani stood by the bookshelves, a photograph in her hand.

"That's my family," he said. "Taken a few months before Sully passed away." He pointed to each individual and named them. "Sully, Gran, Amy, AJ, and, of course, me."

"You and Amy look so much alike. But not AJ."

"We get our hair and eyes from our dad. AJ looks like a Sullivan. Which is convenient, since he is one."

She placed the photograph on the shelf, then gave him a strange look. "Where's your suit?"

"Before we go, I want to tell you something. About someone else in my family. Let's sit down for a minute."

After she settled in a corner of the sofa, Brett sat next to her. Maybe a little too close because she drew her knees into her body, arms wrapped around her legs.

"Comfy?"

She nodded, and he took a deep breath, then exhaled.

"I have a son. His name is Jonah."

Dani's eyes widened as Brett's words clicked with the memory of the photo of his anguished face. "That's why you were at the hospital."

"He's in a coma. From an auto accident."

"I'm so sorry."

"Me too."

Silence surrounded them as Brett leaned his head against the back of the sofa. Dani's mind whirled with the implications. He'd never been married, but he was a father. A dad.

"How old is he?"

"Eight." His dimples creased and twisted as he clenched his jaw. "Eight years old today."

So the present he gave the other man at the hospital last night was for his son. But then . . .

"Why aren't you with him?"

"That's difficult to explain. I only found out about him a couple of months ago."

She unconsciously placed a hand on his arm, then pulled away when she'd realized what she'd done.

He seemed momentarily amused, but then sadness tightened his slender smile.

"It's okay if you don't want to talk about it." The words surprised her, not only because she said them, but because she meant them. His pain had smothered her burning curiosity. "I'm glad you told me, but you don't owe me any explanations."

"I know. But to tell you the truth, it'd be nice to talk to someone about it. And there aren't that many people . . ."

The light bulb sparked above Dani's head. This amazingly handsome and wealthy and most eligible bachelor was lonely.

And he was turning to her for friendship.

The realization awakened something strange in her. An odd mix of being honored but also of power. Especially if he confided in her.

Guilt pressed against her conscience, and she swatted it away. If their roles were reversed, she had no doubt Brett wouldn't feel any remorse at all. But the twinge grew stronger. This wasn't who she was.

She inwardly sighed. Maybe not. But no matter how nice he

had been to her, she had to find a way to make him regret what he'd told the world about her mom.

Sweat dampened her palms. No wonder. Brett's faith in her was akin to piling hot coals on her head. Worse, he didn't even know it. She was a wolf in sheep's clothing. And she didn't like being thought of as either the big bad wolf or the meek helpless lamb.

She slightly shifted, settling deeper into the lush corner of the couch. Brett didn't look so confident now. Certainly not like the millionaire owner of a multimillion-dollar company. She guessed she shouldn't be surprised he had fathered a child. Though it seemed strange he hadn't known about the boy until recently. Why wouldn't the mother have insisted on getting child support, especially from someone as well-off as Brett?

Slow anger rose in Dani's gut. The perfect example of him not getting what he deserved. Skating by on his charm and good looks. Most men wouldn't have been so lucky.

Except he didn't know.

The loud thought rebuked her, insisting she acknowledge its truth. She tried to brush it away, but that wasn't fair. He couldn't very well do the right thing if he wasn't aware of the child's existence.

But *why* didn't he know?

Her thoughts eddied then cleared.

"She was afraid you'd take him away."

Brett faced her, his eyes dark.

"I'm sorry. I didn't mean to say that out loud."

His mouth twisted as if he were trying to maintain control of his emotions. When she caught his gaze, the light was gone from his eyes.

"That wasn't it," he said softly. "She was afraid. But that wasn't why."

He propped his stockinged feet on the coffee table, then ran his palms from his thighs to his knees. His attention seemed focused on the opposite shelves with their silver-framed family photographs.

"Several years ago, when AJ was in his first year at law school, he met a lovely young art student. Meghan." His eyes flicked to Dani, then away again. "They dated for a while, and Meghan became pregnant."

"Is Meghan Jonah's mom?" She narrowed her eyes. "I don't understand."

He ignored her question. "Meghan told AJ about the pregnancy, and he told Sully. Big mistake. Sully had major plans for AJ. Upwardly mobile law career. The state legislature. Eventually the governor's mansion."

"That's ambitious."

"Too ambitious for AJ to be tied to a girl from nowhere."

"So what happened?"

"Sully insisted Meghan have an abortion. Gave her a five-figure check and sent her packing. By the time AJ found out what Sully had done, Meghan had disappeared."

"He didn't look for her?"

"I'm not sure he knew where to look."

"But this is Jonah's mom? Jonah is your son?"

Brett puffed out air, seemingly lost in thought. "Fast-forward to this past June. AJ finds Meghan a few days after . . ." He paused, his eyes momentarily glazing. "After the accident. It was bad. Really bad." He shifted positions as if he couldn't get comfortable. "So AJ arranged to have Jonah flown to the children's hospital here. But it turned out—at least that's when we found out—AJ isn't Jonah's dad."

"You are."

He nodded, his facial muscles tight. "Yep." The word barely escaped his lips.

"AJ didn't know?"

"Not until I told him."

"So Meghan cheated on him?"

"It wasn't her fault." He paused, intent on studying his hands. "It was mine. I wined and dined her. Enjoyed her company. Then said good-bye."

Dani's thoughts whirled, caught up in another eddy. This proved he was capable of anything to get what he wanted. That he didn't care who got hurt or what pain he caused. And yet, his heartache surrounded them, a palpable presence she couldn't ignore. Or push away. Instead it seeped into her soul.

"Oh, Brett." She leaned toward him, her voice quiet and small. "Why would you do that?"

"Meghan was AJ's girlfriend. A young, naïve dreamer with stars in her eyes." He gazed past Dani as if he was looking into the past. "I wanted her because she belonged to AJ."

Unshed tears stung the back of Dani's eyes. Brett placed his feet on the floor, propped his elbows on his knees, and rested his chin on his closed hands. As if he didn't want Dani to see his face.

So handsome on the outside. But with such a cruel heart. What was that verse in the Bible—something about whitewashed tombs?

AJ must despise him.

Except he didn't.

Anger flared again. Did everyone forgive Brett his transgressions? Did Meghan? Though she was just as guilty of betraying AJ's trust.

"Meghan hates me," Brett said as if he'd read her thoughts.

The sorrow in his voice smothered her anger. All her emotions, all her thoughts were overshadowed by how his pain gripped her heart. At that moment nothing seemed to matter except to soothe his hurt. "She won't let you see him?"

He shook his head, then faced her. When he spoke, his voice was so low she barely heard him. "He's my son."

Caught in his gaze, she realized how easy it would be to get lost in those light blue depths.

Like so many others before her.

Perhaps like Meghan.

– 11 –

Brett slowly eased away from the emotional precipice he'd been about to fall over. He knew it would be hard to tell Dani about Jonah. He was man enough to admit he'd been a little anxious about how she'd respond. But he hadn't expected to be the one seeking her comfort.

To find himself getting lost in the luminous pools of her dark eyes.

He placed his arm around her shoulder, pulling her close. Her initial resistance was slight, then she rested her head against his shoulder. He shouldn't touch her, shouldn't give her false hope. But if he hadn't embraced her, he'd have kissed her. The tantalizing mouth, the parted lips, had been too mesmerizing. The urge to lose himself, to escape his pain, almost unbearable.

Resting his jaw against the warmth of her hair, he shut his eyes and focused on relaxing the tension in his muscles. Talking about Jonah had sharpened the pain he'd grown accustomed to living with, its multifaceted blade slicing his heart into a million scattered pieces. But with Dani fitted snugly against him, his breath steadied and the sharpness eased into a dull and heavy ache.

His phone buzzed, and Dani stirred. He tightened his hold. "Not yet," he whispered. "Please."

"What if it's important?"

"I don't care." He breathed in the floral notes of her fragrance, and his lips brushed her hair.

She pushed herself away from him, retreating to the corner of the couch. He swept his gaze over her as desire flared. Resisting the urge to gather her up, he simply squeezed her arm instead.

"If you were anyone else . . ."

"What?"

"If I answered that, you might run out of here. Then I'd have to roam the streets to find another date for tonight's banquet."

As he expected, her cheeks reddened. Pulling a square pillow from behind her, she swatted him with it. He ducked and rolled to the floor, practically getting stuck between the sofa and the coffee table. She swatted him again, and he grabbed the pillow. The quick tug-of-war ended when he let her win. As he sat on the floor between the table and the sofa, the remaining tension seeped from his body.

"For the record, Mr. Somers, you didn't find me by 'roaming' the streets."

"But I did find you." He playfully squeezed her foot as he rose, then stretched the kinks from his back.

She gazed at him, a rare teasing glint in her eyes. "Maybe I found you."

"Maybe you did." Maybe there was more truth to that than he wanted to admit. The moments holding her, brief as they were, had given him more comfort, more of a sense of well-being, than any he'd known with a woman.

Unsettled by the thought, he sat on the edge of the chair across from her. "I've told you my dark secret. Now it's your turn."

Her expression darkened, and she hugged the pillow to her chest. "What makes you think I have any?"

"You're hiding something."

"Nothing of interest to you."

He gazed at her, purposely keeping his eyes soft and nonthreatening. For years, he'd practiced the art of creating a silence, then patiently waiting for the other person to break it. Just another part of The Game, except this one worked equally well in business as it did with women.

Grinning on the inside like the Cheshire Cat, he tried to imagine what she might tell him. It couldn't be anything too serious, given her air of naivety and seeming lack of worldly experience.

Her facial muscles seemed to stiffen as guilt and shame chased each other across her features. She pulled her legs close to her body and bent her head so her dark hair fell forward. Huddled in the corner, hiding behind her hair and a pillow, she appeared helpless. Alone.

Perhaps she had a hidden past after all.

Intrigued, he moved to the coffee table, pushing aside a magazine so he could sit in front of her. "What is it, Dani?"

Silence.

"You can tell me."

She looked up and brushed the hair from her eyes. "Why did you tell me? About Jonah?"

"In case Elizabeth or Tabby mentioned him this afternoon." He shrugged. "And maybe I just needed someone to hear my side. Someone who wasn't family."

"So you told me. A stranger."

"You're more than that."

Surprise brightened her eyes, and he quickly stood. Almost as a defense against the words he hadn't meant to say, he reached for his phone and checked the screen.

"That missed call was AJ. I'm going to leave you alone again. Sorry."

"You aren't afraid I'll snoop?"

He started at her audacity, then chuckled. "Read a magazine." He picked up the latest issue of *Forbes* and handed it to her. "I won't be long."

"Do you mind if I get a glass of water?"

"There's a pitcher in the fridge. Help yourself."

He headed to his closet, then picked through his large assortment of ties while returning AJ's call.

"Are you on your way?" AJ asked.

"Hello to you too."

"Sorry." AJ audibly exhaled. "Hi, Brett. Thanks for returning my call. Are you almost here?"

"We're still at my place." He looped a black-and-silver silk tie over his suit hanger. It perfectly complemented the charcoal gray jacket. "You okay?"

"Shelby had an errand, so I'm alone with two little girls who can't wait for you to get here. But first they want you to stop by King Karl's and pick up a 'p'roni' pizza, as Tabby calls it."

"You know, don't you, that King Karl's isn't exactly on the way."

"I don't think they do. Besides, they say it's tradition."

"Two times." Brett plopped on the foot of the bed. "Two times I stopped there and now it's a tradition?"

"Don't know what to tell you."

"Are you sure you know what you're getting into with those little monsters?"

"Only that I can't wait to find out."

Jealousy poked Brett's gut. Like it did any time he thought too much about AJ and his soon-to-be family. He longed for the certainty AJ had that marrying Shelby was part of some divine plan. Inevitable. Perfect.

With his history, a divine plan would mean retribution. His heart being torn in two to repay him for all the hearts he had needlessly trampled. Even more reason, then, for him to guard his affections. To let no one in.

"You're a lucky man," he said. "You know that, don't you?"

"I do." AJ paused, probably counting his blessings. One, Shelby. Two, her daughters. Three, his own soon-to-be family. "So what about the pizza?"

"Do you think I'd disappoint those two hooligans?"

"Thanks. You know they're crazy about you."

"Only because they're too young to know any better."

After hanging up, he placed his suit in a garment bag, then packed his dress shoes and a few other things. Though he went through the motions on autopilot, his mind whirled as one thought chased another.

Dani's question about why he had told her about Jonah poked at a tender spot deep inside him. All he knew was that he'd said an impulsive prayer, then felt a resolve he'd never experienced before.

But he'd only meant to tell Dani of Jonah's existence.

So why had he poured out the sad, sordid story to her? A woman— little more than a girl herself—whom he'd just met?

It wasn't his style to share his deepest feelings with anyone. He'd learned not to do that long ago, having been taught by great teachers—his parents. He experienced firsthand how often each one lied to the other. And he was very aware of the deceitfulness implicit in his own relationships. He seldom out-and-out lied to the women he allowed into his life, but he always knew the secret they did not.

A relationship with him was on a countdown clock. Once the time ended, he said good-bye.

With that as his plan, women got access to his wallet but not his heart.

Yet he'd shared something important, something significant, with an unemployed brunette. One with a liberal arts degree, no less.

He zipped up the garment bag. Had no one been around to advise this girl?

After the door closed behind Brett, Dani stretched her legs, then wiggled her toes in the plush carpet and closed her eyes.

The apartment was blissfully quiet, the only sound the purring hum of the refrigerator. A fresh, clean fragrance seemed to fill the room. Despite the emotional upheaval she'd experienced while talking to Brett, she sighed contentedly.

How wonderful it must be to live in a place like this. No sirens waking you in the wee hours of the morning. No rank odors. No creepy-crawly things in dark corners.

She shivered, then headed for the kitchen area. The first cabinet door she opened held stacks of dishes, bowls, and mugs. The next held bottles. She pulled down one that was half-filled with rich amber liquid.

Scotch. The brand her stepdad only bought on holidays. Then downed like water.

Repulsed, she shoved it back onto the shelf next to a delicate glass dish. Intrigued by its etched design, she tilted it forward. A ring slipped from the dish, and Dani fumbled to catch it.

Diamonds surrounded the deep purple gemstone set in a platinum band. Enchanted by the ring's elegant beauty, Dani slid it on her finger. It was a little loose, but she trapped it in place with her thumb and admired its loveliness. The diamonds sparkled, and she leaned across the counter to see them radiate their fire beneath one of the trio of pendant lights that hung from the ceiling.

Startled by a noise from the hallway, Dani straightened. Brett appeared, and she quickly crossed her arms to hide her hand, then shoved it into her pocket.

"I just talked to AJ," he said as he laid a garment bag over the back of the sofa. "Apparently we need to pick up pizza."

"Sounds fun." She forced her voice to sound casual and hoped he couldn't hear the pounding of her heart. Or notice that she didn't have any water.

"According to Elizabeth and Tabby, it's tradition."

"Pizza is a tradition?"

"Twice I've brought them pizza. Only twice. Apparently now I have to every time I visit." He gave an exaggerated sigh.

"You know you love it," she said, her voice remarkably calm considering her pocket was laden with stolen loot.

"You're right." His lopsided grin revealed only one dimple. But even that was enough for her breath to catch in her throat.

Especially now that she had unwittingly become a thief. How was she going to fix this?

"Ready to go?"

No, I need you to go away so I can put this ring back where it belongs.

"Ready as I'll ever be."

"Before we do . . ." He perched on the back of the sofa, his hands resting on either side. "I've been thinking that, well, after what I told you, you know, about Jonah, about Meghan." He stopped and licked his lips.

He's nervous?

"I'll understand if you don't want to hang out or go with me to the banquet. Just say the word, and I'll take you home."

"Is this your polite way of getting rid of me?"

"Not at all," he said hurriedly. "It's just, now you know something about me most people don't. I haven't exactly gone around town shouting out the news I'm a dad."

"No, of course not."

"So now that you know the truth about me"—he paused and heaved a sigh—"I probably shouldn't have told you."

"I'm glad you did." And not only because his behavior had been scandalous or because she wanted him to suffer. He'd trusted her with something important. Something personal. She doubted many women could say the same.

Maybe not even the woman who had last worn this amethyst ring.

Her conscience burned as she pushed the ring from her finger and as far into her pocket as it would go. Who did it belong to? Amy? Or an old girlfriend? He'd said he wasn't seeing anyone, but he could still be in love with someone.

The mystery of the hospital had been solved, but another mystery had taken its place.

And a dilemma.

She shouldn't have hidden the ring when Brett walked in on her. After all, she hadn't done anything wrong. But now it was too late. Somehow she had to figure out a way to get the ring back in the dish before he noticed it was gone. Though it didn't look like she was going to have that opportunity this morning.

With both hands tucked in her pockets, she came around the counter. "I'm ready if you are."

"You're not going to ditch me?"

She tilted her head and pretended to scrutinize him. "Not for now."

Definitely not till this ring is where it belongs.

"Then let's go."

*B*rett maneuvered the powerful Lexus along Glade County's rural roads as the sun's heat dried the steaming as-
phalt. The clearing skies held the promise of a rain-free afternoon.
Beside him, the pizza boxes from King Karl's rested on Dani's lap.
He ran his eyes quickly over her. A little shorter than he preferred,
but trim and petite. Even cute.

He risked taking his eyes from the road again for another quick
glance. She was looking out the passenger window, apparently
lost in thought.

Yep, she was cute. Just not the kind of girl he usually honored
with a second look. Let alone invited into his life for an entire
weekend.

Rounding a curve, he frowned slightly. If she hadn't captivated
him with her Regina Lampert act at the hospital last night, he
wouldn't have asked her to the movie. But that invitation was more
out of his loneliness than any real interest in her.

He cut another glance her way, then concentrated on the road.
Not a blonde. Not tall and leggy. Not blessed with an overabun-
dance of a woman's most enticing asset.

A sudden image of Tracie flashed through his mind. Tracie with
her snowy white blouse, purposefully unbuttoned to attract his
attention. He'd allowed himself to be seduced. Allowed Tracie to

believe she was the sharp-clawed cat when in reality their first kiss had started Brett's time clock. He allowed her into his life while the weeks counted down until the day came to close off the credit card, toss her out of her job as his receptionist, and move her out of his apartment.

He shifted in the luxurious leather seat, suddenly feeling agitated, and unconsciously accelerated. That breakup had ended worse than most. But it had ended. That was the point.

"How much longer?" Dani asked. Her voice sounded a little panicky.

His thoughts jerked back to the present, and he let his foot off the gas. The vehicle slowed to a more reasonable speed.

"Only a few more minutes. Are you okay?"

She better not get sick in his car. He'd just had it detailed after making the mistake of taking the little monsters through the drive-thru a couple of weeks ago. Who knew two kids could make such a mess eating French fries?

"I'm fine."

Her knuckles, gripping the pizza boxes, slowly faded from white to their natural color.

Brett found himself wanting to reach out to her, to cover those fragile fingers with his own. But he resisted the impulse. He'd already pushed the limit by embracing her this morning. Hold her hand now, and next thing they'd be "going steady" or some other nonsense.

At least women like Tracie understood the risks they took when they unbuttoned their blouses and unzipped their skirts. They might be angling for marriage, security, the big house and new car when they used their bodies for bait. In their minds, the potential payoff was worth the gamble.

But not a girl like Dani. Even inviting her to meet the family could turn into the anniversary of their first date if he wasn't careful. Except that their first date had been yesterday. Technically this counted as a second.

Did that mean tonight's banquet was a third?

He unconsciously sped up again, and Dani grabbed the door handle.

"What's with you?" she demanded.

"Sorry." The apology came out as a meaningless grumble.

"Why do you keep speeding up like that?"

"Just thinking."

"About what?"

"Nothing important."

"You expect me to believe that?"

He flashed an apologetic smile. "Misty Willow is about a mile up the road, just around the next curve."

"Why is it called Misty Willow?"

"Don't know."

"It sounds poetic. I bet there's a story."

"You'll have to ask Shelby. She knows a lot about her family history. And she likes to talk about it."

Dani didn't reply. At least she no longer had a death grip on the pizzas.

"How about you?" Brett asked.

"How about me what?"

"For as much time as we've spent together, you haven't told me much about yourself."

She slightly hesitated before answering. "Like I said before, there's not much to tell."

He feigned interest. "Did you grow up in Cincinnati?"

"Mostly. Then I stayed there for college."

"For that very useful liberal arts degree," he teased, then tapped her arm. "Just kidding. I'm sure you'll have a great career doing something amazingly significant."

"I would very much like to punch you right now."

He laughed, then gestured out the windshield. As they rounded the curve, the immense brick home came into view. "This is it."

Dani leaned forward as far as the seatbelt would let her.

"Impressed?"

"It's lovely."

"Shelby has put a lot of work in it. You should have seen it a few months ago." He pulled into the long drive. As the tires crunched the gravel, he grinned. "AJ bought this gravel for Shelby. Made her so mad. But I guess it turned out to be a good move after all."

"Why was she mad?"

"Sully hated the place. And before Shelby came along, so did AJ. It'd been empty for a long time, and she blamed him for letting it fall apart."

"Why did he hate it?"

"Aren't you the nosy one?"

Her face reddened. "I didn't mean to pry."

"It doesn't take much to make you blush, does it?" Amused at her discomfort, Brett circled the grassy loop at the side of the house and parked near Shelby's Camry and AJ's Jeep Cherokee. He turned off the ignition, then faced Dani.

"It's no big secret. After Meghan disappeared, AJ dropped out of law school and became a high school history teacher. That ruined Sully's grandiose plans for his favorite grandson becoming the governor of our fair state. So he changed his will. AJ got the farm Sully hated and nothing else."

Before Dani could reply, a bark sounded from near the house, followed by high-pitched squeals.

Shelby's girls, followed closely by Lila, AJ's creamy Labrador retriever, raced from the patio toward them.

"My little nieces-to-be. Spill-happy Tabby and Bookworm Elizabeth."

"How are they your nieces?"

"Technically they're not. But I like the sound of 'Uncle Brett.' Besides, AJ is the closest thing I have to a brother."

He opened his car door, then pretended to fall backward as Tabby pounced on him.

"Let me out," he growled, grabbing her beneath the arms as he exited the car. After enduring her throat-crushing hug, he swung her around, setting off another squeal.

"Again, again."

"After I say hello to your sister." Squatting to eye level, he playfully tugged Elizabeth's long braid. "How you doin', Bitsy? Still getting straight As?"

"I didn't miss any problems on my arithmetic this week. And I read best of anybody," she boasted, then her smile faded. "Mommy said I shouldn't brag."

Brett put his arm around her thin shoulder and rested his chin on the top of her head.

He didn't like kids. Never had. They were a bother, a pain, an annoyance.

But these two were different. Tabby's mischievous antics made him laugh. And Elizabeth's too-serious nature dislodged the stone he had instead of a heart.

He doubted Tabby remembered much of her dad, but Elizabeth did. She had told Brett about her father making up silly stories and the time they'd gone roller-skating, just the two of them.

Brett guessed the memory was so vivid because there hadn't been enough of those special times. Gary Kincaid had been a law enforcement officer, working long hours, until he was killed in the line of duty.

Sometimes Elizabeth's chameleon eyes—sometimes green, sometimes blue—held a faraway expression that told Brett she was thinking of her dad, dreaming about a different time in her life. He knew that look. He'd seen it often enough in Amy's eyes over the years. The look that wished for the past.

He squeezed Elizabeth's shoulder and whispered in her ear. "It's never bragging when you tell me, Sweet Pea. I'm going to be your uncle soon, so I have the right to be proud of you."

Her eyes brightened, and she gave him a quick hug. "You'll be the best uncle ever."

"Yeah, well, I'll be your only uncle ever, so I guess that's not too hard."

"Even if I had a million uncles, you'd be the best."

"Remind me to give you a dollar later for that one," he said as he straightened and glanced at Dani who stood by the hood. "I want you two to meet Dani. She's a friend of mine, so you have to be nice to her. And look. We brought the pizza."

Tabby piped up. "It's tradition."

"I guess it is." Brett took the boxes from Dani and herded the group up the patio steps while Tabby showed Dani a scrape on her leg and bombarded her with questions.

Dani hesitated as they reached the kitchen's screen door. Brett rested his hand on the small of her back and whispered, "They don't bite."

From the tightness of her smile, he wasn't sure she believed him. "If they do," he said, "I'll bite them back."

Her spontaneous smile radiated through him. Not that it meant anything.

Inside the kitchen, Shelby greeted Brett with a quick hug, then shooed the girls out of the room with instructions to wash their hands. In their rush, they almost knocked over AJ, who entered from the hall with a tall glass of iced tea.

"Careful there," AJ said as he balanced the glass. "Don't make me spill this."

Brett caught Dani's gaze. She didn't seem to know whether to be embarrassed or amused. He squeezed her elbow, then made the introductions.

"I'm so glad to meet you, Dani." Shelby shot a teasing look at him. "It's not often Brett introduces us to his friends."

"Friend? She's a hitchhiker I picked up on my way here. Never saw her before this morning."

"Stick with that story if you want," Shelby said. "You aren't working for him, are you, Dani?"

"No . . ." She drew out the syllable.

"I'm glad to hear that." Shelby placed a large salad on the table. "Would you like something to drink? Tea, soda, water?"

"Tea is fine. Is there anything I can do to help?"

"Do you mind getting the napkins? They're in that drawer over there."

AJ edged closer to Brett and elbowed him. "Hitchhiker, huh? What happened to dating your receptionists?"

"Have you seen my latest?" Brett pretended to shudder. "Ancient, I tell you. Must be at least thirty-five."

"We're not dating," Dani jumped in. "Just spending the day together. The electricity is out at my place."

"So you're 'not dating'?" Shelby asked pointedly, though she feigned utter innocence.

"I'm good at that," Brett said. "As you know so well."

"We're not dating and we're not not-dating." Dani's voice held a nervous edge, and she shrugged self-consciously. "We're just . . . hanging out."

"Well, whatever you're doing, I'm glad you're here." Shelby smiled warmly at Dani, then caught Brett's gaze. He read the question in her eyes and slightly shook his head.

He and Dani weren't a couple, would never be a couple.

She was a minor diversion for a lonely weekend.

Besides, love and romance weren't in his immediate future. Too many other things demanded his focus.

Like the small boy lying in a coma. The son he wasn't allowed to see.

– 13 –

*A*fter lunch, Brett and AJ took the girls outside to play croquet. Dani started to stack the plates, but Shelby touched her arm. "I can do this. Go on out with Brett."

"I'd rather help if that's okay." She'd enjoyed the mealtime banter and even endured Brett's version of how she had drenched his pants at the movies. To hear him tell the story, she'd dumped a gallon of soda on him. Though he'd made up for it by glossing over her deplorable housing situation. He'd also downplayed her unemployment and made it sound like her senior thesis had been worthy of an Emmy.

Regretfully two more people were now snared in her budget-cut lie. The dishonesty she hated cast a gloom in this sunlit kitchen where their easygoing conversation and laughter seemed to linger.

"Help is always appreciated." Shelby dumped melting ice in the sink and placed the glasses in the dishwasher. "So I won't say no."

Dani reached for another plate. "Your house is so lovely. Brett told me it was in pretty bad shape before you restored it."

"The worst was the dead things in the attic." Shelby shuddered. "It made me sick. Literally."

"Dead things?"

"Pigeons. Raccoons. It was awful. Thankfully one of our neighbors and his son cleared them all away. I couldn't have done it."

"I can't even imagine."

"I advise you not to try." She shivered again.

Dani picked up the plates and paused by the window overlooking the oval lawn. Elizabeth smacked a striped ball with her mallet, then chased after it.

"This is a great place to raise a family," she said, unable to keep the wistfulness from her voice. She'd have loved to have grown up in a place like this. Huge and warm and comfortable.

"I moved here to give my girls the kind of childhood I had," Shelby said. "It's not going to be easy to leave."

"You're moving?"

"Didn't Brett tell you about the archaeological project?"

"The what?" Dani focused on Shelby, her interest piqued. "No, he didn't."

"This house was once a station for the Underground Railroad. There's a secret room underneath the study where the runaways were hidden." Shelby hesitated, as if momentarily lost in thought. "A few weeks ago, I had an old barn torn down, and we found the opening of a tunnel."

"Where does it go?"

"We're not sure. My grandfather always said there was a tunnel leading from the creek beyond the back pasture. But whether it could be the same tunnel . . ." She shrugged. "We just don't know."

Images of midnight meetings, of secret boat trips and runaways scurrying to safety played in Dani's mind. This house wasn't simply a home. It was history.

"So there's a real archaeological dig happening right here?"

"The beginnings of one. The plan is to open a Civil War museum and research center. Here in the house." Something odd tinged the pride in Shelby's voice. Regret? Sadness?

Or maybe my overactive imagination.

"It sounds like an incredible project. I'd love to . . ."

The familiar heart-tug stirred deep inside Dani's spirit. It always did when she found an interesting tidbit or fascinating topic that beckoned her to explore, to discover. All through college, she had done her best work on the assignments where the spark had accompanied her research.

But she hadn't felt it since graduating. Perhaps because she had cloaked herself in boredom. And self-pity.

"Love to what?" Shelby asked.

"I don't know. Be part of something so important. You must be thrilled."

"I suppose," Shelby said.

Dani heard it again. The hint of something not quite right.

"What is it?" She pressed her lips together. "I'm sorry. Brett says I'm nosy, and I guess he's right."

The tense lines around Shelby's eyes relaxed. "No need to apologize. It's just that for so much of my life, all I wanted to do was come back here. I'm glad about the museum, really I am. But we've barely settled in. It's hard to think of leaving."

"You're moving in with AJ?"

"Oh no. He lives in a one-bedroom cottage with a kitchen no bigger than my bathroom." Shelby added the tableware to the dishwasher, then rinsed her hands. "After the wedding, we're moving to the cutest bungalow you've ever seen. It belonged to AJ's grandmother."

Another family house, probably bursting with happy memories, waited to become a home for Shelby and her daughters. Dani tensed, anticipating the pierce of the jealousy spear. But her green-eyed monster must be sleeping.

"Brett said you're getting married around Christmas."

"That's the plan. AJ and the girls will be out of school." Shelby loaded the last of the tableware and shut the dishwasher door with her foot. "Four months, and we still haven't decided on a color scheme or decorations. Sometimes I wish we could just elope."

"Why don't you?"

Shelby released a deep sigh. "Because my parents are coming. All the way from Mozambique."

"They're missionaries, right?"

"This is their first trip back since Tabby was a baby. So it's more than a wedding, it's like a reunion too. Then there's AJ's students and their families. We can't invite everybody, but he's been part of this community for a long time."

Shelby glanced around, a quick inspection of the kitchen. Apparently satisfied, she leaned against the counter. "From what I gather, folks around here didn't think he'd ever get married, especially not to a Lassiter, and they're not about to miss the grand event."

"Lassiter?"

"That's my maiden name. Our grandfathers weren't exactly friends."

Dani thought about what Brett had said about Sully. The situation with Meghan had changed everything for AJ—his inheritance, his career choice. If Meghan was the reason he'd never married . . . Dani brushed away the thought. Anyone who saw AJ with Shelby could see how much he loved her. Meghan's reappearance wasn't going to change that.

But what about Brett? Was Meghan the reason he had never settled down? He said he pursued her only because she was dating AJ.

Dani pictured Brett staring up at the hospital's colored windows. He longed to see his son. Did he long to see Meghan too?

"It's so hard to believe you only met Brett last night," Shelby said, breaking into Dani's thoughts.

"Why's that?"

"I don't know. I guess it's because you seem so relaxed with each other." Shelby pulled out a chair and motioned Dani to join her at the table. "He seldom introduces the women he's dating to the family. At least that's what AJ told me."

"We're just hanging out, remember?" Dani said lightly, but her stomach knotted. She didn't want to be lumped in with Brett's women even if he did treat her differently than the rest. Besides, there was a good chance he considered her a distraction while his heart mended from his last breakup. The amethyst ring in her pocket seemed to burn against her leg.

Maybe he had bought the ring for Meghan but hadn't given it to her yet. The idea rooted, sprouted, and flourished in the time it took Dani to pull her chair up to the table.

"Even in the short time I've known him," Shelby said, "he's changed."

"What do you mean?"

Shelby tilted her head as if in thought. "He spends more time with AJ now than with his Monday night buddies."

"Who are his Monday night buddies?"

"A bunch of unmarried men trying to hang on to their college days. Least that's what it seems like to me. They have this weird game where they get points for breaking some poor woman's heart." A crestfallen expression crossed Shelby's face. "I shouldn't have told you that. He's not that guy anymore. At least, he's trying not to be."

"Why not?" Dani could guess the answer, but she wanted to hear it from Shelby.

For a long moment, Shelby stared out the kitchen window. Dani followed her gaze. In the room's silence, the gleeful shouts of two delightfully exuberant children called to Dani's own miserable childhood. The spear-wielding monster stirred.

"I think his past caught up with him."

Their eyes met across the table.

"You mean Jonah?"

"He told you?"

"He didn't want me to hear it from someone else."

"That was amazingly thoughtful of him."

Shelby was right. But he'd been amazingly thoughtful, considerate even, since Dani had met him. She wanted to bask in the warmth he'd shown her, the friendly welcome she'd received from Shelby and AJ.

She turned back to the window. When they were grown, Elizabeth and Tabby probably wouldn't remember this particular day. But the joyful glow of moments like this would never leave them.

Or me.

Brett placed his mallet in front of his ball to block Shelby's shot. Only the two of them remained. Shelby had completed the course, but he still needed to go through the last wickets before she hit his ball and won the game.

"Cheater," she snarled.

"A guy does what a guy's gotta do."

"You're only delaying the inevitable. There's no way you can win."

"I never lose."

"Famous last words." Shelby shouldered her mallet and stepped closer. "If you move out of the way, you can help me with dessert."

"Appealing to my stomach? That's a cheap shot."

"Cupcakes," she singsonged, then hesitated and lowered her voice. "I went to the hospital this morning."

Brett bit the inside of his lip and glanced around the yard. AJ perched on top of the picnic table, his face shaded by the bill of his OSU cap. Around the back of the house, just barely in sight, Dani and the girls were swinging on the wooden monstrosity he and AJ had built a couple weeks ago for Elizabeth's birthday. At this distance, Dani looked more like a teen than a college graduate.

"You want to talk to me alone, don't you?"

"Only for a minute."

He nodded, then moved out of her way. Shelby lined up her shot and smacked her ball into Brett's.

Game over.

"Way to go, Shelby," AJ cheered and bounded from the table toward them.

She flashed him a smile. "Brett and I are going to bring out dessert. Why don't you get the girls settled at the picnic table?"

"Gotcha." He reversed direction and loped toward the giant swing set.

When Brett and Shelby reached the house, he opened the screen door. "You haven't changed your mind, have you?"

"About what?"

"Marrying AJ," he teased.

"You know that's not going to happen."

"I'll never forget how angry you used to get at him."

"I'll never forget how you neglected to tell me he was your cousin. You just let me complain about him."

"And all the while, I was thinking, 'The lady doth protest too much.'" He reached for her left hand. The diamond in her engagement ring flashed a spectrum of light as it caught the sun's rays from the window. "Turns out I was right. As usual."

"I wish you'd find the right person. I pray you do."

"You actually pray that?"

"Of course I do." Shelby retrieved the box of cupcakes from the pantry and set them on the table. "And not someone like Tracie, either. Though you weren't very nice to her."

"I don't want to talk about Tracie. Or my love life." Brett turned a chair around and straddled it. No use in avoiding the unavoidable any longer. "So how's Meghan?"

"As well as she can be." Shelby grabbed more napkins from the drawer. "She gave me the cupcakes so we could celebrate Jonah's birthday."

He peeked inside the box. "Chocolate. My favorite."

"Jonah's too."

"That's my boy." The words slid out easily enough but left an odd aftertaste, as if they weren't quite true. Or as if he didn't have the right to say them.

"I took him a few presents."

"That was kind. Thank you."

"Someone else gave Jonah a present too. A little monkey wearing an OSU sweatshirt."

"Sounds like someone with good taste."

Shelby's expression had "Are you kidding me?" written all over it. "Meghan knows it was from you."

"Why would she think that?"

"Brett, she's not stupid."

"I never said—"

"I know you didn't."

"Is she mad?"

Shelby shook her head. "I think she's softening toward you. Just a little."

"What about Jonah? How is he?"

"Poor little guy. Nothing's changed."

"I only want to see him. Just once."

"Give her time. I promise if there's anything I can do or say to get her to change her mind, I will."

Suddenly weary, he rested his chin against his crossed arms on the chair back. Meghan had built an unrelenting wall between them, as strong as any fortress. Never had he felt so helpless.

"I don't know what to do."

"Trust God to work it out."

"Easier said than done."

"Believe me, I know that. But you can't force her."

"I won't. Next time you see her, tell her that."

She rested her hand on his shoulder. "Are you okay?"

"Yeah." He stood and picked up the bakery box. "Let's go celebrate my son's birthday."

- 14 -

The oak tree's spreading canopy cooled the picnic table, offering welcome shade from the glare of the summer sun. The leaves swayed, only lightly touched by a slight breeze. As if caught in an enchantment, Dani closed her eyes and breathed in the fresh fragrance of flowers touched by sunshine. Sitting between Brett and Elizabeth, basking in the peacefulness of the day—could this gorgeous Saturday afternoon be any more perfect?

From the moment she'd arrived, her anxiety had been soothed by the warm welcome she'd received. Shelby and AJ treated her like a long-lost friend instead of a stranger. As if she could be a part of this family's circle instead of an outsider yearning to be let in. The only awkward moment occurred when Brett and Shelby brought out the cupcakes. Tabby had been dissuaded from her notion that they light candles but not from singing "Happy Birthday" to Jonah. Brett had started out fine, his voice a rich timbre that blended with her soft soprano melody. But his body tensed beside her, and he barely choked out Jonah's name. He didn't sing the last line.

She spontaneously reached for his hand under the table. He clasped her fingers, and her skin tingled at his touch. Then Shelby had passed out the cupcakes, and the private moment had ended.

Dani brushed the last of the crumbs from her fingers, then tucked a strand of hair behind her ear.

"Anyone up for a rematch?" AJ glanced at his phone, then frowned. "Though I'm not sure we've got time."

"The girls need their baths before going to the Owenses," Shelby said, then looked across the table at Dani. "Our neighbors are taking them and their son on an adventure while we're gone."

Dani shifted toward Elizabeth. "What kind of adventure?"

"They won't tell us," Elizabeth said, her eyes dancing. "It's a surprise."

"I love surprises."

"Me too."

"How about if we trade places? I'll go on the adventure and you can go to the banquet."

Brett cut in before Elizabeth could respond. "Sorry, Bitsy, no trades allowed. And you"—he pointed at Dani—"you're coming with me." He jabbed his thumb into his chest.

Elizabeth giggled as Dani pretended to shiver with fear.

Brett leaned close. "What you don't know," he said in a stage whisper, "is that our Miss Elizabeth is spending the evening with Master Austin Owens. They're engaged."

Elizabeth's cheeks flushed, though from the glint in her eyes she didn't mind the teasing. "We're not really," she said softly. "Just kind of."

"I heard he carved your initials on the engagement tree," Brett teased.

"That's so he'd remember me if we moved away."

"Well, it sounds serious to me."

Dani nudged Elizabeth. "Is he a nice young man?"

"The very nicest."

"He really is," Shelby said with a soft laugh. "His dad Jason and I were best friends when we were young. They live just down the road."

"Jason carved initials on the engagement tree too," AJ said.

He pulled Shelby close and kissed her cheek. "But God had other plans."

"What's the engagement tree?" Dani asked.

"It's a weeping willow that hangs over the creek," Shelby said. "Not far from where the boats for the Underground Railroad would land. During the Civil War, one of my ancestors fell in love with a Rebel soldier. He was the first one to carve initials into the tree. Since then, it's been a tradition." She narrowed her eyes at Elizabeth. "But only for grown-ups," she said with mock sternness.

"That's so cool," Dani said. "It's like a living family tree."

"It truly is," Shelby said. "We don't have time to go back there this afternoon, but maybe we can another time."

If there was another time. After Brett dropped her off this evening, Dani doubted she would see him again. She smiled politely. "That'd be nice."

"Brett, why don't you show Dani where we found the tunnel?" Shelby asked. "She's interested in our history project."

"Great idea." He caught Dani's gaze. "Shall we?"

"Sounds fun."

"I wanna go." Tabby scurried to Brett's side and grabbed his arm. "I go too."

"Nope," Shelby intervened. "Time to get cleaned up. Go on now. You too, Elizabeth."

AJ stepped away from the picnic table. "I'll go with Brett—"

Shelby grabbed his shirt with one hand and shoved the bakery box, now filled with used liners and napkins, into his abdomen. "I need you in the house."

"Um, okay." He cradled the box and looked at Brett. "I'm going in the house."

"See you in a few." Shelby gave a little wave, then steered AJ away.

Dani willed her body to turn to liquid so she could slide under the picnic table. But nothing happened.

Brett snorted. "Shelby must think she's Yenta."

"You know *Fiddler on the Roof?*"

"'Course I do." He tapped her arm. "You ready to tour the excavation area?"

"Absolutely. I can't even imagine how thrilling it would be to have archaeologists digging in my backyard."

"Don't get too excited. None of them look like Indiana Jones."

"Except for Harrison Ford, who does?"

"Is that your type? The romantic adventurer?"

"Maybe."

"He's old enough to be your grandfather." Brett's playful smile practically took her breath away. "Oh, wait, I forgot. Regina Lampert prefers older men."

"You're never going to let that go, are you?"

"Never."

They sauntered up the graveled drive past the landscaped fence-row. A red wheelbarrow rested among the flowers, reminding Dani of a William Carlos Williams poem. She opened her mouth to mention it when Brett started whistling a tune. It only took a few notes for Dani to recognize "Matchmaker, Matchmaker."

The familiar words sang in her head, and she unconsciously swayed to the music. When Brett noticed, he placed his arm around her waist and took her hand. The whistling changed to singing as they danced in the sunshine.

His natural affinity eased her nervousness at being in his arms. He guided her through an improvised routine that ended with him on one knee and holding the last note as if serenading her.

"You're a good dancer." He stood and brushed dirt off his knee.

"So are you."

"I had good teachers. First my mom and then Gran. How about you?"

At the mention of his mom, Dani tensed. So far he hadn't seemed to notice that she hadn't asked about his parents. Even now, she didn't dare. That conversation could take her places she didn't want to go. And once it did . . . She wrapped her arms around her chest and shuddered.

"You okay?"

"Fine. Just a sudden chill."

"In this heat?"

"I lived in a foster home for a while." This wasn't safe territory either, but now the words seemed to tumble out. "The dad there was really nice. He taught me the basics."

"A foster home," he repeated almost as if speaking to himself.

"Sometimes my . . . my dad had issues." Like drowning his sorrow in a bottle, oblivious to his stepdaughter's painful grief. Like throwing her into the foster care system until his conscience guilted him into sobering up long enough to reclaim her. Ever hopeful the two of them could be a real family, each time she believed his promises. But he never kept them, and the repeating cycle had left her broken.

Brett's expression darkened. "It's tough being a kid."

"Yeah, it is." Tougher for her than for him, though. True, the same crash that claimed her mom had claimed both his parents. But while she ended up with a stepfather who could barely stomach the sight of her, he had been taken into his grandparents' lap of luxury. Securely wrapped in wealth and privilege, he had no idea just how tough a childhood could be.

Brett swung open the metal gate separating the house and yard from the rest of the acreage. The graveled drive sloped gently upward, then disappeared into a pasture. About a quarter of the way up, beyond the lanky stalks of the sunflower house, chain link fencing surrounded what had once been the barn's foundation.

The barn itself had been torn down, but its memories remained. Shelby's grandfather had been accidentally killed in the barn when she was only a teen, and a couple of months ago her great-uncle suffered a fatal heart attack there. Though Richard Grayson had been related to Shelby, he'd been Sully's oldest and closest friend—

perhaps the old man's only friend. And he'd been like an uncle to Brett, Amy, and AJ.

His death severed the only connection Brett had to his grandfather and, coming so soon after Gran's, had left an unexpected vacancy in his life.

Dani stepped through the gate with him, then turned to look at the house. "If I were Shelby, I don't know if I could give all this up. Does the museum have to be here?"

"It kinda does." Not that he wanted to get into all the reasons why—the restrictive terms of Sully's will, the loophole AJ found so Shelby could buy the farm, the lawsuit Amy had filed to reverse the sale.

He rubbed his neck.

"We're working to get the house on the National Register of Historic Places. That way, it'll always be protected."

"We?"

"I'm on the board for the foundation."

"One of the reasons you're being honored tonight, right? Serving on different boards, I mean."

"Do I detect a hint of cynicism in your voice?"

Dani practically stuttered a denial. Amused by her flustered expression, he brazenly appraised her features. The deep brown eyes a bit too large for her heart-shaped face, the nose a little too small and straight, her slightly crooked mouth. Little imperfections that added up to perfection.

The desire to cradle her chin, to give in to the appeal of her naturally pink lips, surged through him. He pointed to the row of shrubs bordering this side of the fence.

"I planted those," he bragged while quelling the sensual thoughts that threatened to lure him into trouble he didn't need. Breaking a young girl's heart wasn't on his agenda.

"You did? Dug the hole and everything?"

"AJ helped." He grinned sheepishly. "Actually, I helped AJ."

"Manual labor. Who would have thought?" she teased.

"AJ's always roping me into doing chores around this place. Now the fence is less noticeable from the house. Less of a temptation for the girls." And less of a visual reminder for Shelby of the tragedies that had occurred there. "The things people do for love, right?"

"You mean AJ and Shelby? They seem to be very happy."

"They are."

He rested his hand between her shoulders and slightly propelled her forward as his thoughts reflected on their conversation. Dani had sounded wistful, almost sad, when she talked about AJ and Shelby. Some clod had probably broken her heart. A high school idiot or college twerp. Maybe both. He shifted his eyes her way and was struck anew by her naïve attractiveness.

If Tracie set the bar at ten, Dani scored a seven. Okay, an eight.

But that kind of numerical rating no longer made sense. In less than twenty-four hours, he felt more connected with Dani than he'd ever felt during his weeks with Tracie. There was no pretense with Dani. No need to hide behind his successful businessman façade. She'd be enjoying today even if he were a small-town laborer living paycheck to paycheck.

As long as that laborer was being honored at tonight's Up-and-Comers Banquet.

They walked past the width of the excavation, but the back of a long equipment shed hid the dig from view. Dani quickened her pace. "This is so exciting. A real dig."

"I'm not sure there's that much to see," Brett said. "The archaeologists have been here doing their thing since the barn was torn down. But it's a slow process."

As soon as they rounded the corner to the gated entrance, Dani laced her fingers into the fence's links and peered inside. Brett chuckled.

"You look like a kid without a ticket to a baseball game."

"This is a thousand times better."

"Says the liberal arts major." He punched numbers into the lock's keypad, then opened one half of the wide double gate. "Come on in, Sparky."

The barn's concrete floor took up most of the enclosed area while the equipment shed stood at one end. Brett led Dani to the other end, where a wooden structure, about six feet square and two feet high, covered one corner of a section of packed dirt.

"This part of the barn's floor was wood," Brett explained. "When it was torn up, the contractor found another wooden floor beneath it. That's when he found the trapdoor into the tunnel. There." He gestured toward the wooden structure.

"It goes straight down?"

"At least three or four feet. Somebody, probably one of Shelby's ancestors, must have filled it in. They're taking out that dirt one slender layer at a time."

"No one knows where it leads to," Dani said, more as if she were talking to herself than him. Brett inwardly smiled as she scrutinized the dig, her eyes bright with enthusiasm as she took it all in.

"Not yet. There's supposed to be a tunnel back by Glade Creek. But it's doubtful it links up to this one."

"So they haven't found the entrance to the other one?"

"Not yet. The tunnel's entrance was under or near an old hunting cabin. It was torn down years ago, but Shelby's fairly certain she knows where it was. That's Phase Three of the project."

"How many phases are there?"

"For now, just three. You're standing on Phase One. Phase Two is establishing the house as a museum. We're working on that now. Then in the third phase, we'll use the wood from the barn to replicate the hunting cabin. It won't be the original, but the barn was built using wood from the property, so it will still have significance."

Dani surveyed the area, her chin slightly lifted, and the late afternoon sun shone on the natural auburn highlights in her honey-brown hair. A radiant glow seemed to surround her, and while Brett scoffed at such an absurdity, he found it impossible to take his eyes off her.

$\mathcal{M}$eghan studied the children's art projects spread out on the sofa in Jonah's room. The colorful birthday greetings the youngsters had created for him warmed her heart.

The creaking of the door drew her attention, and a mass of red hair framed the twinkling blue eyes that peered around the corner.

"Okay if I come in?"

"Please do."

Instead of the usual hospital scrubs, Aaron wore jeans and a buttoned-down shirt. Surprised at his appearance, she chuckled. "You look so different in regular clothes."

"Thanks." He grinned broadly, a cheerful glint in his eyes. "I think."

"I meant it as a compliment," she said hurriedly. "You just surprised me, that's all. It's early for your shift, isn't it?"

"I'm not working tonight." He held out a wrapped box. "This is for Jonah. I hope you don't mind that I got him something for his birthday."

"That's very kind, Aaron. But you really shouldn't have."

He pushed it toward her, his expression hopeful. "Go ahead. Open it."

Meghan untied the slender gold ribbon and removed the tape

from the thick blue paper. She smiled at him, then opened the box. Inside was a plush bright blue robe with matching slippers. Her thoughts scrambled, and the fear that plucked her heart must have shone on her face because Aaron's voice was apologetic when he spoke.

"I know he can't use them now. But he will."

She ran her hand across the downy soft fabric. "It's a generous gift."

"Do you like it?"

"I love it. And Jonah will too."

If he ever wakes up.

The unspoken words hung between them. Aaron started to touch her arm, then let his hand drop to his side. Meghan inwardly smiled at his shy awkwardness. On an impulse, she kissed his cheek.

"Thank you," she murmured.

His face burned almost as red as his hair. "He's going to be okay, Meghan. It may take a while, but he'll wake up."

"I wish I had your confidence."

"Never give up hope."

"Sometimes that's hard."

"Would it help to know I'm hoping too?"

"Yes. I think it would."

Aaron self-consciously cleared his throat, then gestured at the art projects. "What's all this?"

"Birthday greetings from some of the other children here. I want to make a collage to hang on the wall."

"Great idea." He shifted his weight from one foot to the other. "Has it been a good day for you? I mean, given the circumstances, have you celebrated?"

Meghan bit her lip as she considered his question. It wasn't how she ever envisioned spending any of Jonah's birthdays. And she prayed that next year . . . But planning that far ahead was too frightening.

This was the only day she could be sure of.

She fingered the necklace Shelby had given her and glanced at the gifts on the table.

"Yes," she said decidedly. "A friend stopped by with presents. Her daughters made this book." She handed it to Aaron, then reached for the monkey. "This was here when I arrived this morning. I'm pretty sure I know who it's from, but I don't know who he bribed to deliver it."

Aaron's cheeks flamed, and Meghan's eyes grew large. "Is this from you too?"

"No." The sharp denial rushed out. "No, it's not."

"I didn't think so. But you know how it got here, don't you?"

"What makes you think that?"

"Your face." Meghan's growing suspicion tempted her to anger, but Aaron's shocked expression struck her funny bone. "Who's it from, Aaron?" The question didn't come out nearly as harsh as she wanted it to.

Aaron squirmed. "Who do you think it's from?"

"Aaron, please."

"I promised not to tell."

Meghan crossed her arms. She liked Aaron, she really did. His eyes and his smile exuded kindness, and when he examined Jonah, his motions were tender and compassionate. But she couldn't help feeling betrayed.

"How long have you known Brett?" she said.

"Since we were kids."

"So you've been spying on me. On Jonah and me."

"It's not like that. Okay, it was a little like that, but not really."

The stricken expression on his face pulled at Meghan's heart. With his unruly hair and smattering of freckles, he reminded her of a little kid who was in a whole heap of trouble but desperately wanted to make amends.

"I don't understand, Aaron. How could you?"

"I didn't know at first. About Jonah being Brett's son, I mean."

"He told you?"

Aaron nodded. "He's worried about Jonah. About you."

"Brett Somers doesn't worry about anyone but himself."

"He likes people to think that. But it's not true."

"Isn't it?"

"Brett and I go back a long way. My mom was his parents' housekeeper until they divorced. Then she worked for his dad until the plane accident."

"High and mighty Brett was friends with the housekeeper's son?" Meghan scoffed. "I'm surprised his parents allowed it."

"His dad had issues. Lots of them. Even as a kid I knew that. But he was always considerate of my mom. And sometimes kinder to me than he was to Brett."

Meghan raised her eyes and held Aaron's gaze. Part of her wanted to throttle him. But the gentleness exuding from his Santa Claus eyes stanched her anger.

"I didn't see him that much after he went to live with his grandparents," Aaron said, "but we would run into each other around town sometimes. We had a couple of gen ed classes together at OSU when we were freshmen. Before I dropped out to work here."

"You honestly, truly like him. Don't you?"

"Yes. I do."

"Why?"

Aaron's red curls bounced as he tilted his head in thought. "We came from different worlds, you know. From the outside, Brett and Amy looked like the lucky ones. But that house was a battleground. Sometimes I'd be outside doing little gardening chores, and Brett would come out and help. We didn't talk much, just two little boys pulling weeds together. But the point is, he didn't have to do it."

He paused a moment, and his mouth curved upward. "Sometimes we'd play catch. Hide-and-seek. You know, kid games."

Meghan clasped the foot of Jonah's bed. She'd never given any thought to Brett as a child. A memory of Jonah tossing a ball against a wooden fence flashed in her mind. With his light blue eyes and pale blond hair, he had to be a miniature Brett.

Another memory surfaced, and her heart clenched in anguish. She and Travis had fought, a screaming match unlike any they'd ever had, and he'd stormed out. Jonah was supposed to be in bed, but she'd found him cowering behind the couch, hands over his ears.

His fear had broken her heart even as it strengthened her resolve that Travis needed to be gone from their lives.

Had Brett ever cowered the same way?

The ice around her heart melted just a little. She had vowed that her son would be nothing like his father. Yet he'd witnessed her battling the only father he knew. He'd heard them destroy one another with their words.

The angry betrayal she wanted to feel toward Aaron dissipated in the wake of her own guilt.

"I remember this one time," Aaron's voice broke into her thoughts. "It's kind of embarrassing, really."

She twisted to face him and slightly smiled at his bashful expression. "Tell me."

"I wasn't the muscular hunk I am now." He puffed out his chest and laughed. "A bit on the chubby side as a kid."

The image of him as a round little carrot-top broadened her smile. "I bet you were adorable."

"My mom thought so." He laughed again. "Still does, in fact. But then she's biased."

As moms should be. Though not all of them were. Meghan dismissed the dark thought and leaned forward. "What happened?"

"I'd ridden my bike to the comic book store. These kids were giving me a rough time. Calling me names, pushing me around."

"How awful."

"Worse, they wanted my bike. I wouldn't let go of it, so they started to beat me up. Next thing I know, there's Brett and a couple of his pals. He grabbed the ringleader and threw him against the wall. He warned him not to ever touch me or my bike again."

He shrugged. "He was my hero that day."

"So you owe him."

"I don't blame you for being mad at me." He hesitated, then stood and faced her, his words spilling out. "For what it's worth, I told him I wouldn't do it again. But like it or not, Meghan, he is Jonah's dad. He's worried about him. To tell you the truth, I've never seen him like this."

"But *why* does he care, Aaron? For all I know, he only wants Jonah for a plaything. Something to show off."

"I don't think that's true."

"It's the only reason he wanted me."

Aaron appeared taken aback. "What do you mean?"

"What has he told you? About him and me."

"Nothing really. Only that he didn't know about Jonah till after his accident."

"There's a reason for that." Meghan bit her lip as shame washed over her. No matter how hard she tried to push it away, guilt clawed at her heart for cheating on AJ. For lying to him and agreeing to Sully's deal. "You don't know the things I've done."

"I don't need to, and I'm not angling for an explanation. But if you ever want to talk, I'm here for you. And I promise I'll never judge you."

"You are such a sweet guy, Aaron. How is it that you're still single?"

"Still waiting for the right girl, I guess."

A still voice seemed to whisper, *He's waiting for you.*

But that couldn't be true. After what she'd done to Brett, to AJ, she could never be worthy of this kind and amiable man.

"Can I ask you something?" Aaron shifted nervously.

"Sure."

"Would you like, I mean, since it's my night off and it's Jonah's birthday and all, would you want to go get something to eat? Somewhere?"

The question caught her off guard. "I don't know what to say," she stammered.

"How about yes?"

His hopeful expression was like a breath of fresh air.

"It's always hard to leave him."

"We'll go somewhere close. And I won't keep you too long. I promise."

She grinned, her mind made up. "I'd love to. Thank you."

– 16 –

*B*rett adjusted the knot of his silk tie in front of AJ's dresser. They had taken Elizabeth and Tabby to the Owenses' house, then driven to AJ's cottage to get ready for the banquet.

Satisfied with his appearance, he carried his jacket to the long room that ran the length of the rectangular house. The row of windows in the wall's upper half overlooked a grassy slope and adjoining pasture. Slender evergreens, casting their long and narrow shadows, lined the barbed-wire fence at the bottom of the yard.

"Remember when we used to sled down that hill?" Brett said.

AJ pocketed his wallet and nodded. "Those were fun days."

"We didn't have too many of those."

"But we had Gran."

"You know, I think I miss her more than . . ." Brett allowed the unspoken words to hang heavy in the air, trusting AJ to understand.

"She held us together."

"It's too bad she won't be here for the wedding," Brett said. "She'd have loved Shelby. And her girls."

A grim smile tightened AJ's features. He'd been especially close to Gran, while Brett was too much like Sully. But while Brett admired his grandfather's business acumen and ambition, he didn't want to end up like the old man—with embittered grudges and angry vendettas.

That's why he was excruciatingly careful in his business dealings. He did his share of arm-twisting and kept his own counsel, but no one could accuse him of dishonesty. Those principles benefitted him because his financial partners knew where they stood. After a few years of hustling for just the right deals, now others approached him for his expertise and investment.

Of course, it didn't hurt that he had the most gorgeous receptionists he could find greeting his partners when they walked in the door. Serving them a smile-to-die-for along with coffee.

He'd been amused by their reactions to Miss Efficiency, his latest receptionist. Not that he really cared. The development projects he had in the works would see him through the next two or three years. Besides, he had enough money to live on the rest of his life even if he didn't work another day.

"Guess we'd better be going." AJ shrugged into his navy-blue suit jacket and tugged at the lapels. "You see the sacrifice I'm making for you. Wearing this thing."

"I see it, and I appreciate it. Seriously, AJ. Thanks for coming to this thing. It'll probably be long and boring, but . . ."

"We wouldn't have dreamed of missing it." AJ clapped his back. "I'm sorry Amy is."

"She's got better things to do, apparently."

"You want me to talk to her?"

"When has that ever done any good?"

"Never." AJ scooped his keys from the counter. "Are you ready to go?"

"Yeah."

AJ switched off the overhead lights, and they walked outside. Brett paused by the door of the Jeep. The low-hanging sun would set in a couple hours, and the light would shine in Jonah's window. What color would Meghan choose for his birthday?

"You okay?" AJ asked.

"Just thinking."

"About Jonah?"

Brett gave a curt nod and slid into the Jeep. AJ got in on his side and started the ignition. Instead of putting the gear in drive, he twisted in his seat.

"You're his dad, Brett. You have the right—"

"Not legally."

"You could make it legal."

Brett snorted. "Bully her into letting me into his life? She'd never forgive me."

"She's not forgiving you now."

"I know." He yanked the seatbelt and jammed it into the latch. "Truth is, I considered legal action. But that's not how I want it to be between us."

"How do you want it to be?"

"I don't want to marry her if that's what you're thinking. I just want to spend time with my son. Have a say in the medical decisions."

"Sounds fair."

"Yeah, well, try to explain that to Meghan."

"I'm really sorry, you know. About all of it."

"Me too."

They drove in silence till AJ reached the stop sign at the end of his road. "Dani seems nice."

"She is. Too bad this is just a one-time thing."

"You took her to the movies last night. You've spent the entire day with her. How is this a one-time thing?"

"Because after I take her home tonight, that will be the end of it." Unless she still didn't have electricity. He squirmed. Even if she did, he couldn't leave her in that rat's hole. "Actually, she needs another place to live."

"Why?"

"She's staying in one of those pay-by-the-week places by the interstate. It's all run-down. Should be condemned. The storm knocked out her electricity, and it still wasn't on this morning. I can't take her back there."

"Playing the knight in shining armor, huh?"

"I should have called her last night. Because of the storm. That's all."

"I see."

"Don't say 'I see' in that tone of voice."

"I don't have a tone of voice."

"I'm serious about this. Do you have any idea how I can get her out of there without it looking like I'm interested in her?"

"Not off the top of my head. But I'll talk it over with Shelby. Maybe she can think of something."

"Thanks, AJ."

"Don't thank me yet."

As they drove toward Misty Willow, Brett glanced at his cousin. No family resemblance tied them together. And despite living their teen years together under Gran and Sully's roof, they hadn't been close. But then Shelby entered their lives. And so had Jonah.

Uncovering the secrets of the past had somehow ended the jealousy between them. No more rivalry, no more one-upmanship.

Just two cousins who had finally become friends.

Gran must be smiling from heaven.

Dressed in the new-to-her black dress, Dani perched on the twin bed between purple pillows trimmed with pink ribbons and a giant stuffed St. Bernard. A huge stuffed panda bear guarded the other twin bed. Shelby's eyes had shone with pride when she told Dani about AJ winning the toys at the county fair. To the delight of his daughters-to-be, he made every basket into the slanted hoop.

Once again, Dani had to shove the green-eyed monster away. She refused to be jealous of these two little girls just because the man who was going to be their stepfather adored them.

She only wished she had been so lucky.

A knock sounded on the door.

"Dani, are you about ready?" Shelby asked. "The guys are back."

"I just need another minute or two."

"No rush." The clack of Shelby's heels on the wooden floor receded down the hall.

"Or an hour," Dani mumbled. *Or forever.*

She never should have agreed to go with Brett to his fancy banquet. Every expensively dressed, perfectly polished woman there would be appraising her, wondering why Ohio's most eligible bachelor had chosen an unsophisticated nobody as his date.

The answer wasn't flattering—she'd happened to be there when his sister canceled. Serendipity didn't seem so romantic when it happened like that.

Dani took a deep calming breath, then clasped her mother's garnet bracelet around her wrist. The delicate chain was the finest piece of jewelry she owned.

She pressed her fingers against the pocket of her folded jeans. The ring, tucked safely in its depths, seemed to burn her skin through the denim. Somehow she had to get into Brett's apartment and put the ring where she'd found it.

Imagining Brett asking her to his place, perhaps for a romantic, candlelight dinner, was easy. In that daydream, she was poised and lovely, his perfect match, instead of an unemployed, practically homeless nobody.

But in the real world, her imagined dreams never came true. In the real world, moms died in fiery airplane crashes. Stepfathers didn't love their wives' children.

And handsome, wealthy men didn't fall in love with someone like her.

Brett clicked the shutter of Shelby's camera, capturing for posterity the image of her and AJ posing in front of the living room fireplace.

The perfect picture of the happily-in-love couple.

"One more." He started to raise the camera, then hesitated.

Dani appeared in the entry near the fireplace, wearing a black dress and strappy sandals. The angled hem, edged in ebony lace, ended at mid-calf and left Brett ogling her slender ankles.

"I didn't mean to keep you waiting," she said, a nervous tic in her voice.

As he forced his eyes upward, his breath unexpectedly caught in his throat. Her thick hair, parted to the side and held above one ear with a golden clasp, fell in soft waves past her shoulders. His pulse quickened at the obvious appeal for approval in her dark, slightly too wide eyes.

"You look beautiful." An odd huskiness deepened his voice. "I mean it. Absolutely beautiful."

She flushed, which didn't surprise him. But his own reaction did. Tingling spine. Racing heartbeat. He shouldn't feel this way. Not for a naïve youngster still trying to find her place in the world. Certainly not for a brunette.

But he couldn't take his eyes off her.

What was wrong with him?

Shelby reached for the camera. "Let me take your photo. By the fireplace, you two."

Brett offered his hand to Dani. "Shall we?"

She placed her hand in his, and the magic of her touch engulfed him. Holding on to his composure, he led her to the fireplace and placed his arm around her waist. She fit perfectly beneath his shoulder, as if she'd been created just for him. He glanced down at her, unsure what to make of the longing she stirred in him.

"Look at me and smile," Shelby said.

Staring at the camera, he pulled Dani slightly closer.

The moment would pass—it had to—but at least the image had been preserved. Because whatever was going on with him tonight couldn't turn into a fling.

He wouldn't let it.

- 17 -

*D*ani's nervous tension faded during the drive to the hotel hosting the Up-and-Comers Banquet. Brett's humorous stories about a few of the honorees and other Columbus VIPs made her laugh, which made him laugh. Except for a bit of a snarl in downtown traffic, the trip didn't seem to take any time at all.

After Brett entrusted his car to the valet, he tucked Dani's hand into his arm, and they waited for Shelby and AJ to arrive. A few minutes later, the two couples entered the glittering ballroom.

A raised platform stood at one end of the room while round tables covered in black and gold linen graced the floor. Colorful bouquets, dazzling silver place settings, and cloth-covered chairs added to the aura of elegance.

Familiar dread surged into Dani's chest. She didn't belong here, not among all these high-achieving, successful people. Her grip must have tightened on Brett's arm because he laid his hand over hers.

"Are you nervous?" he whispered.

"A little."

"So am I."

She gazed at him in surprise. "Why?"

"I'm not really one for the spotlight."

"You're joking, right?"

"Not really. But I know the secret." He leaned closer. "Act confident, be confident, and no one will be the wiser."

"Easier said than done."

"It's all in the posture." He slid his hand to her back. "Spine straight. Shoulders slightly back. Chin up just a little."

Dani followed his instructions and smiled. "I think it's working."

His approving look sparked a thrill that raced to the tips of her toes.

"If you know the secret," she said, "then why are you nervous?"

"Because I have to go stand on that stage and try to look humble."

Dani barely held back a laugh. "Is that so hard?"

"For me it is." His dimples flashed, and he propelled her forward. "Shall we find our seat?"

After the dinner and keynote speech, the awards were presented. When Brett's name was called, she applauded, then laughed when AJ whistled. Brett looked their way, momentarily met her gaze, and winked.

Throughout the entire evening, he was attentive, even chivalrous. The perfect gentleman. The perfect date.

A few women had approached him during the dinner, their long legs disappearing into scanty skirts, their cloud of perfume enough to make Dani gag. They gushed about the TV interview clip, and it was all Dani could do to keep her emotions in check as his words pounded her brain.

"The incompetent pilot killed—no, murdered—my parents."

After spending the day with him and his family, she'd almost forgotten why she had waited outside his office yesterday afternoon. Why she had stalked him to the hospital.

But his public denouncement of her mom had opened up a Pandora's box of grief and torment. The only way to close it was to publicly humiliate him.

He had to pay for the things he'd said, the hurt he had caused. He'd glided through life on his handsome looks and appealing charm for too long. She was determined to get even with him.

She just needed to figure out how.

Guilt caught in her throat as she glanced at Shelby and AJ. She couldn't hurt Brett without hurting them.

When the banquet ended, Brett stood beside Dani's chair. She reached to adjust the strap of her shoe, and her bracelet caught on the ebony lace edging her dress. The lace ripped, though she barely moved her hand.

Great. The most expensive dress she'd ever owned was ruined. Biting her lip, she tried to see the rip without making it worse.

"Need help?" Brett knelt beside her.

"I can manage, thank you." She struggled with the clasp, but it wouldn't open. She didn't need to look at Brett to know his blue eyes were boring holes in her. Probably wondering what kind of dork he'd gotten stuck with.

She grasped the clasp again, almost got it open, then ripped the lace another inch.

"Hold still." Brett reached for her hand, and she jerked away. Half the lace edging tore with a horrendous rip.

"That's never happened before."

"What hasn't?"

"The ladies usually let me take their hands."

"I guess I'm not a lady."

Amusement flickered in his eyes, and he gestured toward the bracelet. "May I?"

She hesitated, then glanced at Shelby and AJ. Their backs were to her as they chatted with another couple. At least they weren't witnessing her disaster. "Go ahead."

Brett's hand brushed against her leg as he fiddled with the lace-entangled clasp. Thank heavens she had shaved.

"This is what I was talking about earlier," he said. "You're dying inside over something we'll be laughing about tomorrow."

Except we won't see each other tomorrow.

"So why not take it in stride now?"

"You want me to pretend it doesn't matter I tore my dress?"

He raised his eyes to hers. "I want you to smile because this"—he pointed to the hem—"can be fixed. Plus I got to play the gallant rescuer to a lovely damsel."

Beguiled by the warmth of his eyes and his seductive voice, she favored him with a smile. He tapped her chin with his knuckle. "That's my girl."

Her smile froze in place as he focused on disentangling the bracelet. She wasn't his girl and never would be. She was a fraud and a thief who wanted vengeance.

If only he'd been the nasty, conceited snob she'd expected him to be. Maybe then revenge wouldn't taste so bitterly cold.

"All done." He stood, cradling the bracelet in his palm. "This cost someone a bit of change. Gift from an old boyfriend?"

Let him think that. She stood beside him and held out her hand. "May I have it back, please?"

He circled her wrist with the bracelet and clasped it. The feathery touch of his fingers stilled her heart. The room seemed to grow silent, and the bustling crowd around them faded into shadows. His hand closed around hers, and his expectant gaze weakened her knees.

"Thank you," she murmured.

"You're welcome." The whispered words, charged with emotion beyond their simplicity, drew her closer to him. His head lowered; his mouth hovered near hers. "I'm glad you came with me tonight."

"Me too."

A long second. Then another.

He dropped her hand and retrieved the plaque he'd been given from the table. "I guess I should hang on to this."

The room burst to life as the noise of the crowd surrounded her. The paused moment, when only the two of them existed in their own private place, had ended. Her heart yearned to relive the mystery of it, but now wasn't the time.

"What will you do with it?" she asked.

"Put it in my office. I've got a wall—"

"Brett, old buddy." The stranger, stereotypically tall, dark, and handsome, clapped Brett's shoulder. He'd been given an award too, but Dani didn't remember his name. "Congratulations."

"Congratulations to you too."

"These old-timers need to watch out. We're going to take over the city." The stranger placed his arm around the statuesque redhead beside him. Her little black dress encased shapely curves and barely covered her hips.

"Hi, Brett," she said.

"Hello, Minerva." Brett rested his hand at the small of Dani's back. "This is Dani Prescott. Dani, Minerva Allen and Zach Shrouder. He's an old college buddy who inherited his dad's BMW dealership."

"You must be Brett's latest receptionist," Zach said. Dani could tell from the superior expression in his eyes that his appraising gaze found her wanting. "Did he tell you what happened to your predecessor?"

"I don't—"

Brett jumped in. "Dani produces documentaries."

"In Columbus?" Zach eyed her again. "What are you working on?"

"I'm, um, between projects right now." She smiled brightly.

"I see." Skepticism laced his words. "Minerva has done some modeling. Keep her in mind for your next . . . project."

Out of Zach's vision, Minerva rolled her eyes. The unspoken message was clear: the guy's a jerk.

Bolstered by this feminine unity, Dani lifted her chin. "I'd be glad to. We're always on the lookout for talent."

"Sure you are." He snickered. "Brett, can I have a word with you. Alone?"

"Of course." Brett pulled Dani into a side hug. "I'll be right back."

After the men stepped away, Minerva shook her head. "Why do we do it?"

"Do what?"

"Put up with these smug baboons." The corner of Minerva's bright red mouth lifted in a self-deprecating smirk. "Okay, I know why we do it. But they do get tiresome."

"Brett and I aren't really dating. We're just"—she hesitated and shrugged—"friends."

"With men like Zach and Brett, there's no such thing as being 'just friends.'"

"I don't think Brett's like that." As if, after only a day, she knew him so well.

"Tell that to Tracie."

"Who's Tracie?"

"His last receptionist." Compassion filled Minerva's eyes. "I tried to warn her, but she wouldn't listen. We went through two cartons of Chunky Monkey the night he kicked her out of his place."

"He did that?"

"It's what they all do. Brett. Zach. The other members of their little club."

"The Monday night thing?" What had Shelby said? Something about them trying to hang on to their college days. Playing a game.

"They meet every week at a wings place downtown. Boys' night out. They compare notes on their weekend dates and buy beers for the guy with the best story."

Dani glanced to where the men were standing. Brett reached into his pocket and handed something to Zach. A coin, perhaps? The smile of a smug victor creased Zach's attractive features as he made a show of kissing the item then pocketing it. Meanwhile, Brett appeared impassive, almost stoic. Yet something in his stance, the way he held his shoulders—he wasn't happy with whatever was going on between him and Zach.

"Tracie wants payback," Minerva said. "But I told her to let it go. Guys like them never get what's coming to them."

Dani silently agreed. "Why do you stay with someone like that?"

"There are perks." Minerva's face lit up. "Expensive presents. Fabulous vacations. Most of all, connections with all kinds of people I wouldn't have a chance of meeting otherwise."

Dani rubbed her arms, suddenly feeling a chill. "It sounds so—"

"Selfish?"

"I was going to say sad."

"That too, I suppose." She shrugged. "But it's been worth it. Zach doesn't know it yet, but I'm moving to New York in a couple of weeks. My big break may be just around the corner."

"When are you going to tell him?"

"The night before I go." Minerva's expression softened. "Be careful, Dani. Brett will trample your heart if you let him."

The men rejoined them before Dani could answer. Minerva pasted on a simpering smile, then cuddled beneath Zach's arm and smoothed his tie. His hand slipped past her hip, but his eyes focused on Dani.

"Let's go, darling." Minerva's sultry voice purred. "I've planned a private celebration for just the two of us."

Zach directed his self-satisfied smirk at Brett. "See you at Gallagher's, buddy."

"I'll be there."

Brett stared after the departing couple, then rubbed his neck. "I'm sorry about Zach. He's a moron."

"You don't need to apologize for him."

"He's interested in you."

"That's not the impression I got. Besides, what about Minerva?"

"Would you go out with him?"

"Of course not."

"Good."

"Are you okay?"

"I'm fine. You?"

Dani tilted her head as she noted the tension in his jaw and the tiny lines around his eyes. She gingerly laid her hand on his upper arm.

"Are you dying inside over something we'll laugh about tomorrow?"

His eyes momentarily relaxed, and his dimples flashed. "It's a bit more complicated than a torn dress."

"What is?"

"Nothing you need to worry about." He glanced around the room, then offered his arm. "AJ and Shelby are near the door. Shall we join them?"

As he escorted her around the tables, her thoughts circled around Minerva's warning. He couldn't break her heart unless she gave it to him. And that she'd never do.

– 18 –

As they waited near the valet stand for their vehicles, Brett's phone beeped. He slid it from his pocket and glanced at the screen. "It's Amy."

"Probably calling to congratulate you," AJ said.

Brett tapped the button. "Hey, sis."

A deep voice replied. "Is this Brett Somers?"

"Who's this?"

"I'm an intern at Dayton Regional. This phone number is listed as the medical emergency contact for Amy Somers. She was brought into the ER a few minutes ago."

"Amy's in ER?"

"You are Brett Somers?"

"Yes, yes. What happened to Amy?"

"She collapsed. I'm not sure of the details, and there's not much I can tell you at this point."

"Can I talk to her?"

"She's being evaluated at the moment. Perhaps later if you want to call back."

"I'd rather you tell me now what's going on."

"All I know is that she's here. Alone."

"I'll be there soon. Tell her I'll be there as soon as I can."

"I'll do that. Thank you, Mr. Somers."

Brett ended the call and stared at AJ. "It's Amy. She's . . ." His brain wouldn't cooperate with his mouth. "I don't know, she's in the ER."

"What ER? Where?"

"Dayton. He said she was in Dayton."

"What's she doing there?"

"Who knows?" Brett looked around wildly for his car. "I've got to go."

"I'll go with you," AJ said.

Brett nodded, then glanced at Dani and Shelby.

"Don't worry about us." Shelby gave him a reassuring smile. "I'll take Dani home."

The hovel Dani called home broke through the cloud surrounding Brett's thoughts. "No," he said firmly. "No, you can't."

"Of course, I can," Shelby insisted.

"It's not safe. Go to my place." He reached in his pocket for his keys, then realized the valet had them. "Or stay here. I'll get rooms for you."

"What do you mean, it's not safe? That's silly." Shelby said. "We'll be fine."

Dani stepped closer. "Shelby doesn't need to drive me. I can get a taxi."

Brett shot AJ a "help me out here" look, counting on him to remember what he'd said earlier about Dani's so-called home.

"Here's what we'll do," AJ said. "You head to the hospital, and I'll take Dani and Shelby home. By then, we should know more about what's going on with Amy. I'll be there as soon as I can."

"That's really not—" Shelby began.

Brett held up a hand. "Yes, it is."

"I just don't think you should be driving all the way to Dayton by yourself." Shelby crossed her arms. "This is ridiculous."

"Shelby's right," Dani said. "If you're worried about the electricity, I'm sure it's back on by now."

"You don't know that," Brett snapped, then immediately regretted it. He flashed a warm smile at Dani. "Wouldn't you like to stay here? Order room service?"

Indecision furrowed around her eyes, and her thoughts seemed to open before him. She didn't want to be the reason why AJ couldn't go with him; she didn't want Shelby to see her place; she didn't want him to feel responsible for her.

Too late for that.

He stepped closer. "Please let AJ take you home. If your electricity is still out—"

"It's not going to be."

"Probably not. But I can't leave here until I know you're going to be okay." He'd said *please* once already. Now its foreign taste threatened to choke him. He bit the inside of his lip, then cleared his throat. But the plea remained silent.

Except in his eyes.

She scrutinized his face then nodded. His heart flipped with relief.

"There's your car." AJ pointed to the line of vehicles snaking in front of the hotel. "Call me when you get there."

"I will." Brett led Dani to the Lexus. "I had planned to invite everybody back to my place. I'm sorry the evening ended like this."

"Who could have known?" The warmth of her comforting smile momentarily calmed his restlessness. "Your sister needs you. Go."

He gave the driver a tip, removed her bag from the car, then handed it to AJ. Pulling her into his arms, he whispered, "I'll make it up to you. I promise."

Without giving her a chance to respond, he hurried around to the driver's side. Before opening the door, he caught her gaze. He wasn't sure if he saw hope or relief in her eyes. A faint smile lifted the corners of her lips.

The desire to feel their soft lusciousness overwhelmed him.

He slid into the seat, berating himself as he pulled away from the curb. Tonight was supposed to be the end of this little tryst. He should never have made her that promise.

Dani stood at the window, thankful her electricity had been restored, as the Jeep left the parking lot. Much to her dismay, Shelby and AJ had insisted on walking her to the door. They had hidden their reactions behind polite smiles, but Dani knew they weren't happy about leaving her here. Shelby had even urged her to come back to Misty Willow for the night.

She'd have liked that and almost said yes. But pride had stiffened her shoulders, and she'd refused. Besides, it was better this way. AJ's parents had died in that plane just like Brett's. If—no, when they realized her mom had been the pilot, any thought of friendship would be ended.

Dani slid off the strappy heels, then changed into pajamas. After examining the torn hem, she hung the dress in the narrow closet. But the memory of Brett kneeling at her side, carefully untangling her bracelet, wrapped around her.

Such lovely moments. But what a strange day.

She retrieved the amethyst ring from her jeans and placed it and the bracelet in her jewelry box. The painted ballerina rotated on her slippered toe as the metallic notes faltered. A cheap keepsake from her childhood that now sheltered a stolen ring.

Not stolen. Just accidentally borrowed.

She shut the lid, ending the ballerina's pitiful pirouette, then plopped on the bed and hugged a pillow to her chest as she relived the evening.

Brett had promised they'd see each other again. But why? Because he felt sorry for her? Or because there was a nice guy beneath that sophisticated veneer?

The conversation with Minerva replayed itself in her mind and cemented her first impressions. Brett only cared about one person—himself.

And Jonah. And Amy. And AJ and Shelby. And Elizabeth and Tabby.

Okay, he cared about a lot of people but only those closest to him.

That would never include the daughter of the pilot who'd killed his parents.

Brett hurried through the big double doors of the emergency room. A few people, looking drained and unhappy, were scattered around the waiting area. A maintenance man maneuvered a large round sweeper along one side.

Brett wanted to bury his nose in his sleeve to avoid catching some weird virus, but refrained. Instead he strode to the central desk and impatiently waited for the clerk to acknowledge him.

When she did, his voice was businesslike. "Amy Somers. Where is she?"

"And you are?"

"Her brother."

"ID, please."

He went through the identification process and slapped a visitor's sticker against his shirt.

"She's in room 3. Just down that hall." The clerk pressed a button, and an automatic door to the side of her desk swung open.

"Thank you."

Finding the room he wanted, he slipped through the closed curtain. Amy lay on a narrow bed, her eyes closed. Brett sidled between the bed and the wall.

"Amy," he whispered. "It's me."

Her eyes fluttered open, caught his gaze, then closed again. "What happened?" Her voice sounded ragged and weak.

"You tell me," he said gently. "All I know is that you collapsed."

"Didn't feel good."

"What did the doctor say?"

Amy shook her head, and a shudder passed through her frail body. "So . . , tired."

"It's okay," Brett soothed, brushing her long blonde hair from her pale face. Beneath the off-white blanket, she resembled a porcelain doll, though without the rosy cheeks. Darkness encircled her eyes, and mascara caked her lashes.

The IV needle taped to her hand seeped fluid into her vein. He carefully lifted her sleeve and noted the pinpricks where someone had tried to put the needle in her arm. If he'd only been there when she was brought in, he could have told them not to bother.

"Sleep, Amy. I'm watching over you."

She didn't respond.

Brett took a deep breath. A metal chair was wedged near the bed, but he didn't sit down. Suddenly feeling claustrophobic, he closed his eyes.

His own life was a mess. He knew that.

But except for an infrequent hangover, he'd never done much to threaten his health. What was Amy up to?

Hating himself for doing so, he took a closer look at her arms and breathed a sigh of relief. No needle tracks.

Though that didn't mean she wasn't abusing drugs.

He scrutinized her shape beneath the blanket. Amy had always been slender. Above average height. Nice legs.

But now he realized she wasn't just slender but almost emaciated. Why hadn't he noticed how thin she'd become?

True, they hadn't seen much of each other lately. She always had an excuse for skipping out on anything he planned with AJ. He'd chalked it up to either embarrassment or pouting because of the futile lawsuit she'd filed against AJ and Shelby. Nothing like suing your family to ruin a relationship. But neither AJ nor Shelby held a grudge.

Perhaps Amy had another reason for avoiding them.

The curtain parted, and a portly man wearing a white coat entered. "I'm Dr. Asher. And you're . . . ?"

"Brett Somers. Amy's brother. What happened to her?"

"That's what we're trying to find out."

"The intern who called me said she collapsed."

"That's our understanding. I take it you weren't with her."

"I was in Columbus. That's where we live." He massaged his neck. "I don't even know what she was doing here."

"Drinking, for one thing." The doctor studied the screen of his tablet. "The EMTs were called to a nightclub not far from here. Apparently she was alone."

"That seems unlikely."

"No one came forward at the scene, but I don't know any other details."

"They're not important." At least not now. "Is she going to be all right?"

"Eventually. But I'd like to admit her for observation. I assume you can help with the paperwork."

"Of course."

"We appreciate that, Mr. Somers. Someone from admittance will be here shortly."

After Dr. Asher left, Brett cradled Amy's thin hand in his own. He stroked the slender fingers, wrapping them around his palm.

"What were you doing, Amy?" he said softly. "You should have been with me at the banquet. Then this wouldn't have happened."

Anger simmered in his gut. She'd probably been with the mysterious state senator who dreamed of being a congressman. He couldn't risk being seen with his mistress—not even when she most needed him.

Brett sighed heavily.

Amy wasn't the only one with a messy love life.

No wonder, with the examples they'd had.

But even that excuse wasn't good enough. Things had turned out differently for AJ, and his parents hadn't been much better than Brett's.

Somehow AJ had taken a different path, and he wanted Brett

to walk it with him. A path that included trusting in God instead of himself.

For the second time in as many days, Brett struggled to pray. To find the words that would persuade God to watch over Amy. To heal her.

"Brett."

His name on her dry lips sounded weak and raspy. He gently squeezed her hand.

"I'm here."

"Always." She coughed, the effort wracking her body. "Always."

"You know it." He touched her cheek. "You and me."

Her eyes flickered, and she tried to smile. "I don't like hospitals."

"I know."

"Take me home." A tear welled up in the corner of one eye. "Please."

"Not yet, Amy. We need to see what the doctor has to say."

"I'm fine."

"But you're not."

She shook her head, eyes tightly closed.

"What is it, Amy?"

She drifted away from him, back into her private dark world.

– 19 –

An hour or so later, a rap sounded against the doorframe, and AJ came through the curtain. He'd changed into jeans and a T-shirt, the inevitable OSU ball cap in one hand and a bag in the other. He nodded a greeting, then focused on Amy.

"What happened?"

Brett told him about the conversation with Dr. Asher. "No one was with her when the EMT guys showed up."

"Do you know who she's been seeing?"

"Someone she shouldn't have been."

"So he left her alone?"

"Looks that way."

Anger blazed in AJ's eyes, and his mouth tightened into a thin line. Brett had seen that look several months ago, only seconds before AJ decked him. He subconsciously rubbed his jaw. "Dibs," Brett said.

"What?"

Brett pounded his fist into his palm.

"As long as I can watch."

"A ringside seat." Brett snorted. "I'm counting on you to be sure he doesn't hit me back."

"Afraid he'll mess up your good looks?"

"Don't be jealous."

"Not when I got the girl," AJ said, a lighthearted "so there" in his voice. He flexed his muscles in mock bravado.

"I let you have her."

"Sure you did."

The teasing banter somehow released the tension that had been strangling Brett since he'd received the intern's phone call. Having AJ as a friend instead of a rival had its benefits.

"Speaking of girls, how's Dani?"

"Okay, I guess. Shelby invited her back to the farm."

"She wouldn't go?"

"I think she's used to being on her own."

"Doesn't mean she should be."

"What does that mean?"

"I don't know." Brett shook his head, clearing his thoughts of Dani, then glanced at Amy.

So pale and thin. So determined to have her way no matter the consequences. And this is where she'd ended up. His thoughts shifted to Jonah, fighting his own silent battle because his dad hadn't been around to protect him.

He'd failed them. Failed them both.

Because he was just like Amy—caring only about himself, with little concern for anyone who stood in his way.

Until he learned about Jonah. Now his life was like looking in a skewed mirror. Everything he thought was clear and true had blurred into a distorted reflection since his eyes had been wrenched open by a little boy who didn't even know of his existence.

He leaned forward, hands locked behind his head.

"You okay?" AJ asked.

After taking a deep breath, Brett stood and stretched the kinks from his back. "Just tired."

AJ gestured at the bag he'd carried in. "I brought you clothes if you want to change."

"Thanks, I think I will." He laid a hand on Amy's arm. "You won't leave her?"

"You know I won't."

Brett nodded, still focused on the sister who had become a stranger.

In his heart, the mirror skewed again, revealing a dark abyss. He stood on the edge, his arms wrapped around Amy, who struggled against him. They were lost, about to fall. But he wouldn't yell for help.

What was the use when there was no one to hear?

The next afternoon, Brett bought a cup of coffee from the barista in the hospital lobby, then stopped by the gift shop. He purchased a bouquet of pink roses and baby's breath before returning to Amy's private room. It'd been a long night, and Amy had slept fitfully between the routine checks of her vital signs.

Brett had been annoyed this morning when Amy made him and AJ leave while she talked with the physician doing rounds. And his temper almost got the better of him when she refused to tell them what the doctor had said.

At least she was being discharged. For now, that's all that mattered.

AJ had left after lunch, and soon Brett and Amy would be going home too.

When he reached the room, he rapped on the doorframe, then entered. Dressed in cotton capris and a T-shirt, Amy lounged on the bed and stared at the hanging TV.

He placed the vase on the side table. "I brought you a present."

"Lovely."

"Pink still your favorite?"

"When can we get out of here?"

"When are you going to tell me what the doctor said?"

"Nothing of any interest."

"I don't believe that."

"Believe what you want."

"Are you pregnant?"

"Of course not."

One thing to be thankful for.

He drew the padded chair closer to the bed. "Amy, you've got to talk to me. Tell me what happened last night."

"Nothing to tell." Her flat gaze dared him to contradict her. Without any makeup, her features appeared bloodless and drawn.

"You can't blame me for being worried about you."

"No one's asking you to worry."

"Are you kidding me? Do you have any idea what it was like to get that phone call? We were still at the banquet—"

"So that's it. You're upset because I didn't join the 'let's-all-be-family' praise-fest.'"

"Of course not. Though if you'd been there, you wouldn't be here now." He swept his arm around the room.

"Don't you get it, Brett? Now that you and AJ are all buddy-buddy, I'm the family black sheep."

"What are you talking about?"

"AJ's perfect fiancée and I are 'friends' on social media. I see all the precious photos of her and AJ and the adorable antics of her adorable daughters. You're in the photos too." She glared at him. "How do you stand all that cuteness?"

"They aren't like that, Amy, and you know it." He rubbed the back of his neck. The muscles were tight from sleeping in a chair most of the night. "You just need to give them a chance. Allow them to give you a chance."

Her long blonde hair fell forward as she lowered her gaze and picked at the deep purple polish on her fingernails. The Amy he knew couldn't abide chipped polish. She certainly didn't chip it herself.

"You shouldn't have betrayed me." Her voice was almost too low to hear.

"I didn't—"

"You gave up on the lawsuit." She looked at him, her expression filled with disdain.

"That lawsuit never had a chance, and you know it. You shouldn't have filed it in the first place."

"When AJ sold that land, he went against the explicit wishes of Sully's will."

"What difference does that make now? Shelby wanted the farm, and he didn't. Besides, it doesn't matter anymore. The house and most of the land have been donated to the foundation."

She ignored him, too insistent on making her point to listen to reason.

"We could have won. If you hadn't insisted on trying out your own little plan first."

Brett flushed with the memory of his ill-conceived plot to charm Shelby into giving up her farm.

"What were you really trying to do? Claim another conquest from under AJ's nose? I still can't believe how you cater to that woman." She pulled at her T-shirt. "This is hers. These pants are hers. AJ brought them."

"Be thankful she had the foresight to send them with him. Otherwise you'd be wearing my dress shirt and suit pants." The skimpy dress Amy was wearing when she was brought to the ER had reeked of alcohol, stale smoke, and other odors he didn't want to think about. Someone had shoved it into a plastic bag along with her shoes. They might as well have tossed it in the trash.

"All I know," Amy went on, again as if he hadn't spoken, "is if we'd pulled it off, my investment portfolio would be substantially larger. And my clients weren't at all pleased."

"As I recall, you said you didn't care what your clients thought." Brett stared at the whiteboard on the wall but barely registered the info written on it. "Look, if you need another piece of property, I'll find you one."

"So now you want to help me."

"I'm always here for you. You know that."

"You used to be. But things have changed. You've changed."

"I've just gotten tired of . . . tired of the games. Of being alone even when I'm with someone." He raked his fingers through his hair, pressing his nails against his scalp. "We're shallow, Amy. Both of us. I don't want to be shallow anymore."

Tears welled in Amy's light-blue eyes, then slid silently along her cheeks. "You're going to leave me, aren't you? AJ's going to have a new family, and you want to be part of them."

"Yeah. I do."

"You were always jealous of him."

"It's not jealousy to want what he's getting. A beautiful woman who's crazy in love with him. Children who adore him."

"So now you're on the hunt for a widowed mom?"

"I just want to meet someone who cares more about me than the size of my bank account. Someone I can love with all my heart."

"Good luck finding that."

"It's what you want too, isn't it?"

She stared toward the window, her facial muscles tense and drawn. "We don't live in a fairy tale. That kind of dream doesn't come true for people like you and me."

"Why can't it?"

She faced him, her expression exquisitely sad. "We've been hurt too much already. We can't let anyone hurt us again." Her voice cracked, and the tears streamed.

"What is it, Amy? Tell me."

"He left me." The words were broken with grief and heartache. "I collapsed, and he left me."

"Tell me his name."

She shook her head.

"He's married, isn't he?"

She stiffened, giving him the answer.

"Amy, why . . ."

He moved to the bed and gathered her in his arms, comforting her as he had when they were children. Soothing away her demons and monsters. But this time was different. This time he silently prayed for her.

A prayer without words because he didn't know what to say. He only knew that Amy needed divine assistance.

And so did he.

– 20 –

*D*read weighed Brett's shoes the closer he got to the entrance of Gallagher's. He'd considered using Amy's weekend hospitalization as an excuse to skip the regular Monday night beer-and-brag. But with Zach eager to stick his verbal knives into Brett's chest, the only thing worse than showing up was not showing up.

He entered the wings place, flashed his dimples at the teenaged hostess, and headed for the back corner. About seven or eight men, good-looking and with money to burn, gathered around circular tables laden with trays of assorted wings and other appetizers.

One of the men, a former OSU quarterback, raised his glass as Brett joined them. "Here he is. Internet sensation and supposedly Ohio's most eligible bachelor. You scored a touchdown with that one, Somers."

"What did all that publicity cost you?" teased another.

"Just an hour of my time." Brett signaled for a soda, then selected a golden-brown mozzarella stick. Every time he thought his fifteen minutes of fame had ended, someone brought up that video again. Like most people, these guys had probably seen the shortened version being passed around social media—a couple of minutes at most. Thankfully, the simpering probe into his deepest wound wasn't part of the clip, though it was also online for anyone who took the trouble to ferret it out. Remembering the interviewer's insincere sympathy reignited the pain in his gut.

"Don't hate him, men." Zach Shrouder slapped Brett on the back. "Our buddy won't hold that title long. Not when he's dating Little Miss Stars in Her Eyes."

Brett forced a jovial smile. "You got it all wrong, Zach. I'm not dating anybody."

"Does she know that?" Zach smirked, then eyed the group. "I saw her at that Up-and-Comers Banquet Saturday night. All dolled up like Cinderella but uncomfortable in the fancy dress." He faced Brett. "What was with the dangling lace?"

"She caught her bracelet on the hem. No big deal."

"Did you get her home before midnight?" Zach laughed, then swigged his beer. "Cute as she is, your brunette sweetie isn't in the same league as my red-hot Minerva."

You got that right.

Spence Elliott, a rising executive with a local investment firm, about choked. "You're still dating Minerva? Did you decide to keep her?"

"Not a chance. But I'll give her another month or so before changing the locks." Zach pulled a golden token out of his pocket and handed it to Brett. "You owe me a beer."

"That's why I'm here." All part of the game they played. Brett didn't think much of Minerva—she reminded him too much of Tracie—but he hadn't argued with Zach about the merits of their respective dates.

Dragging Dani through the mud of comparison seemed dishonorable. Funny, he'd never felt that way about a woman before.

Zach ordered his beer and gestured toward Brett. "Put it on his tab."

The waitress glanced at Brett, and he nodded. Zach shifted to

talk to someone else, and Brett and Spence took seats at one of
the tables.

"Any photos of your brunette sweetie?"

"I don't need your appraisal."

"I'm just curious." Spence shrugged. "Don't think I've ever seen
you with a brunette."

Brett considered, then found a photo of him and Dani on his
phone. Shelby had taken it at the banquet. "Again, we're not dating."

Spence studied the photo and nodded approvingly. "Not sure
Zach won that round, buddy."

"He thought he did. And I wasn't in the mood to argue."

"So why aren't you dating her?"

"Just not interested." Brett gulped his soda and looked around at
the Gallagher regulars. Their numbers had dwindled significantly
over the years. Some had moved away, but most were married now.
They had children. Mortgages.

A life he'd have scoffed at only a few weeks ago. But now?

"How about introducing her to me?" Spence asked.

Taken aback by the unexpected question, Brett almost spilled
his drink. "You want to go out with her?"

"Sure."

"She's not a . . . a box of candy to be passed around to whoever
wants her."

"Come on, Brett. It wouldn't be the first time one of us has
dated someone else's reject."

"She's not a reject."

A slow smile cut across Spence's features. "You've got a thing
for her. Don't you?"

"Aren't you already dating somebody?"

"Nothing serious." Spence stiffened and shifted his gaze to a
platter of nacho chips and spinach dip. "She's a nurse at that children's hospital. You know the one I mean?"

The back of Brett's neck tingled, his senses on full alert. "Yeah,
I know it."

"She told me something interesting." He lowered his voice. "About you."

"How does she even know who I am?"

"She saw a photo of us at my apartment. Remember when we did that charity golf event earlier this summer?"

"Yeah."

"That picture." Spence coated a chip with the thick dip.

"What did she tell you?"

"That you were arguing with the mom of one of the patients. A little guy who looks a lot like you."

A lot like me. Shelby said the same thing. "It's a personal matter."

"About as personal as it gets." Neither spoke for a few moments, then Spence leaned closer. "We've been friends a long time, Brett. Why didn't you ever tell me?"

Brett spread his hands and sighed. "I just found out myself."

Spence's eyes widened as he ate another chip. "The risk we take, I suppose. Too bad you got caught."

"It happens." Brett forced a lightness in his tone he didn't feel. He twisted in his seat and found Zach regaling a couple other guys with some crazy story. He turned back to Spence. "I'd appreciate it if you kept this between us."

Spence looked over his shoulder in Zach's direction. "I think having a child is a major penalty according to Zach's rules. It might get you kicked out of The Game."

"I don't care about that." Brett hesitated, surprised to realize he really didn't. A couple of these guys, like Spence, were good friends. But the others were arrogant. Condescending. Self-absorbed—he ended the thought, not wanting to admit he was one of them.

He bit the inside of his lip as disgust rose in his chest. They'd been playing this game for years—buying beers for the guys who had the hottest dates at major events, inviting women into their lives, then counting down the weeks until they were tossed aside. Awarding points for a string of made-up rules he now recognized as cold and heartless.

He'd been among the worst.

"I've got to go." He abruptly stood and handed a couple of twenties to Spence. "Take care of my tab, will you?"

"Why are you leaving? If it's because of—I promise. Not a word."

"I'm just tired of it, Spence. Tired of . . . not having any answers."

Before Spence could reply, Zach joined them. "You can't go, Brett. It's against the rules."

"I've got things to do."

"If you leave now, you'll owe us all a round next week."

Brett pulled several bills from his wallet and laid them on the table. "I won't be here. But this should cover it."

Zach reached for the money, but Brett flattened his palm on the bills. "Spence will see to it."

"Sorry. I can't." Spence stood. "I won't be here either."

"What is this?" Zach lifted his lip in his familiar smirk. "A mutiny. Are you really that sore of a loser, Somers?"

"I didn't lose anything, Shrouder. I'll see you around."

As he walked away, Zach called after him. "Tell Cinderella the guys said hello."

Brett fisted his hands but resisted the urge to turn around. Nothing he said to Zach would make a difference. He'd pulled enough similar antics over the years to know.

Spence followed him to the street. "You all right?"

"Fine."

"You know how Zach is. Don't let him get to you."

"I don't care what he says. But I'm not doing this anymore."

"You're really not coming back?"

"No. At least not for a while."

"How about if we try someplace else? Me and my nurse, you and your brunette cutie?"

"Forget it. I'm not setting her up with you, Spence."

"I don't want you to." He stared off in the distance for a moment. "All that in there was a joke. To tell you the truth, this thing with Kristen—it's getting serious. I'm not trading her in for anybody."

"Cupid finally got you, huh?"

"All I know is that she's the best thing that ever happened to me. So how about a double date?"

"I'm not sure I'll be seeing Dani again."

"Whoever then. You've got my number."

"Sure."

"Guess I better go back in and settle the check. See you around."

Brett said good-bye, then ambled toward the parking lot. Zach's leering face juxtaposed with Spence's unexpected admission. Another of their group headed for the altar.

As he angled toward his car, a tall spire caught his attention. Changing direction, he sauntered across the lot to the sidewalk. The summer heat lingered between the buildings, but he scarcely noticed. When he reached the church, he gazed up at the elaborate statues set into the architecture. Ionic columns graced the portico.

All he needed to do was walk up the steps. Go inside the open door. Sit in a pew.

It's something Gran would have liked to see him do when she was alive. He wished he had. But instead he'd left the churchgoing to AJ. That kind of life wasn't for him no matter how much Gran had wished it.

His life was his own—all mapped out—and there had been no place for God in it.

Until Meghan returned with Jonah.

Now things didn't seem so clear. The map held hidden pitfalls he'd never anticipated. Beginning with Meghan's deceit.

He closed his eyes. That wasn't fair. He was the one to blame for what happened. He'd only seduced her because she was dating AJ. Just a way to hurt his cousin for being Sully's favorite. The heir apparent and namesake.

He'd succeeded more than he could have imagined.

Sully died without mending the rift between him and AJ. Brett hadn't minded that either. With AJ out of the picture, he did as he wished with Sully's business. It all had worked out fine.

Until now.

He looked up at the half-open door again. AJ had found answers in a place like this. Enough to bring him peace from the past.

But Brett found it hard to believe that would be true for him too.

He returned to his car and, without giving it much thought, drove to the hospital.

What color would Jonah's window be tonight?

Meghan straightened Jonah's blankets, then placed Brett's birthday monkey beside his pillow. "John Jacob Jingleheimer Schmidt" softly played, one of Jonah's favorite silly tunes, and she could almost believe a slight smile touched his pale lips.

If only that were true.

"What color of lights do you want tonight, my sweet boy? Would you like yellow for the sunshine or blue for the sky? Or how about orange now that autumn is coming?"

She stroked his soft blond hair, then raised her eyes to the open door as Aaron stepped inside.

"How is he?" he asked.

"No change."

"How are you?"

"About the same." She gestured at the monkey. "Much as I hate to admit it, this was a great idea. The music seems to relax him."

A shadow flickered across Aaron's features, but it was quickly dispelled by his congenial smile. Perhaps she'd imagined it.

"Brett would be glad to know that," he said.

She frowned and plucked an imaginary piece of lint from the blanket. "I tried writing him a thank-you note. But I couldn't get the words right."

"How hard is it to say thank you?"

From anyone else, the question might have sounded like a rebuke. But not from Aaron.

"You could tell him for me."

Aaron hesitated, then shook his head. "You can't put off facing him forever."

"But I can put it off as long as possible."

"To what end? Like it or not, he's Jonah's dad."

"I don't like it." She crossed her arms and stuck out her lower lip.

Aaron chuckled at her pouty-face. "Writing a thank-you note is a good first step."

"I don't know his address."

"I do."

"And then what?"

"Let him see his son."

A sudden chill raised goose bumps on Meghan's arms. It was the right thing to do, yet the thought of Brett in the same room as Jonah terrified her. She'd tried to sort through the fears, to put them in perspective and consider them rationally.

But that never worked. Brett had money, and he had power. So far he hadn't taken any legal steps to establish his paternity, but that didn't mean he wouldn't. Her deeper fear, though, was that he'd seek custody. He might, especially if he blamed her for Jonah's accident.

From the moment she learned of her pregnancy, she'd vowed to be a good mom. To protect her child from harm.

And then this had happened.

Brett couldn't blame her any more than she blamed herself.

rett ran his eyes up and down Amy's thin frame as she stood in the doorway. Even though she was wearing one of his cast-off sweatshirts, she obviously had lost weight. Once again, he berated himself for not noticing sooner.

"Aren't you going to let me in?"

"Why are you here?"

"Nice to see you too."

She snorted, then padded into her apartment and lounged on the sofa, her slippered feet propped on the coffee table. He lowered himself into a nearby chair as guilt squeezed his gut. The last time he'd been here was the day Shelby had discovered he and AJ were cousins. Unwilling to go home and face Tracie, he'd sought refuge on Amy's couch.

That had been weeks ago.

"I stopped by your office. Turns out my phone calls aren't the only ones you're not returning."

"Don't lecture me." She pulled a throw pillow onto her lap, then studied her nails. Bright pink polish had replaced the chipped purple.

"You can't blame me for being worried. What did the doctor say?"

"I'm just overtired, needing a rest. That's it."

"I don't believe you."

"Please don't give me that 'I can tell when you're lying' look."

"I *can* tell when you're lying." He leaned forward, resting his elbows on his knees. "You've got a tell."

"So you *tell* me, but you never *tell* me what my *tell* is."

"Why would I do that?"

She scooched further into the sofa's soft cushions, clearly annoyed. "Why are you here? Don't you have work to do? Multimillion-dollar deals to make?"

"Actually, I do." He'd gone to the office that morning. Had tried to focus on the paperwork in his inbox and pay attention to the callers on the other end of the phone. But he'd been unable to concentrate on even the most mundane task.

Jonah and Amy commandeered his thoughts. And much as he dreaded admitting it, Dani preoccupied his heart. He hadn't talked to her since leaving her at the banquet, even though he'd promised to call.

Broken promises didn't bother him much. Not usually.

Maybe it was better she realized he was a conceited jerk. Exactly the sort of man she had first accused him of being.

"Then leave me alone and go do it," Amy said.

He mentally shook away his dreary thoughts and inwardly sighed. "Who is he?"

She didn't even bother to answer, just closed her eyes and leaned her head against the back of the couch.

"You won't see him again, will you? After what he did?"

"See who?"

"He's not worthy of you, Amy."

Silence surrounded them. When she spoke, her voice was as small as a child's. "Maybe I'm not worthy of him."

He reached for her hand and squeezed it gently. "That's not true. How could you ever think that?"

She lifted her eyes to his. "Why is it so easy for you to change?"

"It's not . . . I haven't."

"One day, we're partners. Conniving against AJ. Now you're doting on his fiancée and her children as if we can be one big happy family. But we can't."

"Why can't we?"

"Since when do you like children?"

"Since . . ." He searched his memory, trying to pinpoint the moment Elizabeth and Tabby were no longer an annoyance. But there wasn't one moment—only a string of moments that led them straight into his heart.

"Since I found out how easy they are to like. No complications. No secret agendas. I swing them around and bring them pizza and they like me." He let go of Amy's hand and plopped back in the chair. "I can be the uncle they've never had."

"Uncle? Won't they be some kind of cousin? Actually, they're not going to be related to us at all. Not really."

"Maybe not. But I like them thinking of me as an uncle. And you know what, they've never had an aunt either."

"I'm not exactly aunt material."

"When they're all grown up, what are they going to remember about you, Amy? Because the memories they have—those are up to you."

Her features briefly softened, and for a moment, she was once again his lovely little sister instead of the world-hardened adult she'd become. But the veil returned, and her mouth tightened. "I don't care what they think of me."

"Then don't be surprised when they don't."

Her eyes narrowed, and he could almost see the steam coming from her ears. The comment must have stung.

Good.

Somehow he had to get through to her, had to convince her to stop shutting them out. She'd never find peace by alienating those who loved her. Why couldn't she see that?

The hypocrisy of his thoughts gripped his temples. Their situations might not be exactly the same, but it hadn't been that long ago that he'd protected his heart as fiercely as she now protected hers.

"You don't have to babysit me, you know."

"Are you trying to get rid of me?"

"Stay if you like. But I'm going to take a nap."

"Can I get you anything? Bring you anything?"

"I'm fine."

He stood, pulling his keys from his pocket. "I'll stop by tomorrow. Text me or call if you want me to stop somewhere on my way."

She simply nodded, avoiding his gaze.

He started for the door, then turned back. "I'm here for you, Amy. Always have been. Always will be."

She merely nodded.

Brett closed the door behind him, then leaned against the outer wall.

How do I help her?

The question surprised him, not because he'd had it, but because he hadn't asked himself. He'd asked God. And he desperately needed God to answer.

22

*D*ani left the interview shortly before noon on Friday and hurried to her car. Once inside, she texted Shelby. *Running late. Be there soon.*

She'd done well enough at Monday's interview with the bank manager to get this second one. They'd hinted the job was hers but said an official offer couldn't be made till next week. She hoped she'd soon be earning a paycheck instead of depleting her meager savings.

So why wasn't she more excited?

Peering through the windshield at the imposing structure, she imagined walking through its doors every weekday for the rest of her life.

The thought filled her with dread.

It's temporary. Something to pay the rent on a real apartment. To make do until something better comes along.

She parked in an empty space not far from the downtown restaurant where she was meeting Shelby. The invitation had been a welcome surprise, and the *yes* was out of Dani's mouth before she could stop it. Now guilt nibbled at her spirit. She liked Shelby, and under other circumstances perhaps they could have been friends.

To ease her conscience, Dani promised herself not to pump Shelby for information about Brett. At least then Shelby wouldn't be involved in any scheme Dani concocted to teach Brett a lesson.

Especially now that she was even more determined to do so.

Despite his reluctant good-bye and promise to call, almost a week had gone by without even a text. Why had she expected anything else? He'd been lonely and invited her to the movie. He'd needed a date and invited her to the banquet. No doubt someone else had caught his eye, maybe a nurse at the ER or a friend of his sister's, and driven all thoughts of Dani from his mind.

Men like him never kept their promises.

She found Shelby at an outside table shaded by an overhang and slightly cooled by a ceiling fan. Before taking her seat, Dani removed her tailored jacket and arranged it on the back of the metal chair. "Sorry I'm late. I'm still learning my way around town."

"Don't worry about it. How did the interview go?"

"Really well. I'm hopeful." Except she didn't want the position. And yet she did. But only for the paycheck.

"Will you like working at a bank?"

"It's a job." Time to change the subject. "Thanks again for inviting me over last Saturday. I had a great time."

"I'm glad you could come. I know how hard it is to move to a new city."

"Easier than moving to a new country." When Dani was at the farm, Shelby had talked about her family's move to the mission field when she was a teen. Apparently, the transition had been difficult, and Dani pretended to sympathize. But she'd trade her childhood for Shelby's any day.

"That was definitely harder," Shelby said. "Though so was coming back to the States. I guess sometimes we don't appreciate what we have until it's too late."

You think? Dani dismissed the ungracious thought as quickly as it arose. Shelby wasn't to blame for her rotten childhood.

The waiter arrived with menus, and they both requested iced tea.

"Could you bring an extra tea?" Shelby asked. "Someone else is joining us."

A tremor shot up Dani's spine at this unexpected news, and her mind whirled. It couldn't be AJ, not on a school day. But that only left one other person.

"Be back soon with your tea, ladies."

The waiter left, and Shelby glanced at her watch. "It's not like Brett to be late."

"Brett's coming?"

"Didn't I tell you? I'm sorry, I meant to. Tabby must have distracted me."

Shelby's apology sounded sincere, and Tabby had interrupted their phone conversation a couple of times. But the butterflies Dani had managed to control during the interview now flitted wildly. She grasped for something, anything, to say. "How's Amy?"

"Okay, I guess. They only kept her overnight, and she's refusing to tell AJ or Brett anything the doctor said."

"They aren't close?"

"In some ways, yes. Some ways, no," Shelby said. "I don't know her very well. We live in such different worlds. She's involved in politics and all this legislative stuff while I'm busy corralling children and being a bore."

"You're not a bore."

"Tell that to Amy." She glanced past Dani's shoulder and waved. "There's Brett."

Reminding herself to breathe, Dani sternly ordered the butterflies to settle. He greeted Shelby with a quick kiss on the cheek, then sat in the chair between them.

When he gazed at Dani, her heart stopped. She didn't want him to affect her this way. Didn't want to be charmed by his gorgeous dimples or drawn into the crystal depths of his eyes.

But his very presence overwhelmed her.

"Hi," she murmured.

"You're looking very professional today. And lovely, of course."

"I had an interview this morning."

"So I heard." He turned to Shelby. "Did you talk to her yet?"

"I was waiting for you."

"Talk to me about what?" Dani asked, once again silently reprimanding the butterflies.

Shelby rested her arms upon the table. "Don't take this the wrong way, but we talked about you last night."

"You and Brett?"

"And AJ."

"Why?"

"We wanted to know if you'd be interested in working with our foundation."

Dani glanced from Shelby to Brett, then back again, her mouth slightly open. The butterflies flitted, but for a different reason. Excitement surged through her as the familiar heart-tug flared.

"You mean with the archaeological dig? And the Underground Railroad museum? Are you serious?"

"Very serious," Brett said. "I don't know about you ladies, but I'm starving. How about we order lunch and then we can talk?"

The waiter returned with three icy glasses of tea. After he left with their orders, Brett shifted in his chair and nodded at Shelby.

"I think it's important we document our progress with the archaeological dig," she said. As she talked, her enthusiasm grew and her gestures became more animated. "But it's also important to put everything in context. We need someone to conduct research, interview the archaeological team, find out more about the history of the area. Things like that."

"We know there's interest," Brett said. "Someone approached us about doing a documentary."

Distaste flickered in Shelby's eyes. "I didn't like him very much."

"Why not?" Dani asked.

Brett spoke up. "He didn't have the same vision we do."

Dani glanced at the tension in Shelby's eyes, then focused again on Brett. They were hiding something, making an excuse for their refusal to work with this mystery individual. But why?

As if sensing her curiosity, Brett flashed a disarming smile. "If this were your project, how would you approach it?"

Dani considered a moment, mentally reviewing what she'd learned about Misty Willow and its history during her visit. "I suppose I'd want to delve into the history of the house, the people who once lived there. Find out more about their role in the Underground Railroad both before and during the Civil War. Then, like Shelby said, interview the archaeologists and everyone else involved with the excavation."

"That's what I think too." Brett raised his eyebrows at Shelby. "What about you?"

"Even if we never produced a documentary," Shelby said, "I'd still like to have an organized record of what we're doing. The work that's taking place."

"The beginnings of an archive," Brett said.

"That's right." Shelby looked away from them, as if she were seeing something they couldn't. "I want my family to be remembered. For my grandchildren to know their heritage."

"We're going to make that possible," Brett said. "I promise."

He turned to Dani with a self-conscious shrug, and somehow she knew his thoughts mirrored her own. Compared to Shelby, who could recite the names of her ancestors several generations back, Brett and Dani were practically rootless. Though Brett, with a sister and a cousin, a grandmother he'd apparently adored, had more of a grounding than Dani did.

Her father was a nonentity in her life. Someone her mother had refused to talk about. She'd had no grandparents, no aunts or uncles, no cousins. Only her mom and her stepdad.

Until the crash that claimed her mother's life.

Then she'd had nobody.

"What do you think, Dani? Will you help me?" Shelby's softly spoken question interrupted the painful train of Dani's thoughts.

She pushed aside her yearning for what she ached to have and let her imagination fill with possibilities. Besides a documentary, they could create video shorts, guided audio tours for the museum's displays, even curriculum.

Her mind whirled with ideas, though doubt tempered her eagerness.

This wasn't just a job—it was a dream job. A rare opportunity to fuse her love of history, storytelling, and film into something that mattered. Into a legacy.

She'd be a fool not to grab it with both hands.

Except working for Shelby meant she couldn't plot trouble for Brett. Could she?

For the past few nights, the fiery monsters he'd unleashed had tormented her. In her dreams, Brett stood at a distance while flames licked at her feet. When she begged him for help, he shouted the words she despised above all others: *Murderer. Your mother is a murderer.*

When she awakened, gasping for breath and clutching her pillow, she again vowed to find some way to get back at him.

But here, where the summer sun shone bright and clear beyond the patio and the air smelled warm and fresh, the vengeful monsters appeared small and petty.

"Better than a bank job, right?" Brett asked.

Dani's jumbled thoughts perched at a crossroad. Hearing her mom's name publicly vilified had stung. Deeply. If she took the bank job, she could pursue her quest for Brett's comeuppance without feeling guilty for taking advantage of his kindness.

But he was right—her creativity would wither each time she stepped foot inside that huge hive of worker bees.

"It's definitely intriguing," she said.

"Tell her about your idea," Shelby urged. "This is so exciting. Brett is brilliant."

"Yes, I am," he agreed, then focused again on Dani. "But this is basic business. The dig will shut down once the weather gets bad. Though there's plenty to do, you may have some downtime.

However, if you set up as an independent contractor, you could do research and creative projects for other clients to fill in any gaps."

"You mean I'd have my own business?"

"If you want. And I can help you with the paperwork. Recommend an attorney for the legalities."

"Why would you do that?"

"Frankly, it saves the foundation money in the long run. Since you would be an independent contractor, we won't be providing any benefits."

Shelby pulled a folder from her bag and handed it to Dani. "But on the flip side, you'll get paid more than if you were an employee. Isn't that right, Brett?"

He tapped the folder. "The numbers are in there."

Dani opened the folder and scanned the document. It included a suggested list of projects and an extravagant compensation plan that included an upfront retainer fee. She'd be able to move into a real apartment, one with curtains and clean furniture. Get new tires for her car. In time, trade in her car. All sooner than if she accepted the position at the bank.

"This is very generous," she said.

"Is that a yes?" Brett asked.

Her heart shouted "Go for it!" but doubt and fear choked the words. She glanced at the project list again. The items weren't much different than what she'd done for her senior thesis—more complex in scope, definitely. But basically they involved research, organization, and presentation.

"Why me?"

"Why not you?" The challenge in Brett's eyes was softened by something else—hope, perhaps? Not likely, and yet . . .

"We love your enthusiasm," Shelby jumped in. "Besides, I don't think it's a coincidence you and Brett were at the hospital at the same time. I mean, what are the odds he'd meet someone with your education and experience? To me, you're an answer to prayer."

Me, an answer to prayer? Dani mentally shook her head.

Shelby could believe what she wanted. But Dani knew the truth. That night at the hospital wasn't a coincidence, but God had nothing to do with it. He'd abandoned Dani long ago.

Brett placed the napkin on his lap while the server passed out their plates. He, Shelby, and AJ had spent most of Thursday evening discussing the proposal for Dani. This morning, he and Shelby had held a video conference with the three other board members of the Lassiter nonprofit foundation. In less than half an hour, a unanimous consensus had been reached.

"We'll need to check a few references, of course," he said. "Just routine. That won't be a problem, will it?"

"No, of course not." Somehow the tone of her voice seemed at odds with her words.

He'd expected her to jump at the offer, had imagined her eyes shining with gratitude. Instead, she appeared hesitant. Maybe he shouldn't have ignored her all week.

He hadn't meant to. Hadn't even wanted to. But each time his thumb hovered over her number, he forced himself to pocket the phone. The promise he'd made the night of the banquet ate at him like an omitted tax deduction. But the bottom line was he liked her too much to pursue her.

At least that's what he told himself on his late-night excursions. For the past week, he'd taken supper to Amy, who wouldn't leave her apartment. She still refused to tell him anything, but diagnosing her symptoms didn't take a medical degree—he just didn't know which eating disorder she was battling.

From her place, he went to the hospital, standing vigil beneath the colored lights. Next stop: Meghan's apartment. And finally, a drive to Dani's so-called apartment complex before heading home. A strange restlessness compelled him to make each stop. Otherwise he couldn't sleep. Without meaning to, or understanding why, he'd turned into a crazed stalker.

He rubbed the back of his neck. "We're open to negotiation if you want to counter."

Surprise, then mischief, replaced the uncertainty in her eyes. "Give me your car?"

He snorted, then exchanged glances with Shelby. Her smile gave him the go-ahead.

"How about we give you another place to live?"

Obviously stunned, Dani leaned back in her chair. "What?"

"We won't have official offices until after the wedding," Brett said. "So here's our plan. AJ moves into Gran's bungalow now, and you move into the cottage."

"It'd be so much more convenient to have you nearby," Shelby said, then laughed. "Though I promise we won't take advantage of that."

"The cottage is a little rustic," Brett said drily. "But it's got all the modern conveniences. Indoor plumbing, running water."

A smile teased the corners of Dani's mouth, and he ached to reach for her hand.

"It's too much," she said. "I can't . . ."

"But you'd be doing us a favor," Shelby said. "It's not a good idea for either house to be empty."

Brett could almost hear Dani's thoughts, they seemed so intense. Somehow he had to persuade her to move into the cottage and out of that hovel masquerading as an apartment. But for once, he was at a loss for the words to close the deal.

Maybe that was the problem.

This wasn't a sale, but her future. If she accepted their offer, she'd be dependent on them for her paycheck and her housing. That would give any rational person pause.

"It doesn't have to be permanent," he said. "Stay at the cottage until you find something you like better."

"We'd like you to do that even if you say no to the job," Shelby added with a shiver. "Dani, you know that place where you're staying isn't safe. And it's not charity because . . . because it just isn't."

Brett shook his head. "Real smooth, Shelby."

"Just trying to help." She turned to Dani. "Please say yes. You're the only person I want to work with on this project."

Dani ran her eyes down the document, then closed the folder. "How soon can I start?"

Relief whooshed through Brett's spirit. "Right now. I don't want you spending one more night in that place."

23

*D*ani flattened a cardboard box and placed it on a stack of others beneath the pool table that took up one end of the long room. She paused to once again admire the large stained-glass scene of a country landscape hanging in front of the side window. Within the rustic frame, vibrantly colored wildflowers grew along a creek beneath the outstretched limbs of a sheltering tree. The glass sections were divided by dark leading.

Whoever had built the rectangular cottage had essentially divided the long house into two halves. The front half was one room with windows across the front. The back half had been divided into the kitchen, with a door leading outside, a tiny bathroom, and a bedroom. The space near the main door may have been a second bedroom at one time, but the walls closing it in had been removed. AJ used it as an office. A slender desk stood beneath a window, and an antique rocking chair nestled in a corner.

The entire place held an air of coziness and warmth, a refuge from a world that could be cruel and unyielding. Her new home, at least for a little while. No more cringing in the dark, fearful of all the outdoor noises. No more living out of cardboard boxes.

Dani sighed with contentment as she gazed out the front windows. Elizabeth and Tabby chased Lila, their retriever, and each other around the sloping yard. Apparently the dog had belonged to AJ, but she'd slowly been claimed by Elizabeth and now lived at Misty Willow.

The murmur of voices grew louder as Brett and AJ entered the long front room from the bedroom. Each carried an armful of clothes.

"This is the last of them," Brett said to Dani. "I never would have thought AJ was such a clotheshorse."

AJ guffawed. "Says the man with the walk-in closet bigger than my bedroom."

"Oh, come on. It's not really that big," Brett protested. "Besides, I wear suits almost every day, and they take up a lot of space, AJ has exactly two—a navy blue and a gray. The same ones he's had since college."

"No need to replace them," AJ said.

Brett made a face behind AJ's back, and Dani giggled. He rewarded her with a heart-stopping flash of his dimples. The men left the cottage, still debating the merits of their wardrobes, as Shelby entered from the kitchen carrying a kitten-in-a-basket cookie jar.

"Are they almost done?" she asked.

"I think so," Dani said. "I still can't believe I'm going to be living here."

"I hope you'll like it. And that it won't be too quiet for you."

"It won't be." She pointed to the jar. "That's so cute."

"It's kind of special. AJ had one just like it that belonged to his mother. The first time I was here, Tabby broke it. Naturally, I was mortified."

"I would have been too."

"AJ was sweet about it, though. So I went online and found a replacement. It was the first gift I ever gave him."

"What was his first gift to you?" Dani held up her hand. "Wait, I already know. The gravel for your driveway, right?"

"Real romantic, huh? Though to tell you the truth, I did appreciate it. The ruts were horrible."

"Aw, true love."

"Yeah." Shelby cradled the cookie jar, a slight smile on her lips. "I'm going to find a safe spot for this in AJ's Jeep. Be back in a moment."

Dani inwardly sighed, then pulled a few books from another box. Shelby and AJ's romance was a fairy tale come true. Though from what Brett said, it hadn't started out that way. Dani didn't want to be jealous of Shelby, but she longed for a romantic story of her own.

When Brett and AJ returned from a trip to the bungalow, they manned the grill while Dani put the finishing touches on a three-bean casserole in her new kitchen. Because the bungalow was already furnished, AJ had only taken his clothes and most of his personal belongings from the cottage. Everything else he'd left for Dani.

Her own place.

The thought of it elated her spirit, and she couldn't help grinning.

"You're happy to be here?" Shelby asked. She stood on the opposite side of the kitchen counter and grated cheese for the salad.

"There's a warm feeling to this place. Like *it's* happy."

"It's been loved."

And it's been a refuge. While helping her pack up her belongings at Baines Lodging, Brett had talked about his grandmother coming here to escape the hubbub of city life. When AJ got hired as a teacher at the local high school, it became his home. And his haven.

What Brett left unsaid, but Dani somehow understood, was that both Gran and AJ needed a place to escape from Sully. The man had held tremendous influence over his wife and grandchildren. But nothing they did ever seemed to please him.

Kind of like her stepdad.

Elizabeth popped in the kitchen door. "Steaks are ready," she said hurriedly, then raced back to the grill.

They ate beneath the shade of a trio of silver birches and enjoyed the light evening breeze that stirred their branches. The little girls played tag with Lila and the adults chatted about everything and nothing.

A warm feeling of contentment filled Dani's spirit as she joined in the easy banter and laughter. This was the life she dreamed of. Hanging out with friends. No angry undercurrents or hidden land mines.

Though that wasn't quite true.

But with Brett's lazy smile, accented by those gorgeous dimples, directed her way, she ached to forget the searing pain that had caused their paths to cross and simply relish this moment.

When Tabby crawled onto AJ's lap, Shelby rose to clear their dishes.

"Why don't you take the girls home?" Brett said. "I'll stay and help Dani."

"I don't like leaving a mess," Shelby protested.

"That kitchen isn't big enough for more than a couple of people." He winked at Dani. "We can handle it, can't we?"

"Sure."

"Well, I'm impolite enough to let you," AJ said. "Unless Dani wants me to stick around. I'm used to playing chaperone."

"This isn't the prom," Brett retorted.

Shelby leaned over his chair and stage-whispered in his ear. "Just behave yourself after we've gone."

"What is this?" Brett said, mock injury in his voice. "Scout's honor, I will."

AJ guffawed. "Well, that's reassuring. You were never a Boy Scout."

Dani chuckled at the indignant expression on Brett's face. She was admittedly flattered by Shelby and AJ's teasing protectiveness, though they had to know Brett had no designs on her.

Shortly after the Jeep pulled out of the drive, Brett dried the last glass and put it in the cupboard.

"One downside to this kitchen," he said. "No room for a dishwasher."

"I didn't have one at my last place, either."

"Or any other amenities." Brett exaggerated a shudder.

"You're disparaging my former home."

"This is your home now."

Dani glanced across the counter through the front room windows as she rinsed the sink. Twilight had slid into dusk in only a few minutes. Once again, contentment surged through her. As of today, the cottage was her refuge. Perhaps she could escape the past here.

"Do you have plans for the Labor Day weekend?" Brett asked.

"Shelby asked me to a picnic on Monday."

"Me too."

"Are you going?"

"Are you?"

"I promised to bake my world famous brownies."

"How about if I come early and help?"

"You know how to bake brownies?"

"I'm a bachelor. Who do you think cooks for me?"

"Restaurants."

He pressed his hand against his heart. "You smite me, Dani. You really do."

She rolled her eyes and flicked water at him from her wet fingertips.

"Hey!" He laughed, then twisted his towel, a teasing gleam in his eyes.

"Don't you dare hit me with that," she said, giggling. He had her trapped in the tiny kitchen unless she went out the back door.

"I think I have to." He lightly flicked the towel so it missed her.

"Don't you dare." She lifted her hands, palms outward to protect herself.

"Or what?" His voice sounded like a growl.

She giggled again. "Um, I won't let you help with the brownies."

"Do I get to lick the spoon?"

"If you put down the towel."

"You've got a deal." He snapped the towel, then hung it over the oven door. "Happy?"

"Very." She dropped her hands and glanced around the kitchen. "I think we're done here. Thanks for helping me clean up."

"Glad to help." He led the way from the kitchen and paused by the pool table. "How about we play a game?"

"I'm not very good."

"Glad to hear it. I'm a poor loser."

"Why doesn't that surprise me?"

With a grin, he handed her a cue stick, then racked the balls. "You have plans for tomorrow?"

"Thought I'd do some research."

"Getting started on the new job, huh?"

She lined up the cue stick and hit the white ball into the others. They scattered across the green felt.

"I need to get caught up."

"What can you do on a Saturday?"

"Internet searches. Visit the local library. Come up with a plan." She hit the three ball into a side pocket, then eyed the table. "What are you doing?"

"Nothing special." He moved out of her way as she lined up another shot. The five ball slid into a corner pocket. "I thought you weren't very good at this."

"Just lucky." She calculated her next shot. As she slid the cue stick between her fingers, Brett bumped her elbow. The ball went wide of its mark.

"Oops."

"No fair."

"Told you I hate to lose."

"Still my turn." She moved around the table and pointed the cue stick at him. "You stay away."

"Tell you what. Winner chooses what we do tomorrow."

"I'm working tomorrow."

He deliberately shook his head. "Not on a holiday weekend. And since I'm kind of your boss, you have to do what I say."

"Do I really?"

"Yep. And I say your first day is after Labor Day."

"I have a better idea. I win, I work tomorrow. You win, we do it your way."

He pursed his lips and stared at the ceiling as if in serious thought. "Compromise?"

"I'm listening."

"You win, you work half the day, play half the day. I win, play all day."

"As long as it's still my turn."

"Your turn."

She hit one more ball before missing the pocket, then Brett hit a few. They took turns clearing the table until Brett called the eight ball in the side pocket and easily won.

"I want a rematch," Dani said.

Before Brett could respond, an ornate wooden clock chimed the quarter hour. "You should have sent that with AJ," he said.

"I think it's charming."

"It'll drive you nuts." He glanced at the time, and a frown pulled at the corners of his mouth. "I'll take a rain check on another game if that's okay. Now that you're out here in the boonies, it'll take me longer to get home."

Even longer if he stopped at the hospital. Because she knew as sure as if he'd told her that was what he was going to do. Stand outside and stare at the lights. Lift his eyes to heaven and what? Pray for a miracle?

He didn't seem like someone who spent much time praying. But an injured child could drive anyone to his knees.

Dani placed her cue stick in the rack. "Next time I'll beat you."

"You'll try, you little pool shark. Who taught you to be a hustler?" He waved his hands. "Sorry. You don't need to answer that."

"It's okay." The apologetic look in his eyes told her what he was thinking. She'd learned to shoot the same way she learned to dance. "Except it was a foster mom instead of a foster dad."

"You're kidding."

"I'm not. She played in amateur tournaments. And she made the best meatloaf I've ever had."

"Sounds like a fun lady."

"I liked her."

"How long were you with her?"

"For almost a year. Then my dad decided he wanted me home again. I thought this time, things might be different. But they never were."

She gave a slight smile to cover her discomfort, but it seemed enough for him to understand she didn't want to end this amazing day wallowing in the past.

"I almost forgot. I got you a little housewarming gift." He opened a drawer in a nearby side table and pulled out a small box. "I put it there for safekeeping. Open it."

Inside the box, she found an antique key, a miniature trowel, and a delicate purple flower attached to a key ring.

"Symbols from *The Secret Garden*." The gesture touched a hidden place in her heart. "Thank you. I love it."

His features relaxed into a pleased smile. "I'm glad. Did AJ give you a house key?"

"He left it on his desk."

"It's your desk now. Okay if I get it?"

"Sure."

He disappeared into the office area. When he returned, he held out his hand for the key ring. "Allow me."

Once the key was on the ring, he handed it back to her.

"This means a lot to me, Brett."

"I hoped it would."

"Have you read *The Secret Garden*?"

"Truth?"

"Please."

"Finished it last night."

"What did you think?"

"I think everyone should have a special place to call their own. I hope you've found yours here."

"I hope so too."

"You're going to be all right out here. And if you need anything, AJ is just down the road. Do you have his number?"

"Shelby gave it to me. Hers too."

"We should have dognapped Lila. She'd have been company for you."

"And break Elizabeth's heart? I don't think so."

They walked to the front door, and Brett paused with his hand on the knob. "About tomorrow, do you golf?"

"Only on a putt-putt course."

"Miniature golfing it is. I'll be here around ten."

"I'll be ready." She stuck her thumbs in the side belt loops of her jeans. This was so awkward. He should just go. But before or after he kissed her? At that moment, she couldn't say which option she preferred.

He seemed ill at ease too. She sensed his thoughts were now with Jonah, not with her.

"You should go," she said. "The lights are probably already on."

"You're reading my mind."

"Sometimes you read mine."

He held her gaze, and her body tensed as electricity charged the space between them.

"Good night, Dani." He leaned forward then straightened. "Sleep well."

"Good night, Brett."

He opened the door and walked out into the night.

Dani lifted her face to the hot water streaming from the shower head. The heat rose around her, cleansing her from the grossness of the pay-by-the-week rooms and the strain of the day. Here, in this tidy cottage, she felt fresh and invigorated.

That morning, she'd awakened on the verge of panic, worrying about the bank interview. Knowing she needed the job as much as she abhorred the thought of it. Fearful she'd do something stupid and be turned away.

Now here she was, eager to start on an exciting project that held significance. She'd be bringing history alive, sharing the past with the present. Best of all, she'd be her own boss. It was more than she had ever dared to dream.

She toweled herself dry, then slipped into pjs and slippers. Padding into the long room, she made sure, once again, that the doors were locked and all the blinds were closed.

A home of her own.

The words had repeated themselves throughout the afternoon and evening, and she was as much in awe of them now as she had been the first time they entered her thoughts. A hidden retreat where she could hide from the world.

Though not from the past with all its heartaches and misery.

In the kitchen, she put on a kettle of water to boil for tea. Almost giddy with happiness, she imagined herself the star of her own movie. The down-on-her-luck unemployed homeless waif being handed the keys to luxury by a handsome . . . gallant . . . The giddiness faded.

She wasn't destined for the feel-good story with the perfect ending. Not if her happiness depended on Brett.

Despite herself, she was falling under his spell. Because if he'd attempted to kiss her this evening, she would not have resisted.

Only one thing could thwart her treasonous heart. She booted up her laptop and clicked on the research folder. One lousy news clip, watched for the millionth time, would reignite her anger.

A few seconds later, the video appeared. Not the abbreviated version that soared around social media. The entire video. Of its many downloads, probably half were hers.

She clicked the play button and endured the fluff preceding the part she hated.

The impeccably dressed interviewer leaned slightly forward in her chair, her interest almost palpable even through the camera lens.

"You've enjoyed great success," she said. "A man who seemingly has it all. A charmed life, some might say. But you also know what it is to face tragedy."

Brett graced her with a disarming smile, but his eyes slightly hardened. "I'm not here to talk about the past."

"But the past is what makes us who we are in the present. Wouldn't you agree?"

Brett's smile broadened, but for the first time Dani noticed the stiffening of his jaw. He was determined to be polite, but he was no longer amused by the woman's flattery or flirting.

"Everyone has a past. Some are happier than others. But what I care about is the present and the future. What I can do today that will make a difference tomorrow."

"And yet the past got you where you are today." Her voice rose in girlish delight. "It was your grandfather's wealth that propelled you into the property investment business. You've said that yourself."

"True."

"What effect did your parents' deaths have on your decision to take over Sully Sullivan's empire?"

"It's hardly an empire. And it would be mine even if my parents hadn't died. That's what Sully wanted."

"You and your sister were raised by your grandparents, isn't that right?" The woman's cloying voice gave Dani the creeps. Why hadn't she noticed the cold-heartedness before? The hard gleam behind the sympathetic gaze? "After your parents' fatal crash, I mean."

Tell her off, Brett. You don't have to listen to her anymore. She doesn't really care. You know she doesn't.

"We were."

"Such a tragic accident," the woman said, her voice low and simpering.

Dani wanted to reach through the screen and slap her.

"Accident?" Brett practically spat the word, and his eyebrow arched. "My parents died. My aunt and uncle died. And not because of a mechanical failure but because of a pilot who didn't do her job."

Before she could hear the rest, the venom against Mom that had sent her into an emotional tailspin, Dani shut the lid. But that didn't keep the barely controlled anger of Brett's words from resonating through her brain like a relentless pinball caroming off one sharp edge and then the other.

She could no longer blame Brett for what the accident, his grandfather, or the courts had done to her mom's reputation. Not after seeing his pain instead of his arrogance in the interview.

But her grief-stricken heart still ached, and the questions she'd thrown up to God remained unanswered. After all, she'd lost someone she loved in that crash too. Someday she'd have to tell Brett that.

– 24 –

*D*ani placed the backpack she'd been carrying onto the picnic table, then stretched the kinks from her back and arms. Sun pennies sparkled in Glade Creek, and the slight breeze smelled fresh and warm. Another gorgeous day in an already memorable holiday weekend. On Saturday she and Brett had played two rounds of miniature golf with so much mischievous cheating they gave up keeping score, browsed the local antique stores, and had dinner at a little Italian café in town. A mini Cary Grant marathon whiled away a lazy Sunday afternoon. And now here she was at Glade Creek, eager to enjoy a Labor Day picnic with Brett and his family. She breathed in the sun-scented air and sighed with contentment.

"I can't believe we're the first ones here." Brett removed a water bottle from his backpack and took a swig. "That was a longer hike than I expected."

"I'm just glad we found this place," Dani said as she sat on top of the table. "That backpack was getting heavy."

"I told you I'd carry it."

"You were carrying your own."

"I could have carried both." Brett flexed his biceps. "I big strong man."

"I not helpless woman."

"But you sure are a cute one." His fingers brushed her arm, then he took her hand. He pointed toward a massive weeping willow near the bank. Its graceful fronds swept over the creek and into the water. "Let me show you the engagement tree while it's just us."

"The one with all the initials?"

"Come on. I'll show you."

She let him pull her from the table, and he held onto her hand while they sauntered to the willow. Her head insisted the gesture didn't mean anything. Just Brett being Brett. But his touch, no matter how casual, exhilarated her.

Time to focus on something else. Like the rural landscape in front of her.

"There's something almost mystical about the way the sunlight filters through the fronds. It'd make a lovely photograph."

"Did you bring your camera?"

"Wish I had."

"Me too. That'd be a great wedding gift for AJ and Shelby. Are you interested in helping me with that?"

"I'd love to."

"Great." Brett pushed aside the fronds, and they ducked into the shadows of the ancient tree.

"Look here." He pointed to the carved initials. "These are Shelby's ancestors. When they became engaged, they added their initials. And this"—he pointed to a metal heart securely attached to a limb—"is for the latest couple."

The heart's engraved inscription read "Shelby & AJ."

"Why didn't they carve their initials into the trunk like everyone else?"

"This is more tree-friendly. A new tradition."

Dani pointed to a set of initials: J. L. + E. W. "This carving somehow looks older than the others. Is it the first?"

"Could be. Shelby can tell you when she gets here. I know

the story of this one." He pointed to S. L. + J. O. "Shelby was a teenager when her boyfriend, breaking family tradition, carved these."

"Who's J. O.?"

"Jason Owens. He and his family live up the road from Shelby."

"They took care of Elizabeth and Tabby when we went to the banquet."

"That's right."

"A teenage romance, huh?"

"I guess. But Shelby's parents zipped her away to Mozambique." He walked around the tree, then knelt. "Like father, like son."

Dani knelt beside him. The carving appeared fresher than the others. "E. K. and A. O. Elizabeth and her young man."

"You mean the scurvy rat who's trying to run off with my niece." He slightly smiled, seeming to revel in his role of indulgent uncle.

"She's not really your niece, you know."

"I know, but it's what we decided."

"Who's we?"

"Elizabeth, Tabby, and me. Instead of being ordinary old cousins, I'd be their uncle and they'd be my nieces." He cocked his head. "I think I hear them now."

They emerged from the shelter of the tree as the whine of a motor grew louder. Only a moment later, a utility four-wheeler pulling a trailer appeared from beyond a low rise.

Brett nudged Dani. "We need one of those."

"Maybe they'll give us a ride back."

"The walk too much for you?"

"I thought it was too much for you," she teased as they wandered back to the picnic table. AJ parked the vehicle nearby and waved.

"You got a new toy?" Brett asked.

"Better than carrying Tabby all the way back to the house."

"Voice of experience?"

"Carried her to the cottage once. That was enough."

Their conversation ended as the two little girls pounced on Brett, each insisting on being spun in a circle. He obliged, whirling them one at a time as Lila bounced and barked.

He set Elizabeth on her feet, then knelt in front of her.

"I saw your initials on the tree," he said, his voice as serious as he could make it.

Elizabeth's pixie face turned crimson, and she unconsciously leaned forward. "Mine and Austin's?"

"Are you really going to marry him?" Brett asked solemnly.

"Someday. When we're all grown."

"What if you meet someone else? Someone you like better?"

"There's no one I could ever like better than Austin."

"He's a lucky kid."

"Are you going to put your initials on the tree?"

"Naw. That tree's just for Lassiters."

"But you're part of our family now. Isn't he, Mommy?"

"He will be soon," Shelby said. "How about if we give you your own branch?"

Elizabeth clapped her hands together. "That would be tremendous, wouldn't it?"

"Sure would, Bitsy," he said, poking her ribs. "Now I just have to find someone to marry me. How about you? Can I steal you away from Austin?"

Elizabeth giggled then squealed as he whirled her around again.

Dani stuck her hands in the back pockets of her shorts. She was an outsider to this family tableau, and at this moment she was acutely aware she didn't belong. Not really.

It'd been less than two weeks since Brett asked her to the movies. But it seemed she'd been playing this charade for most of her life.

The thought caught in her throat. For the first time, she associated her deceit with *Charade*, the movie that had inspired the name she'd originally given Brett. Except it was Cary Grant's character who had hidden his identity, not Regina Lampert. Even as she fell in love with him, Regina knew she couldn't trust him. Not until the final scene, anyway.

The chances of Brett falling in love with her were as slender as a Hollywood film classic not having a happy ending. And while he might be Cary Grant gorgeous, she certainly was no Audrey Hepburn.

In the movie, Regina forgave the man she loved for deceiving her, but if Brett ever discovered the truth about Dani, he'd never speak to her again.

A physical ache squeezed her heart at that possibility.

The notion to eventually tell Brett the truth had made sense late last night, but in the stark reality of this sun-soaked day, she knew she never could. At least not the truth about who she was. But she should tell him about her mishap with the amethyst ring.

"You okay?" Brett stood next to her and ran his finger along her bare arm. "You look a little sad."

"No, I'm fine," she said, forcing a smile. "Just thinking."

"About?"

The confession stuck in her throat. "Nothing important."

"Hey, Brett," AJ called. "How about giving me a hand with this stuff?"

"Coming," Brett said over his shoulder. He turned back to Dani. "If something's bothering you, I hope you'll tell me about it. I'm a good listener."

"Are you?" The question popped out of her mouth before she could stop it.

"When I want to be." He leaned closer, his mouth tantalizingly near her ear. "I want to be when I'm with you."

Before she could respond, he jogged over to help AJ unload the trailer. Dani tried to catch her breath.

He didn't mean it. Not really. That's what guys like him did. Flirt with lonely women to boost their own vanity.

So why couldn't she just accept that and enjoy his attention while it lasted?

Because she wanted something more.

As Brett and AJ set up the charcoal grill, her heart practically burst from her chest. Both men were handsome in their own way, Brett blond and almost Nordic, AJ dark and athletic. But something deeper lay beyond their good looks.

With a jolt, Dani realized her glimpse into Brett's heart was rare—an intriguing facet hidden from the women he dated.

None of them, not even Tracie, had seen him with Shelby's daughters. They didn't know how he teased and played with them. How sweet he could be with shy Elizabeth.

Or the fun and playful side she'd seen this morning as they got in each other's way making potato salad and baking brownies.

It was as if God was giving her a peek into the joy of belonging to a family. But why? She couldn't keep her secret forever. And even if she could, her initials would never appear on the engagement tree.

Suddenly aware that everyone was busy preparing for the picnic except her, she hurried to the table and unzipped her backpack. Shelby had already laid a blue-checked cloth over the table and was clipping the corners so they wouldn't fly away in the random gusts.

"Brett and I made brownies this morning," Dani said as she removed the container from her pack.

"Brett? He baked?"

Dani laughed. "He stirred. And licked the bowl."

"You've cast a spell on him."

"I . . . no, I haven't."

"It's a good thing," Shelby said reassuringly. "Everything that's happened recently has been like a wake-up call for him, but I know it's not been easy for him to break old habits. You are exactly what he needs."

"We're not dating, you know. We're not a couple."

"Are you sure about that?"

"Pretty sure."

Shelby glanced toward the men, then back at Dani. "I wish you were. He seems to be a better 'Brett' when you're around."

"I guess I'm still surprised he ever gave me a second look."

"Don't say that. He needs someone like you. Someone genuine. Authentic."

Dani busied herself pulling more food containers from the backpack as the sharp arrows of Shelby's words pierced through her heart. *If only she knew.*

– 25 –

The sun cast long shadows across the creek as Brett helped AJ pack the trailer. He couldn't remember the last time he'd had such a leisurely day. They'd grilled chicken and hot dogs, eaten way too much, fished, played tag with the girls and Lila, chatted and laughed with one another. He'd even dozed for a short while until Tabby sprinkled creek water on his head.

All his worries about Jonah, Meghan, and Amy seemed to be banned from this tranquil place.

He anchored the grill in place, then leaned on the trailer, his arms resting on the frame. In the creek, Dani waded with Shelby and the girls in the shallow water off a sandbar. The pure joy of the children's giggles resonated in the quiet.

AJ followed his gaze. "Looks like fun, doesn't it?"

"Too bad this day has to end."

"You're welcome to come back to the house. We don't have any plans except to give those two a bath and send them to bed."

"I'll leave the 'daddy' chores to you," Brett said, clapping AJ's shoulder. "Are you sure you're ready for that full-time?"

"Can't wait."

"You could always elope."

"That'd be fine with me. But Shelby doesn't want to do that again."

"I'd forgotten she'd eloped before."

"This time it'll be a family event." AJ adjusted his OSU cap. "Think Amy will honor us with her presence?"

Brett shrugged, and the sun seemed to disappear behind a cloud.

"I invited her to come today," AJ said. "Left a voicemail. But she never called me back."

"I'm not surprised."

"Is there anything I can do . . ."

"She doesn't want anything from anybody." The tranquility of the day cracked, and Brett pushed away from the trailer. "I don't want to talk about Amy. Not right now."

AJ grimly nodded. "Got it. So you coming over?"

Brett glanced at Dani again. "Could we take a raincheck?"

"You've got other plans?"

"Nothing definite."

"She's not one of your blonde babes," AJ said, lowering his voice.

"I know that."

"Then be sure you don't break her heart."

"That's not going to happen." Brett gave an amused smile. "Apparently, I'm not her type."

"She said that?"

"She has firm opinions on the kind of guy I am. In her world, a great-looking guy like me is arrogant, conceited, snobbish . . ."

"In other words, she's got you pegged."

"Ha-ha."

"She doesn't really believe that, you know."

"You think not?"

"I know not. I've seen the way she looks at you when you're not looking at her." AJ removed his cap and examined the bill for a moment. "I've seen the way you look at her too. When you think no one's looking."

"What does that mean?"

"You're not as indifferent to her as you'd like me to believe."

"What are you, some kind of romance expert? Just because you're in love, you think everyone else is in love too."

"I teach high school. Believe me, I know 'the look.'"

"In case you haven't noticed, neither Dani nor I are in high school."

"You never grow out of 'the look.'"

"You're crazy. There's no 'look.'"

"If that's true . . ." AJ hesitated, as if searching for the right words.

"What's bugging you?"

"You want me to be honest?"

"No, AJ. Lie to me."

"If you really don't care about Dani, then why do you keep seeing her? It's almost as if by going out with her you're trying to make up for what happened with Meghan."

"That doesn't even make sense."

"Come on, Brett. Doesn't she remind you of Meghan when she was still in college? Dani can't be much older than Meghan was then."

Brett looked at him, dumbfounded. "I suppose so, but—"

"They're just not your usual type."

"My usual type? I'm so tired of that."

"Like it or not, you have one. And it wasn't Meghan and it's not Dani."

"You know, you're not her father."

"Someone has to look out for her."

"You think you have to protect her from me?"

"You tell me. Do I?"

Brett stared into the distance, wishing he could find an answer somewhere along the horizon. What if AJ was right? In some strange way, maybe he was trying to atone for what he did to Meghan by spending time with someone who resembled her.

A motivation like that delved further into his psychology than he wanted to go.

"Look, AJ. I'm not sure what this thing is with Dani. I'm not even sure it matters. I enjoy her company, and she seems to enjoy mine. What's the harm with us just hanging out with each other?"

"Nothing. As long as you're sure that's all it is—for you and for Dani. I'm not convinced."

"Because of 'the look.'"

"And because it's obvious she's not all that . . . experienced."

Brett's jaw tensed, and he blew out air. "You want to know the truth?"

"That would be nice."

"She's the only good thing in my life right now. All this stuff with Meghan and Jonah, and now Amy . . ." He bit his lip as the worries he'd held at arm's length throughout the day washed over him. "With Dani, there's no pressure to be a certain way. There's no drama. We just have fun together. I need that right now."

"That makes sense."

"We're just friends." He glanced her way. She'd banded her hair into a makeshift bun before wading into the creek, and loose strands curled against her temples. Even at this distance, her eyes sparkled, and her cheeks were pink as if kissed by the sun. He wasn't sure he'd ever seen her so happy.

A satisfied smile tugged at his lips. "I've never had a friend quite like her before. It's kind of nice."

"First step, cuz."

"Seriously, AJ. She's like a breath of fresh air. But that's it. That's all it can ever be."

"Why's that?"

"I'm done with this conversation." He clapped AJ on the back, then walked away. His cousin might be his closest confidant. Certainly he was a truer friend than the guys at Gallagher's. But Brett wasn't into kumbaya moments. Not with AJ or anyone else. He had to figure this out for himself.

Though it wasn't that hard. Certainly wouldn't take hours on a therapist's couch.

He didn't want to be his dad. He didn't want a marriage like his parents had. That was what it was all about for both of them, he supposed. For him and for Amy. At some subconscious level, she probably pursued her senator because deep down she knew there was no future with him. And maybe that was why Brett dated the women he did. Women he definitely was attracted to physically, but that was all. Playthings to be shown off for a time and then discarded.

A pang pierced his heart, and he rubbed his chest. He'd never felt as guilty about his behavior as he did at that moment. His mind raced for excuses, for justification for the way he'd treated Tracie and the ones who had come before her. But nothing he could think of had any substance. He was a sleaze. Worse than a sleaze.

As if sensing his eyes upon her, Dani met his gaze. Her radiant smile, bright as the low sun shining behind her, pressed against the guilt that threatened to engulf him.

His breath caught at her loveliness in that moment.

A few weeks ago, he'd never have believed he could find happiness in a pasture near a creek overhung by an ancient willow tree.

Yet today he had. More happiness, more peace than he'd known in a long time.

Dani threw the trash from her backpack into the bin beneath the sink, then pulled the liner up.

"Let me get that," Brett said as he reached for the bag.

"I can do it."

He glowered, but his eyes showed he was only teasing. "It'll just take a minute." He tied the bag, then headed out the door.

"Thanks." How nice to have someone take out the trash. A simple gesture, but an appreciated one.

Dani sighed contentedly as she filled the sink with soapy water to wash the containers they'd brought back from the picnic.

Brett returned and closed the kitchen door behind him. "Did you have a good time today?"

"A great time." If only he knew how often she had dreamed of holidays like this one. She had vague memories of picnics and silly laughter, but those had ended when her mother died. Everything had changed then, as if the summer sun had slipped behind a cloud and never come out again.

Until now. A feeling of blissful happiness swept from the tips of her sneakered toes to the top of her messy bun.

"You really like them, don't you? AJ and Shelby?"

"I do. They make me feel really welcome."

"What about the little monsters?"

"You shouldn't call them that. They're adorable girls." She pointed to a towel and handed him a dish. "They sure are fond of you."

"Don't tell anybody, but I'm kinda fond of them too." A shadow momentarily darkened his eyes, but he quickly flashed his dimples and dried the dish.

Dani didn't need to read his mind to know he was thinking of Jonah. She wished she could do something to alleviate his pain. He must have hurt Meghan very much for her to be so cruel to keep him from his son. Or perhaps she enjoyed the power she wielded over him.

Dani's conscience twinged. What if she were in Meghan's shoes? Dating one man, pregnant with his cousin's child. Would she have told the same lie? Stood up to the powerful grandfather? Confronted Brett?

She frowned.

"What are you thinking?"

"Nothing much."

"For a moment there, you looked a little upset. Something bothering you?"

"I was just wishing something."

"You may not know this, but I'm a master at making dreams come true."

"Not this one."

"Give me a try."

She scrubbed a nonexistent spot on the brownie baking pan. "I was wishing I could make your wish come true."

"My wish?" His puzzled look changed to understanding. "You mean Jonah."

"Yeah." She handed him the pan, then pulled the plug from the sink.

"I'd like that too. But for now, all I can do is stare up at his window."

"I'm sorry that's the way it is, Brett."

"You and me both." His voice caught, then he grinned and reached into his backpack. "I've got a surprise."

The subject of Jonah had closed shut. Dani didn't have the heart to pursue it further. "What kind of surprise?"

He held up a DVD. "*Bringing Up Baby*. Cary Grant and Katharine Hepburn."

Dani took the box from him. The cover showed the two actors but also included an inset of them, almost like a still from the movie, holding the pet leopard. "I haven't seen this one in ages."

"I thought we could watch it this evening. Unless you're tired of me."

"You sure you're not tired of me?"

"Nope. So are you up for this zaniness?" He flicked the DVD cover with his finger.

"You bet. Can I get you something to drink first?"

"What do you have?"

In the tiny kitchen, he was closer to the refrigerator than she was. "Check it out."

Brett opened the door and peered inside. "Juice. Lemonade. Root beer." He turned to look at Dani. "Nothing stronger?"

"Not in my house." She grimaced. "Well, at least not in AJ's house while I'm living here. Even that sounds pompous, doesn't it?"

"Your place, your rules." He grabbed a couple bottles of root beer. "Want one?"

"Sure."

He unscrewed the caps and handed her a bottle.

She took a sip, then waved the DVD. "I'm surprised you own this movie."

"I own the entire Cary Grant collection. All seventy-six of his movies."

"You're kidding."

"I told you, I used to watch them with my grandmother."

"I guess I figured she was the one who had them."

"She had videotapes of her favorites." He paused a moment, swiveling the root beer bottle before meeting her gaze. "In the past few years, watching movies with Gran wasn't exactly a priority for me. It became something she and AJ did together on Sunday afternoons after church. Not quite my thing." He smiled uncertainly, the dimples disappearing almost as quickly as they appeared. "I'd give anything to watch this with her again."

Compassion filled Dani's spirit at the sadness in his eyes. "When did she die?"

"Just a few months ago. In April."

"I am sorry."

He pressed his lips together and nodded. "Me too," he said, then he cleared his throat. "Anyway, after that I bought every single movie we had ever watched together and a lot more that we never got around to. Trying to alleviate my guilt, I guess."

"I'm sure she understood."

"I hadn't told anyone that." He sounded surprised. "Until now."

"I'm glad you told me."

"Me too." He reached for her hand. "What is it about you, Dani Prescott, that makes me spill all my secrets?"

"Have you told me all your secrets?"

"Well, maybe not all of them. But you do seem to inspire my confidence."

"Believe me, it's unintentional."

"What about you?"

She averted her gaze, intently focused on hanging the dishtowel just so. He shifted his position and lifted her chin. "Come on. You've got to tell me at least one of your secrets."

"Okay." She leaned against the counter and crossed her arms. His closeness in the tiny kitchen was making her light-headed. "I'm craving another one of those pizzas we had the other day. Do they deliver out here?"

"You're hungry?"

"Kind of."

"Lucky for you, I have their number. I'll give them a call and find out."

"Great. I'll set up the DVD." She grabbed the movie and headed for the TV. Relief at having successfully distracted him bubbled inside her and was quickly followed by a gush of happiness. He had confided in her. Shared his deepest hurts.

And she wasn't tripping over her own feet, and she no longer blushed every time he said something to her. She could even carry on a conversation without embarrassing herself.

A breakthrough of gigantic proportions.

She pushed buttons on the remote, then placed the DVD in the player.

"You're in luck," Brett said as he joined her. "Pizza will be here in about forty-five minutes."

"Great. How much will it be?"

"Why are you asking?"

"My treat."

"I don't think so."

"My house, my rules."

"My rule is I pay."

"This isn't a date."

"Doesn't matter."

"It matters to me," Dani said. "I wouldn't have suggested it if I expected you to pay for it."

"Which is one reason you're so adorable." He plopped onto the sofa, removed his shoes, and put his feet on the trunk that served as a coffee table.

The offhanded remark settled into Dani's heart. She didn't want it to go so deep, but it couldn't be stopped.

He thinks I'm adorable? Me?

She settled in the chair next to the sofa, and they clanked their bottles together when the movie started. There had never been a more perfect evening.

– 26 –

$\mathscr{B}$rett scanned the document on his computer screen, trying to focus on the important clauses while ignoring the legal mumbo jumbo. He'd met with his attorney a few days after Labor Day, and she'd emailed him the final document that morning. Once signed and executed, the trust fund for Jonah would be in place. The attorney only needed Brett's final approval to make it happen.

Which left only one question. Did Brett tell Meghan before or after he signed the papers?

He looked away from the computer screen when his assistant rapped on the doorframe. Kimberly O'Neil, an organized and efficient former Realtor, had immediately proven herself capable of more than answering phones and serving coffee to clients. She filled a void in the office Brett didn't know existed.

"You have a moment?" she asked.

"Sure." He leaned back in his seat and gestured at the folder she cradled in her arm. "What do you have there?"

She sat in the chair opposite his desk and rested her hands on top of the folder. "I contacted the references Ms. Prescott emailed me. Each one had great things to say about her."

"But?"

"I may have dug a little deeper than she wanted me to. Than perhaps you wanted me to."

"Why's that? Is she a corporate spy? In witness protection?"

"Nothing so exciting." Kimberly glanced at the folder, then back at Brett. "Her references included a professor, her boss at a retail store where she worked part-time while in college, and a producer she worked with who now lives in Cleveland."

Brett immediately intuited the same lapse Kimberly had. He rotated his cell phone against the desk. "She didn't list a reference from her last employer?"

"No."

"But you contacted him? Her?"

"Him. A Mr. Gerald Greene, who's the station manager. He also had positive things to say."

"Then I don't understand the problem."

"I thought you said she lost her job at the station because of budget cuts."

"That's right."

"Mr. Greene said she resigned. That he was sorry to see her go, and he'd work with her again given the chance."

"No budget cuts?" Rotate, tap. Rotate, tap.

Kimberly opened the folder and placed her finger on the page inside. "He said she showed great promise and potential. That she was creative and imaginative."

"Maybe I misunderstood her."

"He also said—"

Brett held up his hand to stop her. He'd heard enough. Kimberly closed the folder and placed it on the desk. "I typed my notes. They're all in there."

Brett nodded his thanks, and she returned to her desk. He swiveled to face the wall of windows, barely registering the familiar skyline as he focused on one fact. He hadn't misunderstood Dani.

She'd told him she left the TV station due to budget cuts. Why the lie?

Rotate, tap. Rotate, tap.

Dani grabbed her phone a second before the call went to voice-mail and answered without looking at the screen.

"Hello?"

"Hey, sunshine. What are you up to?"

Brett.

"Research."

"Are you with Shelby?"

"No, I'm at the OSU library."

"You're kidding. On a Friday afternoon?"

"I met with Professor Kessler earlier at his office, so it seemed a good time to check out the library's resources."

"Does all that research make you hungry?"

"I suppose so."

"Then how about I treat you to supper."

"I think it's my turn to treat you."

"Well, I decided to play chef. Show you I'm more than just a handsome face. Think you can find your way to my place?"

The opportunity she'd been hoping for. "Sure. Sounds fun."

"When can you get here?"

"About half an hour or so."

"Great. See you soon."

She ended the call and cradled the phone to her chest. This could be her chance. She removed the ring from the inner pocket of her bag. Beneath the fluorescent lighting, the diamonds and the amethyst sparkled. Such a lovely ring.

She'd return it, and Brett would never know it had been missing.

She shoved the ring deep into her pocket, then gathered her belongings and left campus.

Brett opened the door after her knock, looking as handsome as ever in pressed khakis and a polo. He flashed a dimpled smile. "You're late."

"Came as soon as I could." She put her hand in her pocket to ensure the ring was still there. Not the safest place for it, perhaps, but at least it was accessible.

He invited her in, then closed the door. "Couldn't pull yourself away from the research?"

"Just takes time to put things away. And I wasn't parked that close to the library."

"Parking on campus is never easy."

"How's your day been?"

"I've had better."

"Something wrong?"

"Nothing that won't work itself out. May I offer you a drink?"

"Tea if you have it."

"I do." He filled two glasses with ice and pulled a pitcher from the fridge.

"Something smells good. What are we having?"

"Bruschetta. Lasagna. And cannoli for dessert."

"You fixed all that?"

"Bruschetta, yes. I put it in the oven right before coming to the door. The lasagna is authentic Italian from a quaint little place near my office—it's also in the oven. And we'll have to walk to the bakery down the street for the cannoli."

Dani perched on a barstool and grinned. "I thought you were playing chef."

"Hey, it's in my oven. That's all that matters." The timer rang, and he snatched up a potholder. "You're going to love these."

A yummy, mouth-watering aroma wafted from the oven as he removed the bruschetta. After placing the baking dish on a trivet, he turned to the cupboards. Dani held her breath when he opened the door where the ring belonged. But he merely took two small plates from a stack on the second shelf.

"So what did you learn today?" he asked as he handed her a plate and a napkin.

"I found a map of a Civil War prisoner-of-war camp that was located right here in Columbus." Between bites of the tomato, basil, and garlic bruschetta, Dani told him about a few of her other discoveries. "I started making a list of possible photos we could use for displays. Some may be copyrighted, though, which means getting permission and maybe buying rights. That'll cost money."

"Remind me to give you Eldon Laine's phone number. He's our accountant, so he can help you come up with a budget. But don't worry too much about cost. We're not going to skimp on quality." A dimple flashed, and he picked up a napkin. Leaning across the counter, he dabbed the corner of Dani's mouth. "You missed a bit of tomato."

She momentarily closed her eyes as her cheeks warmed beneath his touch.

"I love when you do that."

"Do what?"

"Turn all pink. It's cute."

"No, it's not. It's embarrassing."

"Trust me. Cute."

Definitely time to change the subject. "So what did you do today?"

"The usual. Bribed a city councilman, green-lighted a toxic waste dump, embezzled money from orphans."

"Wow. You were busy."

"All I really did was plow through paperwork." His face slightly clouded, and he came around the counter to sit on the stool next to her. "Though something odd came up. I need to talk to you about it."

The hair prickled on the back of her neck at the tone of his voice. "Sounds serious."

"My assistant talked to the station manager in Cincinnati this afternoon. He said you quit."

Judging by the heat on her cheeks, Dani's face was no longer a blushing pink but fiery red. She expected this might happen, though part of her had hoped that Brett's asking for the references was only a formality. That his assistant would be too busy with other work to thoroughly check her employment history. It was a gamble she had taken and lost.

"Why did you tell me that story about budget cuts?" Brett asked gently.

"It was the story I told my dad." She raised her eyes to his. "I just thought it best to stay consistent."

"But why lie to him?"

To avoid a confrontation. So he wouldn't berate her for being foolish. For being stupid.

She couldn't tell Brett any of those things. It was too humiliating. Perhaps the time had come to tell him the truth. At least a little bit of it.

"He can be cruel when he's angry." Tears stung behind her eyes. She took a deep breath, then blew it out. "Besides, he's not really my dad."

"Stepdad?"

"Yeah."

"Where's your father?"

"I wouldn't know him if I passed him on the street."

"What happened to your mom? I mean, I know she died, but . . ." His hand stroked her arm. "I'm sorry. You don't have to talk about it if you don't want to."

Dani focused on her plate, biting her lip.

Tell him now.

She opened her mouth, but the words wouldn't come. The vengeful turmoil eating at her heart had dissipated, one tiny molecule at a time, beneath the featherweight of Brett's kindness. His and Shelby's and AJ's. Maybe they never needed to know her secret.

"It was an accident." Dani swiped at a tear as it moistened her cheek.

"My parents died in an accident too. I guess we're both orphans, huh?" Brett asked with a wry chuckle.

She caught his expression before he looked away. For that brief moment, she hadn't seen the handsome, confident man who sat in front of her but a grief-stricken boy. The same hurting boy who, tempered by maturity, responded to the insistent questioning of the interviewer. Words of pent-up anger casting blame on the person who'd robbed him of his mom and dad.

His blame was misplaced, but so was Dani's. She had come to Columbus to punish Brett for slandering her mom. But how could she punish him for experiencing the same loss she had? The same plane crash had devastated both their lives. If only she'd realized that before leaving Cincinnati.

Her stepdad was right. She was foolish. Stupid.

"Let's talk about something else," Brett said.

"Good idea."

"So why did you quit your job?"

Tell him.

She couldn't. But she didn't want to lie to him anymore either. "I had a reason. It's personal."

"Because of a guy?"

Taken aback by the question, it took her a moment to realize what he meant. She took a deep breath. "Kinda."

"But you're not seeing anyone." His tone was incredulous, then wary. "Are you?"

She shook her head and inwardly smiled at his obvious relief. Though it didn't mean anything. He needed a distraction while he worked out the other problems in his life. And she was it.

"I'm sorry I lied," she said. "About the television station. I'll give Shelby my research notes, and it won't take me long to get moved out—"

"Wait a minute. What? You're not leaving."

"I can't stay." Her conscience screamed at her to tell him the truth, but her heart was too afraid. He'd despise her if he knew she'd been stalking him.

"Look, I understand how difficult family relationships can be.

Believe me, I know. And you don't have to tell me anything you don't want to about your stepdad." He scooted his stool closer. "But this job situation is out in the open now, at least between us. I should probably tell Shelby, but she'll understand."

"You don't want me to go?"

"I'm glad you quit. Whatever the reason."

"Why?"

"Because if you hadn't, you'd never have met me."

His boastful smile warmed her heart, but again her conscience pressed. One thing she had to do. No matter the consequences.

Dani pulled the ring from her pocket and held it out to him. He took it from her, his eyes darting from the ring to the cupboard where it had been kept, and then to Dani.

"How did you get this?"

She couldn't hold back the tears any longer. "It was an accident. I didn't mean to snoop."

"You were snooping? When?"

"Not really." She hiccuped. "But you had teased me about snooping, remember? Last time I was here. And then I wanted a drink of water. I was looking for a glass, and . . ." She hiccuped again as the words tumbled out. "I saw the dish. It was so lovely. The ring fell in my palm and then you came in and startled me and I didn't know how to explain. I panicked, and I didn't want you to think I was snooping and"—she paused to hiccup and catch her breath—"the next thing I knew it was in my pocket."

She sniffed, then wiped her nose with her napkin. "I'm not a thief, honest, I'm not. I wanted to return it, but there was never a chance. At least not without you finding out." Another hiccup, then she buried her face in her hands.

Immediately Brett wrapped his arms around her. Snug in his embrace, she let the tears flow.

A moment later, realizing his shoulders were shaking, she raised her eyes. He pressed his lips together, but soon his suppressed chuckles turned into teary-eyed laughter.

"What's so funny?" she blubbered.

"You. Your 'theft' is like something out of a zany slapstick comedy."

"You're not angry?"

"Only amused. And hungry. What about you, my little snoop-dog? Feel like eating?"

"You are the nicest, kindest man I've ever met." Really? Had those words just come out of her mouth?

Brett's eyes clouded, but he smiled and tapped her nose. "I hope you always believe that about me. It's not true, though. I'm neither nice nor kind."

"You've been very kind to me."

"And you're a little vixen whether you know it or not."

"I'm a what?"

"Never mind."

"Who does it belong to? The ring?" *Please don't say Meghan.*

"I think its Tracie's. I found it after she, um, after she left."

"Your girlfriend?"

"Ex-girlfriend."

One more thing she had to know. "Did you give it to her?"

He gave a careless shrug. "I probably paid for it."

"Probably?"

"Tracie liked to shop."

"I can't possibly imagine buying an expensive ring with someone else's money. And not even telling him."

"That's one of the many differences between you and Tracie. A difference I appreciate, by the way."

"Though maybe it's not much different. Look at where I'm living."

"It's part of your compensation package. There are no strings attached with the cottage."

"Were there strings with Tracie's ring?"

"There were expectations."

No need to ask what those were. But it hurt that the man of her dreams had such a cavalier past.

"She knew what she was getting into," he said, his voice defensive. "It's all part of . . ."

"The Game?"

"What do you know about that?"

"Not much, really. But enough to know I don't want any part of it."

"Another difference between you and Tracie."

"So who broke up with whom?"

"How about we talk about your love life instead of mine."

"Yours is much more interesting."

"Tell me about just one guy. To make us even."

"I didn't have time to date. Not with school and a job." Sometimes more than one job so she could stay in school. Waitressing, daycare, housecleaning. She'd done them all and more.

"No broken heart in your past?"

"Nope," she said, almost chirping. The fake cheeriness hid the pressure descending on her chest. No broken heart in her past. But there might be one in her future. They weren't playing Brett's typical game, but she wasn't immune to his charm.

She needed to stop seeing him, stop thinking about him, stop dreaming about him. Each moment they spent together increased the risk of him finding out who she really was. And yet, she couldn't stop.

A timer buzzed, and he returned to the oven. "That's the lasagna. How about we eat on the patio? There's usually a nice breeze this time of day. And the view's not too bad this high up."

"Sounds wonderful." She slid from the stool and grabbed her bag. "I'm going to freshen up a little, if that's okay."

"Just don't take too long. Dinner's about ready."

Dani closed the bathroom door and leaned against the pedestal sink. She'd told the truth, sort of, about the job and confessed to taking the ring. Now there was only one secret between them.

A secret she had to keep.

– 27 –

_D_ani dabbed her mouth with the linen napkin, then placed it beside her plate. "That's the best lasagna I've ever had."

"I'll let the chef know the next time I see him. He loves compliments from pretty young ladies." Brett reached into his pocket, then slid something across the table. "Here's another ring you might like to see. Just don't take it home."

"Ha-ha." She shot daggers at him, then examined the ring, a brilliant solitaire diamond. "Is this a platinum band?"

"White gold. It's probably an antique."

"It's stunning." She almost asked if it belonged to his mother but stopped herself. Bringing up his parents was never a good idea. But she had to say something. "Where did you get it?"

"I found it in the office safe after Sully died."

"It belonged to your grandmother?" Dani tilted the diamond one direction then the next, catching the setting sun's rays within the prism.

"Unfortunately, no."

"Then who?"

"You're inquisitive."

"Only intrigued. Besides, you _did_ show it to me."

"So I did. From what I understand, Sully planned to give it to the woman he loved. But when he came home from the Korean War, she was engaged to someone else."

"How sad for him." For the first time, Dani felt a twinge of sympathy for the man she considered a monster. Not just because of the things Brett had told her, but also because of the things she'd read in the investigative reports about the airplane crash. Sully Sullivan had made sure the fault was placed on her deceased mother. What Brett had said in the interview was true. If she had survived, she might have been charged with manslaughter. Or worse.

Dani's thoughts created a whirlpool that threatened to drown her, but Brett's voice broke through the waves of sickness and stilled the eddy.

"Depends on who you ask," he said.

"I don't understand."

"The woman he was in love with married Thad Lassiter."

"Shelby's grandfather?"

"Sully bought this ring in Seoul, brought it all the way back from Korea. But when he found out that Thad and Aubrey were engaged, he locked it away."

Another sympathetic twinge. But the bitter old man's youthful heartache was no excuse for what he'd done. For how he'd used his power, his influence, and his money to malign her mother.

"He never forgave her, did he?"

"I'm sure he didn't."

"There's more to the story?"

"I wish I knew why Gran married him."

"She must have loved him."

"I suppose."

"Was she terribly unhappy?"

"She was . . . stoic." His pressed lips curved slightly upward, and warmth softened his eyes. "I wish you could have known her."

"You think she'd have liked me?"

"She would have loved you."

His words floated into a deep and hidden place in Dani's heart, a treasure worth more to her than Sully's diamond ring.

Brett hadn't intended to say what he did, but he meant every word. His grandmother would have loved Dani.

The longing to spend another day with Gran, to hear her gentle laugh, to feel the soft touch of her palm against his cheek, welled up within him. The grief, only a few months old, rubbed his insides raw.

For all of Sully's acumen, he'd been too blind to see how fortunate he'd been to have Joyanna as his wife.

The last time Brett asked Aubrey's elderly brother about the ring, Richard had floated into the past, lost in the days before Aubrey's wedding to Thad. He'd wanted Aubrey to change her mind and marry Sully instead.

"Then I can marry Joyanna," he'd said, his voice a pitiable whimper.

It was the last conversation they'd had. A few days later, Richard had died in Shelby's barn.

"The ring seems to symbolize spurned love," Brett said to Dani. "And I don't know what to do with it."

"I don't know either. Though if that's how you feel about it, you probably shouldn't give it to anyone you're seriously involved with." She handed the diamond back to him as if its radiance had burnt her hand.

"You mean you'd say no if I got on one knee and offered it to you?" He held up the ring, his voice teasing.

"I'd say no whatever you offered me."

"You cut me to the quick, Dani Prescott." He clutched at his heart. "Love spurned again. I tell you, this ring is bad luck."

"Don't blame the ring just because your grandfather lost the girl. It's sad that something so lovely was hidden away. After all, things turned out okay, didn't they?"

"I think that's debatable."

"But if he hadn't married your grandmother, you wouldn't be sitting here right now. I'd be talking to someone else. Or maybe I wouldn't be here either." Her face took on a strange expression, but her thoughts were hidden from him. Clouded and somehow sad until a sudden light sparked in her eyes, and a strange insight lasered into his mind.

"You wish that, don't you?" he asked.

"Wish what?"

"That Sully had married Aubrey. That we weren't here together."

"Of course I don't." But her tone didn't convince him. She forced a smile, then stacked their plates. "Did I tell you the lasagna was delicious?"

He gripped her hand to stop her from gathering the silverware. "Why does it matter to you who Sully married?"

"I was just thinking that maybe he wouldn't have been so unhappy. Maybe he would have been a nicer man. All the circumstances of his life might have been different."

"Maybe." In his gut he knew she was hiding something from him. But what? Sully's broken heart didn't have anything to do with her.

He stood to help with the dishes. "So any ideas on what I can do with this ring?"

"Sell it. Pawn it."

"And pass the curse on to some other innocent soul?"

"There's no curse." Dani rose too, and her eyes brightened. "But we could make up a story. He bought it in Seoul, right? Maybe it once belonged to a Korean prince. Do the Koreans have princes?"

"I have no idea. And I'll leave the stories to your crazy imagination."

"I think the ring first belonged to a handsome but poverty-stricken young man who was deeply in love with a beautiful young woman. She came from a wealthy family, so her father didn't want her to marry the handsome young man."

214

"If he was so poor, how did he afford the ring?"

"He worked hard and saved all his money. For years and years. Then he bought the ring and took it to the girl's father."

"Who threw him out and told him never to come back again."

"Who said, 'I've never seen anything so fine as the love you have for my daughter. Marry her and be happy.' So you see, it's a ring of happiness and the truest, deepest love."

"That's a great story but highly unlikely. Maybe I should just throw it in the Scioto River. End its unlucky streak."

"You know, I never thought of you as the superstitious type. You're too practical. Too business-y."

"Business-y?"

"Yeah."

"We all have our flaws. Even you."

"What flaws do I have?" She held up a hand. "Nope. Don't answer that."

"Just look at your face."

"What's wrong with it?"

In the soft light of the afternoon sun, a rosy blush touched her cheeks and her dark eyes shone with a radiance that wrapped around his heart. "It's perfect."

Brett paid for the cannoli and two bottles of water, then followed Dani to one of the few wrought-iron tables lining the sidewalk outside the bakery. They'd walked the few blocks from his apartment, her fingers interlaced with his. Holding her hand had been the natural thing to do, as if she belonged to him and he belonged to her.

But not in the smothering confines of a relationship built on selfish expectations—greed on the woman's part and lust on his. He'd dated numerous beautiful women. Showered them with expensive gifts. Given them access to his credit card.

Then unceremoniously sent them packing on an arbitrary

timetable that stoked his ego. It'd been fun, he thought. But his callousness had hollowed out a chunk of his heart and left him cold and empty. He didn't want to live like that anymore.

Dani somehow managed to sit cross-legged in the iron chair as she daintily nibbled the cream-filled pastry. The girl had an appetite—also a pleasant change from the constant diets of his usual arm candy.

But that's what made Dani different. She wasn't on display for the drooling pleasure of other men. Nor did she aspire to use her body to snag his name. That plan never had a chance of working, but several women had tried it.

She popped the rest of the cannoli in her mouth and brushed the crumbs from her fingers. "Why are you staring at me?"

Because you enchant me.

"Didn't I tell you?" he said instead. "Best cannoli in town."

"It was yummy. Thank you."

"Glad you enjoyed it. I like a gal who's not afraid to eat."

Her eyes narrowed in puzzlement. "I'm not sure if that's supposed to be a compliment or an insult."

"A compliment. I promise." He flashed a reassuring smile, then rotated the water bottle against the tabletop's latticework. "Maybe I should buy a few for Amy."

"Why don't you?"

"Because she'd probably throw them in the trash as soon as I walked out the door."

"She doesn't eat dessert?"

"She's not eating anything."

"Is that why she collapsed?"

"That's my guess. She won't talk about it, so I don't know whether it's anorexia or bulimia. But it's one or the other or something similar."

"I'm sorry, Brett. It must hurt for her to shut you out like that."

Instead of answering, he studied her expression, suddenly vulnerable to how she responded to him. She shifted position and hugged one leg as the sole of her sandled foot rested on the chair's edge, but her eyes held his, clear and steady. She cared that he hurt, not to win points with him but because she honestly, truthfully cared.

"Do you have any idea how beautiful you are?"

She broke eye contact and stared in the opposite direction. Would he ever be able to pay her a compliment without her blushing? In a way, he hoped that day never came.

"What are you going to do?" she asked, still intent on avoiding his gaze. "About Amy, I mean."

"I've given her information about a few places that specialize in eating disorders. Highly recommended facilities. But she won't admit she needs help." He took a long drink from his water bottle, then twisted the cap. "I've considered kidnapping her, but apparently that's against the law. Even when your motive is a good one."

"She'd hate you for doing that."

"You don't have any siblings, do you?"

"There's just me." She faced him and gave a wry smile. "The lonely only."

His lips momentarily curved upward in response to her rhyme. But he didn't feel like smiling. "I've always taken care of Amy. Protected her when I could. When she'd let me."

His pulse stirred beneath Dani's sympathetic gaze. "I'd risk her hatred if it meant she'd get well."

Neither said anything for a moment or two. A group of teens neared the bakery, their chatter lively and raucous. The uneven purr of a dozen automobiles increased as Brett became more aware of the silence between him and Dani.

He'd said too much. Exposed another secret place in his heart and handed it to her for safekeeping.

Something he'd never done with other women. So why did he with Dani?

Her fingertips brushed his, and he loosened his grip on the bottle to take her hand.

"I'll be your getaway driver," she said, bending her head to peer into his eyes. "If you need me."

Her expression, mischief graced with tenderness, eased his misgivings. Her lovely freshness, given the chance, could knit his heart's frayed pieces into something whole and new. But now was not the time. Not when his life was this out of control.

Maybe if AJ had never found Meghan. If Brett didn't know about Jonah.

And if Amy would face the truth and get the help she needed instead of burdening him with her issues.

Then he could fully enjoy being with Dani. No worries, no concerns to cloud their time together. For the first time in his life, he would be free to explore a relationship built on mutual respect and trust.

If everything else in his life wasn't so wrong.

Without letting go of her hand, he stood, then drew her to her feet. "Let's just walk, okay?"

"Where to?"

"Wherever our feet take us."

Both literally and perhaps metaphorically. Though again he was getting ahead of himself. He couldn't pull her into his world until it was a tidier place. Only God knew how long that would take.

Only God knew.

The thought startled him. This time, for the first time, it wasn't a meaningless phrase but almost a prayer.

– 28 –

The oven buzzer rang, and Dani pulled a container of bubbling macaroni and cheese from the oven. She'd spent another too-short day, this time at the Ohio History Center, engrossed in research. The hours had flown by as she delved into a past of both brutality and courage. Her list of possible photographs was growing, and she also had scribbled the broad outlines of a potential narrative. Tomorrow she'd share her ideas and the research she'd gathered over the past several days with Shelby.

She scooped mac and cheese to a plate, then settled at the pub table in the front room. From her vantage point, she could see the silver birches through the long row of windows.

The openness of so many windows had been a little unnerving at first. But she'd already grown accustomed to it. The bungalow AJ had moved into wasn't too far away, but it was hidden by a stretch of woods. Only at night could she see a few outdoor lights, set high on poles, from the horse farm on the other side of the road.

The secluded cottage was a restful place, serene and quiet, and its tranquility seeped into her spirit. Of course, anything was an improvement over the pay-by-the-week hovel, but the cottage was more than that. Kindness imbued the place, and perhaps the laughter of lingering memories.

She took a deep breath before biting into the gooey mac and cheese dish. AJ was lucky to have this place, and she was even luckier he had moved out so she could move in. He didn't seem to have any ulterior motive either. He just did it.

Unless Brett had forced him. Maybe Brett was paying the rent.

But why would he do that? The man was a giant conundrum, and not at all what she expected. He'd surprised her by confiding his concerns about Amy. From the expression on his face, he'd been surprised too.

After leaving the bakery the other night, they'd walked hand-in-hand around the downtown area. Window-shopping and people-watching. But once they reached his apartment building, he escorted her straight to her car, mumbling something about how it'd been fun and to drive home safely.

No good-night kiss. Not even a peck on the cheek.

Not that she'd been expecting either. Except maybe just a little bit. A couple of hours later he sent a text.

Are you at the cottage?

I am.

That's good. Night.

Night.

Nothing else.

Since then, they'd talked several times on the phone, but he hadn't asked her out for this past weekend. Not that she wanted him to.

She took another careful bite of the hot mac and cheese, then popped the DVD she'd purchased at the history center into the player. Much better to focus on Ohio's past than the inner workings of a millionaire jet-setter.

Though to be fair, he was hardly that. What had he said that night they met? He never flew. Easy enough to figure out why.

She was about to hit the play button on the remote when her phone rang.

Brett.

Her heart fluttered despite her best efforts to remain indifferent.

"Hey, there," she said.

"Hi. Did I catch you at a bad time?" His voice sounded odd, almost distant.

"Not really. Is everything okay?"

"Fine. Have you eaten yet?"

"Just about to. Why?"

"Don't sound so suspicious. I was hoping we could go somewhere. Eat together."

"Is something wrong?"

"The truth is," he said, then sighed heavily, "I left Amy's place and just started driving. Next thing I know I'm at the Glade County line. And I'm hungry, and I know it's not polite or following the 'girl rules' to call like this, but you'd be doing me a big favor if you said yes."

Dani's head spun with his patter, and she clung to one phrase that stood out. "What are 'girl rules'?"

"You know, the guy can't ask for a date on the same day he calls. That kind of thing."

"I guess I missed that subject in school."

"Which is what makes you so adorable."

And her heart up for grabs for any gorgeous guy who paid her a compliment. "I don't know, Brett. I just took supper out of the oven, and I'm about to watch this DVD on Ohio history. Research for the project." Then something else he'd said ricocheted between her temples. "Glade County line? Where are you?"

"About to pull into your drive."

"You're kidding." She hurried to the window by the front door as his Lexus stopped outside the closed gate.

"If you won't have supper with me, then I'll have to raid AJ's refrigerator."

"Or you could go back home."

A moment's silence filled the air. When he spoke, his voice was soft. "I'd rather not."

"What's wrong?"

"Nothing. It's just . . . nothing."

Something else he'd said—he'd been to Amy's. And they'd probably argued.

"Do you like mac and cheese? The frozen kind you bake?"

"I'm not sure I've ever had it."

Really?

"I guess there's a first time for everything. Come on in."

As he stepped out of his car to open the gate, she scrambled into the small bathroom, ran a brush through her hair, and gave her teeth a ten-second cleaning. By the time he knocked on the door, she was ready to face him.

"Hi," she said, smiling. "What a pleasant surprise."

"You don't really mind, do you?" he said sheepishly. "Honestly, I didn't realize I was here until I was . . . here."

"Is Amy okay?"

"She's fine." The tone of his voice said otherwise. "Stubborn as always."

"Do you want to talk about it?"

"Not really." He flashed a cheerless smile. "Are you sure you don't want to go into town? There's a diner that has great burgers. Or we could see a movie. The theater is ancient, and I have no idea what's playing, but I could find out." He dug his phone from his pocket.

"What about watching the documentary?" She pointed toward the TV screen. "We might find info we can include in the museum. Or pick up ideas for our own film."

"Work instead of play, huh?"

"When you enjoy what you're doing, it's not really work, is it?"

"Good point." He shrugged and pocketed his phone. "The documentary it is."

She stepped back so he could enter, and he closed the door. "Can I get you something to drink?" she asked. "There's not much to choose from. Lemonade. Tea. Coffee."

"How about an Arnold Palmer? Half lemonade, half tea."

"You've got it."

He followed her to the kitchen, then leaned against the doorframe as she put ice and the beverages into a tall glass. "So, are you all settled in here?"

"I'm still pinching myself to be sure I'm not dreaming."

"It's not a dream, Dani."

"You sure?"

"I'm sure." He shifted and glanced toward the kitchen window. Dani followed his gaze and wished she could follow his thoughts. Through the paned glass, the hill sloped upward, a copse of hardwood trees visible above the crest. The cottage nestled against the slope, belonging to the landscape as much as the nearby oaks and maples.

"I used to love coming here when I was a kid," Brett said. "Gran's special place out of the city. Away from Sully."

"From what you've told me, your grandfather was a hard man."

"He craved power. And he didn't care who he hurt to get it."

"Do you? Crave power, I mean?"

"I don't want to end up like him. But I do want to be successful. To grow my business. Make lots of money." He reached for the glass she held and tilted it toward her. "What about you? What's your big dream?"

Dani paused, holding the lemonade pitcher with the refrigerator door half open. She couldn't remember the last time—perhaps any time—someone had asked her that question.

"Must be serious," Brett said. "You're lost in another world."

She placed the pitcher inside the refrigerator and closed the door. "Just thinking."

"I'll give you $100 for those thoughts."

"That's extravagant."

"You're worth it."

"I wouldn't bet on that."

"Let me be the judge."

"Let's sit down first." She grabbed an extra plate and utensils, then slipped past him in the narrow space between the kitchen wall and counter.

Once they were settled on the high stools of the pub table, she released a deep breath. "My big dream is to write, maybe even direct, an award-winning script."

"A Hollywood movie?"

"Eventually, yes."

"Then shouldn't you be living in LA? Or at least New York?"

"That takes"—she paused, stumbling over the word *money*—"resources. And as I'm sure you've noticed, that's a scarcity for me right now."

"Are you talented?"

She drew back from his bluntness, then plunged her fork into the mac and cheese. "I think so. But you know, it's not just talent. It's hard work and discipline. Connections."

"So what's your plan? Have you written a script?"

"A few."

"And . . ."

"And what?"

"Can I read them?"

"I don't think so."

"Why not?"

"I thought you dabbled in real estate."

He stiffened with pretend indignity. "I more than dabble, thank you very much. But just because I'm a brilliant businessman doesn't mean I'm not interested in creative pursuits. So tell me about them."

"You really want to hear?"

"I do," he said around a mouthful of mac and cheese.

"Okay." She took a deep breath. "A short story I wrote for one of my classes won an award. So then my professor suggested I turn it into a script, and the film department chose it for one of their projects the following semester. It received an honorable mention in a collegiate film festival."

"Congratulations."

"Thank you."

"What's it about?"

She searched his eyes for any sign of teasing, but he appeared genuinely interested. "Did you know there were German POW camps in the United States during World War II?"

"I don't think so, no. Were there really?"

"Dozens of them. My script is about a young boy whose father is in Europe fighting in the war. He misses his dad, and he hates the Nazis. On Christmas Eve, he finds an escaped German POW in his barn. He wants to kill him."

"Do you have a copy? I want to see it."

"Sure, but—"

"Let's watch it."

"What about the Ohio history DVD?"

"That'll keep. Come on. Get your movie."

She groaned and laid her head on her arms, then peered up at him. "You can watch it. But if you don't like it, you're not allowed to say so."

"How about this? If I don't like it, I'll say, 'Wow, Dani. You certainly put a lot of time and effort in this cure for insomnia.'"

She punched his arm.

"Ouch." He rubbed the sore spot. "Okay, I won't say that."

"You can say, 'That was very interesting. Thank you.' Nothing more."

"Got it. 'That was very interesting. Thank you.' I think I can remember that."

She made a face at him, then headed for the bedroom to retrieve the DVD from the closet.

When she returned to the long room, Brett was sitting on the couch with a second helping of mac and cheese. "This is good stuff," he said, waving his fork. "You sure it's not homemade?"

"When do you think I had time to make macaroni and cheese from scratch?"

"I just wouldn't have guessed it was frozen."

"It's Bob Evans brand. My favorite."

"I eat there. Sometimes."

"When was the last time?"

He made a face as if deep in thought. "I . . . couldn't tell you."

"You're such a snob. You're even a food snob."

"I'll prove to you I'm not. Have you ever had Boyd's Bodacious BBQ?"

"Nooo. Never even heard of it."

"Tomorrow night. They have a live band and classic car show on Thursdays." He raised his fork as she was about to protest. "No excuses. I'll pick you up around six."

"I'm guessing from the name that I don't need to go shopping for a new dress?" she said coyly.

"You probably shouldn't wear anything you're too fond of. It can get messy."

"So you like BBQ?"

"Surprised?"

"A little."

"You're the snob, Dani. I've told you before. You think it's me, but it's really you."

"I have to admit you're not what I expected."

"'Expected'? What does that mean?"

She focused on the DVD player so he couldn't see the flush creeping up her cheeks. "Oh, you know. That night at the hospital this handsome guy appears out of nowhere. Driving a Lexus. It sets up certain expectations."

"You mean stereotypes."

"You didn't have stereotypes about me?"

He tilted his head as if appraising her. "Guilty. You're not what I expected either."

Dani gave an inward sigh of relief. Once again she'd almost tripped on her stalking secret. She switched out the DVDs, then flashed a teasing smile at him.

"That's because I'm not your type," she said airily.

– 29 –

You're better than my type.

As the unexpected words resounded in Brett's head, an odd warmth curled in his stomach unlike anything he'd ever felt before. Whenever he thought of a future with only one woman, he pictured a tall blonde, gorgeous, sophisticated, poised, and perfect. Yet here was this petite brunette, cute in her own way, who kept turning his picture of the ideal woman upside down and inside out.

How had she managed, without even trying, to finagle so many dates with him when he wasn't even dating? Okay, truth be told, he was the one finagling. But she didn't have to always say yes.

Some dating sabbatical.

Never had he spent so much time with a woman when sex wasn't an integral part of the relationship. But he hadn't even kissed Dani. Not that he hadn't been tempted a time or two. Or ten . . .

He studied her as she pushed a button on the remote and waited for the menu to pop up. Her brown hair was pulled to one side so that the space behind her ear was visible. An overwhelming urge to kiss her there, in the smooth space near her earlobe, came over him. But his desire didn't stop there. She shifted her weight from one foot to the other, and he admired her slender curves. What would it be like to pull her to him right now? To hold her close while exploring all she had to offer?

He closed his eyes, but the vision stayed with him. Somehow he needed to control his lust, but he'd spent too many years giving it free rein. No woman he pursued ever refused him. In fact, most, like Tracie, had made the first move. All he did was wait. It was part of The Game.

But he'd be waiting a long time if he expected a first move from Dani. She seemed oblivious to even his most practiced "looks." Probably why he found her so appealing. Something different and new intrigued him. That's all it was.

"Guess I was right."

Dani's voice brought him from his reverie, and he had to think back to what she'd said. *I'm not your type.* Did she expect him to deny it?

"But you're not my type either," she said.

Her cheeks flushed slightly, and her voice held a bit of bravado. Good for her. Inwardly he smiled. She could be so easy to tease.

"You have a type?"

"Maybe not a type." Looking thoughtful, she settled in the chair next to the couch.

"If not a type, then what?" He casually propped his feet on the trunk. "Oh, I know. You're dreaming of Prince Charming. Just waiting for him to ride in on his white horse and sweep you off your feet."

"Nothing like that." She gestured toward the TV. "I thought you wanted to watch my film."

"First things first. You've cut me to the quick, you know. Stabbed me in the heart even," he teased. "I'm not your type, but who is? I hope not AJ, because he's taken."

"Of course not AJ."

"Who then?"

"No one in particular. I just want a guy who's . . ."

"Handsome?"

"Looks don't matter."

"Women say that, but it's never true."

"Okay, they matter a little."

"A lot."

"Unlike you, I'm not that shallow."

"You think I'm shallow?"

"Aren't you?"

He held her gaze, wanting the banter to continue, wanting to confess the truth.

"Your silence is your answer," she said triumphantly.

"I guess it is." He reached for the remote and, shifting slightly in his seat, pushed the play button. "Movie time."

As the film started, he surreptitiously glanced at Dani. When she turned to him, the pleading expression in her dark eyes tugged at his heart.

"Please don't hate this," she said quietly.

"How could I?"

She shrugged, a pitiful movement that pulled his heart from his chest. At that moment, it took all his willpower to stay on the couch. Why did AJ have that chair anyway? If Dani was already beside him, he could put his arm around her shoulders, feel her hair against his cheek as she leaned her head on his chest.

How easy then to forget the film and kiss her soft lips.

Maybe it was best she was sitting in the chair after all.

He squirmed and focused on the TV screen. The title image showed a boy outside a barn on a wintry night. A man wearing a POW uniform stood in the shadows. A star, reminiscent of the one that guided the wise men to Bethlehem, radiated light around them.

To his own surprise, Brett became totally engrossed in the film. As the final credits rolled and Dani's name appeared on the screen, he shook his head as if to awaken from the experience.

"That was amazing. You're amazing."

"Don't tease."

"I'm not. Okay, to be honest, I was expecting some fluffy story. But this . . . I'm beyond impressed."

She turned away, and the light reflected a small glimmer on her cheek. Scooting forward on the couch, he lightly pressed his forefinger beneath her silent tears.

"Why are you crying?"

"I haven't seen it in a while. I guess I'd forgotten how good it is." Her hesitant smile almost did him in. "That sounded like bragging, but I didn't mean it that way."

"It's better than good." His hand lingered against her damp cheek. For the tiniest second, she leaned into his hand, then moved away. He clasped his hands in front of him. Better for both of them if he didn't touch her again.

"You have a gift, Dani Prescott."

"You really liked it?"

"More than liked it. You've got a way of, I don't know, pulling heartstrings without being banal."

"Thank you. That means a lot to me."

"Maybe we should hire someone else to—"

"What?" Her eyes grew large. "You don't want me anymore?"

Brett blinked, momentarily confused by her outburst. He wanted her very much. But that's not what she meant.

"I think you should concentrate on a documentary, that's all. Instead of it being something we might do, let's make it a priority. Someone else can take care of the other projects."

"But I want to do it all. The documentary, the displays, all of it."

"You're sure?"

She started to answer then focused on the television screen. The DVD had returned to the main menu, and the same musical theme repeated itself.

"What are you thinking?"

She faced him, then sighed. "Have you ever had a time when everything seemed to be too perfect?"

"I suppose so."

"That's how I feel right now. The perfect job." She gestured around the cottage. "The perfect place to live."

"Then why so glum?"

"Because when things are too perfect . . ." She hesitated. "Some dreams just aren't meant to come true."

"I don't believe that. And neither should you." He shifted to the trunk, his knees pressing against hers. "Unless it's not a dream worth having."

"But it is."

"See?" He squeezed her hands and smiled. "Harness that passion, that drive, and someday you'll write that award-winning script."

"You really think so?"

"You're not a quitter, are you?"

She tensed, then seemed to consciously relax. "Things have been a little rough lately."

That was an understatement, he was sure. "Want to talk about it?"

"You'd never understand."

"Give me a chance."

He wanted a chance.

A chance to what? Understand her world?

But how could he? Even though his own childhood must have been difficult, he had a financial cushion that softened any blows he endured. Any doors he couldn't open with his good looks and charm were opened by his checkbook. He hadn't worked two, three, sometimes four jobs to pay his tuition. He'd never seen his dream as a star shining dimly in the night sky, drawing his attention like a magnet but always too far away to grasp.

The image of him outside the hospital pounded into her mind.

The way he stared at the lighted window. How he'd leaned against his car, bowed by a weight he couldn't escape. In that unguarded moment, she'd witnessed his vulnerability.

But she couldn't let him see hers.

She pulled her hands from his and stood, intending to gather their plates. But he rose too, and she gripped his arm to steady herself in the awkward space between the trunk and the chair. Loosed from her hold, his hands naturally gravitated to her waist. His gentle touch surged through her body, and her pulse raced with a desire she'd never experienced before.

His chin rested near her temple, then slid to her own. Before she could take a breath, his mouth was on hers as his grip on her waist tightened. Her senses seemed to spring to life apart from her as she simultaneously breathed in his expensive aftershave, felt the slight prickling of his stubble against her skin, and exalted in the tantalizing pressure of his kiss. Her response was quick and out of her control as she melted into his embrace. Her lips sought his with a passion she never knew she possessed as her hand crept to his neck.

Time slowed as Dani lost herself in the exquisite moment. Brett's fingers slid beneath the hem of her T-shirt, soft as a butterfly's wing against her bare skin, before his palm pressed against the small of her back.

Intoxicated with the sensations flooding through her, she gasped as he suddenly grasped her waist with both hands and pushed away.

"I shouldn't have done that." He tried to step backward, beyond the trunk, while holding on to her as if reluctant to let her go.

Feeling betrayed, not just by him but by her own desire, she averted her gaze.

"Dani." His warm voice caressed the space between them, but she still couldn't raise her eyes to his. He pressed his forehead against hers. "I lost control. It won't happen again."

She nodded as hot tears stung her eyes, but she didn't understand why.

She only knew she wanted him. Despite his arrogance, his conceit, and despite her own misgivings, she was falling in love with him.

A hopeless love.

An impossible dream.

– 30 –

Brett wanted nothing more than to pull Dani into his arms again. To kiss her lovely lips. To make her his own. Taking a deep breath, he struggled against his desire.

Only one option remained.

"Good night," he whispered, then quickly walked out the door. Once outside, he paused on the concrete slab serving as a porch and took several more deep breaths.

What had he done?

Why had he done it?

Digging his keys from his pocket, he strode to the Lexus. A few seconds later, he'd driven through the gate. When he got out of the car to close it behind him, he looked toward the cottage.

What must she be thinking?

He considered returning, to apologize, to make some attempt at an explanation. But he didn't dare. She was too vulnerable, too alluring, and he was too . . . well, it had been about three months since he'd kicked Tracie out of his life.

Once again, remorse smacked him for how he'd treated his former receptionist. The unexpected pang clutched at his chest.

After latching the gate, he slid back into his car and drove the half mile to AJ's bungalow. The house where Gran had lived out her last days before her death.

The outside light shone above the porch, but AJ's Jeep wasn't in the driveway. It didn't take a genius to know where he was. On a Wednesday night, he'd be at church. And after that, a couple miles over as the crow flies with Shelby and her daughters.

Fortunately, Brett knew where to find the spare key. He let himself in, turning on a few lights as he headed for the kitchen. After grabbing a sports drink, the only thing AJ had in the fridge besides a quart of milk, he unscrewed the bottle's cap and walked out to the screened porch. He plopped onto the rattan settee and took a long drink.

Though Glade Creek couldn't be seen from here, the night creatures inhabiting it could definitely be heard. The deep croaks of bullfrogs interspersed with other sounds he couldn't identify. A whippoorwill crooned its lonely call.

He closed his eyes, wanting to hold on to the memory of Dani in his arms, the tenderness of her mouth, the softness of her skin beneath his fingertips. As if in a dream, her image blurred and it was Meghan he was kissing, not from desire but from conquest.

He'd taken her from AJ, and at that time, nothing else mattered.

Disgust filled his gut, and he retched after hurrying to the restroom. The vomit burned his throat as it spilled into the toilet bowl.

He was rinsing his mouth when the front door opened.

"Brett?" AJ called. "Where are you?"

He rinsed again, then wiped his mouth with a towel. "Coming."

They met in the living room.

"What are you doing here?" AJ took off his OSU ball cap and tousled his smashed-down hair. "Are you okay?"

"Fine. Hope you don't mind I came on in."

"Not at all. Just surprised to see you."

"A little surprised to be here."

"What's going on?"

"I don't know." Brett pressed his lips together and swallowed the lump clogging his throat. "Things don't . . . I'm not . . ."

"Did something happen to Amy?" Concern squeezed AJ's voice.

"She's . . . Amy."

"Is it Jonah?" The concern plummeted into panic.

Brett almost shook his head again, but Meghan's image stopped him.

"Why did you do it, AJ?"

"Do what?"

"Find Meghan. Why did you go looking for her?"

AJ blew out a breath and passed his hand over his eyes. "You'll think I'm crazy."

"Try me."

"God told me to."

"Honestly?"

"Honestly. You want something to drink?"

Brett passed his hand over his chest and abdomen. "I'm fine, thanks."

"Then let's sit down." AJ led the way to the porch, and they settled into the cushioned chairs. The only light came from inside the house.

AJ hung his cap on his knee, an odd, almost awe-filled expression on his face. "This may sound crazy."

"I want to know."

He paused a moment, searching for the right words. "Somehow I knew I could never be the man I needed to be for Shelby if I didn't make amends with Meghan. So I did an online search, got a lead, and, well, you know the rest."

"So you made a deal with God?"

"It wasn't quite like that. I didn't know how things would work out with Shelby. There were no guarantees."

"But God told you to find Meghan?"

"He did."

"You heard his voice?"

"Not like I hear you. It was more like a strong impression. A . . . a whisper into my soul," AJ said softly. "Sometimes I wish I hadn't."

"Why not?"

"Maybe it would have been better if we hadn't known about Jonah. The truth, I mean."

Brett rolled the thought around in his mind, twisting it into different shapes, viewing it from different angles. "I needed to know. And so did you. Besides, if you hadn't found him when you did, he might be . . ." He couldn't finish the sentence, though he admitted its melodrama. Because of AJ, Jonah was getting the best possible care, but even that hadn't been enough to bring him out of his coma.

"It's changed things, you know," Brett said.

"What things?"

"It's changed me. I knew Meghan was pregnant when she left. Even suspected she lied to you. But I never dreamed she'd go through with the pregnancy." In the dim light of the porch, surrounded by the night's darkness, he felt safe talking about things he never could have said in the daytime. Not even to AJ. "Knowing about Jonah, knowing I have a son, makes me want to be someone better than I am. For his sake."

"I understand that. I feel that way about Elizabeth and Tabby, and they aren't even mine."

"But they will be. You'll be the dad they remember. The man who walks them down the aisle someday."

"Don't even talk about that. My heart can't take it."

Brett chuckled, then turned serious again. "I was over at Dani's a little while ago."

"Has she settled in?"

"Looks that way. She was going to watch a DVD on Ohio history this evening. Research."

"Do you really think she's got the experience for a job like this?"

"Maybe not, but she has the passion. Why? Has Shelby said something?"

"Shelby enjoys her company. They get along great."

"I'm glad." Even with the poor lighting, Brett sensed AJ's eyes upon him. "What are you thinking?"

"You really want to know?" AJ asked.

"Don't tell me she's not my type."

"I wasn't going to. But she could be if you let her."

"She's just a girl. A *nice* girl."

"What's wrong with that?"

"Me." Brett leaned forward, elbows on knees, and bowed his head. "I'm what's wrong."

"What did you do?"

"I . . . kissed her."

"Like a"—AJ made a smooching sound—"kiss?"

Brett glowered, then shook his head. "Never do that again."

"More than that, huh?"

"Let's just say it was a substantial kiss."

"I don't think I want to hear any more."

"No more to tell. I kissed her and then I left."

"Without saying anything?"

"I said good-bye."

"Brilliant."

"I think she was crying."

"And you left her?"

"I couldn't stay. There's something about her that . . . I couldn't stay."

For several minutes, they listened to the nocturnal symphonies. Once again, the ethereal whippoorwill sang its three-noted melody. Another one, further away, answered the lonely call.

"What are you going to do?" AJ asked quietly.

Brett shrugged. "Can you believe it? For the first time in my life, I don't know what to do with the women in my life."

"Women?"

"Dani. Amy. Meghan."

"Didn't you just meet Dani?"

"Four weeks day after tomorrow." Since the Labor Day picnic at Misty Willow, he'd spent as much time with her as he dared allow himself. It seemed he could barely go twenty-four hours without calling or texting her. He'd given up his sham of a dating sabbatical.

His life made no sense.

"Do you love her?"

"It's too soon for that. Isn't it?"

"Don't ask me. I think I fell in love with Shelby before I even met her."

"Because of the letter she wrote you?"

"Yeah."

"How did you know for sure? That you loved her?"

AJ thought a moment, then said quietly, "I couldn't breathe without her."

Brett rested his head against the back of the chair. He could breathe just fine on his own. But Dani drew him to her again and again without even trying. And when he was with her, he was more his true self than at any other time. No expectations to meet. No pretense.

No games.

Just a slip of a girl winding his heart around her finger. And totally oblivious to what she was doing. "It's confounding, isn't it?"

"Yep."

"Maybe God is telling me the same thing he told you."

"You mean . . ."

"I have to make things right with Meghan. If I don't, I'll never . . ." He stopped and took a deep breath. "I'll never make it with anyone."

When Brett closed the door behind him, Dani rushed to the window. She peered through the crack between the blind and the window as he slid into his car. When he got out to shut the gate and looked toward the cottage, she backed away from the window.

What had just happened?

If she needed any more proof that her middle name was "loser," this was it. Her face flamed as she relived her eagerness to accept his embrace. What must he think of her?

Even worse, what would have happened if he hadn't pulled away?

She curled up in a corner of the couch and hugged a pillow to her chest as she fought back hot tears. If things had continued, he'd have discovered her inexperience. Though he'd teased her about being a "nice" girl, he probably had no idea how right he was.

Never before had she been so tempted to break her resolve to wait for Mr. Right. A promise she'd made to herself after spending too many hours consoling lovesick girlfriends who had been dumped by love 'em and leave 'em idiots. Immature jerks who boasted about their conquests and gave no thought to the wreckage left behind.

Agonizing pain struck the side of her head.

Brett was no different.

She knew it. To the depths of her heart she knew it.

If he hadn't left, and she hadn't gotten control of herself, she was sure her story would be the same. One night of romance, then he'd have walked out of her life.

But he'd done that anyway.

If only she'd pushed him away first. Next time she would, holding on to her resolve no matter how difficult it might be.

Except there wouldn't be a next time. His brusque departure made that clear.

The pain in her head increased. Hopefully AJ had left something in his medicine cabinet. Finding ibuprofen, she downed a couple, then washed up the supper dishes.

As she was turning off the kitchen lights, her phone buzzed. A text message. She closed her eyes before looking at the screen.

Shelby.

She should have known it wouldn't have been Brett.

Via text, they agreed on a time to meet the next day, then Dani headed to the bedroom. She settled beneath the covers and gingerly laid her head on the thick pillow. Hopefully her headache would be gone by morning.

But what about the ache in her heart?

Brett returned home after a detour to the hospital, where a clear green light shone from Jonah's window. He took a glass of iced tea to his bedroom and set it on top of a mahogany nightstand along with his phone and wallet. He started to sit on the bed to take off his shoes, but something drew him to the ebony box on top of his dresser. The rings, the amethyst and the diamond solitaire, were nestled inside.

He sat on the edge of the bed, opened the lid, and picked up Tracie's ring.

Or was it?

She'd probably bought it with his money, impatient for him to buy a ring for her. But that had never been part of his plan.

Still clutching the ring, he leaned against the headboard, stretching his legs along the comforter and crossing his ankles. Tonight's events played in his mind, from the argument with Amy to the rare heart-to-heart with AJ. And in between, the refuge of Dani's company. Until he lost control.

How was he going to make things right with her?

He stared at the ring, angling the diamond chips surrounding the stone to catch the light from the nearby lamp. AJ believed, actually believed, God told him to make things right with Meghan. But that was what Brett had been trying to do since he'd learned of Jonah's existence.

Anything he did for her, for Jonah, had to be done in secret because she refused to forgive him.

Somehow, by staring into the depths of the amethyst stone, he confronted what was expected of him.

He tried to resist the message pressing against his spirit. It demanded too much of him, and Tracie would never understand.

But the impression persisted. He needed to apologize to Tracie, for his sake as much as hers.

And then what? Apologize to every woman he'd ever dated? He couldn't think about that right now.

He put the amethyst ring back in the box and took the solitaire from its case, then angled the fine diamond in the lamplight. Dani had been intrigued with the ring and its story. Sully, the returning war veteran, had loved Aubrey then lost her. The anger he harbored found its revenge decades later when he took over the mortgage on Misty Willow. The grab had probably been illegal, but Aubrey's husband had died in a horrible accident before he could save the farm. Stricken with grief, Aubrey died soon after.

The repercussions from those long-ago events echoed through the years. Decisions made. Vengeance executed. Hearts broken.

If only Sully could have foreseen the misery unleashed by his rage. Perhaps things would have been different.

Even in the meager lamplight, the diamond—a symbol of lost love, of spurned love—sparked its mesmerizing fire.

"Why did Sully hold on to you," Brett murmured, "when all you meant to him was pain?"

– 31 –

The next day, Brett opted to eat lunch in the office as he worked through the numerous folders on his desk. The pile that faced him would have been even worse without Kimberly's organizational expertise. Certain files he expected to read through now came with an abstract, a template she created that provided pertinent information in an accessible format. The corresponding paperwork was labeled and tabbed for easy reference.

Still, he had several more projects to review before he could call it a day. Not that he minded. The heavy workload kept his thoughts from being consumed with Dani. Absorbed by work, now he thought of her every other minute instead of every one.

He needed to do something to make amends for walking out on her. But neither a text nor a phone call seemed appropriate. Of course, there was always flowers.

But what message would that send? What message did he want to send?

After a sleepless night trying to figure it out, he still didn't know.

And what about their date tonight? With anyone else, he just wouldn't show up. His conscience pricked him as he remembered doing exactly that with Shelby. She had discovered he and AJ were cousins—a relevant fact Brett had purposely kept from her—a few hours before their planned first date.

But Shelby knew Brett would back out. And she wouldn't have gone out with him if he'd shown up at her door.

This situation wasn't the same. If Dani was expecting him and he didn't show up, she'd be hurt. If she expected him to back out and he showed up—well, at least he wouldn't be a jerk. And maybe by then, he'd have figured out some way to explain his rude departure without sounding like the sleazeball she already thought him to be.

He had to keep the date, that much was certain, no matter how awkward the circumstances. Time to call in reinforcements.

He'd just hung up from talking with AJ when his phone rang. The jeweler, returning his call. After a brief chat, he clicked the end button, then swirled around to gaze at the Columbus skyline. He tapped his phone against the chair arm.

Before going to bed last night, he'd gone online and searched his credit card statements. A four-figure amount had been spent at a local jewelry store only a week after he and Tracie began dating.

The jeweler remembered Tracie. No surprise there. Heads turned wherever they'd gone together, and Brett's chest had puffed with pride at the obvious jealousy of every other man in the vicinity. The shallowness he'd indulged in now made him sick.

But at least he had the answer. Tracie had purchased the ring with his credit card. Whether or not she'd left it behind on purpose, he didn't know. But since it was purchased with his money, he had no obligation to return it to her. If that had been her ploy, to have an excuse to see him again, it wasn't going to work.

Though he supposed if that had been her plan, she would have contacted him by now. Perhaps she accidentally left it behind.

The jeweler had offered, albeit reluctantly, to take the ring back. Brett almost agreed, but the same sensation he'd felt when examining the ring last night pressed upon him again.

But how could saying "I'm sorry" make any difference?

He couldn't fathom an answer, but the feeling wouldn't let him go.

Taking a deep breath, he dialed Tracie's number. The phone rang, then went to voicemail. He ended the call and typed out a text. *We need to talk.*

He hesitated before sending it.

Chances were, she wouldn't respond. Unless he piqued her curiosity. Or she thought there was a possibility of them getting back together. She might not miss him, but she undoubtedly missed his money.

He deleted the message and typed a new one. *Any chance of seeing you this weekend? I'd like to talk.*

That should do it. She'd make him wait for an answer till at least tomorrow. But in the end, she'd agree to meet. She wouldn't be able to help herself.

Tracie thought she was clever and irresistible. But actually she was only predictable.

Not at all like Dani. He never knew what she was going to say or do. Like that first night, telling him her name was Regina Lampert.

It had happened again.

Without meaning to, his thoughts had seesawed back and forth, then returned to the naïve waif who never seemed far from his mind.

He ran his fingers over his mouth as the memory of their kiss lingered around him. Gaining control of his thoughts before they wandered down the road he didn't dare travel, he swiveled back to his desk and grabbed the next folder on the pile.

Concentrating on work was the only way to keep Dani out of his thoughts.

Dani's phone only rang a few times during the day, but each time, her heart seized in her throat. She both hoped and feared it'd be Brett. But it never was. So did that mean they still had a date for this evening? What if she got ready and he didn't come? What if she didn't get ready, and he did?

Either way, this was going to be awkward.

"Is something wrong?" Shelby's voice broke into her thoughts. "You look like you're a million miles away."

"I'm sorry. I guess I was." Dani glanced at her notes. "Let's see, I have interviews set up with the archaeology crew for next week. Dr. Kessler arranged for the film department to help out with that. While they're here, perhaps they could shoot footage in the secret room."

Shelby had shown Dani the trapdoor in the hallway closet that accessed the room one Sunday afternoon while AJ had the girls preoccupied outside. Though Elizabeth knew the room existed, Shelby didn't want her knowing where it was.

Descending the ladder had been like stepping back into the past. Plywood covered most of the dirt floor, and wooden bunks formed an *L* against two of the brick-lined walls. The only other furniture was a ramshackle table.

Part of their renovation plan included placing straw-filled mattresses covered in ticking and antique quilts on the bunk beds. But Dani wanted *before* footage too.

"Elizabeth will probably be in school when the film crew is here," Shelby said. "I'll ask Cassie Owens to watch Tabby so she won't be underfoot."

"We also need to videotape you talking about your family and the history of this place."

"Will you give me a script?"

"More like an outline. That way, you'll be more natural."

"I don't know, Dani. I get nervous just thinking about it."

"The trick is to tell the stories as if you're talking to a good friend. Like you've told them to me. And it doesn't matter if you flub something up. We'll work all that out in editing."

Shelby released a pent-up sigh, then smiled. "I'm so glad Brett found you. God has answered all my prayers. Even the ones I didn't know to pray."

Dani's eyes narrowed in confusion. "Does that happen often?"

"What?"

"What you just said. God answers prayers you didn't know to pray."

"Fairly often, yes."

The concept seemed strange, even mysterious. Dani hadn't prayed since she was a child, but throughout her life she experienced unexplained times when she'd felt oddly protected. A foster home placement that got canceled at the last minute when the dad was arrested for selling drugs. A family stopping to help her when she had a flat tire on a lonely road. Could it have been God? Was he paying attention to her when no one else did? Did he answer the unprayed prayers of her heart?

"Why do you suppose God answers prayers you don't pray and then doesn't answer prayers that you do?" Dani asked. "I know people say he always answers prayer. The whole 'yes, no, wait' thing." A minister who came to one of the group homes she'd stayed in for a while had stressed those three responses to every prayer.

"I can't explain it," Shelby said. "I'm not sure anyone can. Sometimes awful things happen to the best people, and we don't know why. When my grandparents died, I was devastated. It still hurts. But I believe with all my heart that God's love is steadfast. No matter what happens."

"Did you blame God?"

"I was angry with him." Shelby gestured around the room. "I came back here to reclaim my grandparents' home, a heritage that was rightly mine."

"Then why are you giving it up?"

"It's complicated. I'd like to live the rest of my life in this house, but the foundation protects the land from developers. That's the best way for me to protect the Lassiter heritage. Besides, I realized my grandparents' legacy wasn't just a house or a farm. It was their godly examples, their standing in the community. The people who loved them."

Dani sunk in her seat, her body suddenly tired, as if bowing under the weight of a heavy burden. She didn't have a heritage to protect, only one to hide. Her deepest, darkest secret was her private relief that her mom had married. As much as she grew to loathe her stepdad, she'd been grateful not to share Mom's last name.

When the plane crashed, all of Dani's classmates seemed to know about it. Even before the blame had been placed at Mom's feet, Dani had been ashamed—and ashamed of her shame. It was as if her mom had done something awful simply by dying. The other students stared and whispered, and Dani had retreated into a dark and lonesome place.

She changed schools almost as often as she changed homes. Being the new girl meant not fitting in, and she stopped trying. She was in college before she trusted anyone with the truth about the plane crash. Only Jeanie, her friend in Boise who was once her roommate, knew that Leslie Mercer, the pilot responsible for the deaths of four prominent members of Columbus society, was Dani's mom.

At Shelby's touch on her hand, Dani practically jumped out of her seat. She laughed self-consciously and apologized. "I guess I was somewhere else."

"I won't pry," Shelby said. "But if you need someone to talk to, well, I know what it's like to need a friend."

Dani sucked in her lip to bite back the secret her heart wanted to spill. Shelby knew what it was like to lose family she loved. She'd understand Dani's sorrow at losing her mom. But AJ wouldn't. Dani didn't want him to know the truth, and she couldn't burden Shelby with keeping the secret from her fiancé.

Nor could she find the courage to tell Shelby what happened last night. Her face warmed at the memory of Brett's arms around her, his kiss overwhelming her senses.

His quick departure.

Confessing her stupid attempt at playing detective was completely out of the question. In the perfect vision of hindsight, the scheme to somehow humiliate Brett sounded like the farfetched plot of a third-rate movie even to her. Shelby would be appalled.

Dani didn't know whether to feel like a failure because she didn't have the brains to come up with a solid plan or to feel like a doofus for even attempting one. She did know that leaving Cincinnati had turned out to be a good thing. Already she loved the cottage and Misty Willow.

But how long would she be able to stay?

"Did you and Brett have a fight?"

"No," Dani said slowly, but her cheeks flushed. "You make it sound like we're a couple. We're not."

"But we're all going out tonight, right?"

"What?"

"AJ texted before you got here. He said Brett invited us to go to Boyd's with you this evening."

So he wasn't going to cancel. But he didn't want to be alone with her either.

"He hadn't told me."

"If you'd rather we didn't—"

"No, I want you to come," Dani said hurriedly. "Please do."

"Only if you're sure."

"It'll be fun."

"I think so too." Shelby smiled, then gave an exasperated sigh. "But Brett should have asked you first before inviting us. Typical of him. He's not the most thoughtful guy in the world."

Perhaps not from Shelby's perspective. But he'd been more than thoughtful to Dani—creating a job for her, finding her a home. But Shelby obviously knew a different side to him. The one Dani had expected to find.

"Too used to getting his own way, I suppose," she said, trying to be flippant.

"You suppose right." Shelby chuckled. "Though he does surprise me sometimes. He dropped by once when I was trying to make the flower bed out front and having a horrible time with the tiller. He finished the job for me. Didn't even care about getting his clothes dirty."

Dani hesitated, then spit out the question before she could change her mind. "Have you met any of the women he's dated?"

"Only Tracie. And only once."

"Did you like her?"

"To be honest, I felt sorry for her."

"He broke her heart, didn't he?"

"She didn't really love him, but, well, it doesn't matter, does it? She's out of his life, and you're in it."

She was in it all right. More than Shelby or even Brett knew. Their lives had become entwined the day her mom had agreed to fly Brett's parents to Martha's Vineyard. Some fancy charity event they attended every year.

"They think a private charter impresses that crowd," Mom had said. "I doubt it does, but so what? We put up with their fancy airs and pocket their money."

From anyone else, the words would have echoed with their own arrogance. But not from Mom. She didn't merely say them—she acted them out. Strutting around the room with her nose in the air, then jamming her hands in her pockets with a smile and a laugh. Dani had laughed too.

Less than twenty-four hours later, her secure world had been turned upside down, inside out, and set on a trajectory that zigzagged from her stepdad's custody to foster care and back again.

At least Brett had been spared that.

"You're far away again." Shelby's soft voice entered Dani's thoughts. "We could take a break if you want."

"No, it's fine. I was just thinking."

"About Brett?"

Dani scrambled for a response. "And Amy. He's worried about her."

"I know. AJ is too.".

"Why won't she let them help her?"

"With Amy, one never knows."

"He's a good man, isn't he?"

"Brett? Yes, I believe he is." Shelby laid down her pen and rested her chin on her hands. "He's changed in the past few weeks. Before, he and AJ were practically estranged, but now they're in touch almost every day."

"What changed him?"

"I can't say for sure, but I think it started when he found out about Jonah. I wish Meghan would forgive him. I pray for that every day."

"What's she like?"

"She's nice. I really like her. And she's very talented."

"Oh?"

"Mmmhmm. She's an artist. Actually, she made that stained-glass piece in the cottage."

"She did?" Each morning, the sun's rays set the red, yellow, purple, and green of the glass ablaze. "I've fallen in love with it."

"AJ bought it because it reminded him of Glade Creek," Shelby continued. "Of course, Meghan doesn't get to work much now, but she volunteers at the hospital. Does arts and crafts with the patients and their siblings."

"I suppose she's blonde and beautiful."

"Actually, she resembles you in a way. Same coloring and same, I don't know, petiteness? Is that a word?"

Dani returned the expected smile, but inside her heart ached even more. Now everything made sense. Brett wasn't interested in her. She was just a drab substitute for the talented woman he really wanted.

And why not? Meghan was the mother of his son.

How could Dani compete with someone who had that kind of leverage?

When had she started wanting to?

If she were honest, it began that first night. Hard as she tried to keep him out, Brett had effortlessly burrowed his way into her heart. But she needed to face the facts and not be swayed by his charm.

His only interest in her was platonic. All he cared about was the woman who could give him what he wanted most—a relationship with his son.

Did Meghan realize the power she held over him? How cruel it was to keep him away from Jonah?

It's not my concern.

She needed to put aside all these distractions and focus on doing the best job she could with the Misty Willow project. Her resolve would keep her focused.

At least until six o'clock this evening.

– 32 –

*M*eghan gave the waitress a shaky smile as she took the double-sided menu. She still couldn't believe she was this far away from the hospital. She wouldn't be if her friend Dawn hadn't come to the city on business and volunteered—no, insisted— on staying with Jonah while Meghan went out on her first official date with Aaron.

Even so, Meghan's stomach flipped at the thought that Jonah might awaken while she was gone.

"I thought we declared this a no-worry zone," Aaron said. His eyes twinkled with gentle humor.

"I'm trying. Honest."

"If anything happens, I promise you'll be back at the hospital before you can say Jack Frost."

"That fast, huh?"

"Even faster."

Holding on to his reassurance, she skimmed the menu. "So what do you recommend?"

"A little bit of everything."

"Seriously?"

He chuckled. "Okay, what's your favorite? Beef, pork, or chicken?"

"I suppose the healthy PC answer is chicken, but I confess. I love beef."

"Then I recommend the brisket."

"What about you? What are you having?"

"The same."

"You don't have to do that."

"It's my favorite too."

They laid the menus aside, and Meghan nervously placed her napkin in her lap as she looked around the rustic room. All those years ago, when she'd been a starry-eyed college student, AJ had mentioned bringing her to this place a few times. But for one reason or another, it never happened. Not that she'd told Aaron that.

She was still surprised he'd asked her out. Even more surprised at the flutter in her stomach and the delight she'd felt when he did.

"I take it you come here often," Meghan said. Their waitress and a couple of others had greeted Aaron by name when they walked in.

"Been coming here for years. It's a little out of the way but worth it. Especially on Thursday nights." He glanced toward the makeshift stage. "Though it looks like we're a little early for the band."

"That's my fault. I'm sorry we couldn't have come later."

Aaron was shaking his head before she could finish her apology. "I'm just glad we're here," he said, almost sheepishly. "That's all that matters."

"I'm glad too." Meghan slightly flushed, then sipped her water. She had to admit it felt good to eat somewhere besides her apartment or the hospital cafeteria. And to have company instead of eating alone.

Still, even with Dawn by Jonah's side, Meghan hadn't been comfortable staying out too late. Aaron understood her apprehension and seemed determined to ease her fears. She didn't think she'd ever met anyone so good and kind.

"Do you ever get angry?" she blurted, then flushed again as Aaron gave her a strange look and laughed.

"What made you ask that?"

"I don't know. It's just, you're always so patient and so sweet. All the children love you."

"They do?"

"They talk about you during arts and crafts time. They're very fond of you."

"I'm fond of them too."

"So do you? Get angry?"

Aaron slightly shook his head, then hesitated. "There are times when I wonder . . ."

"What?" Meghan prompted.

"I wonder why. Why are these particular children afflicted with diseases and injuries?"

"Let me know if you ever find the answer."

"I don't suppose there is one. At least not this side of heaven. But anger doesn't make anyone feel better. It doesn't heal or soothe or solve anything."

"I'm not sure I agree with that. Sometimes it feels really good to scream and shout and even break things."

Aaron's good-natured chuckle filled the air with cheer. "Do you know what Aristotle said?"

"Nooo," Meghan said. "I don't think so."

"I won't get it exactly right, but he said something about the key to anger is having the right amount at the right time about the right situation. We're not good at that. People in general, I mean."

Meghan mulled the words around in her mind. He was right, of course. Anger too often seemed more detrimental to the person feeling it than to anyone else. Despite what she'd said, she was proof of that. Though no one could blame her for being angry when her son had been in a coma for weeks.

Right amount at the right time.

She needed to think about that some more but not now.

"Let's find something more cheerful to talk about, shall we?" she asked. "What do you do when you're not at the hospital?"

"I read a lot. Travel when I can."

"Travel where?"

"Promise not to laugh?"

"I promise."

Aaron gave a self-conscious chuckle. "I'm trying to see a game at every major college football stadium."

"Football?" Meghan exaggerated her disbelief. "I should have known. How many have you seen?"

"Most of the ones within five hundred miles, including all fourteen stadiums in the Big Ten Conference."

"Wait a minute. Shouldn't there only be ten stadiums in the Big Ten?"

"They've expanded over the years. I've already got tickets for games at Clemson, Florida State, and Notre Dame, though I've been to that last one before."

"Any other hobbies?"

"Why don't you tell me about yours instead?"

"I've learned to knit. Other than that, I don't really have any."

"Then tell me about life as an artist."

"It's not very glamorous. Sometimes it's even lonely spending hours by myself in my studio." A studio she hadn't stepped foot in since Jonah's accident. The lease ended next month, and she needed to decide whether to renew it. But how could she make decisions about the future when Jonah's prognosis was so uncertain? Only God knew when they'd be able to go home. *If* they'd ever go home.

"Your studio is in Michigan?"

"A little town just over the state line called Brennan Grove. I rent a house there on the edge of town. My studio is in a converted barn. It's perfect, actually. One section is all windows. That's where I hang my stained glass pieces when I'm working on them. To see how the sun shines through the colors. I like experimenting."

"You must miss being there."

"I do. There's nothing quite so . . . . fulfilling . . . as knowing you've captured the image that was inside of yourself onto a collection of colored glass. To make something whole out of pieces."

The on-edge tension she carried with her like an extra appendage lessened while her conversation with Aaron ebbed and flowed, delightful and engaging. For a little while, as difficult as it was, she put her worries to rest.

Brett took a deep breath, then knocked on the cottage door. When Dani opened it, he braced himself for whatever welcome she gave him. But he couldn't help an appreciative smile at how attractive she appeared. Her brown hair brushed her shoulders, and the dusky blue sundress she wore flattered her figure. The lovely mouth shimmered with pink gloss, and a dusting of blush accented her cheeks.

"You look lovely," he said. Words he'd said hundreds of times to dozens of women. But he'd never meant the compliment as much as he did at this moment. "I mean it. You're beautiful."

"Thank you." Dani flushed slightly, her hand gripping the knob as if unsure whether to open the door wider or close it on him.

"These are for you." He handed her the bouquet of assorted flowers he'd picked up on his way to the cottage. Usually he ordered a stunning arrangement of roses or tulips delivered to his chosen recipient. But this time he joined the florist in selecting a unique collection of daisies and miniature carnations, then tying their stems together with a broad pink gingham ribbon.

Dani deserved more than his "usual." He wanted everything about his relationship with her, even if it turned out to be no relationship at all, to be different.

"They're . . ." She bit her lip, then the corners of her mouth turned up into a smile. "They're festive."

"You like them?"

She nodded as she inhaled their sweet fragrance. "Very much. Do you want to come in?"

"Only for a moment. I hope you don't mind, but I asked AJ and Shelby to join us."

"I know. Shelby told me."

"Is that okay?"

"Absolutely. Do you suppose AJ has a vase somewhere in this place?"

"I'll help you look." He followed her into the tiny kitchen, then stopped by the counter. "Tell you what. You stay on this side of the counter and let me see what I can find."

She appeared to mull the meaning behind his words, then slightly exhaled. "Good idea."

As she slipped past him, he resisted the urge to take her into his arms. Instead he opened cupboard doors until he found a large mason jar under the sink. He held it up with a grimace. "This is the best I can come up with. Guess I should have brought a vase."

"It's perfect." She gently laid the flowers on the counter, then untied the bow holding the stems together. After arranging the bouquet, she tied the ribbon around the lip of the jar. "How's that?"

"Looks nice."

"Country chic." She centered the jar on the pub table. "They fit with this place. As if they belong here."

"Like you belong here."

"I'm not sure where I belong."

"But you'll stay here until you can figure it out?"

"I suppose I will." She slightly shrugged. "As long as AJ lets me, anyway."

"He won't be moving back in."

"No, I guess not."

"About last night. I shouldn't have left the way I did. I can't really explain it except to say, I guess I got a little scared."

"Of me?"

"Of how I'm beginning to feel about you."

"I don't understand."

"Neither do I." He squeezed her fingers. Even that gentle touch swarmed through him. "We better go."

"I need to grab a jacket in case it gets chilly later." He let her fingers slip from his, and she disappeared into another room. When she returned, she dropped her purse and jacket in a chair and held up her camera.

"I want to take a photo of the flowers. Do we have time?"

"Sure."

She snapped a few shots, then placed the camera in its bag.

"Why don't you bring that with you? We can take a few photos to celebrate our anniversary."

"Today's our anniversary?" she said doubtfully.

"Okay, it's a day early. But tomorrow is the four-week anniversary of when we met." He should take her somewhere nice to celebrate. Candlelight. Soft music.

"I thought only women thought of things like that."

"What can I say? I'm a romantic."

"What happened to our other weekly anniversaries?"

"We spent the first one moving you into this place, and last week you were confessing your thievery."

"Great. Is that going to be our story?" Her eyes rounded, and she hurried to correct herself. "I mean, *the* story. *Your* story. You know what I mean."

"It sure is." He glanced at his watch. "AJ and Shelby will think we stood them up if we don't get going. Plus, Boyd's fills up quickly on Thursdays. It's classic car night, and there's a band that plays the oldies but goodies."

"I'm ready." Dani gathered her things, and Brett carried the camera bag.

Less than fifteen minutes later, Shelby and AJ slid into the backseat of the Lexus.

"I haven't been to Boyd's in months," Shelby said as she fastened her seatbelt.

"I didn't know you'd ever been there," AJ replied.

"Just once."

Brett glanced at her in the rearview mirror, then headed down the driveway. "Ancient history."

"You went there with Brett?" AJ asked, his tone incredulous.

"That was before I knew the two of you were cousins."

"New rule," Brett said. "No talking about the past."

"But you are so much fun to tease," Shelby answered. "And I don't get the chance very often."

Stopping at the end of the drive, Brett glanced at Dani. A slight smile curved her lips as she returned his gaze. A sense of contentment settled over him as he pulled onto the road. A pretty girl beside him. His cousin in the backseat with his bride-to-be. An enjoyable evening before them.

If only he could be content with such simplicity every day of his messed-up life. For tonight, he vowed, he'd banish his worries about Jonah and Amy from his mind and concentrate on the people he was with.

Good food. Good companions.

It was going to be a great evening.

The band was going strong, entertaining the crowd with an eclectic selection of classic country-western and golden oldies. The hostess led Brett and Dani to their booth, but AJ and Shelby were stopped along the way by a few teens at a nearby table.

"His students," Brett explained to Dani as he slid into the booth beside her. "Can't take him anywhere around here without students or their parents wanting to talk to him."

"He's a popular teacher?"

"And coaches football. When's the last time you went to a high school football game?"

"Not since high school."

"Maybe we could go tomorrow night. Cheer AJ and the team."

"First an OSU game, now high school. You're making a lot of plans for us."

"Suppose I am. First things first, though. How about we go to Bicentennial Park on Saturday for a picnic? We can even bike the Scioto Mile."

"I left my bicycle in Cincinnati."

"Not a problem. They have rentals."

"One question. What is the Scioto Mile?"

"It's an 'urban oasis,'" he said, making air quotes. "Mainly it connects the downtown area to the river. There's a huge fountain in the middle of the park. It's a Columbus landmark, so you've got to see it."

"Sounds fun."

"Okay if I pick you up about ten?"

"Wouldn't it be easier for me to meet you in Columbus? That way you won't have to backtrack."

"Easier, yes. But not very gentlemanly."

"I think I can overlook that. At least this once." She picked up one of the menus the hostess had left on the table. "What are you getting?"

"What I always get. Best pulled pork north of the Ohio River."

"I'll try that too."

"You won't regret it."

As AJ stepped back for Shelby to slide into the booth, his attention seemed caught by someone across the room. He nodded and waved, then took his seat.

"Who is that guy over there?" he asked Brett. "He's familiar, but I can't place him."

"What guy?"

"On the other side of the stage. Red curly hair."

Brett scanned the crowd, then smiled. "Aaron Wiley. He used to come over sometimes after school." He casually waved, and Aaron nodded in return. But his amiable smile appeared frozen in place.

"He works at the children's hospital, doesn't he?" AJ asked.

"Yeah. He used to give me updates on Jonah."

"Used to?" AJ asked.

"I quit asking. He's always been a good friend, but I didn't want him getting into trouble." A little white lie, but what did it matter?

"Is that who delivered your birthday gift to Jonah?" Shelby asked. "Meghan told me he's really good with the children. They love him." As soon as the words were out of her mouth, she gazed at Brett, an apologetic look in her eyes.

"It's okay. And yes, to answer your question, he did." Hard to believe that was only a month ago.

"Dani and I already know what we're getting," he said, forcing cheer into his voice. "What about you two?"

"Brett," AJ said quietly, then nodded his head toward Aaron's table. Brett glanced that way, and the blood rushed from his head. Aaron walked toward them. And with him was Meghan.

Brett took a deep breath, then stood as they approached. "Aaron," he said, holding out a hand. "Good to see you."

Aaron clasped his hand. His usually warm smile was slightly reserved. "Good to see you too, man."

"Hi, Meghan," Brett said.

"Hello, Brett." She turned toward the table and smiled at Shelby and AJ.

"It's so great to see you outside of the hospital," Shelby said warmly.

"I almost feel like a normal person." Meghan laughed nervously. "My friend Dawn Lahm is in town. You met her, AJ, at the gallery."

"I remember her."

"She's here for a few days to attend an art symposium, so when Aaron asked me out, well—"

"She said yes," Aaron interrupted.

"Good for you," Shelby said, then looked pointedly at Brett.

"Where are my manners?" Brett introduced Dani to Meghan and Aaron. While they greeted each other, he tried to steady his racing heart.

"We don't want to interrupt your dinner," Meghan said hesitantly. "But I wanted to thank each of you for Jonah's birthday presents."

She took a deep breath as she faced Brett. "I can't be sure, but it seems Jonah rests easier when he's listening to the music you loaded into the little monkey. It was a nice thing for you to do."

"If there's anything . . ." He swallowed as his voice caught. "Anything he needs, that you need. All you have to do is say so."

"There is one thing." Meghan turned to Shelby. "Like I said, Dawn is here for this conference. There are all kinds of displays and presentations. She'd like me to go with her on Saturday. I know it's an imposition, but would you be able to stay with Jonah for a little while? I wouldn't be gone too long."

"I'd love to," Shelby said. She glanced at AJ, who seemed to quickly take the hint.

"I've been promising to take the girls fishing," he said. "We'll do that while you're gone."

"It's settled then."

Meghan looked hesitantly at Aaron, then turned to Brett. "If you'd like, you could stop in. While Shelby is there."

Hope surged through Brett's heart. "You mean it?"

"I'll take your name off the 'not allowed' list tomorrow."

The back of his eyes burned as he tried to formulate a response. He cleared his throat and looked around the room before meeting her gaze. "Thank you, Meghan."

She didn't answer but looked up at Aaron. Unshed tears glistened in her eyes.

"I promised Meghan I wouldn't keep her out too long. Good to see you all." He held out his hand to Brett again. "See you later, buddy."

"Later." Brett took his seat as Aaron escorted Meghan from the restaurant. When they were out of sight, he let out a low breath. "I heard her right, didn't I?"

Shelby beamed. "You did. Oh, Brett, I'm so glad."

"I wonder what made her change her mind?" AJ said.

"I don't care," Brett responded. "I'm just glad she did."

Without thinking about it, he reached for Dani. She clasped his hand between both of hers as he leaned his temple against hers. "I get to see my son," he said quietly.

"I heard," she whispered. "That's great news."

"I get to see my son," he said again, a little louder, then whooped. "I get to see my son."

- 34 -

*E*arly the next afternoon, Dani drove to Misty Willow to meet with Shelby. Outside the rain came down in sheets, chilling the late summer day. The surly weather reflected her own mood. After Meghan had left their table last night, Dani had to fight the bitterness rising within her as Brett's renewed good spirits washed over all of them.

She was glad Meghan had relented. Glad Brett could see Jonah.

But had there ever been any doubt? The man lived a charmed life. Eventually he got anything he wanted.

In his excitement to see Jonah, he seemed to have forgotten their plans to go to Bicentennial Park on Saturday. He hadn't mentioned it again, not even when he took her back to the cottage. In fact, he'd appeared eager to get away, probably so he could race to the hospital and stare at his son's window.

Dani tried to clear the bitter thoughts, but they were as incessant as the pouring rain. If only she had windshield wipers for her mind. She didn't like the jealous pettiness that held her in its grip, especially not for a man who was only biding his time until someone new came along to catch his attention. Because she couldn't kid herself that he cared enough about her to be thinking about forever.

The question reared again—why was *she* thinking of forever?

Somehow the dream of spending the rest of her life with Brett, of being part of his family, had taken hold of her heart. She tried to squash it as a ridiculous fantasy, but deep within her soul, she yearned for her future to be entwined with his.

She pulled into the graveled drive, then parked behind Shelby's Camry. An umbrella was useless against the downpour, so she pulled the hood of her jacket over her head, grabbed her tote, then raced through the rain toward the house.

The screen door opened as she ran up the steps of the concrete patio.

"Come on in," Shelby urged as she stepped back from the door. "Can you believe this rain?"

Dani scurried inside and removed the jacket. "Cats and dogs."

"I'll say. Would you like coffee? Tea?"

"Tea would be nice."

"Coming right up."

Dani set her tote on the kitchen table, then stooped to pat Lila. The retriever's long pink tongue caught Dani's chin before she could turn away. "Hello to you too, girl."

She straightened before Lila got in another lick. "She's such a nice dog."

"The best. We joke that AJ had to marry me if he wanted to get her back. She and the girls became inseparable over the summer."

"Speaking of, where is Miss Tabby?"

"In her room for quiet time. She'll be out before too long though."

As they talked, Shelby put together a tea tray, then nodded toward the door leading to the hall. "Let's set up in the dining room. I'll be there in a sec."

Dani crossed the short hall and entered the square room. A long oak table stood in front of a mantel and what had at one time been a fireplace. Apparently one of Shelby's ancestors had closed all but two or three of the fireplaces. Shelby had once mentioned that reopening them was on her restoration list, but now the work wouldn't be done until after the wedding.

A streak of lightning flashed past the long double windows as Shelby came into the room and placed the tray at one end of the table.

"Will they still play football tonight?" Dani asked. Not that she cared. Brett had suggested they go to the game, but apparently he'd forgotten all about that too. From the look in his eyes, when he talked about their anniversary, she thought he might have something else planned. Perhaps even a romantic candlelight dinner. But one word from Meghan, and thoughts of Dani had gone right out of his head.

"Oh yeah. Nothing cancels a game," Shelby said. "But I already canceled on AJ. I don't want to take the girls out in this."

"You don't think it'll let up?"

"Not according to the forecast. What about you and Brett? Any plans for tonight?"

"I'm not sure."

"If not, why don't you hang out here? We'll pop popcorn and watch movies."

"Thanks, but—" Her phone beeped, and she glanced at the screen. "Talk about timing. Do you mind if I take this?"

"Go ahead."

Dani took a deep breath, then tapped the button as she wandered into the kitchen. "Hi, Brett."

"Staying dry?"

"Trying to. How about you?"

"The storm gives me an amazing view out of my office windows."

"I can imagine."

"Any leaks in the cottage?"

"None that I know of."

"That's good."

A moment's awkward silence followed, but Dani didn't know how to fill it.

Brett cleared his throat. "Amy called me a few minutes ago."

"Oh?"

"She wants me to come over later. I know we talked about going to the football game tonight, but, well, with the weather this bad, I thought maybe we could go another time."

"Sure. If you really want to."

"I do. And I'm sorry about canceling on such short notice. Especially considering what day it is."

Their four-week anniversary. As if that really mattered.

"In fact," he continued, "I was going to surprise you with dinner reservations at M Restaurant. You can see the Scioto River from the terrace. But now . . ."

But now his sister needed him. And tomorrow he'd be with Jonah.

Not that he needed any excuses. He had gotten too involved with her, made too many plans. Now he wanted out. Maybe he was angrier about the amethyst ring than he let on. Or maybe he was just tired of being with Miss Nice.

"You still there?"

"Yeah, sorry." She forced lightness into her voice. "I hope everything is okay with Amy."

"If it had been anyone else . . ."

"Don't worry about it. I understand."

"You're a gem, you know that?"

"Actually, this works out. Something came up for me too."

"Not a date with someone else, I hope."

She lightly laughed but didn't answer.

"Is it?"

"Not really. Just plans with a friend." Which wasn't a lie if she hung out with Shelby.

"I didn't realize you knew anyone else from around here."

"There's a lot about me you don't know."

"But I want to." A voice sounded in the background, probably his assistant. "Listen, I need to go. Talk to you later, okay?"

"Okay. Bye." She hung up the phone and gazed out the kitchen window. Rain obscured the fence on the far side of the driveway, but a variety of flowers and plants grew there thanks to Shelby's green thumb and hard work.

Shelby loved Misty Willow because her ancestors had cleared the land and built this house. They had hidden slaves, protected them, and helped them on their journeys.

Dani had been here only a few weeks, but she loved it too. Somehow she connected with the peace of this place. So different than the upheaval of her childhood, the squalor of her stepdad's home. She'd worked and studied hard to escape that turmoil.

But the claws reached for her, threatening to pull her back into a life of struggle, with little sunlight or nourishment for growth.

She wouldn't let them. She couldn't.

Brett was right. If she wanted to pursue her dreams, she needed to go where that dream could be pursued.

New York. LA.

But the thought of venturing to such bustling cities made her shiver. Deep in her heart, she wasn't sure that's what she wanted. Not really.

At the banquet, Brett had said he'd rather be a big fish in a small pond than a minnow in the sea. She understood that. In the movie meccas, she'd be a tiny voice amidst thousands of other tiny voices. Her chances of success weren't great.

There had to be a different way. Somewhere she belonged. A place that belonged to her.

Maybe Boise was that place. She could call her friend Jeanie, see if the position was still open. And even if it wasn't, she could take Jeanie up on her invitation to come out for a visit. Send out more résumés and begin a new life away from this place. Away from Brett.

Sighing, she pocketed the phone, composed her features, and returned to the dining room. Shelby had stacked several photo albums and scrapbooks on the table. She looked up as Dani entered, but her smile quickly faded.

"What's wrong?"

Dani mustn't have been as composed as she thought. "Nothing really. That was Brett."

"And?"

"Amy wants to see him this evening. He couldn't very well say no."

"Is she okay?"

"He didn't say, and I didn't ask. He doesn't really like to talk about her."

"Then spend the evening with us. It'll be fun."

"Maybe I will. Right now, though, I want to look through your albums. Hear more stories."

For a couple of hours, and with only minor interruptions from Tabby, Dani took notes and asked questions as Shelby talked about Isaac Wyatt, a long-ago ancestor who fought in the American Revolution. When Ohio land was set aside for veterans as part of the Virginia Military District, he claimed his homestead. In 1842, Isaac's great-grandson James cleared out a site a few hundred yards from the original house and built this brick one. The original wooden house was eventually torn down and its wood used for the outbuildings.

When Elizabeth arrived home from school, Shelby declared snack time. "I'm done for the day," she said. "How about you, Dani?"

"I think I'll go . . ." She paused, stumbling over the word *home.* "I'll go back to the cottage and review my notes while everything's still fresh in my mind."

"Will you come back later? We'd really love for you to."

"Maybe I will." *Though I'd have so much more fun curled up in a chair feeling sorry for myself.*

She gathered her things and slipped into her jacket. At least the downpour had lessened into a light rain.

"I know I've said it before, but I'm so thankful you're here," Shelby said as they walked to the door. "I can't imagine trying to pull all this information and research together without your help."

"I love doing it."

"There's another reason I'm glad you're here."

"What's that?"

"Because of Brett. He needs you."

"I'm not sure Brett needs anyone."

"But he does. I wonder if you don't need him too."

Shelby's soft voice cut through the heaviness of Dani's thoughts and whirled inside her heart. Could that be true? Did she and Brett need each other?

"We're just friends."

"AJ tells me Brett has never spent as much time with any 'friend' as he has with you."

"Only because he's lonely."

"He may be. But believe me, he has whatever today's equivalent of a little black book is that would put Don Juan to shame." Shelby touched Dani's arm. "If he's spending this much time with you, it's because he wants to. You mean more to him than you know. Probably more than he knows."

Twenty-four hours ago, Dani would have grabbed Shelby's words and hugged them to her heart. She might not have truly believed them, but she would have hoped in them.

But not now.

Meghan had come back into Brett's life, dangling a visit with Jonah like a brass ring on a carousel. Brett had grasped for it with both hands. And rightly so. Seeing Jonah was his deepest wish. One she had wished she could make happen for him.

How could she blame him for forgetting about their Saturday plans? For breaking the anniversary date he'd made so much of?

Unless . . . what if he wasn't really seeing Amy tonight? What if he was seeing Meghan instead?

That made so much more sense. Last she knew, Amy wasn't returning his phone calls and wanted him to stay out of her business. But all of a sudden, she'd called and Brett was running to her side? It didn't seem likely.

"I've got to go," she said suddenly, forcing a smile.

"The invitation is still open. Come for supper if you want. Nothing fancy, but it'll be fun."

"Thanks, I'll let you know." With a quick good-bye to the girls,

Dani pulled the jacket over her head and raced to the car. When she got inside, she wiped the rain from her face.

But not the tears.

There was no way to stop their aching sting.

Brett himself had said she reminded him of Meghan. She'd been the second fiddle all along, the poor substitute. The one he hung around with while he waited for Meghan to come back to him.

Of course she would. Despite their history, he was the father of their child. Handsome. Wealthy.

Money could buy a lot of forgiveness.

And Brett was willing to give Meghan anything she wanted for the chance to be with his son.

Dani didn't have a chance.

Again, she asked herself—when had she wanted one?

erched on a stool at the restaurant's bar, Brett glanced at his watch and quietly fumed. He should have expected Tracie to keep him waiting. But fifteen minutes?

He'd rather be with Dani. Not only was that not happening, he'd even lied to her about getting a phone call from Amy. He should have insisted on meeting with Tracie earlier. Then he and Dani still could have gotten together. But Tracie, a come-hither purr in her voice, named the time and the place. Whether from guilt or because he didn't want her to back out, he'd agreed. Now he only wanted to get this over with and go home.

As he sipped his soda, his attention was drawn to the foyer.

Tracie. Making her grand entrance. Looking like she'd just stepped from the pages of an upscale fashion magazine.

He stood, momentarily unable to curb his admiration for her luscious beauty or the pride swelling in his chest that this gorgeous blonde was here to meet him. The jealous stares of the other men in the place created a palpable energy.

"Darling," she whispered in his ear as she kissed his cheek. Her intoxicating perfume swirled around him. "I've missed you."

"Then why didn't you call?" he said, then wished he hadn't.

He needed to say what he came to say then leave. He swiveled the stool so she could join him at the bar.

"Because then I would have lost."

"Lost?"

"I know how you are with your little games." She shifted slightly, purposefully, displaying her gorgeous cleavage. "But I have a few games of my own."

"First one to call . . ."

"Loses."

"So that makes you the winner?"

"I guess we'll see."

Strange how empty and vacuous she suddenly appeared to him. The beauty faded into an overly made-up mask. The body that had once enchanted him no longer held any appeal. It had no heart.

Though neither did he. At least not where Tracie was concerned.

"I'm not here to play games."

"Oh." She drew out the word, then gazed at him beneath her heavily mascaraed lashes. "Why are you here?"

"I thought we should talk."

"My ears are all yours. And anything else you want."

He ignored the obvious double entendre and heavily exhaled. "You're not going to believe this."

"Try me."

"I found a ring in my apartment." He held it out to her.

"My birthstone?" She eagerly snatched the ring, then pushed it onto her finger. "I thought I'd lost it."

The way she grabbed the ring, as if it was a long-lost family heirloom, snapped at Brett's already taut nerves.

"It may be your birthstone," he said, "but technically it's my ring."

"You aren't planning to give it to someone else, are you?"

"What do you think?"

She extended her arm and admired the ring. "I think it's beautiful. And it will always remind me of you."

"Because you bought it with my money."

"I bought a lot of things with your money."

"That's not the point."

"Then what is?"

He opened his mouth, then closed it again. An argument was the last thing he wanted. A similar thought must have been going through Tracie's mind. She softened her expression and pressed her fingers against his arm.

"I've missed you, Brett. Remember what it was like, the two of us dancing at all those charity events?" She slid her fingers into his hand. "We were always the most attractive couple, you and me."

"I'm not here to reminisce," he said, keeping his voice as even as possible. He couldn't explain why, but her fingers felt wrong against his. An impossible fit. He eased his hand away.

Tracie's eyes narrowed, and the fine lines around her mouth tensed. "Why did you want to meet me?"

He took a moment before answering. This conversation had already gone places he hadn't intended and reflected an ugly side of himself he'd rather ignore. But he couldn't be that person—not anymore. "I want to apologize."

She arched her elegantly shaped eyebrow. "I see. For what exactly?"

"For how I behaved. For ending things without telling you why. I'm . . . I'm sorry."

She leaned against the back of the stool, arms folded across her chest. "Who told you?"

"Told me what?"

"Was it Minerva?" She snorted. "She probably told Zach and he told you. Is that right?"

His mind tried and failed to fill in the missing pieces. "I have no idea what you're talking about."

"Fine. We'll play it your way. After your little 'I'm Ohio's most eligible bachelor' interview went viral, I did an interview of my own. With the *Weekly Blast*. Are you familiar with it?"

"It's the local equivalent of the *National Enquirer*. So what?"

"So they're going to run a story all about the *real* Brett Somers. The one who sexually harasses his employees then fires them."

"You know that's not what happened."

She gave a slow, deliberate shrug. "People believe what they want."

"If they print that story, I'll sue for libel."

"They're used to dealing with you corporate types, and they love to be threatened." A callous smile stretched her lips. "The story will be that much better. And no matter how strongly you deny my allegations, they'll still be out there."

"You're crossing a line, Tracie."

"And you didn't?" Her eyes suddenly reddened. "I thought we had a future together."

"Why would you have thought that?"

"Oh, I don't know. Maybe because you gave me a credit card. Told me to go shopping."

"An arrangement I've had with almost every woman I've ever dated."

"It was different with us."

"No. It wasn't."

"You can't mean that."

He didn't respond. There was nothing else to say.

She sighed heavily, then stood. "Never contact me again."

Her departure wasn't nearly as confident as her arrival. Guilt tightened its hold on Brett's gut, and then anger.

Anger at his own arrogance.

Perhaps Tracie's interview was God's punishment for his sins. The consequences of his actions. At least now he knew it was coming, a tornado on the horizon.

For the second time in just a few hours, Dani braved the rain to drive to Misty Willow. After a long cry and a hot shower, the thought of a lonely Friday night in the quiet cottage unnerved her. It didn't help when lightning streaked across the long row of windows or claps of thunder boomed just outside the walls. So when Shelby called to ask her over again, she jumped at the chance. She even said yes to spending the night after learning the bridge between the cottage and Shelby's road sometimes flooded.

The girls greeted her with gleeful squeals, pulling her to their room as soon as she'd taken off her jacket and wet shoes.

"We're going to have a slumber party," Elizabeth said. "In front of the TV. So Mommy said you could sleep in our room if you wanted."

"Choose my bed, my bed." Tabby jumped up and down with excitement.

"Or sleep with us." Elizabeth pulled Dani across the hall to the living room and pointed to rolled-up sleeping bags piled by the couch. "Those are for Tabby and me, but you can sleep on the couch."

Shelby entered the room with a tray of fresh veggies, chips, assorted crackers, and a steaming baking dish.

"That smells delicious," Dani said.

"It's a dip recipe I got from Cassie Owens: bacon, cheese, and jalapeño. We'll save the popcorn for later." Shelby scooted the girls to their room to change into pajamas, and Dani helped lay out the snacks on the unusual coffee table. Thick planks stained a deep espresso rested on four immovable iron wheels. It fit the décor of the room perfectly, an upscale country style. The mason jar holding Brett's flowers would look perfect on it.

No more thinking about Brett.

Before long, everyone settled on the couch with snacks and comfy afghans as the storm raged outside. Lila stretched in front of the unlit fireplace, her nose resting peacefully on her forelegs.

Elizabeth and Tabby selected the first movie, an animated story about bees that Dani hadn't seen before. With the girls snuggling on either side of her in the dimly lit room, she relaxed into the moment. Tabby's feet pressed into her thighs, but she didn't care. She craved times like this, a family gathered together on a stormy night, not doing anything memorable.

Except creating another warm and fuzzy memory of happy times.

She'd once known moments like this. On wintry evenings, she and Mom had curled up together for movie nights, feasting on freshly baked cookies and sipping steaming cups of hot chocolate covered with marshmallows. But those special together times ended when Mom married. It seemed all the little traditions she'd shared with Mom changed when her stepdad moved in. She didn't mind at first—in fact, she was ecstatic to finally have a dad. They had new traditions like pancakes on Saturday mornings and walking to the ice cream stand on Sunday afternoons for a double-dip cone.

Until Mom died. He'd been lost without her and found solace in all the wrong ways. Soon he became someone Mom wouldn't have recognized.

Near the middle of the second movie, Tabby squirmed and cuddled closer. Dani put her arm around the little girl's shoulder and stroked her hair. "That feels nice," Tabby murmured sleepily.

Dani silently agreed. Nice to be here on a stormy night. Nice to be sandwiched between two fun little girls. Nice to belong, even if only for a little while.

36

Brett took a deep breath, then slowly opened the hospital door.

"Come on in," Shelby said quietly.

Taking another deep breath, he walked softly toward the bed. The little boy lying in it looked almost lost beneath the covers and the tubes. His sandy hair needed a trim, and his long dark lashes brushed his pale cheeks.

Shelby stood on the other side of the bed. "Let me introduce you to your son. This is Jonah." She leaned down and whispered in the boy's ear. "Jonah, your daddy is here. He wants to say hello."

Brett glanced at her, unsure what he should do. What he should say. She gave him an encouraging nod. With one finger, he brushed the bangs from his son's forehead.

His son.

"Hi, Jonah," he said quietly. "How have you been, buddy? You know, you've been here a long time. Too long. But I know you're going to get better. And when you do, we're going to have so much fun. We can go fishing with your Uncle AJ. Would you like to do that? Or we can go to a football game. Watch the Buckeyes beat Michigan."

His throat caught, and he swiped his hands over his eyes. He'd thought he had it made, living a life that was the envy of his peers.

Trading one beautiful woman for another. Free to make his own decisions, to live life on his terms.

But this is what he had missed. The chance to be a father to a little boy who was growing up without one. Except for that reprobate Meghan had taken up with. He'd proved not to be any kind of dad.

Bile swirled in his gut, and his face tightened.

"What is it?" Shelby asked.

"Just thinking of Meghan's husband. What I'd like to do—"

"You mean her *ex*-husband."

"Doesn't matter. It's his fault Jonah's lying here." His voice caught again. "You'd think she'd have been more careful about who she married."

"And who she slept with." Shelby's words, laced with a touch of sarcasm, punched the air from Brett's lungs.

If anyone was to blame, it was him.

He avoided Shelby's gaze by staring at Jonah. Meghan's drunken ex had walked away from the horrific accident that put Jonah in this coma. Barely a scratch on him. While Jonah . . . And yet it needn't have happened.

Shelby reached across the bed and gripped his hand. "I'm sorry I said that, Brett. You have every right to be mad. Just don't be mad at Meghan."

"I deserved it." He blew out a breath, trying to get his emotions under control. "If I'd been a better man . . ." His voice broke, and he swallowed hard. "I . . ." He shrugged his shoulders, not wanting to shock Shelby with the word he'd almost said. "I seduced her. I let Sully bully her and I let AJ take the blame. And I hardly gave her another thought until AJ found her."

He couldn't keep the tears at bay any longer. "I'm responsible for this." He spat the words past the lump choking him. "God forgive me, this is all my fault."

Arms against the rail, he bent his head, not sure he could have stood without the bed's support.

Immediately Shelby was by his side, one hand resting on his arm, the other rubbing his back.

"I just want Jonah to be okay," he said huskily.

"I know. It's what we all want."

"You've been praying."

"Every day."

"Then why isn't God listening to your prayers?"

"He's listening."

"But not doing anything."

"It seems that way, I know. But look at how God has protected Jonah."

"Protected him?"

"Jonah could have died in that accident. But he didn't. And it wasn't a coincidence that AJ found Meghan when she needed him most. Because of that, Jonah is getting the best possible care." Her eyes pleaded with him to understand. He wanted to, but a giant stone blocked his heart.

"Even if the worst happens, we'll all know that everything that could be done for Jonah was done. Neither you nor Meghan will be haunted by that."

"He looks so small."

Shelby gave him a half hug. "He has your eyes."

Brett's glance darted to her, then back to Jonah. "How do you know?"

"Meghan told me. The very same blue."

"Really?"

"Um-hm. She told me she'd forgotten how much he looked like you till you came to the hospital that first time. It panicked her."

"Why?"

"You've got money. To hire attorneys. To give Jonah things she can't. All she has is him." She gestured toward the small boy, then smoothed his blanket. "She's afraid you'll take him. That's why she's kept you away."

"What changed her mind?"

"If I had to guess, I'd say Aaron. He has a very high opinion of you." Her lips curved into a mischievous grin. "I don't know why."

Brett straightened and arched his back. "What can I tell you? He knew me before I became the world's biggest jerk."

"I met him again this morning. He seems a bit smitten."

"That's not a word you hear every day."

"But it fits."

"What about Meghan?"

"She definitely likes him. But I think she's too worried about Jonah to be interested in a relationship."

"Aaron's a good man. Better than me." He rotated his shoulders and paced the room, suddenly restless. Returning to the bed, he gripped the rails. "Do you think it's true what the Bible says? That part about the sins of the father being visited upon the children?"

"You know that verse?"

He ignored the question. "I pretty much followed in my dad's footsteps. Except I didn't make the mistake of marrying someone first." He gestured toward Jonah. "If he grows up to be like me . . ."

"We're all influenced by our childhoods." Shelby looked thoughtful, again as if she were weighing her words, wanting to say the right thing. "But we still make our own choices."

"You think I can be someone different? Like AJ?"

She smiled broadly, her eyes shining at the mention of AJ's name. His cousin was lucky to be loved so deeply. "Why don't you just try being the best of Brett?"

"Sounds like a top ten list."

"Jonah needs someone to look up to. Even if his first years have been difficult, that doesn't mean it's too late for you to be a significant part of his life. To be the dad he desperately needs."

Brett stared at his son, letting Shelby's encouraging words glide over the stone in his heart, melting it with their warmth. His life could have been so different. He could have been a dad coming home every day to a woman he adored, the mother of his children. Now he'd never have that. At least not with Meghan and

Jonah. But Shelby was right. That didn't mean he couldn't have a relationship with them. That he couldn't be part of Jonah's life from here on out.

At least Meghan was giving him that chance. And maybe she'd give Aaron a chance too.

"All I want is to be his dad. The best dad I can be."

"I know."

"And maybe someone's . . . special someone." The word *husband* wouldn't slide past his lips. He wasn't sure he was ready for that yet.

"Oh?" Curiosity lengthened the simple syllable.

"Must be something in the air. I think I'm feeling a little smitten myself."

"With Dani?"

"What do you think of her?"

"I like her. She's hardworking. Has a lot of creativity and vision. Plus she's fun to be with."

"Was she at your house when I called yesterday?"

"I was telling her my family history."

"Did she, you know, talk about me?"

"That would be breaking the girl code."

"Come on. We're family. Almost. What did she say?"

For a few seconds, Shelby stared at the monitors, then seemed to make up her mind what to tell him. "She thinks you spend time with her because you're lonely."

Brett's eyes widened, and he poked his chest with his finger. "Me? She thinks I'm lonely?"

"Not the case, huh?"

"I've got a list this long"—he held out his arms—"of gorgeous young women who are just waiting to see my name pop up on their cell phone screens. Lonely."

"You do have a high opinion of yourself." Shelby shook her head but smiled. "Anyway, I told her the same thing. Though not in those words."

"So she thinks she's doing me a favor? I can't believe this."

"Quit being a baby. She didn't mean it like that."

"Then how did she mean it?"

"Confession. I was being nosy."

"And?"

"Maybe playing matchmaker." She scrunched up her features. "Just a little."

"I don't need your help finding a girlfriend."

"I just want to see you happy. And you know you're not going to be as long as you're running around with women like Tracie."

"So you think I can be happy with Dani?"

"You're different when you're with her. More at ease and, I don't know, relaxed maybe."

"Did you tell her that?"

"I told her I thought God brought the two of you together. You've got to admit it's kind of strange the way you met."

"True." He thought back to that night at the hospital, and how much had changed since then. He never would have believed that he'd actually be here with Jonah instead of staring up at the colored lights. "I've been praying. Or at least trying to. I don't always know what words to say."

"Just say the words that are in your heart."

"You make it sound so easy."

"That's because it is. God is always listening."

"Maybe to you. But I've probably broken every commandment there is."

"I've broken commandments too."

"Not like me."

"It's not a contest, Brett. It's a relationship."

"I'd do whatever God wanted if he'd save my son."

"God's son already paid the ultimate price to save you. And Jonah."

Her words caught him up short. He'd been to church often enough as a kid to have heard the sermons, to know the basics.

But none of the preaching or teaching had affected him as much as Shelby's comeback. For the first time, he was struck by the magnitude of what God had done all those centuries ago.

Could he have done what God did? Sacrificed his only son to save someone else?

Never.

He gazed at the small boy, quiet and still beneath the blanket, and a swell of love threatened to burst his heart. He could barely stand the enormity of what he felt for this child. To think that God's love was even greater. It was unfathomable.

It was true.

"I really am sorry for what I did to Meghan. How I left her alone when she needed someone. And I'm sorry I wasn't there for Jonah."

Unable to trust his voice any longer, Brett stared out the window into the bright morning sky and deeply sighed. To trust in God didn't mean giving up anything that really mattered but discarding his old life for a new one.

One with Jonah, at least as much as Meghan would allow him.

And maybe one with Dani.

She'd been understanding about him breaking their date for today. Even happy for him. But he'd make it up to her and plan something special for next weekend. Something special for his special someone.

- 37 -

ani stood in the foyer of the church, smiling and nodding as she tried to remember the names of everyone Shelby had introduced to her. After leaving Misty Willow on Saturday morning, she'd driven to the university library, muted her phone, and gotten lost in research. When she finally checked her phone, she'd found one missed call from Shelby. And nothing from Brett. Feeling lonely and forlorn, she'd immediately said yes when Shelby invited her to church and dinner.

They were about to enter the sanctuary when someone tapped her elbow.

"Hi, beautiful." Brett's dimpled smile beamed, drawing her into its warmth. "Shelby. AJ."

"Glad you could make it, cuz," AJ said.

"Thanks for inviting me."

Brett asked about Friday night's football game, and Dani faced Shelby, whose attempt to appear nonchalant wasn't working.

"Why didn't you tell me you were asking him too?" Dani whispered.

"Because I didn't want you to back out."

"Did he know I'd be here?"

"AJ talked to him, not me."

As if he heard his name, AJ turned to them. "It's time to go in."

Brett stepped to her side and placed his hand at the small of her back. "Shall we?"

She nodded, and they followed AJ and Shelby to a pew.

Once they were settled, Brett bent toward her. "This is a nice surprise. I didn't know you'd be here."

"I didn't know you'd be here."

"Were you invited to dinner afterward?"

"Yes. You?"

"Yes." He nodded his head toward AJ and Shelby. "Yentas."

She stifled a giggle, then stood with the rest of the congregation in opening prayer. He clasped her hand and whispered, "I've already found my perfect match."

His stomach full after a Sunday dinner of roast beef, fingerling potatoes, and a large tossed salad, Brett perched on the porch railing, his back against the wooden column, while AJ lounged on the swing. The first of the falling leaves dotted the long front lawn, and chrysanthemums bloomed along the fencerow.

"You should have seen the bouquet I gave Dani," Brett said. "I helped the florist choose the flowers. I've never done that before."

AJ looked at him skeptically. "Are you sure you're my cousin?"

"It's crazy, I know. But the usual roses just didn't seem right for Dani."

"So *you* created the bouquet."

"I just selected what I thought Dani would like. And she loved it."

"Wish I could have seen it," AJ said drily.

"She took pictures."

"Naturally. That's what women do."

"They're on her camera." He suddenly stood. "Which she left in my car. I'll show you."

"No need to do that, cuz."

"I can't have you doubting my floral-picking skills." Brett puffed out his chest, then hurried around the side of the house to where his Lexus was parked. As he returned to the porch, he removed the camera from its case and turned it on. The last photo Dani had taken of the bouquet appeared on the screen. He handed the camera to AJ.

"See?"

AJ examined the photo. "Gotta admit. You did good." He flipped the screen a few times, then stopped. "She's taken photos around the cottage too. These are really nice."

"Let me see." Brett took the camera and looked at a couple of the photos. "My girl's got talent."

"Your girl?"

"As long as she agrees." Brett flipped past a few more photos, then stared at the screen. A hot ember flared as he looked at the previous one and the one before that. His face burned and his hands shook so that he almost dropped the camera.

"I don't believe this," he muttered.

"What's the matter?"

Brett handed AJ the camera, then ran both hands through his hair. It couldn't be.

"Is this you?" AJ's gaze was intent on the small screen.

"It's me."

"Where are you?"

"The hospital." She'd taken his photograph outside the hospital. Recorded his image during one of the lowest moments of his life.

Why?

His thoughts flashed back to that night, the night he'd given Aaron a birthday gift for Jonah. Dani had watched it all, photographed it all.

Including his anguish.

She had to see he had been in pain. But she'd taken his picture anyway.

And never told him.

Shelby's words to Dani flashed through his mind. *I don't think it's a coincidence you and Brett were at the hospital at the same time.*

No, apparently not.

Taken in by Dani's innocent girl façade, he'd trusted her. Provided for her. And she'd never said a word.

And then there was the ring. He'd accepted her story of innocently pocketing it out of embarrassment. But now he wondered. Sure, she returned it. But who knew what motivated the girl.

She'd lied.

Lied about her job at the station. Lied about why she was at the hospital. Even lied about her name when they first met.

"I don't get it, Brett." AJ's voice pounded into his thoughts. "Why did she take these?"

"I don't know." He grabbed the camera and stared at each photo again, burning their images into his brain. Anger built with each one until he couldn't contain it any longer. "But I'm going to find out."

He entered the front hall and checked the living room. Empty. He turned, intent on finding Dani. AJ blocked his way.

"What are you going to do?"

"Move, AJ."

"Not till you get control of yourself."

Brett shoved past him and headed through the hall to the kitchen, AJ hurrying behind. Dani sat at the kitchen table while Shelby put the finishing touches on a chocolate-frosted cake.

Seeing the camera in his hands, Dani's eyes grew round and she slowly rose. She opened her mouth to speak, but no words came out.

"What's going on?" Shelby asked as AJ placed a protective arm around her waist.

"Maybe we should leave them alone."

"No," Brett said. "She's lied to all of us. We deserve an explanation."

"Lied?" Shelby said, incredulous. "About what?"

Brett glared at Dani, steeling his heart against the fear and pain showing in her lovely brown eyes. When he spoke, his tone was hard and unyielding. "Why were you at the hospital that night?"

"I can explain." Dani grabbed for her camera, but he held it out of her reach.

"We're listening."

"I . . . I followed you there." Tears welled in her eyes, and she seemed uncertain what to do with her hands. Finally she crossed her arms in a tight hold.

"You *followed* me?"

She bit her lip and nodded.

"I don't understand—" Shelby began, but AJ shushed her.

"I didn't know you were going to the hospital," Dani said, her voice threatening to break at any moment.

"You took pictures of me." Brett's voice dripped with accusation. "You lied to me again and again and again."

He smashed the camera against the table.

"Stop!"

"Why did you take those photos?"

"Give me my camera."

"Not till you give me some answers. Why did you do it?".

Her face contorted from shock to anger. "To sell them."

The words, colder than ice water, smacked into him. He couldn't have heard her right. That was something Tracie would do. But not Dani. "To . . . what?"

"I needed the money." Her voice teetered on the edge of panic.

"I don't believe you."

She reached for the camera again, but he was quicker. He slammed it against the table again, then threw it to the floor.

Broken pieces and the shattered lens skittered across the tile. He was vaguely aware of Dani dropping to her knees with a painful moan. Part of him wanted to gather her up, tell her he was sorry. But her angry words snaked through his head and tied him in knots.

He needed time to think, time to let his anger ease. As he pushed through the kitchen's screen door, he glimpsed Dani, still kneeling on the floor and gathering the broken pieces of the camera.

She might as well have been picking up the pieces of his heart.

He strode up the lane and past the excavation area. Wrong choice, because even this place held memories he now wanted to forget.

She was supposed to be the one good thing in his life. Somehow Meghan's animosity and Amy's issues hadn't pressed against him quite as hard with Dani to think about, to spend time with, to tease.

But his affection for her, his concern for her, even his desire for her, had been built on deceit.

Besides, everything Dani had right now she owed to him—her job, a place to live.

How could she have done this to him? Was it some kind of sick game?

He bent over, hands on knees, and breathed heavily.

A game.

Not much different than the game he'd played with countless women over the past several years. He remembered the hurt in Tracie's eyes the last time he saw her. He had discounted the pain because he didn't believe it. She had never really loved him, he was sure of it. Only his name, his good looks, and his bank account.

But his callousness at the end had still hurt her.

He plopped onto the ground at the edge of the cornfield, forearms resting on his knees. The world seemed topsy-turvy, his happy-go-lucky life turned inside out. First with Meghan and Jonah, then with Amy, and now with Dani.

What was he supposed to do?

His phone buzzed, and he glanced at the screen. AJ. He ignored the call.

What Dani said didn't make sense. If she'd taken the photos to sell them, why hadn't she?

There had to be another reason she'd followed him to the hospital that night. Watched him. Stalked him.

She must have been proud of herself for snaring him into a date. Then another and another.

But why?

Was it her plan all along for him to fall for her? And then what? Sell her story to the local tabloids? Maybe Dani was more like Tracie than he wanted to believe.

A sour ache clenched his gut.

Well, if that was Dani's scheme, she'd played her cards like a pro. He'd never even seen it coming. Not from a slip of girl unlike any woman he'd ever dated.

She had somehow managed, with her supposed innocence and naivety, to sneak through his defenses and into his heart. He'd been so busy trying to look out for her, to help her, he'd been oblivious to her stealth.

What a fool he'd been.

He sat there awhile longer, letting his angry thoughts swirl into a confused mass that seemed impossible to untangle.

A few months ago, he'd had life all figured out. But this summer had brought nothing but trouble. From AJ. From Amy. From Tracie. And now Dani.

He wanted his old life back, the one where he was in control, the one where he didn't get hurt.

The one where he hurt others.

A roar gathered in his stomach and pushed through his throat, but he refused to give it voice. Instead he smacked the hard-packed dirt with the side of his fist as grief and anger contorted his face.

A sound behind him caught his attention, and he looked around just in time to stop Lila from pouncing on him. A few feet away, Elizabeth stood, her feet rooted in the dirt path as if she were a statue. Her eyes, large and uncertain, stared at him.

To keep Lila from licking his face, he stood and brushed his pants, then managed a smile. "Hi, sunshine." His voice sounded weak and pitiful, and he took several deep breaths. "Your mom send you after me?"

She silently shook her head, then took a few steps toward him.

"I saw you," she said as a large tear glistened on her delicate cheek. "Why are you so sad?"

"Come here." When he stretched out his arms, she ran to him, and he inhaled the sweet fragrance of a soap-scrubbed youngster.

Elizabeth wrapped her arms around his neck. "Did I do something to make you sad?"

"No, sweetheart. No." He adjusted the way he held her and gazed into her elfin face. "Of course you didn't."

"Who did?"

Instead of answering, he hugged her close.

Dani did. Dani made him sad. And he wasn't sure he could forgive her. But the pain he felt went deeper than her deceit.

He was sad because of who he'd become over the years. His pride, his arrogance, his indifference to others had brought him to this place where everything in his life was turned upside down.

"I could sing you a song," Elizabeth said as he set her feet on the ground. She tightly gripped his hand as if afraid to let him go. "Would that make you happy?"

"It might." The sound of a car engine caught his attention. Someone was leaving, probably Dani.

Good riddance.

Elizabeth tugged at his hand.

"What are you going to sing?"

Instead of answering, she sang the chorus to "You Are My Sunshine." Not really a surprise, since he often sang the song to her and Tabby.

"Don't you want to sing too?" she asked when she finished.

"Not today." All he wanted was to go home. Lie on his couch. Forget the photos he'd seen.

"I know something else."

"What's that?" The photos. His anguish hit him again.

"'I trusted in the Lord when I said, "I am greatly afflicted."'"

He was lost in his thoughts, and Elizabeth's solemn recitation scarcely registered. "Say that again."

"'I trusted in the Lord when I said, "I am greatly afflicted."'"

"What is that? Do you even know what *afflicted* means?"

She glared at him. "Sad."

"Why do you know that?"

"My Sunday school teacher where we used to live told it to me. After Daddy died. She helped me remember it so I'd be close to God when I cried."

"It's a Bible verse?"

"Psalm 116:10. You should memorize it."

Brett's thoughts slipped back to the days surrounding his parents' deaths. The news reporters, the sensationalism. All the wrong things people said—meaning well, he supposed, though back then he had no patience for anyone's grief but his own. They didn't understand, they couldn't understand.

Elizabeth had been, what? Four or five when her father was killed. Did the words even exist for telling a child that young that she'd never see her dad again?

"You miss your dad, don't you?"

Elizabeth focused on something beyond him and nodded.

"Can you teach me that verse?"

She smiled slightly and repeated the Scripture. Brett said it after her, then they said it together.

Trust.

He'd never trusted anyone but himself. Until he met Dani. But she'd been as deceitful as any of the other women he'd dated. Worse even.

His conscience squirmed. Maybe not worse. But different. Her deceit had been different, and that somehow made it worse. With the others, he'd suspected their false motives from the start. But Dani had appeared so innocent. It was like she had an unfair advantage.

Like the unfair advantage he'd always had when he started his countdown clock to a breakup.

Trust in the Lord.

Easy to say. Almost impossible to do.

"Did it help?" he asked Elizabeth. "Saying that verse."

"Most of the time. I prayed Daddy would come back, but he didn't." She picked a wild daisy from a nearby clump and absentmindedly pulled the petals off, one by one. "I thought I'd be afflicted forever."

Brett knelt beside her and covered her hands with his to keep her from destroying any more petals. "What's bothering you, Elizabeth?"

Her chameleon eyes, more blue than brown today, searched his as if wondering if she could trust him.

That word again.

Trust.

Maybe this was where it had to begin . . . with being worthy of a seven-year-old's trust.

"You can tell me, sweetheart. No matter what it is."

She swallowed hard as if making up her mind. "Is it bad to be happy that I'm getting a new daddy?"

"Of course not." He gently tucked a strand of hair behind her ear. "You love AJ, don't you?"

"More than this." She stretched her arms wide, and the flower stem dropped to the ground.

"He loves you too." He put his face close to hers so they were almost nose to nose, then lowered his voice. "And so do I."

She threw her arms around his neck. "I love you too, Uncle Brett." She placed a kiss on his cheek, then ran down the graveled drive with Lila loping beside her.

Brett straightened, his thoughts swirling as Elizabeth hopped on her bicycle. Even at his darkest moments, bowed to his knees with worry over Jonah, he'd resisted the temptation to bargain with God. Somehow he sensed that a God who was no more than a business partner, a heavenly entity open to negotiations, wasn't much of a God at all.

Yet it seemed that the more he tried to be a good person, some-one who Jonah—and even the little monsters—could be proud of, things had only gotten worse. Amy was a mess. And Dani . . . He shook his head. He didn't want to think about Dani.

I trusted in the Lord when I said, "I am greatly afflicted."

It sounded so simple. So why was it so hard?

He wandered to the stone circle and plopped in a lawn chair. A few minutes later, Shelby and AJ came through the screen door.

"It's Meghan," Shelby called as she hurried to him and thrust her phone into his hand. "Such good news. Talk to her."

The world seemed to slow as he put the phone to his ear. "Meghan?"

"He's awake, Brett. Jonah's awake."

Brett bowed his head, pressing the phone against his chest as he concentrated on breathing. AJ clapped his back. "Great news, cuz."

Brett nodded, then lifted the phone again. "When can I . . . is it possible . . . ?"

"This afternoon, if you want. Shelby and AJ are coming. I'm not sure he'll still be awake, and even if he is, it may only be for a moment, but, I'm so happy and I just . . . I need someone to celebrate with me."

"We'll be there soon, Meghan. Thank you." He cleared his throat. "Thank you."

He handed the phone to Shelby, then bent over, hands on his knees. This was what he wanted more than anything else in the world. But somehow the world was still off-kilter.

– 38 –

*D*ani dropped the broken camera into the chair, then curled up on the sofa in a tight ball. The anger and pain she'd seen in Brett's eyes gripped her heart until she thought it would shatter into a million pieces.

She should have told him the truth. But instead, in her shock and anger, she'd spouted another lie, wanting to hurt him as much as he had hurt her by breaking her camera.

Selling the pictures had never been an option. Not really.

What was she supposed to do now?

She half-expected, half-hoped that he would come over. That after his anger subsided, he would want to talk to her. To straighten things out. Perhaps even make up.

But the long minutes turned into dreary hours. And he didn't come.

Spent of tears, she restlessly napped, then woke with a headache. She glanced at her phone, but no one had called.

Not Brett, though that wasn't a surprise.

But not Shelby either. Apparently they weren't such close friends after all. Shelby had seemed shocked by Brett's behavior, even angry on Dani's behalf. But in the end, Brett was family. And Dani wasn't.

She placed the phone on the table and entered the tiny bathroom. After washing her face, she changed into pajama pants and a comfy pullover, then wandered through the cottage. Her time here had been too short, and she wanted to imprint every memory into her heart.

Because she couldn't stay. The refuge, the exciting project—they were over. All because she hadn't told Brett the truth. But then, they never would have been hers if she had.

She needed to decide what to do now. Where to go.

Her options were so few.

She reached for her phone and found Jeanie's name.

"Dani! It's so good to hear from you."

She might as well get right to the point. "I've been thinking about that offer. Is the position still open?"

"Not the sales job, but we have another opening. Nothing glamorous, just basic office work, really."

Office work. If only she'd taken the bank job. Though now that Brett hated her, she couldn't stay in Columbus. It'd be too awful if they accidentally bumped into each other.

"I know it doesn't sound like much," Jeanie continued. "But it's a foot in the door, and with your background I bet you'd be promoted. There's rumors that one of the call screeners will be leaving soon. You'd be good at that."

"Do you think they'll hire me?"

"I already told my boss all about you when that sales job opened up. Please say you'll come, Dani. It'll be so much fun working together."

"How soon can I start?"

"How soon can you get here?"

"Two or three days."

"It can't be too soon for me."

A moment's silence hung between them. The weight of this decision bowed Dani's shoulders. She was so afraid to go, but she was even more afraid to stay.

Jeanie's gentle voice came through the speaker. "What changed your mind?"

"The new job isn't working out so well after all."

"Sounds like there's more to it than that."

"We'll talk when I get there, okay?"

"I can't wait. Promise you'll be careful, and stay in touch. It's a long drive."

"I will. Thanks, Jeanie."

She hung up the phone and plopped on the bed. So much for all her dreams and hopes. Perhaps she wasn't meant for awards or the limelight, but couldn't she at least do something fun? If she wasn't careful, she'd be spending the next ten years in a boring office, her dreams nothing but dust.

Not the legacy her mom would have wanted for her.

But then Mom wasn't around to see whether or not her dreams came true.

Sighing heavily, she rose from the bed, padded to the pub table, and booted up her laptop. For the next couple of hours, she typed and organized her research and a bibliography, then created a PowerPoint presentation of possible photographs for the museum's displays.

Once the documents were printed, she stacked everything in neat piles on the table. Then she changed clothes and drove to town to find enough boxes for her meager belongings. In the morning, she'd return the DVDs and books she'd borrowed to the library on her way out of town.

By Tuesday evening, she'd be with Jeanie. Settling into a new life far away from Brett and Misty Willow.

A new beginning.

One with no lies.

Brett arrived at the hospital before AJ and Shelby, who'd driven separately and dropped the girls off at the Owenses' first. The drive to Columbus had given him time to think, but his thoughts brought him no peace. The good news about Jonah doused his anger but not his hurt.

When he reached the hospital lobby, he debated whether to wait for AJ and Shelby but decided against it. A minute or two alone with Meghan might be just what he needed.

The pretty nurse responded to his smile with one of her own. "I'm here to see Jonah Jensen."

"Your name, please."

"Brett Somers."

She consulted a list. "Ms. McCurry said you'd be coming. Along with a couple of other people."

"They'll be here soon."

"Great. It's room 927."

"I know where it is. Thank you."

Standing outside the door, he took a deep breath, then knocked softly.

"Come in."

He entered, his eyes drawn immediately to Jonah's bed. "Is he really okay?"

"He's really out of the coma. But still sleeping a lot. They say that's normal."

"Normal." He breathed the word.

"He's going to be okay, Brett. In time, he'll be okay."

He raised his eyes to Meghan. "Thanks for letting me come."

"I'm so happy, I want to shout it to the world."

"Me too."

"Where are Shelby and AJ?"

"On their way." He stroked Jonah's arm. "So what happened?"

"He opened his eyes this morning. And then his arms flailed. It scared me, but I called the nurse and, well, that's normal when people come out of a coma. Then a couple of hours ago, he squeezed my hand. He said *Mommy*." Happy tears glistened in Meghan's gray eyes. "I never heard anything so beautiful in my life."

⟪~⟫

The adrenaline rush eased from Meghan's body, and she stifled a yawn. It'd been a long and exciting day. A great day.

Finally her son slept—not in a deep coma but the peaceful sleep of a tired little boy. For the first time in months, perhaps she'd be able to sleep too. Without the help of any pills.

She sank onto the couch and rubbed her hands over her eyes, looking up when the door squeaked open. Brett entered carrying two cans of ginger ale.

"I thought you were going home."

"Me too." He feigned a careless shrug. "But after AJ and Shelby left, I changed my mind. Is that okay?"

"I guess."

"We should celebrate." He held up the cans. "This is the best thing I could find in the vending machines."

"At least it doesn't have caffeine."

"Exactly." He popped a tab, then handed the can to her. "You need to get some rest. Are you staying here tonight?"

"I don't think I'd sleep if I left him."

"Do you need anything? Want anything?"

"Only for Jonah to keep getting better."

"He's going to."

"And then what?"

"What do you mean?"

"What are you going to do? Legally, I mean."

"I just want to be part of his life. That's all."

He lifted the ginger ale to his lips and took a drink. The dimples flattened, then disappeared. But they didn't tug at her heart like they once had. Their quick romance had been the biggest mistake of her life.

And the biggest blessing.

"We could talk about a couple of things," he said.

"What things?"

"For one, where you're going to live when Jonah is released from here."

"I haven't thought that far ahead."

"Don't go back to Michigan. Please." He flashed his dimples. "You've got to raise him a Buckeye."

The playful expression in his eyes eased her tension, and she shook her head. "You and AJ. It's all about OSU."

"You said he liked the monkey."

"I have a life in Brennan Grove, you know. So does Jonah."

"I know it's asking a lot." The playfulness disappeared as he grew serious. "But I am asking you, Meghan. More than asking. I'm begging you. Stay here. Raise him here."

She hadn't given much thought to the future, fearing to make any plans while Jonah was still in his coma. Fearful to face the demands she'd been sure Brett would make. Deep in her heart, she knew he wouldn't want his son to be half a day's drive away.

What did she really have to go back to?

Her little house and studio. Dawn's art gallery. Familiar places. A community she knew.

But the small town hadn't been all roses. And a couple hundred miles between her and Travis wouldn't be a bad thing.

"What are you thinking?" Brett asked quietly.

"Maybe it's time to make a fresh start."

"You mean it?"

"I'm not making a decision tonight. Or even tomorrow. But I'm not sure we could go back even if I wanted to." Jonah's doctor had already hinted that therapy might last several months. It all depended on how much the little guy needed to relearn.

"But you'll consider staying here."

"I'll consider it."

He nodded, seeming to release a heavy weight from his shoulders. It was almost hard to believe this was the same gorgeous man who'd oozed self-confidence as he flirted with her at his grandparents' Christmas party all those years ago. She'd been flattered, excessively so, at his attentions, and imagined herself madly, wildly in love.

But the whirlwind romance had ended as quickly as it had begun, leaving her humiliated, ashamed, and broken. The scheme to ensnare AJ had been the desperate attempt of a frightened and heartsick woman barely out of her teens. She hadn't counted on his grandfather's stepping in to offer a solution. One that gave them both what they wanted.

Sully protected his favorite grandson from scandal. She got more money than she'd ever seen at one time and his promise she could raise her child with no interference from the Sullivan family.

Because despite what Sully told AJ at the time, the money had never been for an abortion. He didn't want his great-grandchild in his life, but he didn't want that life destroyed either.

It was the secret they had shared, only the two of them, and a promise she'd had every intention of keeping.

Until Jonah was injured and AJ walked back into her life.

She'll consider it. For now, it was the best Brett could hope for. He almost wished he loved her, that for Jonah's sake, their story could have a happy-ever-after ending. But real life didn't work like that. Even if he proposed, she'd never accept. The scars of the past ran too deep.

"There's something else I need to tell you," he said.

"What's that?"

"I set up a trust fund for Jonah."

"You didn't need to do that."

"I owe you eight years of back child support."

"You've probably already paid that for his hospital bills."

"You're not supposed to know about that."

Her shoulders sagged as if she were too tired to argue, too weary to do battle. "Is this a bribe so I'll stay in Columbus?"

"It's already done. The money is Jonah's no matter where you live."

"No strings? No conditions?"

"None."

A light chuckle filled the air. He'd forgotten how lovely she sounded when she was amused.

"You're not angry?" he asked.

"We did okay, Jonah and me. At least until things became so awful with Travis. But this"—she waved her hand around the hospital room—"this changed everything. Whether I like it or not, Jonah is a Somers. He should benefit from that."

"I agree."

"You don't think that makes me a money-grubbing social climber? That's what your grandfather called me, you know. He said I wasn't good enough for AJ."

"He had it all wrong. We weren't good enough for you. Neither one of us."

Not back then. AJ had disappeared to sulk, taking too long to make up his mind to fight for Meghan. And Brett, who suspected the truth about Jonah's paternity, took sophomoric joy in watching the relationship between Sully and AJ crumble around them. He'd taken immense pleasure in stepping into AJ's place as the favorite grandson and scarcely thought of what Meghan might be going through.

"But we're here for you now. Anything you need or want."

For the first time the smile Meghan gave him reached her eyes. If the hospital bed hadn't been between them, he might have put his arm around her. Or pulled her into an embrace.

Maybe it wasn't too late for them after all.

The thought sprang up, then as quickly wilted.

The woman he wanted in his arms wasn't in this room.

"Mommy?"

The whispered voice snagged Brett's heart, and he hovered beside the rail. Meghan jumped from the couch and brushed Jonah's hair from his forehead.

"I'm here, sweetheart."

The little boy's eyes flickered, then opened. He gazed into Meghan's eyes and sighed wearily. "Can I pick the color?"

"What color?"

He closed his eyes and took several deep breaths. "The color of the light."

Meghan startled, her gaze flickering to Brett then back to Jonah. "Sure. Which one do you want?"

"Green." The light blue eyes opened again. A hint of a smile touched his lips, and dimples creased his pale cheeks. "My favorite."

"Green it is." Meghan turned on the ambient light, bathing the room in serene tranquility.

Gratitude and wonder lodged in Brett's throat. Finally, he experienced the color instead of observing it through the window like a prodigal observer. Joy overwhelmed him, and his knees buckled.

Thank you, God. Sobs broke past his defenses. *Thank you for saving my son.*

- 39 -

*D*ani stuck her laptop on the floor in front of the passenger seat, then turned to take one last look at the cottage. Nestled into the hillside, it appeared a natural part of this little corner of the world.

Her little corner for too brief a time.

Another disappointed dream but with only herself to blame. She should never have agreed to move into this refuge. Never should have allowed herself to believe she could be happy here. Not when her secret, a ticking time bomb, could explode in her face at any moment.

She'd meant to delete the photos.

But staring at them had allowed her to glimpse the man behind the façade of gorgeous dimples and debonair charm. The man who was slowly revealing his heart to her.

She could never push the delete button for a single image.

And now he hated her.

She slammed the car door harder than she intended. The sound reverberated against the small hillside and into her heart, a harsh and noisy ending to the brief happiness she'd known here.

A long night of crying had spent her tears but left her eyes red and puffy. Hopefully, she could face Shelby without falling apart.

She drove past AJ's bungalow, turned left at the stop sign, and rounded the curve to the Misty Willow homestead.

You don't have to do this. Just keep driving.

The temptation beckoned, but she made the turn into the graveled drive. Brett wouldn't have the satisfaction of thinking her a coward or the opportunity to criticize her for leaving without telling anyone.

Though why did she care what he thought?

Shelby rose from kneeling beside a bed of fading annuals and removed her gloves as Dani parked her car.

"Hey, there," she said. "Are you okay?"

Shelby had called last night, leaving a message, and Dani had responded with a brief text saying she was fine but didn't feel like talking.

"I'm fine."

"About yesterday. Brett knows he—"

"I can't talk about it. Please don't make me."

Shelby nodded, then eyed the box Dani had retrieved from the car. "We weren't supposed to meet this morning, were we? I'm sorry, I must have forgotten."

"No, we weren't meeting." Dani set the box on the picnic table. "I wanted to give you these."

"What are they?"

"My notes, a couple of mock-ups of display ideas. A DVD I bought. Well, you bought. The foundation bought." Her voice faded, and she cleared her throat.

Shelby's eyes flickered over the car filled with boxes and clothes. "Dani—"

"Please. This is hard enough as it is." She fumbled to remove the key ring Brett had given her from her pocket, then handed it to Shelby. "Here's the key to the cottage."

Shelby stared at the key, her expression dumbfounded. "You're leaving? But there's no need for you to."

"I can't stay."

"What did Brett say to you?"

"Nothing." Dani crossed her arms against a sudden chill. "We haven't talked."

"So you don't know about Jonah?"

"Did something happen?"

"It's good news. Meghan called shortly after you left yesterday. Jonah came out of the coma."

"He's going to be okay?"

"They're still running tests, but everything looks positive."

"I'm glad." She was glad. At least she wanted to be glad. But truth be told, Jonah's recovery gave her another reason to leave. Even if Brett and Meghan didn't love each other, they both loved Jonah. The little guy would be first in Brett's thoughts and in his heart for a long time. As he should be. Deserved to be.

She refused to be jealous of an injured child. But the green-eyed monster wasn't so easily dissuaded.

"Why don't you come in? Have a cup of tea, and we'll talk."

Another temptation.

"I need to go."

"I wish you wouldn't."

"It's for the best."

"At least talk to Brett first."

"I don't think he's interested in a chat."

"Then talk to me. I can't believe you were going to sell those photos. That's not who you are."

"You don't really know me, Shelby."

"Maybe not. But I still don't believe it." She grasped Dani's arm, her touch light and comforting. "Why were you at the hospital that night?"

Dani's body tensed and her eyes burned. She bit the inside of her lip, then exhaled a heavy sigh. "I didn't expect to meet him. That was an accident."

"But you knew he was there?"

"I followed him from his office."

309

"To take his picture?"

"Not really."

"Then why?"

"I can't tell you that." Dani's heart pounded against her chest. It all seemed so silly now. Why had she ever thought such a stupid scheme would work? Instead of finding a monster, she'd found a friend. More than that. She found someone she cared about. Maybe even loved. "Turns out he's not the man I thought he was. And I'm sorry for . . . for everything."

"You can't leave here without some kind of explanation."

"Please don't think me ungrateful. You, all of you, have been so kind. But remember that radio station in Boise I told you about? There's an opening there, and I've decided to take it."

"So just like that, you're moving out west?"

"I really have to go. It's a long drive."

"I'm going to call Brett. He needs to—"

"No, Shelby. Please don't."

"But why not?"

"I hurt him. But right now, he's happy about Jonah. Don't spoil that by reminding him of me."

Shelby shook her head, her expression grim. "Is there anything I can say to change your mind?"

"Just promise me you won't call him."

"I promise. But I don't understand."

Unable to say any more, Dani hugged Shelby good-bye and hurriedly slid into the driver's seat. Shelby grabbed at the car door.

"Please stay in touch. I'm praying for you."

Dani responded with a weak smile. She welcomed Shelby's prayers, though she didn't know how much good they would do. Prayer couldn't turn back time or transform Brett's anger into affection.

With tears blurring her vision, she pulled out of the graveled drive and headed for the interstate that would take her west.

Brett spent the day in meetings, negotiating contract terms here, putting out a fire there. Toward the middle of the afternoon, he received a text from Amy asking him to stop by around 6:30. He finished up the current project, then drove to the hospital. Thankfully, the reconciliation with Meghan meant he could see Jonah whenever he wanted.

Before he'd left yesterday evening, they had vowed never to tell anyone how they'd cried together in the corridor outside Jonah's room. The episode had been embarrassing for both of them, but also a release of pent-up emotions that ended in semi-hysterical laughter. Jonah's parents might not be in love with each other, but neither were they bound by suspicion and fear. Not any longer.

Today the Columbus sky seemed bluer, the sun more radiant. Only two dark clouds hung on the horizon.

Amy and whatever she was up to.

And Dani.

He'd think about Amy when he saw her later.

But it wasn't so easy to push Dani from his thoughts. Or his heart.

Now that the initial shock of finding the photos had faded, he regretted his bratty behavior. If nothing else, he owed her a new camera. She'd probably never forgive him for breaking hers.

And he wouldn't blame her. His conduct had been inexcusable.

The memory of her kneeling on the kitchen floor, gathering up the broken pieces, pierced his spirit. Right then, he should have knelt beside her. Begged her forgiveness. Gathered her in his arms.

He wished he had.

– 40 –

*B*rett punched the up button on the elevator in Amy's apartment building and eyed the lights above the door.

"Hey, Brett."

He turned and grinned. "Hey, AJ. What are you doing here?"

"I received a text summons from Princess Amy."

"So did I."

"Any idea what she wants?"

"Couldn't tell you."

The elevator dinged, and they made small talk until they reached Amy's floor. She opened her door a few moments after Brett knocked and greeted him with a kiss on the cheek. Her long blonde hair, freshly washed and brushed to a sheen, hung past her shoulders. The sapphire blue dress she wore enhanced the crystal blue of her eyes. Though still too thin, her body exuded an energy that had been missing since her collapse.

"Who are you and what have you done with my sister?" Brett teased.

"Leave her alone," AJ said, returning Amy's fragile embrace. "You look lovely."

"Thank you." She playfully tugged at the bill of his OSU ball cap. "Take that thing off so I can see your eyes."

"Sorry. I forgot I was wearing it."

"Because you're always wearing it." She ushered them into the apartment. "Fix yourselves something to drink. Whatever you want."

"I'm good," Brett said. "AJ?"

"Nothing for me, either."

"Suit yourselves." She lowered herself into a chair, smoothing the long skirt over her knees. The gauzy fabric covered her once shapely legs. Now her skinny ankles appeared barely sound enough to support her.

"So what's this confab all about, Sis?"

"Maybe I just wanted to spend a little time with my two favorite men."

"We're always your favorite when you want something."

"Don't be so cynical, Brett."

AJ laid his cap on the coffee table, then relaxed into the soft contours of the couch. "Did Brett tell you the good news?"

Her gaze moved lazily from AJ to Brett. He sat opposite her, a leg propped on his knee. She arched an eyebrow. "Tell me."

"Jonah woke up yesterday." Brett's voice quavered, and he cleared his throat. "He's going to be all right."

She stared at him, her expression impassive, then her eyes softened. "I'm glad, Brett. Really I am." Her gaze flickered between him and AJ again. "Look at you both. Only a few months ago, you were independent bachelors. Now you both have children in your lives. Strange how quickly things can change."

"It's a good change," AJ said quietly. "I just wish Gran was still alive to . . ."

"I wish that too." Amy pulled a strand of her hair through her fingers. A habit she'd had since they were children. "Though I doubt she'd be very happy with me right now."

"She loved you," Brett said. "She'd want you to be well."

Amy held up a palm. "No lectures, okay?"

"I can't help it if I'm concerned about you."

"I know. Actually, that's why I asked you to come."

Brett exchanged a glance with AJ. "What do you mean?"

"There's nothing wrong with me. Nothing too serious, anyway."
She jutted out her lower lip, then stared at the large ceramic bowl
centered on the coffee table. After a few moments, she raised her
eyes and smiled. "But since you two won't leave me alone, I've
decided to check into a clinic."

Brett realized he'd been holding his breath and exhaled relief.
Another answered prayer? After all these days of not knowing
what to do, where to turn?

AJ reached for Amy's hand. "This is a big step. I'm proud of you."

"Which one?" Brett asked, his voice still sounding dry and rough.

"It's in Richmond, Virginia."

"I remember reading about that place." He nodded approval.
"When do you go?"

"Now." A wan smile curved her lips. "Before I change my mind."

"Let's do it," Brett said.

"Are you sure? Now that . . ." She heaved a giant sigh. "I'm sorry.
It still seems surreal to me that there's a little Brett Jr. in the world."

"His name is Jonah."

"Does he look like you?"

"He has the Somers eyes."

"Lucky boy."

"I doubt he feels that way."

"That's not what I meant."

"I know it's not. And I know what you're thinking, but you're
wrong." He chuckled. "Well, you're right, but you're also wrong."

"What am I thinking?"

"That I won't take you to Richmond because I won't want to
leave Jonah. You're right that I don't want to leave Jonah. But I'm
still taking you to Richmond. Whenever you want to go."

"Tomorrow morning?"

"Tomorrow morning it is."

"I want to go too," AJ said.

A faint smile curved Amy's lips. "That's sweet of you. But I know you can't leave your students."

"For something like this, I can."

"What about your fiancée?"

"Shelby cares about you, Amy. She only wants to be your friend."

"Maybe when this is all over, when I get back . . ."

"We'll have a cookout at Misty Willow. And you'll be the guest of honor."

"You two really are my favorite men. All the time."

"What about the mysterious state senator?" Brett asked, then wished he hadn't as Amy's expression darkened. Her jaw clenched, and even the angles of her cheekbones sharpened.

"He no longer matters."

"Then tell me who he is."

"Why? It's not like you're going to go beat him up."

"You're right." Brett rubbed his jaw. "I'll send AJ."

"You don't have to send anyone. I've taken care of him."

"How'd you do that?"

"Not with my fists." She flexed her hands, and her dark nails glistened. "Let's just say, he won't be running for office again."

"I thought he had his eyes on a congressional seat."

"He thinks he does. But he'll soon find out differently."

"How can you be so sure?" AJ asked.

"He made the mistake of confiding in me more than he should have. Now he'll either return to life as John Q. Citizen or face jail time."

"You can make that happen?"

"I have powerful friends."

"Guess I better be glad you only hit me with a lawsuit," AJ said.

"I am sorry about that. Though you deserved it."

"Let's pretend that never happened," Brett said. "We've got a long day of driving tomorrow. I'm going to stop by the hospital first, so what time should we plan on leaving?"

They worked out travel arrangements, then Amy walked them

to the door. After AJ said good-bye and stepped into the hall, Brett pulled his sister into a hug.

"I'm scared," she whispered.

"I know. But you're also very brave. Gran would be so proud."

"Will you visit me?"

"As often as they'll let me." His lips brushed her hair. "Get a good night's sleep, okay?"

She nodded.

"See you in the morning."

"Night."

He joined AJ at the elevator bank.

"Do you think she's right about that senator?" he asked.

"Imagine so," Brett said. "I'd still like to know who he is."

"Me too." AJ unconsciously made a fist.

"What about turning the other cheek and all that stuff?"

"I'll turn my cheek when someone hurts me. But it's hard to stand by and do nothing when it's Amy."

"Or Jonah. Meghan's ex is another scumbag I'd like to get hold of."

"Did you go to the hospital today?"

"Before I came here."

"How's he doing?"

"He's alert for longer periods." Brett smiled at the memory. "We talked. Just for a minute."

"What did he say?"

"Thanks for the monkey. That he wants to see the Bucks play."

"Another fan."

"Looks like."

"Does he know who you are?"

"Meghan told him I'm a family friend. We agreed he needs to get stronger before telling him the truth."

"That's probably wise, but it's gotta be hard."

"Worthwhile things often are." He followed AJ into the elevator and pushed the button for the lobby. "Are you in a hurry to get home?"

"Why do you ask?"

"Thought you could help me pick out a new camera for Dani."

"You're not mad at her anymore?"

"I broke it. I need to replace it." What he felt didn't matter.

AJ shuffled uncomfortably and adjusted his ball cap.

"Are you going to help me or not?"

"Dani's gone."

Gone? The air whooshed from Brett's lungs as the harsh word reverberated in his head.

"Gone where?"

"Boise."

"But why?"

"To take a job at a radio station."

"She had a job here." This couldn't be happening. "When did she leave?"

"This morning."

"And you're just telling me now?"

"I only found out a little while ago. Shelby told me before I drove up here."

As they stepped into the lobby, Brett pulled out his phone and navigated to his recent calls screen. "Why didn't Shelby tell me? Maybe I could have stopped her."

"Dani made her promise not to. Who are you calling?"

"Who do you think?"

The phone rang several times, then went to voicemail. Dani's cheery voice identified herself and promised to return calls as quickly as possible. When the beep finally sounded, his mouth went dry.

"It's me, Brett." A pause while he struggled with what to say. "Just call me, okay. Please. Call me."

He ended the call and slipped the phone in his pocket. His thoughts twirled in a maelstrom of emotion. The photos she'd taken—he couldn't believe she meant to sell them. But if that was the lie, then what was the truth?

"I can't believe she left."

"You're really upset about this." The surprise in AJ's voice needled and scratched.

"What exactly did Shelby tell you?"

"Dani stopped by this morning. Her car was completely packed. She left a box with notes about the project, I'm not sure what else. And said she was leaving."

"Nothing else? Nothing about me?"

"She told Shelby it was an accident—meeting you. Except that she followed you to the hospital from your office. So that doesn't make sense."

Unless she'd told him the truth. All she wanted from him was photographs for the tabloids.

His heart refused to accept that explanation. Somehow he couldn't reconcile the Dani who wrote such a moving script about a lonely boy missing his dad with someone who'd profit from his despair. No, the Dani he knew, the Dani he cared about, would never do such a thing.

He'd been in anguish when she took those photos. But then the ambulance had come, siren blaring, and caught his attention. He turned toward the street corner, and for reasons he still didn't understand, he'd been captivated by her presence. Why else would he have crossed the street in that moment when only Jonah mattered?

"I don't think I've ever seen you like this," AJ said. "You want to . . . wait a minute. It's Monday night."

"So?"

"It's not that late. Aren't you going to Gallagher's?"

"I gave that up."

"Because of Dani?"

"No," Brett said more harshly than he intended. "Because I . . . because I just got tired of it. The juvenile games. The sophomoric rivalry. All of it."

"Because of Dani."

"She had nothing to do with it."

"Keep telling yourself that, cuz. I know better."

"There you go again. The curse of the newly-in-love. Always playing matchmaker."

"I didn't set you up with her." A grin spread across AJ's tanned features. "Maybe God is your matchmaker."

"Great. Now you're directing *Fiddler on the Roof.*"

"Hey, it fits."

"You need to get out more, AJ."

"I'm happy right where I am."

As an older couple approached the elevators, Brett and AJ moved to a seating area. Brett perched on the arm of an upholstered chair. "What am I going to do about Dani?"

"Go after her."

"She lied to me."

"And you've never lied to a woman. Not even to Dani?"

Only once.

But mostly, he'd told her things about himself he'd never revealed to anyone else.

"Tell me something," AJ said. "Are you mad because she left you before you could leave her? Or are you, in fact, head over heels in love with her?"

"I don't fall in love."

"You don't like kids either. Unless, of course, their names are Jonah or Elizabeth or Tabby. And you don't like picnics or fishing or history. Though it seems like you've been having a good time at Misty Willow lately. And the Lassiter Foundation wouldn't be nearly as strong as it is without your leadership."

"What are you trying to say, AJ?"

"Only that you're not the same guy you were a few months ago."

"That doesn't mean I'm going on a wild goose chase clear across the country to get down on one knee and propose to a little snoop who wants to be Audrey Hepburn."

"What are you talking about?"

"It doesn't matter."

"No one asked you to propose to her. Just bring her back."

"What if she won't come?"

"Use the infamous Somers charm."

"I'm not sure that works on Dani."

"Maybe that's why her charm works on you."

"Maybe." He thought a moment. The trip to Richmond would take two or three days, depending on how long they stayed. "How long do you think it takes to drive to Boise?"

"At least a couple of days."

"If I leave here Friday, I'll only a few days behind her."

"A few days where she puts a deposit on an apartment. Starts a new job." AJ shook his head. "You should fly out there. As soon as we get back."

Brett stiffened and his head spun. "You know I can't do that."

"I'll go with you."

"You're going to fly?"

"I don't want to, but I will. Besides nothing says 'I love you' like facing your deepest fear."

"What fear did you face before telling Shelby you loved her?"

"Finding Meghan."

Brett smirked. All AJ had to do was a little bit of internet research and drive to Michigan. But he wanted Brett to board an airplane and fly across the country. In the air. Without touching the ground.

He couldn't do it. Not even for Dani.

The very thought of flying churned his stomach and turned his skin green.

But the thought of being without Dani, of living his life without her, churned his stomach too. She might not come back, but he had to know why she'd left. Why she'd followed him to the hospital.

And the real reason she'd taken those photographs.

Dani pulled off the interstate somewhere in southwestern Iowa. After a long day's driving, she was still less than halfway to Boise, but her eyes refused to stay open much longer. She peered through the windshield at the motel and took a deep breath. Brett wouldn't approve of the motor inn, but then Brett wasn't paying the bill. It'd probably be a couple of weeks or more before she got another paycheck, so she had to stretch the money in her bank account as far as possible.

About a half hour later, she was settled on the bed, freshly showered and towel-drying her hair. Her car was parked right outside the room, and she had pushed a chair in front of the locked door. The TV was turned on, more for the company than the entertainment.

Her phone buzzed, and she looked at the screen.

Brett.

Again.

She reached for the phone, staring at his name, but resisted the temptation to answer. There was nothing to say. Not anymore.

She waited for the buzzing to cease, then waited for the voicemail tone to ring. But it didn't. He hadn't left a message. Despising herself for her weakness, she clicked on the only voicemail message she had saved on her phone. His voice came through the tiny speaker.

"It's me, Brett." A pause. *"Just call me, okay. Please. Call me."*

Tears trickled down her cheeks as she played the message again and again.

Images played through her mind. His muffled laughter when she confessed to snooping. The lasagna he was so proud of though he hadn't made it. Their conversation on his high-rise patio about the diamond his grandfather had bought in Seoul and brought home after the war to give to the woman he loved.

A woman who loved someone else.

The conversation seemed stuck in her mind.

If only Sully and Aubrey had married. They'd have had other children. And perhaps those children wouldn't have cared about flying to a charity event. Perhaps they would still be alive.

Perhaps her mom would still be alive.

Did all her grief trace back to Aubrey's fickle heart?

Those thoughts had chased themselves around her mind as she cleared up the dishes after their lasagna dinner. Thoughts she'd hidden from Brett's probing eyes because he often seemed to know when she was keeping something from him. It was eerie, how often their thoughts were in sync with one another.

But it didn't mean anything.

Because anything he'd felt for her had been destroyed when he saw his images on her camera's screen. And anything she'd felt for him had been destroyed when he broke her camera.

So why did she miss him so much?

− 41 −

*B*rett called Dani before picking up Amy from her apartment, again after getting settled in a Richmond hotel room that night, and a few more times as he and AJ traveled home on Wednesday. But she didn't return his calls.

On Thursday, he went to the office and tried losing himself in paperwork. He had a huge pile to get through since he promised to visit Amy over the weekend. But his mind wouldn't concentrate on the plans and dollar amounts and contractual terms.

Finally he swiveled his chair and stared through the window at the city's skyline. Absentmindedly he reached for his phone and tapped the end on the chair arm.

Everything he wanted was his. All his problems were being resolved.

Jonah visibly improved every day.

Amy was getting the professional help she needed.

Business thrived and his portfolio fattened.

But somewhere out beyond the Mississippi was a young woman who'd left town in a broken-down junker. And she'd taken his heart with her.

He'd given it a lot of thought while driving back and forth to Virginia. Dani had made her decision, and he had to forget her. To think instead about all the things that were right in his life. How God had answered his prayers for Jonah and for Amy. He couldn't expect God to resolve this too. Especially considering his history with women.

An eye for an eye.

After the way he'd treated Tracie and those who'd been in his bed before her, he couldn't blame God for teaching him a tough lesson. He just never expected to be on the receiving end of deceit and rejection.

Or for his heart to ache with such intensity.

He swiveled around to his desk and faced the dwindling mountain of folders. A slender blue corner poked out from the thick manila stack.

The folder Kimberly had given him a couple of weeks ago. The one with Dani's info.

He slid it from the pile and flipped open the cover to the first page. *Dannaleigh Christina Prescott.*

"That's a mouthful," he muttered. Unusual but lovely. Like Dani herself.

The rest of the page covered routine information. Previous employment, college graduation date and degrees. Prior addresses.

A lot of prior addresses.

Two were group homes for foster children. She'd been at one several months and the other for over a year.

His eyes scanned the page, then turned to the next. Kimberly's interview notes with the references Dani had provided were neatly formatted. Her notes from the call with the station manager were on the third page.

Here, neatly outlined in bullet points, was the information Brett had refused to hear. The stark black type provided no nuance against the white paper. Only cold facts.

If Dani hadn't resigned, she would have been fired. The station manager didn't want to let her go, and wouldn't have if he hadn't been under pressure from higher-ups at the station.

With the folder in hand, Brett entered the outer office. "Are you busy?"

Kimberly turned from her computer. "Just putting the final touches on the Van Tassel project."

"Tell me about your phone call with Gerald Greene. The station manager in Cincinnati."

"You know how it is with these executive types. They won't give out much information that's helpful."

"But he said she was forced to resign."

"After a little sweet-talking, yes. But he also said he wasn't comfortable with that decision. He said something about 'politics being everywhere.'"

"Could you get him on the phone for me?"

"Sure."

Brett wandered back to his desk and picked up his cell phone. Rotate, tap. Rotate, tap.

Kimberly's voice murmured through the open door. A moment later, she called to him. "Mr. Greene on line one."

"Thanks."

He reached for the desk phone and punched the button. "Hello, Mr. Greene. This is Brett Somers."

"What can I do for you, Mr. Somers?"

"I wanted to talk to you about Dani Prescott."

"What about her? Is she okay?"

Only Dani knew the answer to that question.

"I understand there are laws about providing references and all that, but I'm not Dani's employer. I'm a . . . friend."

"I know who you are, Mr. Somers."

"You do?"

"I've seen the YouTube video. You had the ladies here in an uproar for a week or so."

"Dani saw that?"

"She did."

Brett rubbed his forehead. Never again, no matter the reason, would he ever consent to an interview.

"That whole thing got out of hand."

"Don't apologize for being Ohio's most eligible bachelor. Though if you've hurt Dani in any way . . ." He let his voice fade, but his meaning was clear.

Brett inwardly sighed. Hopefully the direct approach would turn out to be the best approach. "Dani is in Boise. Or maybe on her way. I'm not sure."

"Why?"

"To take a job at a radio station out there. By any chance have you heard from her?"

"Not since she packed up and left."

"Why did she quit? What happened?"

After a moment's hesitation, Mr. Greene said, "Give me one reason why I should tell you that."

Brett hesitated a moment himself. *Direct approach*.

"Because I . . . I want to convince her to come back."

"Why?"

"Because I care about her."

Mr. Greene let out a breath. "Does she care about you?"

"We had a fight."

"It must have been a doozy if she took off for Boise."

If only you knew. If he did, Greene might reach through the phone and grab Brett by the throat. "It was."

"And now you're sorry."

"She won't return my calls."

"I don't understand why you're calling me."

"It's a little hard to explain."

"Try me."

"I met Dani outside a hospital." Brett leaned back in his chair and closed his eyes. "She was taking pictures of me. Secretly."

"I see."

"Do you? Because I don't."

"Mr. Somers—"

"Please. It's Brett."

"Okay, then. Brett." Greene hesitated, then heavily exhaled. "Do you know who Dani's mother was?"

"No." Brett frowned in confusion. What would Dani's mother have to do with her leaving?

"So she didn't tell you."

"Tell me what?"

"After your secretary called for a reference, I did a little research. I wanted to know something about the people who'd hired one of my favorite assistant producers. That's when I made the connection."

"What connection?"

"Does the name Leslie Mercer mean anything to you?"

Brett gasped as if he'd been sucker-punched. Cotton filled his mouth. "I don't . . . what does she . . ." His grip on the phone tightened. When Dani had said her mom died in an accident, he had assumed a car accident. No wonder their conversation had upset her so much.

"Leslie." He choked on the name, then paused and cleared his throat. "Leslie Mercer is Dani's mother?"

"You talked about her during that interview."

Now it was his voice that pounded within his head. *That incompetent pilot killed—no, murdered—my parents.*

"That part wasn't in the YouTube clip."

"Not the one that went viral, but it was online."

"Dani watched it?"

"Yes." A sigh came through the phone. "It's why she was forced to resign."

"I don't understand."

"She used company resources to do her own investigation of the plane crash. I'd have let it go, but a colleague with more ambition than sense caught her. Next thing I knew, Dani had moved to Columbus."

Brett buried his head in the palm of his hand. His voice had deserted him, and hot tears stung his eyes.

He'd fallen for the daughter of the pilot responsible for his parents' deaths.

Was this God's sense of humor?

If so, he wanted none of it.

"Brett? Mr. Somers? Are you still there?"

"She should have told me."

"Could you tell me again how you met?"

"Outside a hospital. I don't think she meant for it to happen, but I saw her." He shook his head. "I'm sorry. I need to go."

"Mr. Somers—"

He laid the phone on the receiver, unable to listen to any more. To trust his voice not to break. The events of the last few weeks played like a movie in his mind. Dani on the street corner, the siren blaring around them. The painful expression in her eyes.

Her initial refusal to tell him her name.

Her wariness, the barriers she'd placed between them.

Had it all been some crazy ploy? But to accomplish what?

Only one person had the answer. And she wasn't returning his calls.

Heat shimmered outside the window, and a sudden wave of claustrophobia overwhelmed him. He loosened his tie, but when the wave didn't recede, he yanked it from his neck. He had to get out of there.

He strode past Kimberly's desk with a curt, "I'll be back later."

"What about your meeting with—"

The door closed, shutting out her voice. The meeting didn't matter. Nothing mattered except to drive.

He headed out of the city, taking the familiar route to Misty Willow even though he didn't plan to stop there. Shelby couldn't help him sort through his tangled emotions. Besides, Misty Willow was too close to the cottage. He didn't dare go there—not where memories of Dani lingered in the rooms.

The verse Elizabeth taught him pressed into his mind. *I trusted in the Lord when I said, "I am greatly afflicted."*

Like Elizabeth, he thought he'd be afflicted forever. But Jonah had awakened, and Amy was in therapy. Brett hadn't made any bargains or tried to negotiate with God; he'd only opened his eyes to the world he had created for himself and decided to leave it behind.

Only one affliction remained.

At a crossroads, he turned and headed toward Glade County High School.

The final class bell rang shortly after Brett arrived. He sent AJ a text, then waited for him at the football bleachers. A few minutes later, AJ jogged toward him.

"What are you doing here?" he asked. "Is Jonah okay?"

"He's doing fine. I stopped in this morning, and he was eating Jell-O." Brett smiled at the memory. "He likes strawberry, but he can't have anything red right now."

"Why not?"

"In case he gets sick. Red Jell-O looks too much like blood."

"Makes sense. How much longer will he be in the hospital?"

"Don't know. He tires easily, but Meghan said each day he's doing a little better."

"That's great news."

About forty or fifty teens, wearing pads and practice jerseys, dropped gear on a nearby bench. Two coaches followed them, and the team huddled around them.

"You need to join that?" Brett asked.

"Not till after they warm up. Then we do drills." AJ adjusted his ball cap, his gaze focused on the team. "Any word from Dani?"

"She hasn't called me. And I've given up calling her."

"She isn't answering Shelby's calls either."

Brett lowered himself to a bleacher and set his feet on the metal seating in front of him. With his elbows propped on his knees, he focused on the players as they lined up on the field and went through their warm-ups. He needed to tell AJ the truth about Dani. This wasn't the best time or place. But he'd get no relief from the burning in his gut until he spewed out her secret.

"I talked to Dani's station manager. From her last job."

AJ leaned against the railing as if he had all the time in the world. "Tell you anything interesting?"

"Yeah." Brett rolled the distasteful words around in his mouth. If he'd seen AJ immediately after talking to Greene, he'd have spit them out in all their hateful brutality. But the drive to the high school, along roads bordered by pastures and fields, had softened the claustrophobic grief that pushed him from his office. His stomach ached with anger, but he was no longer sure who he was mad at.

Dani for deceiving him or himself for allowing her to?

Or some other reason—like holding on so tight to his own childhood sorrows that he'd hidden his heart in a deep, dark place. Determined not to let anyone too close and unwilling to love.

Until Dani showed up, with her own hidden heartaches. At least he'd had his grandparents, and Amy and AJ. She'd had no one.

"What did he say?" AJ's voice broke into his thoughts. "Must have been important for you to come all the way out here."

"Maybe I shouldn't have. Except I thought you should know."

"Know what?"

Brett took a long, slow breath, then exhaled. When he spoke, he somehow managed to keep his voice low and even. "Dani's mom piloted the plane."

"The plane that . . ."

"Yeah."

AJ's body stiffened, and his back slid along the railing until he hit the bleacher. "She knew? All this time, she knew it was us? We were us?" His head shook, almost like a spasm, as if trying to sort out the words he meant to say.

Brett related the conversation he'd had with Greene, surprising even himself with how calmly he mentioned Dani's mother's name. AJ pulled off his ball cap and wiped his arm across his forehead.

"You okay?" Brett asked.

"I moved out of the cottage for her, Brett. You and Shelby gave her a job. Was that her plan? I don't get it."

"Neither do I. Except she told Shelby it was an accident that we met. I've been going over and over it. I insisted she go to the movie with me that night. I was the one who wanted her out of that slum she was living in. Every time we got together, it was me pushing for it, not her."

AJ didn't say anything. On the football field, the players counted and grunted in unison.

"She lost the only family she had when that plane went down," Brett said. "The only family that mattered."

"Sounds like you've forgiven her."

"It wasn't her fault."

"She should have told us. Before we all got so buddy-buddy."

"Maybe she didn't know how."

"She got to you, didn't she?" Bewilderment and hurt hoarsened AJ's voice.

"There's just something about her that . . . I don't know. My world's a better place when she's in it."

"What are you going to do?"

"I'm not sure."

AJ clapped Brett on the shoulder, then shifted his focus to the field and stood. "I need to get out there."

Brett rose too. The burning sensation in his gut had dissipated only to be replaced by a restless emptiness. A whistle blew on the field, and the team divided into smaller groups.

"Are you okay?" Brett asked.

"I will be. Are you?"

"I miss her."

"Then you've got a decision to make." AJ stepped off the bleachers, then turned and jogged backward. "Let me know what it is."

He pivoted and sprinted toward his players while Brett struggled to tame his restless feelings.

After leaving the high school, he drove to the cottage and parked in front of the gate. As he walked up the gentle slope, memories flooded over him—childhood visits with Gran, a few barbecues with AJ. But mostly, every minute he'd been there with Dani.

Helping her move in. Baking brownies. Movies and pizza.

Never setting a countdown clock, at first because it didn't matter and then because he didn't want to ever say good-bye to her.

He still didn't.

Somehow he had to make her understand how sorry he was— for what he'd said about her mom, for breaking her camera. For being a world-class jerk.

Nothing says I love you like facing your deepest fear.

AJ's words taunted him.

Brett stared at the empty cottage. Now that Dani was gone, it seemed to have lost some of its luster. He had to persuade her to come back. To come home. No matter what the cost.

He broke every speed limit racing back to Columbus, rushed into his office a few minutes after five, and stood before Kimberly's desk. "Good, you're still here. Can you do something for me?"

She gave him a wry smile. "Something personal?"

"Afraid so."

"Sure. What is it?"

"Find a camera shop in Boise. A mom-and-pop place, not one of the big box stores." He pulled out his wallet and handed her a credit card. "Buy the best camera they have, a couple of lenses."

"Any dollar limit?"

He shook his head. "They have to deliver it. Today. I don't know where yet, but I'll let you know as soon as I do."

He pivoted, then turned back to Kimberly again. "One more thing. Charter a flight for tomorrow."

"For you?"

He audibly exhaled. "For me."

He returned to his office and searched online for Boise radio stations, then dialed the first number. Turning on the Somers charm, he'd find where Dani was working. And then he'd bring her home.

– 42 –

*D*ani closed the last file drawer and stood, arching her back to ease the pain while once again swallowing her disappointment. After a tour of the station, a few introductions, and filling out paperwork for human resources, she'd done nothing but file a tremendous backlog of documents. Jeanie promised the mundane task was temporary. But how temporary?

Had she really left everything behind to become a file clerk?

She should have swallowed her pride and gone back to Cincinnati. Her stepdad probably would have let her stay with him long enough to find a job.

Flipping burgers.

Walmart greeter.

Anything to bring in some money until she could find her own place.

Now she was sleeping on Jeanie's couch and doing a job she hated.

Her phone buzzed, and she checked the screen. Gerald Greene. What could he want?

She ignored the call.

At least it hadn't been Brett.

Though in truth, she was disappointed it hadn't been. She couldn't talk to him, but that hadn't stopped her from listening to his voicemail over and over again. And now when she played the YouTube clip, it was the same one that had gone viral and not the longer part of the interview.

Only the laughing Brett, the dimpled Brett.

In those moments, she allowed herself to remember what it felt like to have her hand cradled in his, to cheat at miniature golf, to wade in a sun-dappled creek beside an ancient willow.

To remember the warmth of his lips and the magic of his kiss.

All things she needed to forget if she were ever to find happiness in this world. If her heart was ever going to heal.

"Some of us are going out after work," Jeanie said. "Interested?"

"I think I'll pass," Dani said. "I'm still a little road-weary."

"No wonder, making that trip as fast as you did."

Not wanting to spend any more money than necessary on lodging, Dani had driven from east of Omaha to Boise in one long, mind-numbing stretch. Jeanie hadn't been too keen on being awakened in the wee hours of the morning, but her ill humor never lasted very long. She'd simply shown Dani the bathroom and the couch, then headed back to her own bed.

The drive had been awful, but worth it. She'd had all day yesterday to mope around the small apartment feeling sorry for herself and indulging in torture by watching every Cary Grant movie she could find online.

The tears had flowed as Cary saved Ingrid from the Nazis, saved Audrey from a thief, and saved Katharine from a wild leopard.

She'd never enjoy her favorite classics again without thinking of Brett's dimpled smile and gorgeous eyes. Or how often she'd lied to him. Spilled soda on his pants. Responded to his fervent kiss.

"You should call him." Jeanie's voice broke into Dani's thoughts.

She shook her head. Jeanie didn't know the whole story—only

that Dani needed a refuge from a romance gone bad. But even if she did know the whole story, she'd probably say the same thing. Ever the optimist.

"Sure you don't want to go with us? It'd be good for you to meet some new people."

"Another day."

"If you say so." Jeanie glanced at the files. "Sorry to saddle you with this. But it's the easiest thing to start the newbies on."

"I get it."

"I'll be back to check on you in a little bit."

One slow hour passed and then another. Dani had just about reached the end of the stack when someone she hadn't met dropped another pile of papers in the inbox. She inwardly groaned but smiled at her new co-worker.

Only temporary. It had better be only temporary.

A few moments later, Jeanie appeared. "You need to come to the reception desk," she said excitedly.

"Why?"

"A surprise."

"For me?"

"Come see."

Bewildered, Dani followed Jeanie through the maze of cubicles to the front office. The man standing by the receptionist's desk wore a gray polo and black slacks. His hand rested on a large bag emblazoned with a camera logo.

"Are you Dani Prescott?" he asked. His jovial smile puffed his cheeks.

"Yes. I am."

"I have a delivery for you. Just need you to sign right here." He handed her a clipboard and pen.

Momentarily confused, her gaze flickered from the receipt to the bag and back to the receipt.

"There's been a mistake. I didn't order anything."

"You'll find a note inside the bag. It'll explain everything."

"Is it from *him*?" Jeanie sidled next to Dani and elbowed her. "How romantic."

With everyone watching her, Dani was too self-conscious to do anything except sign her name. "Thank you," she said as she handed the clipboard back to the man.

"You're very welcome, miss. And if you need anything else, just come down and see us. We'll take good care of you."

"I will. Thanks."

"Open it," Jeanie urged.

"I'd rather wait till I get back to your place."

"Party pooper."

"It's best, trust me." The last thing Dani wanted to do was read a message from Brett in front of people she'd just met that day. Or even in front of Jeanie. If the tears started to flow, she'd have to tell the whole stupid story. Including her ridiculous plan to humiliate the man she then managed to fall in love with.

Because there was no doubt in her mind that the bag contained an expensive camera from Brett.

She faked an enthusiastic smile at everyone in the reception area, then carried the bag to the filing room. She was almost there when a thought slammed into her brain.

Brett knew where to deliver the camera.

That meant he knew where she worked.

But it didn't matter. All he could do was call. And all she had to do was never answer the phone.

Brett stood next to the chartered plane, a Cessna Citation Encore, and gripped his bag till his knuckles turned white. The ever-efficient Kimberly had arranged the charter to fly Brett from the Glade County airfield. AJ was skipping his morning classes to give Brett a pep talk before he got on the plane.

"Are you sure you're okay?" AJ asked.

"How many times are you going to ask me that?"

"Probably once a minute until you get on that thing."

"It's safe, right?"

"So they say."

"You're not being much help."

AJ clapped him on the back. "Actually, I'm very proud of you. Surprised, but proud."

"Sure you can't come with me?"

"I wish." AJ checked his watch. "But I can't miss all my classes."

"I thought she'd call after the camera was delivered." He didn't need to explain who *she* was.

"I'm sorry she didn't."

"You're not mad at her?"

"I talked to Shelby about it last night. Some things still don't make any sense, but Dani didn't cause that plane to crash."

"So if I persuade her to come back, she can still live in the cottage?"

"And Shelby said she still has a job."

Brett grinned his appreciation, then grew serious again. "What do you think she'll say when I show up?"

"Haven't a clue."

They were silent for a few moments while the pilot finished his pre-check.

"What would you be doing?" Brett asked. "If you were in my place?"

"Do you love her?"

"I miss her."

"But do you love her?"

Brett focused on the horizon, as if the answer could be found in the distant clouds instead of his own heart.

"I want to say the words to her first," he finally said. "This time, when I really mean them, I want to say them to her first."

One corner of AJ's mouth turned up in a slight smile. "Then go say them."

"Pray for me?"

"You know it."

"Thanks." He pulled AJ into a quick guy-hug, exhaled, and headed for the plane. If this was what he had to do to get Dani back, then he'd do it.

He settled into his seat and buckled the belt for takeoff. Closing his eyes, he leaned his head back against the seat and said a prayer of his own. A prayer for safety on the flight. A prayer that Dani would at least listen to what he had to say.

A prayer without words for the selfishness of his past and a changed life and a new beginning.

– 43 –

*D*ani shoved the folder in its proper slot and pushed the heavy drawer shut. After a sleepless night, she'd decided to return the camera. Though technically, ethically, morally, and even legally, Brett owed her a new one, she couldn't accept it.

If she did, he would always be a part of it, his handsome face a silent shadow in every shot she took.

Besides, she needed a clean break from him. Keeping the camera required certain social niceties, such as writing a thank-you note. She'd already tried that last night, before she'd made up her mind to return the gift.

Nothing she wrote worked. No words expressed the right amount of gratitude accompanied by distance surrounded by a "now leave me alone" air.

Jeanie appeared in the doorway, a Cheshire cat smile on her face. "You're wanted at the front desk."

Dani crossed her arms and sighed exaggeratedly. "Another delivery?"

Jeanie's eyes crinkled in amusement.

"What is it this time? Because if it's a new car, I'm keeping it."

"Come see."

Jeanie grabbed her arm and led her through the office maze. Dani prepared herself to say no to whatever delivery person waited for her.

She turned a corner and gasped.

Brett stood by the receptionist counter, an uncertain smile tugging at his lips.

"Hi, Dani." He held out his hands, palms up. Empty hands. "I was going to bring flowers, but I didn't want you throwing them at me."

"What are you doing here?"

His gaze flicked at the receptionist then Jeanie before resting again on her.

"You wouldn't answer my calls. So what else could I do?"

The sheepish look on his face tugged at Dani's heart. The Brett she expected to find when she went to Columbus would never have gone after a woman who'd left him. At least that's what she'd thought. Yet here he was.

"You drove all the way out here?"

"I, um, I flew."

"On a plane?"

The uncertainty that tensed his facial muscles lessened. "On a plane."

Oblivious to anyone's presence but his, Dani focused solely on Brett. "Why?" Her voice was barely a whisper within the three or four yards that separated them.

"To take you home."

"This is my home now."

"It doesn't have to be."

The time had come. No more secrets. "You don't know who I am."

He closed the distance between them but didn't touch her. He seemed afraid of spooking her, that she might turn tail and dash away if he tried.

"Yes, I do, Dannaleigh Christina Prescott. I know who your

mother . . ."—he paused and took a deep breath—"I know your mother died in the same crash that killed my family."

"How did you find out?"

"Gerald Greene told me." He reached for her hands, holding them loosely in his own. "I'm sorry for what I said in that interview. If I had known, if I could take it back . . ."

Tears formed in her eyes and slid quietly along her cheeks. "I wanted to hurt you for what you said about my mom. But I wouldn't have sold the photos. I'm sorry I took them."

He leaned forward, touching his forehead to hers and gazing into her eyes. "All I care about is that God brought you into my life when I needed you most. The circumstances don't matter."

His arms closed around her, and she buried her head in his shoulder.

"Please come back with me, Dani," he whispered into her ear. "I love you."

"You love me?"

"With every beat of my heart."

His assurance floated inside her.

"I love you too," she said softly.

He pulled something from his pocket, then pressed the key to the cottage into her hand. "I think this is yours."

Her fingers closed around the Secret Garden key ring, and she breathed a muddled thanks to God for answering the prayers she'd been too afraid to pray. Prayers born from loneliness and heartache. Prayers for belonging and love.

The key to the cottage was hers again. She was going home.

"Let's get out of here," Brett said quietly.

She wiped her eyes, then gasped. "Oh, Brett. I got mascara on your shirt." Her words tumbled out, broken but swift. "I'll clean it. No, I'll have it dry-cleaned. There has to be a cleaner—"

He put his fingers against her lips. "Uh-uh. I'll have it framed. To remember this moment."

"Frame—"

The word ended as his lips covered hers, drawing her into a love she never dreamed possible with the only man who was exactly her type.

As the charter plane taxied to a stop at the small Glade County airport, Dani patted Brett's hand. "We're here."

He loosened the death grip he'd had on the armrest. "That wasn't so bad," he said.

She laughed at the fear mingling with relief that still showed on his face. "This is the most romantic thing anyone has ever done for me." She kissed the corner of his mouth. "You're the bravest man I know."

"Just promise me one thing."

"Anything."

"Never make me fly halfway across the country after you again."

"Would you?" she teased.

He pretended to glare, then flashed his dimples. "In a heartbeat."

"Then I promise."

"Good." He stood, a little unsteadily, then followed her off the plane. "I wish I hadn't told Amy I'd visit her this weekend. Then we could have driven from Boise."

"It's a long drive."

"Worth it, though. You and me, the open highway." He sang the opening line to Willie Nelson's "On the Road Again."

Dani grinned widely. "I love that song."

"Me too."

"How long will you be in Richmond?"

"Only a couple of days. The invitation's still open for you to come too."

"I doubt Amy wants to meet me right now."

"Probably true. Anyway, I'll leave later today, drive till I get there. Come back Monday evening. Is that soon enough for you?"

"It'll have to be. Though you know," she teased, "you'd get there faster if you flew."

"Not happening." Brett pulled her close for a lingering kiss, then held onto her hand as they walked toward the office. "As soon as I settle the tab for this thing, we can be on our way."

The kiss left Dani giddy with the happiness that had surrounded her since Brett had escorted her from the radio station.

They'd walked the city streets, then eaten supper in a local diner.

And they talked. Serious, no-holds-barred, vulnerable conversations.

She told him why she had followed him to the hospital, and how her longing for vengeance had faded as their friendship had deepened. He confessed his lie and told her about his meeting with Tracie.

As hurtful as it was, they also talked about the accident that had destroyed their childhoods. Brett had never questioned Sully's version of the crash—why would he? But neither was he surprised to learn his grandfather had coerced authorities into a second investigation when the first cleared Leslie Mercer of any wrongdoing.

But that was the past. Though Brett promised to find out the truth, both he and Dani wanted to focus on the present. And the future.

Earlier this morning, they had sold her car, loaded her meager belongings onto the plane, and flown home.

Home.

The cottage was hers again for as long as she wanted. The job was hers again until the project was complete. Nothing had changed except the hidden places of their hearts. Those had been opened, revealed, and soothed. No more secrets, and no more sorrow that would mar their love for one another.

And she did love him. Madly. Wildly. Thoroughly. Just as she was assured he loved her.

After the boxes and luggage were moved to his Lexus and the pilot given a hefty tip, Brett pulled out his phone, looked at the screen, and grinned. "The little monsters know we're back. They want us to stop at King Karl's for pizza."

Dani wrapped her arms around him and smiled. "It's tradition."

"How about we start our own tradition?"

Her heart skipped a beat as he flashed his gorgeous dimples, swung her around, and then soundly kissed her.

− 44 −

December

Pristine snow covered the creek banks, sparkling like tiny diamonds beneath the winter sun. The fronds of the willow softly rustled, and their ends dipped into the chilled water. Brett's boots crunched through the thin crust of snow and left their imprints behind. He inhaled the icy air, then exhaled a deep sigh of contentment. The winter wonderland was as beautiful as he'd hoped it would be.

Christmas was only days away, to be closely followed by AJ and Shelby's wedding. Then they'd be ringing in the New Year with its promise of fresh starts and hopeful resolutions.

He didn't need to wait till then. His fresh start had already begun.

Whenever he imagined a moment like this, the setting had been completely different. A romantic candlelight dinner in a five-star restaurant. Soft music. Impeccable service. He wore a fine suit and silk tie; the anonymous leggy blonde across from him looked glamorous in a skintight mini and strappy heels.

The reality, a brown-eyed brunette bundled into a thick jacket and mittens, crunched the snow beside him.

A mere slip of a girl who had spilled, snooped, and giggled her way deep into his heart.

And he wouldn't want it any other way.

He cleared powdery snow from the top of the picnic table, then sat on it, his feet planted on the bench. "Sit by me?"

She settled beside him, wrapping her arms around his and burying her red-tipped nose in his sleeve.

"Cold?" he asked.

"A little. But it's breathtaking out here." She laughed softly. "Literally and figuratively."

"Worth the hike?"

"Absolutely."

They sat in silence for a few moments, enjoying the solitude of the winter day. Brett glanced at Dani, barely visible beneath a scarlet-and-gray stocking cap, a souvenir from her first Ohio State Buckeyes football game.

In the months since they'd flown back from Boise, his world had turned right-side up again.

No, not again. For the first time ever.

Jonah had left the hospital walking on his own two feet, and the family—Brett, AJ, and Amy—plus Dani, Shelby, and the girls, had crowded into Meghan's small apartment to celebrate. Amy brought presents for the children and behaved herself admirably with the adults. Aaron was there too, exchanging shy smiles with Meghan when they thought no one was looking.

Brett's fifteen minutes of notorious fame flashed then burned without any of the drama Tracie had predicted. Instead he'd been lauded in the mainstream press for a generous donation to the children's hospital for families in need. The timing may have been a bit calculated, but not the intent behind the gift.

Dani now had an official office in one of the upstairs rooms at the Misty Willow homestead, and a second room held potential display mock-ups, archival items, and the beginnings of a Civil War library. Once Shelby and the girls moved out of the house, it'd be transformed into the planned museum and research center. If all went well, the grand opening would take place a few months later with a daylong festival.

The past may have been rough and flawed, Brett mused, but the present was as fresh and pristine as the newly fallen snow. This was the perfect moment.

He reached into his backpack and drew out a book-sized package.

"I got you a gift," he said.

Dani's brown eyes sparkled. "What's the occasion?"

"You're here with me. That's all I need."

"You're sweet." She leaned forward for a quick kiss, then carefully loosened the broad pink ribbon. Finally she unwrapped the paper to reveal a mahogany box.

"Oh, how lovely."

"Look inside."

She opened the lid, and her eyes widened with delight. Pink tissue paper lined the box, and nestled inside was an engraved heart that read *Dani + Brett*.

She lifted the heart and stared at him, her mouth open.

Brett chuckled. "Shelby promised me a branch on the engagement tree."

Dani gulped and cradled the heart. "We're going to put this on the willow?"

"That depends." He nudged Dani, and her lovely brown eyes gazed into his. "We've had a rough time of it, you and me. Scarred by our pasts. Finding it hard to love. But God gave us the chance to find a deeper love with each other than we've ever known before."

He pulled a ring from his pocket and held it between his fingers.

"Sully shut this away because it symbolized something painful to him. But then you came along, and you didn't see just a diamond. You saw beauty, and you saw a story."

He paused for a moment, wanting to say the words exactly right.

"We may be imperfect. This diamond. Me." He flashed a smile and tapped her nose. "Even you. But we're better together than we could ever be on our own. Together we're imperfectly perfect."

He pulled her upright, then got on one knee. The snow crunched, and an icy dampness chilled his jeans, but he didn't mind. He gazed into the face of the woman he loved and thought only of her and his hopes for their future.

"Dannaleigh Christina Prescott. Please say you'll marry me."

Unshed tears glistened in Dani's eyes, and the entire world seemed to pause as it waited for her answer.

"Yes," she said as the tears graced her flushed cheeks. "I will."

He removed her mitten, then slipped the diamond onto her finger. "We're writing our own story," he said as he stood and drew her into a lingering kiss.

A story of two lonely people brought together by a shared childhood tragedy who finally found their hearts in each other.

And a deeper love than they ever dared imagine.

EXCLUSIVE PEEK INTO

BOOK #3 IN THE

Misty Willow Series

SUMMER 2017

he June sun beat on Gabe Kendall's bare head and tapped into his childhood memories of the horse farm. He leaned his arms on the weathered fence and let his mind bask in the remembrance of long summer days under tranquil blue skies.

The pastures, lush and green. The paddock with its packed dirt circuit. The stables, once alive with the soft snuffles of contented horses and the familiar smells of oiled leather, and fresh hay, and good old-fashioned hard work.

Except for the glow of memory, nothing was the same.

The horse barn, the machine shed, even the nearby house were smaller than he remembered. Perhaps a consequence of seeing his uncle's place for the first time with grown-up eyes. Or maybe his imagination had tricked him into thinking everything about the place was bigger. God knew he'd experienced too many nights when the only way he could lull himself to sleep was to conjure up happier times.

But the emptiness and the silence weren't because of an adult perspective or the glow of childhood memory. A forlorn air hung over the place, heavy with regret and heartache.

If only Rusty were still alive. The fence would be white, the pasture grass pristine, the paddock graded smooth.

Except then he'd know what Gabe had done. And the knowledge would have killed him.

Soft footsteps approached behind him. "It's not how you remembered. Is it?"

Aunt Tess stared into the distance. Her jet-black hair, evidence of her great-grandmother's Native American heritage, held streaks of gray. She wore it plaited in one thick braid that nearly reached her waist.

"I should have been here." He put his arm around her, pulling her into a sideways hug and breathing in her familiar scent. Charlie cologne. At least one thing hadn't changed.

"You're here now." Her voice caught, but she quickly regained control. "I'd have visited you. If you'd let me."

"I couldn't."

"You're too full of pride. Just like your uncle."

"I miss him."

"So do I." She flashed a smile. "But it's nice having you here again. Just like old times."

He pressed his lips together and slowly inhaled. In the past few years, he'd steeled himself against showing weakness. But a few kind words from his only uncle's widow and he'd turn into a blubbering idiot if he wasn't careful.

Time to change the subject.

"See you still have the truck." He nodded toward the dusty two-tone Ford F-150 parked beside the detached garage. The once vivid red had faded, and the tan sides hadn't fared much better. The dent where Gabe had accidentally hit a fence post still marred the rust-spotted fender. But hey, he'd only been twelve at the time.

"I kept it for you," Tess said.

"You should have sold it."

"Wasn't mine to sell. Besides, it's not worth much to anyone but you and me."

"Rusty taught me to drive in that heap."

"I remember. Your mom wasn't too happy."

"I think she just pretended to be mad."

"Perhaps." She squeezed his arm. "Look at you. So like Rusty when he was your age."

"Except he never disgraced the family."

"Neither have you."

"You haven't talked to my dad lately, have you?"

She avoided his gaze for a moment. When she turned toward him again, a warm smile brightened her face. "Come inside, and we'll get you settled. Just took a batch of snickerdoodles out of the oven. Those still your favorite cookies?"

"Anything you bake is my favorite."

"Let's go then."

Gabe hesitated, and her expression changed from puzzlement to understanding. "You want to ride."

"It's been a while since . . . you know."

Since I've been on a horse. That's what he meant to say. But the longing inside him ran deeper than the need to be in a saddle again. He craved the freedom, the solitude, of a long ride in fresh air and sunshine.

"Take Daisy. First stall on the left. She can use the exercise."

"That land on the north side of Glade Creek still belong to you?"

"For now." She sighed heavily. "That reminds me. I have this thing to go to tonight."

"What thing?"

"A reception at the old Misty Willow homestead."

Something niggled at his memory. A scandal of some sort. "Do the Sullivans still own that place?"

"No. And yes." She chuckled. "Promise you'll go with me, and I'll catch you up on all the news after your ride."

"You've got a date." He headed for the barn, then turned and walked backward. "But I'm not wearing a tie."

"You are so like your uncle."

He'd always wanted to be. If only life hadn't taken a different turn.

So this was the place.

Amy Somers clambered on top of the rustic picnic table and drank from her sports bottle. Normally she didn't care for the taste of the vitamin-enriched water, but the long hike from the cottage had made her thirsty.

Sun pennies glinted on the creek's broad surface, and long-stemmed cattails gathered in clumps along the bank. Wild daisies, purple clover, and Queen Anne's lace rose from the grassy field. The ancient willow balanced on the edge of the creek, its elegant fronds dipping their ends into the sparkling water.

Family picnics took place here. Burgers and brats, potato salad and coleslaw followed by exhilarating games of tag, mostly futile attempts to catch fish, and restful catnaps.

At least that's what she'd been told. She'd never been here before today.

Not that she hadn't been invited. Staying away had simply been easier.

She sipped more water, then propped her slightly pink arms across her knees. Sunburn. Another joy of country living. A summer-scented breeze momentarily cooled her skin, and she added sun-screen to her mental shopping list.

The same breeze lifted the willow's fronds so it appeared as if they danced beside the creek.

The misty willow. The engagement tree.

First AJ and then Brett had proposed to their respective brides in this quiet, peaceful, bug-ridden place. Her cousin, she understood. Like Gran, AJ preferred the rural community over the hustle and bustle of life in the big city.

But her brother had her flummoxed. Less than a year ago, Brett had been named one of the city's top young professionals. His thriving business, inherited from their grandfather, was poised to become a major regional development firm. His future seemed golden.

Until he turned his back on all of it—the lucrative investment opportunities, his luxury apartment, Monday nights with the guys—and settled into a three-bedroom ranch up the road from the cottage. True, it had the most elegant upgrades of any ranch-style house in Glade County. Amy made sure of that, steering her sister-in-law to only the finest granite countertops, deluxe appliances, and high-end cabinetry during the rehab.

But it was still a house in the middle of nowhere among people who weren't like the Somerses. People who didn't know the difference between a dessert spoon and a soup spoon. Who'd rather have barbecue and iced tea than filet mignon and a fine wine.

She swiped angrily at the tears that unexpectedly dampened her cheeks.

Brett and AJ were the only family she had, and now she'd lost them. They'd fallen in love, married, and lived within two miles of each other.

They thought she'd moved from Columbus to be closer to them. One big happy family. Didn't they know her at all?

The truth . . . she could hardly bear to face the truth herself, let alone tell her brother and cousin. She'd already had enough of their pity.

Enough!

She started to scoot off the picnic table, then paused, her senses on full alert. Movement across the creek caught her attention. A chestnut horse ambled toward the bank, and the rider lifted his hand in a friendly wave.

Even in the middle of nowhere, she couldn't find privacy.

Acknowledgments

My family and friends know so many things I don't, and I'm grateful they're willing to share their knowledge and know-how with me. Special thanks to the Alexander clan: Hebe, Adam, Tony, Ashley, Bryon, and Lauren. Thanks, too, to Windy Cobourne, Daniel and Danielle Giaquinto, Diana Huff Pitts, Karen Preskar, Dusty Ruth, Peggy Seaburn, and Tom Thacker.

A festive, confetti-sparkled thanks to the wise and witty Facebook friends who answer my odd questions. Your enthusiastic answers energize me and warm my heart.

After my discerning and opinionated first-reader team perused the manuscript, we talked about it over lunch at Panera in Lakeland, Florida. Thanks to Carol Anne Giaquinto, Bethany Jett, Joy Van Tassel, and Mandy Zema for creating that memory with me. (You know I love you!)

Hugs and prayers to my Kindred Hearts: Clella Camp, Karen Evans, Laura Groves, and Jean Wise.

Thanks also to the Imagine That! Writers: Patricia Bradley, Reneé Osborne, and Chandra Smith.

I'm grateful for my agent, Tamela Hancock Murray, and my

fantastic team at Revell: Vicki Crumpton, Kristin Kornoelje, Michele Misiak, Karen Steele, and Cheryl Van Andel.

Heart-deep appreciation goes to my mom, Audry Alexander, who blessed me with a love of reading and believed in me always.

Love always to the treasures of my heart: Bethany, Jillian, Nate, and their families.

I am richly blessed, and I thank my heavenly Father for each one of you.

Johnnie Alexander is the award-winning author of *Where Treasure Hides* and *Where She Belongs*. Johnnie is an accomplished essayist and poet whose work has appeared in the Guideposts anthology *A Cup of Christmas Cheer*. In addition to writing, she enjoys reading, spending time with her grandchildren, and taking road trips. She lives near Memphis, Tennessee.

MEET
Johnnie Alexander
AT JOHNNIE-ALEXANDER.COM

Can love redeem
A BROKEN PAST?

JOHNNIE ALEXANDER

WHERE SHE *Belongs*

A NOVEL

In this emotionally rich contemporary romance, a young widow
determined to reclaim her cherished family home clashes with the
handsome yet infuriating current owner who has let it fall into ruin.

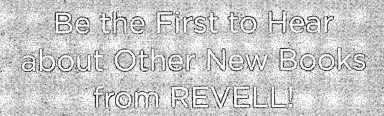